WORLD WAR II

BRITISH AREA OF
OPERATIONS

✦ 1939-1943 ✦

HOLLAND

GERMANY

Cologne

Aachen
Monschau

Liége
St Vith
Remagen

Frankfurt

astogne

LUXEMBOURG

Metz

British Despatch Rider

Palace of Westminster
Home of Parliament

AS TIME GOES BY

OTHER BOOKS AND AUDIO BOOKS
BY JERRY BORROWMAN:

Three Against Hitler (with Rudi Wobbe)

A Distant Prayer (with Joseph Banks)

'Til the Boys Come Home

I'll Be Seeing You

AS TIME GOES BY

A WORLD WAR II NOVEL
BATTLE OF BRITAIN

JERRY BORROWMAN

Covenant Communications, Inc.

Cover design and endsheet maps by Jessica A. Warner, © 2007 Covenant Communications, Inc. Cover painting *HMS Hood Opens Fire upon the Bismarck* by Ivan Berryman © Cranston Fine Arts, www.naval-art.com. Endsheet sketches: Parliament building and motorcycle courier © Cindy Schmidt.

Published by Covenant Communications, Inc.
American Fork, Utah

Printed in Canada
First Printing: April 2007

13 12 11 10 09 08 07   10 9 8 7 6 5 4 3 2 1

ISBN 978-1-59811-324-2

This book is dedicated to
Marcella Borrowman,
my wife and best friend for more than thirty years.
How I love traveling the world together
as we share the journey of life.

ACKNOWLEDGMENTS

I'd like to thank all those who read the manuscript during its development. Fortunately, I had the benefit of some remarkable editors, both British and American.

David Pickup is a barrister who lives in Lancashire, England. He enjoys the distinction of recently being appointed as a judge, the first member of the LDS Church in England to receive such an honor. David did a thorough reading of the manuscript to correct errors in my descriptions of English culture, government, and geography. His work was invaluable, and I am deeply indebted to him for the time and effort he spent during a very busy period in his life.

Val Johnson, managing editor for the international magazine *Liahona,* is a good friend who volunteered to do a technical line-by-line edit and also made suggestions to the story.

David Mitchell, a former editor at LDS Church magazines, provided unique insight to the story in that he grew up in London and remembered firsthand the Battle of Britain and the experience of living through World War II. He later served in the British military before moving to the United States. David's role in strengthening the book took a poignant turn in that just a week after I reviewed his suggestions with him by phone, he passed away unexpectedly. I'm very grateful to have known him even briefly.

Finally, it was a pleasure to work with Covenant editor Kirk Shaw for the first time. Kirk has been delightful to associate with.

I also have the benefit of some very skilled family members and friends who shared their thoughts on the story. I owe particular thanks to my son Scott, a legal editor; my brother Wayne, who served a mission in England; my daughter Kelissa, who mentors English students at Idaho State University; and my daughters-in-law Eden and Hilary. A number of other very good friends provided feedback as well, including Evan Rowley, Lane Jensen, and Blake Hill.

Finally, my sincere appreciation to the staff at Covenant Communications and to all those who work for the booksellers who bring my books to the public.

PREFACE

After reading many hundreds of books on World War II in the past forty years, the most influential and inspiring for me is the six-volume series *The Second World War* by Winston Churchill. Not only was Churchill one of history's greatest leaders and statesmen, but he also was an outstanding writer and storyteller.

Perhaps because of his profound influence on my early thinking about the war, I have always felt a special debt of gratitude to the people of the British Empire for standing alone against the fury of Nazi Germany for nearly two years before Russia and the United States were drawn in as allies. The world would be a very different place today had the British not had the courage and fortitude to withstand the terror of the Blitz while building their strength for an eventual counterstrike that secured the foundations of freedom and stability for the great democracies of Europe and the Americas at the end of the war.

And so this book is written in tribute to our friends and allies in England and her Commonwealth—a friendship magnified in the adversities of the most devastating conflict in world history.

Part One

THE BATTLE OF BRITAIN

Chapter One

A STATE OF WAR

London—September 3, 1939

Lord Philip Carlyle leaned on the elegant mahogany wireless that stood in the parlor of his town house in the fashionable Queen Anne neighborhood of London. At the appointed moment of 11:15 AM, the rest of the family gathered around as the tube amplifier crackled to life and the dial of the station selector started to glow warmly. They were joined by millions of other British households who were also tuning in to listen to the voice of Prime Minister Neville Chamberlain as he announced the reaction of the Nazi government to the British ultimatum requiring them to withdraw from Poland, which they had invaded two days earlier. Many realized that the very fate of the British Empire hung in the balance. At the appointed moment, the twelve-inch speaker crackled a bit, and then Chamberlain's high-pitched voice uttered those fateful and discouraging words . . .

> *This morning the British ambassador in Berlin handed the German government a final note stating that unless we heard from them by eleven o'clock that they were prepared at once to withdraw their troops from Poland, a state of war would exist between us. I have to tell you now that no such undertaking has been received, and that consequently this country is at war with Germany.*

Philip Carlyle glanced at his watch and then reached out to turn the radio off, even though Chamberlain wasn't finished with his entire text. "I just can't listen to the man justify his poor handling of Germany," he said with contempt. His wife, Claire, jumped when the air was shattered by a deep growling sound that quickly grew in intensity.

"What's that?" Claire asked anxiously.

"An air-raid siren," Philip replied. "I can't believe it! Hitler's sending his bombers!"

"What do we do?" Claire asked in a panic.

"It's all right, dear. Even if they've sent a wave of bombers, it will take a few minutes for them to arrive. We need to get everyone to the cellar and wait for the all clear."

"Come on, children," Claire said, hustling them up and out of their seats. "We've got to hurry!" Their seventeen-year-old son, Dominic, groaned, but Claire would have none of it.

"Will you gather up the staff and get them downstairs?" Philip asked the butler. Soon the group was huddled anxiously in the cellar, waiting to hear the concussions that would indicate an attack. Whenever anyone started to talk, Claire shushed them, saying, "I want to hear what's happening." But everything was silent.

After a wait of just twenty minutes, the all-clear siren sounded, indicating that it had been a false alarm.

They tromped up the stairs to the dining room, and the cook hurriedly prepared some sandwiches. Philip picked up the conversation where it had left off. "Well, that's perhaps the sorriest thing I've ever heard. After two decades of appeasement, we're at war again. And this time Germany is stronger than ever while we're so unprepared." No one replied, because they'd heard all this before.

A disciple of Winston Churchill, Lord Philip Carlyle had been one of the few politicians who consistently spoke out for action against Germany while she was still militarily weak and while it was still within the rights of the Allied victors of the Great War to supervise the German people. But under the Chamberlain government, and even under the Stanley Baldwin government before it, precious time had slipped away as the Nazis had rearmed Germany right under the Allies' noses.

"But surely France is prepared, Philip," Claire said hopefully. "They have the largest army in the world and have fortified the Maginot Line across the entire length of their border with Germany. Certainly the Nazis don't want to tackle both Britain and France. Don't you think they'll sue for peace now that they have what they want?" It was this exact sentiment—that a reasonable person would eventually be satisfied—that had emboldened Chamberlain to sign away Czechoslovakia's freedom at Munich just over a year earlier, right on the heels of the forced takeover of the Sudetenland and the bloodless Anschluss in Austria. But Hitler was not a reasonable person. All these compromises made the borders of Nazi Germany look like a puddle of black ink spilled on a map of Europe. The compromises had been accepted because of the Allies' desperate desire to avoid another Great War. Hitler kept promising that if he was just given enough *Lebensraum*—enough breathing room—the Germans would settle into their rightful place as one of the great nations of the world and finally become a responsible member of the international community. Except that each demand led to yet another, and then another, each one more unreasonable and outrageous than the last. Finally he had gone too far, even for Chamberlain.

"But he wants Poland, Mother, and we guaranteed her borders," Michael, the older Carlyle son, said. "We have no choice but to go to war. Hitler has never backed down, and we certainly can't give in again."

Claire turned to look at Michael. The sight of his earnest, nineteen-year-old face made her wince, and instinctively she raised a handkerchief to her face as though to suppress a cough, while trying to hide the alarm on her face. Home on leave from the

Royal Naval College in Greenwich, Michael would be one of the
first to be called into active service.

"Perhaps when Hitler sees that we really mean it this time, he'll
withdraw," Claire replied helplessly.

"I don't see why Poland has anything to do with us," Dominic
said fiercely.

This drew an immediate sigh from Philip, who turned to look
at his seventeen-year-old. Dominic's words sounded too much like
what Chamberlain had said in a speech in 1938 when he'd been
about to abandon Czechoslovakia to the Nazis. Even now the
words made Philip's blood boil. *"How horrible, fantastic, incredible
it is that we should be digging trenches and trying on gas masks here
because of a quarrel in a far-away country between people of whom we
know nothing."* He shuddered, recalling Chamberlain's words, and
then remembered something Churchill had replied with at the
time with his rapier wit: *"An appeaser is one who feeds the crocodile,
hoping it will eat him last."*

As Philip looked at Dominic, he saw his son facing him
squarely, as if hoping for a fight. In spite of his best effort not to
prejudge Dominic's comment, Philip couldn't help but feel that it
was said in selfishness, as were so many things in Dominic's life. At
seventeen, Dominic was just months away from being draft age
himself, which might account for his lack of patriotism.

"This is our fight, Dominic," Philip said evenly. "Tyranny is
never content to live within its boundaries and always seeks to
extend its influence."

Dominic smiled mischievously. "Well, at least Subleftenant
Carlyle here will get his chance to go to war. It's what you've been
training to do for the past four years," he gibed, purposely exagger-
ating the British habit of pronouncing the word as "subleftenant."

Michael flared, as expected. "Nobody wants war, but I'll be
proud to serve!"

"Perhaps you'll have the distinction of firing the first shot,"
Dominic replied pleasantly. He'd always known how to get his

older brother's goat and loved to egg him on. "Why, who knows, maybe you'll even be the first to be wounded or killed—imagine what an honor that would be!"

"That will be enough, Dominic!" Philip reprimanded, and the boy shrank at his father's rebuke. Michael had actually started to rise out of his chair as if to hit Dominic, but he settled back in when Philip took control. Claire and their fifteen-year-old daughter, Grace, simply looked miserable. It was almost always like this when Michael and Dominic were together.

Dominic wasn't quite finished. Turning to Michael, he said, "Well, it may be your fight, but it certainly isn't mine. We're Americans, and Europe's wars have nothing to do with us. Why would you want to serve with the British instead of with your native country?"

It was an old argument. The Carlyle children had all been born in Salt Lake City after Philip Carlyle had accompanied his American friend Dan O'Brian home from England at the end of the Great War in 1918. Philip had rescued Dan when he'd been wounded by a German gas attack on the American trenches, and he had ultimately brought him to Carlyle Manor to recuperate. As a chaplain for the Church of England, Philip had felt it his duty to help the earnest young American who had lost so much on the fields of France.

Philip recalled the last war, and all its carnage and horror flooded his mind.

The sound of Michael's voice brought Philip back to the present. "It's a matter of honor, Dominic. England can't turn her back on an ally. We guaranteed Poland's borders, and now they've been violated. And you know as well as I do that we're both British and American." His voice was heavy with the exasperation that was typical of these discussions.

Having accomplished his goal of stirring things up, Dominic changed tack without even acknowledging the British-vs.-American argument. It had been fought so many times in the past that it was no longer interesting. "Mr. O'Dyer says that the whole Polish thing was just a bluff on the prime minister's part to get Germany to back down. Now that his strategy has failed, Mr. Chamberlain will find another reason to give in again, and real war will be avoided." Then, to add drama to what he said, he spoke the ultimate controversial argument: "And perhaps Germany will give some decent leadership to Europe."

That lit another fuse, and Philip inhaled slowly. Mr. O'Dyer was an instructor at the public school where Dominic now boarded, having been expelled from the more prestigious academy he had attended for the previous eight years until the most recent incident of cheating had finally caught up to him.

"Mr. O'Dyer is Irish," Philip said as evenly as possible. "And many Irishmen believe that their interests are more closely allied with Germany than with England. It's no wonder that he'd say that." Then, before Dominic could respond, Philip added, "But he's wrong. We are allies of the Poles because the Nazis have proven they have no scruples. It's past time to stop them before they carry their hatred across all of Europe and England."

"Well, it's got nothing to do with me, because Germany has done nothing to America."

Philip bit his lower lip until the salty taste of blood caused him to ease up.

"Please," Claire said. "Certainly we don't need to argue at a time like this. These events are larger than all of us, and there's nothing we can do anyway."

"There's something I can do," Michael said quietly. "I can request transfer to the active duty roster. And that's exactly what I want to do."

"But it's too soon," Claire replied quickly. "You should finish school and see how things develop. You're only a term away from completion." Then, choking back her emotion, she whispered, "You're too young."

Michael didn't reply, but he also didn't back down.

"I suspect they'll truncate your program and transfer you anyway," Philip said. "Having made the decision to go to the naval college, you're bound to active duty. So I'd just go back to school and see what they have in mind."

Dominic didn't like having the spotlight turned to Michael, so he interjected, "Well, I'm not joining anything."

"No, I suppose you wouldn't think that it has anything to do with you, Dominic," Michael said coldly. "Maybe you should return to America until it's over, since I'm sure you wouldn't want to run any of the risks of living here when hostilities break out."

Even Dominic was unnerved by this rebuke and started to reply, "It's not that I'm a coward or anything . . ."

"That's enough," Claire interrupted. "It's bad enough the English and the Germans are at war. We don't need to be at war here in our own family."

"I'm sorry," Michael said, going quiet.

Philip sighed. "We'll have time to talk about what this means for each of us in the days to come. Nothing has to be decided right now. In the meantime, I should go up to Parliament, since I imagine there will be a flurry of activity there that I should be part of." He gave Claire a quick kiss, hugged Grace, and then put on his coat. There was an early chill in the air—perhaps even nature was subdued by the unhappy turn of events.

As he stepped out onto Dartmouth Street to begin the four-block walk to the Houses of Parliament, the dark reality that England was at war yet again settled in.

* * *

"I'm sorry I lost my temper with Dominic. I'd promised myself I wouldn't, and there I was, angry again." Philip was staring at the ceiling as Claire snuggled over to his side and laid her head on his shoulder.

Philip was one of the most even-tempered men Claire had ever known, showing incredible patience regardless of whatever provocations he faced—and he'd faced many since their marriage in 1920. His father, the previous Lord Carlyle, had been furious when Philip had joined the LDS Church, threatening to disown him if he didn't renounce his "lunatic" affiliation with the Mormon culture. Because of primogeniture, the English law declaring that family property is held in trust from one generation to the next, he couldn't legally disinherit Philip, and since Philip was his only child, it was unthinkable to allow the title to lapse. But Lord Carlyle had made it clear that Philip wasn't welcome at home as long as he remained outside the Established Church. It wasn't that Philip's father had doctrinal qualms—he'd never shown much interest in religion—but rather that Philip's joining the Mormon church was a political and social faux pas that he viewed as foolish and selfish. For his part, Philip had been content to live the life of a professor of religion at the University of Utah and would have happily raised his family there in relative poverty without any thought for what he had left behind in England had his mother not implored him to come home and claim his title when Lord Carlyle died unexpectedly in 1930. It was a proud name, long affiliated with the Carlyle estate, which had been given to the family by a royal grant more than a century before. Philip's mother, Lady Carlyle, had also come from a prominent family and was anxious to maintain the long traditions that Philip's birthright conferred upon him. Even though she'd shown little motherly affection for Philip through the years, as was common in that level of society, he still felt the burden of duty that she imposed on him with her appeal. And so he'd reluctantly returned to claim his title and take his place in the Lords, even though he'd faced some religious bigotry from a few of the more zealous lords at first. "And yet you've never complained in spite of it all," Claire said quietly into the darkness.

"What?" Philip asked. "I was just apologizing for losing my temper with Dominic."

"I know. And I was just thinking of all the times when you should have lost your temper in this stuffy little country of yours, and yet you haven't. It's a puzzle why you can tolerate so much from others yet lose your patience so easily with our boy."

"If that was meant to comfort me . . ."

"I become exasperated with him too," Claire admitted. "I don't know why he never puts himself in other people's shoes to act in their best interest."

Now it was Philip who smiled. She was right. Dominic seemed to lack empathy. His own self-interest always came first, putting him totally at odds with the character traits that Philip most admired: selflessness, duty, and honor. It was disturbing that Dominic seemed to relish dominating younger, weaker children but often feigned an injury when competing with his equals. It caused both fear and anger within Philip as he thought about what it all meant for his son's future.

They lay quietly for a few moments before Philip said, "Well, I suppose Dominic is right that this isn't his quarrel. He is an American, after all, and has every right to refuse to join the British, particularly since our laws will never bestow our title or property on him." In spite of himself, Philip took comfort from that thought, since Dominic was not well suited for managing the complex affairs of the estate. Then a cold chill went down his spine, settling into an uncomfortable knot in his stomach. "Unless something happens to Michael . . ." he whispered.

"You can't think that way," Claire said. "The future is reserved for God to see. We have to go on as best we can in the present."

Philip relaxed. Claire's common sense always calmed him. Perhaps it was the practicality of her American upbringing or just a reflection of her personality, but it always seemed to work. "Well, what should we do with Dominic and Grace then? When the Germans attack London, it won't be safe here. Besides, when Dominic reaches eighteen, it will provoke a scandal if he fails to enlist like the other boys his age. Perhaps they should go to America."

Claire ignored the last part of his comment. "Do you think they would be safe out at the manor?" she asked. Philip knew that she preferred living in their town house in London since it gave her people to talk to. There was a vibrant branch of the Church in London, and Claire served in the Relief Society. Carlyle Manor, on the other hand, was safely out in the country. It was a large old house surrounded by endless rolling hills tended by tenant farmers. Most of the landed gentry of their social standing enjoyed plenty of social activity, as the various families of the aristocracy visited one another for galas and dinners, but Claire had two strikes against her—she was an American and a Mormon. Some called her Lady Carlyle only grudgingly, and very few invitations or visitors ever came. It made living at the manor lonesome for her and the children.

"Who knows where we'll be safe," Philip said, trying to sound as confident as possible. "I doubt that many bombs would fall out in the countryside, but if the Germans actually invaded the country, they'd consider Carlyle Manor perfectly situated as a garrison for a German general and his staff. No, I think we need something more permanent for the children." His voice betrayed even more strain when he said, "And perhaps for you."

Claire sat up in bed. "You can stop that thought right there, Philip. I will not go back to America without you. I didn't marry you for time and all eternity only to make exceptions for the times when there are challenges. We will stay here together."

Philip relaxed again. On the one hand he hated the thought of his wife being exposed to danger. But the thought of being without her was even worse. Seizing the moment, he said, "So are we agreed that Dominic and Grace should go to Arizona?"

There was a rustling sound in the darkened corridor near the bedroom where they were talking. Philip and Claire looked up to see Grace peek her head around the corner. "I don't want to go to America." There was a defiant look in her eyes.

"How long have you been listening?" Philip asked.

"Long enough to know that you're trying to send us out of the country. Well, I don't want to go." Claire stretched out her arms, and Grace came running to her.

"It wouldn't be forever," Philip said tenderly.

"It might be if something happens to you or Momma." Grace stiffened as he reached over to try to comfort her. With all the uncertainty about the war, he wanted to protect her more than anything in the world and wished she could see it that way. But he knew better.

"You still think I'm a silly little girl who doesn't understand the danger. But I do understand, and I can take care of myself. The last thing I want is to be stuck in Arizona with Aunt Karrie, worrying about what's happening to the two of you. That would be the worst thing of all!"

Philip didn't want to be unkind, but he needed her to understand the seriousness of the situation. "I know you're growing up, Grace, and becoming a woman. But I also know that you have no idea how horrible this thing can get. If the Germans decide to invade, they'll first drop bombs by the hundreds of thousands of pounds, just as they did in Poland. And then, heaven forbid, if they do manage to land troops, they'll take whatever they want from whatever houses they capture." He stopped for a moment to get control of his breathing. "And I can promise you that a young girl would not be safe in such circumstances." He let the words hang heavily in the air to make sure their full meaning had time to sink in. "Do you understand what I'm saying, Grace?"

She was quiet for a few moments. "I understand—but I can't believe it would ever come to that. England beat the Germans in the last war. Why should it be different this time?"

"I wish it were the same, but many things have changed in the last twenty years. Germany is armed and ready for war while we're not. And in those days the aircraft were small and fragile with hardly the range to even reach our shores. But it's not like that now. Today the English Channel is just a minor obstacle. Besides, the Germans are out for revenge," he said, frowning. "No, it's not like the last war—not at all."

"Then why don't you and Mother come with us? If it's so dangerous, why must you stay?"

Philip sighed. The answer seemed impossible to convey. How did you teach your daughter about obligations that were created hundreds of years before her birth? Fortunately, Claire stepped into the conversation.

"Your father is part of Parliament, and we have to be here to share in the country's trouble. I'm not British, but I have to stay with him—because I love him. There will be much to worry about in the days to come. It would be such a relief if we didn't have to worry about you and Dominic."

Philip saw Grace suppress a sob. He reached his arm around her shoulder and drew her close but didn't say a word. This time she yielded, allowing him to stroke her hair.

"I don't know why all this has to happen. I just don't know what I'd do if something happened to either of you," Grace said amid sobs.

"I know," Philip said. "None of us understands why it has to happen. But it has." They sat lost in thought for a few moments. Finally, Philip said as cheerfully as possible, "Still, we don't need to talk about it anymore tonight. We're all safe and together for the moment. We should be grateful for that." And with that they sat quietly holding each other in the face of the oncoming storm.

* * *

After Grace had gone to bed and Philip and Claire were settling down to sleep, Claire said, "I'll cable Karrie tomorrow to see if it's all right."

"We could offer to extend their house a bit . . ."

"That would take a phone conversation. I'm sure she'd be embarrassed by the offer."

"Well, I'll have to insist on providing for the children's financial needs," Philip protested. "Otherwise, we can't let them go."

"Calm down, dear. I'll work this out with my sister. In the meantime, you need to get some sleep so you'll be rested for your summons tomorrow. Do you have any idea what they want?"

"I honestly don't. I'm sure it's not a cabinet post, since I don't have the experience. Besides, they frown on elevating ministers from the Lords instead of the Commons."

"But it's the prime minister himself who wants to see you?"

"Mr. Appeasement himself." Philip paused a moment in frustration, then continued. "I'm not sure I'd want to serve in his government. Under his leadership, England has become weak and unreliable."

Claire rolled onto her elbow and looked directly into Philip's eyes. "The idea is that you should be calming down right now so you can fall asleep—not getting your dander up over Mr. Chamberlain. I'm sorry I brought the subject up."

Philip laughed. "Fine . . . I'll let him rest in peace tonight and find out what he's got in store for me tomorrow." They kissed and Claire rolled back to her side, tucking her knees up against the back of Philip's legs. They lay quietly for a few moments.

"He's not all bad, you know?" Claire piped in.

"Chamberlain? I think he is."

"No, Dominic. He has a vulnerable side. Sometimes I think all his bravado is a mask for his fear. Coming to England was very hard on him."

"I know," Philip said quietly. "I've tortured myself a thousand times wondering if I did this to him. Whenever he challenges me, I see a look in his eyes that is at once both defiant and yearning—as if he secretly wished that we could connect. But there have been so few times that it's happened." Philip found himself biting his lip again.

Claire was quiet for a moment, and Philip couldn't decide whether it was because she wanted to tell him something unpleasant and was trying to figure out how to phrase it or because he had surprised her with his comment and she was thinking about it. Finally she replied, "I don't know the answer, Philip. He's a hard boy to understand. It seems like he goes out of his way to irritate people, particularly you and Michael, as if he relishes the conflict. But other times, when no one else is around, he can be very tender when he talks to me. If people could see that side of him, I think he'd get along better . . ."

Philip decided not to respond when her voice trailed off.

Claire yawned. "I guess that's another thing that will have to wait for tomorrow. Suddenly I can't keep my eyes open."

Philip snuggled close again, and with that, Claire settled deeply into the pillow. It wasn't so easy for Philip, who lay very quietly, thinking about the events of his life over the past twenty years. It almost seemed like a dream now—his injuries in the war, moving to Salt Lake City against his father's will, and starting a family when he thought he was past the age of marriage. Now he was about to be asked to assume some kind of role in the prosecution of a war that he felt could have been avoided had England, France, and America shown any kind of resolve in standing up to Hitler, the Austrian corporal who had seduced the German people.

Chapter Two

THE LORDS

London—December 1939

One of Philip's requirements as a viscount was to sit in the House of Lords, acting on legislation and suggesting amendments. The influence of the Lords had been diminished through the years such that they could not act on any expenditures or taxes and could at best delay legislation passed in the House of Commons for a two-year period. Still, the Lords had significant influence in their review of legislation because they could propose amendments before sending the legislation back to the Commons. Few had more influence than Philip's father. He had become a master at the review-and-revision function of the Lords, and his advice and endorsement were often sought on matters of controversial legislation. Had Philip not moved to America for such an extended period, he would have easily stepped into his father's place of power.

But he had left the Church of England after serving as a church chaplain in the Great War and so had lost most of his political and spiritual connections. In the early days it was difficult for him to even be heard on the floor of the magnificently decorated chamber that housed the Lords because of his relative anonymity. Eventually, Philip had adopted a strategy of working diligently behind the scenes on his committee assignments, where his competence and insight came to be valued. His allies soon forced the Leader to recognize Philip by having Philip give their reports on the floor. After nearly a decade, few people consciously thought about his leaving the Church of England. Philip had proven his competence to the point that even the theocrats in the government seldom gave him trouble.

One of the benefits of the family's wealth was that they could afford a comfortable house in one of the most fashionable districts in London. From a practical point of view, the Carlyle home was ideally situated close to both the prime minister's residence at Whitehall and the Palace of Westminster, where Parliament met, on the languid waters of the Thames River.

On this particular occasion, Prime Minister Neville Chamberlain had asked Philip to meet him at Whitehall for a brief conversation. Philip hoped this meeting would be more routine than his last visit to the prime minister's office, when Chamberlain had invited him in September to join the cabinet.

It was just a short walk before Philip found himself seated in the anteroom, waiting to be summoned. After perhaps ten minutes of pretending to read a magazine, Philip was invited into the office, where he was surprised to see Winston Churchill standing by the prime minister.

"Good morning, Lord Carlyle. Please, have a seat," Chamberlain invited without any warmth, in his usual stiff manner. As the three settled in, Churchill flashed Philip a devilish smile, perhaps in recognition of Philip's support during the previous decade when Churchill had been out of favor and out of office. On more than one occasion, Churchill had surreptitiously asked Philip to use his privileges to get information about the government's plans and preparations for the nation's defense, which Churchill then used in writing the many popular articles and books that he submitted to the press. They agreed that as one of the victorious powers in the Great War, Britain should have intervened in Germany many years earlier, when Hitler first started to rearm. Had the British done so, they would have avoided the war that was now a reality. Philip had had to be careful in feeding

Churchill information, since the outspoken man was a constant thorn in the side of the government, but he had felt it the right thing to do, in spite of the potential risks to his own standing. Now Churchill was at the prime minister's side, which was an interesting turn of events.

"Well, let's get right to the point, Lord Carlyle. The government has asked Winston to join the cabinet as First Lord of the Admiralty." At this Philip brightened and congratulated Churchill. Chamberlain was impatient at the interruption. "Yes, well, in his characteristic manner, the First Lord has submitted a torrent of ideas that range far beyond the work of the Navy about how we should organize things now that we're ostensibly at war." Philip could sense the strain in the prime minister's voice and recognized that Churchill's appointment had been a political move to appease the public, not a sincere desire on Chamberlain's part to have him in the cabinet. The public loved Churchill and saw him as vital to the prosecution of the war. "At any rate, one of the topics that has come to our attention is rather top secret in nature, and Churchill has recommended you as a man who is discreet enough to provide some leadership in this area." Philip's stomach muscles tightened instinctively.

"I'd be pleased to serve wherever I can be of greatest value."

"Very good, then. Why don't I have the First Lord explain it to you," Chamberlain concluded dismissively.

"It has to do with the cabinet, Philip," Churchill began. "With the potential bombing of London, it's felt that we need to have a secret facility where the cabinet can function even while under attack—a secure facility that allows the government to remain sited in London, where we can maintain the morale of the public."

Philip nodded thoughtfully, which Churchill took as instant acceptance, so he continued. "We've actually previously reinforced the cellar of the new public offices building on King Charles Street and have created what is known as the central war room. Of course we have civil servants assigned to staff it, but we really need cabinet oversight. What we'd like is for you to accept an assignment as a minister without portfolio. That way you can join the cabinet and provide oversight of the facility without the nature of your work being made public. One of the prime functions of the staff will be to certify the credentials of those individuals who have access to the various facilities of the war room. The main task will be to keep this cabinet facility secret while making certain that those individuals who have a need to know can quickly get to where they are needed. It's a very sensitive spot that will require great discretion."

Philip was a bit staggered by this, since it wasn't at all what he'd expected to hear. "But if I may ask . . . why me? I've never had a ministerial role—just legislative."

"Ah, that's why we thought of you." Churchill's eyes twinkled. "It hasn't escaped notice that you've had to demonstrate some rather exceptional diplomatic skills in winning the confidence of the Lords, some of whom—how can I say this delicately—were rather hostile to you at first."

Philip laughed out loud—which was not a very British thing to do. "I think *hostile* would be a fair word."

Chamberlain interrupted. "Yes, well, that's the point. The quarters are very close down there, and men of towering egos will be interacting with professional staff in extremely tense situations. It's felt that we need someone who can show patience in such a setting to keep things civil. Is that something you feel you can help us with?"

Probably the biggest two egos I'll ever have to deal with are in this room with me right now! Philip thought. He suppressed his smile, although he guessed that Churchill was thinking the very same thing. "I'd be honored to serve, prime minister. I'll make whatever arrangements are necessary to give my best effort to the country."

"That's settled then. We'll be in touch to get you the necessary clearances, and you can meet with my private secretary to secure all the details." The prime minister stood abruptly, signaling that the meeting was at an end. He shook Philip's hand in a cursory way and allowed Churchill to see him to the door.

"Nice to have you on board, Carlyle. I wish I could have brought you to the Admiralty, but you were Army in the last war, so it might not look right," Churchill said as he escorted Philip to the door.

"I understand. Thank you for your recommendation in this instance, although I don't know what I'm in for."

"What you're in for is a seat at the very center of the government, where you can be privy to all that's going on. I doubt they'll use the facility much in the beginning, but when the war heats up, it will be a vital spot indeed. I'm glad you'll be there." And with that, Churchill closed the door and Philip walked out to the anteroom.

Philip pursed his lips and nodded. Now he understood. Churchill was thinking of him as his inside man who could keep track of the goings-on of the cabinet and war ministers. In this war, Churchill would need every good man.

* * *

Liverpool—February 1940

"I still don't see why I have to go," Grace whined. "All my friends are here, and I don't want to be in America if something bad happens to you or Papa!"

"Grace," Claire said quietly. "We've been over this again and again. Aunt Karrie is expecting you. With everything that's going on, it's just too hard to have you children spread out at different schools here. I have enough to worry about. At least I'll know that you and Dominic are safe in Arizona, and I can have peace on that score."

"Besides," Philip added, "the train trip from London should have convinced you that you're not alone. Millions of children are being sent out of the city. It's just that only a few are fortunate enough to have relatives in America, where it's safe."

Grace tightened her expression, determined not to cry, but she quickly lost the battle. She was still at that awkward age between childhood and young adulthood, and her emotions often spilled out on difficult occasions. To mask her tears, she looked around at the Liverpool dockyard. Rather than leave from London, which exposed them to all the dangers of the English Channel, they'd traveled by railcar to the western side of the country, where they were boarding a high-speed luxury liner bound for New York City.

Catching her sullen expression, Philip moved closer and gave Grace a hug. She was taller than most of her fifteen-year-old friends, although her rather average build made it so she didn't look particularly tall. Her dark brown hair was combed neatly and fell to her shoulders, and her striking blue eyes finished the picture.

He sighed. The thought of missing out on seeing her grow into a young woman was distressing enough to tempt him to let her stay. But it just didn't make sense. Fighting his own instincts, he said, "This really will be better, dear. Hopefully the war won't last long, and you'll be back before you know it. In the meantime, think of yourself as having a grand adventure. You'll enjoy the desert colors and the sunshine of Arizona."

"We'll probably suffocate in the heat," Dominic said sullenly. Philip didn't react outwardly. Dominic had wanted to go to Salt Lake City—not because he was particularly close to anyone there but mostly because it was different from where his parents wanted to send him. Besides, he knew that his Aunt Karrie and her husband were tough disciplinarians, and Dominic always did his best to avoid people like that.

"It's going to get pretty hot here as well," Philip finally replied in as pleasant a voice as he could muster. "So I think you're getting the better end of the bargain."

"At least I won't have to get woken up by those annoying air-raid sirens that keep turning out to be false alarms," Dominic said with an edgy tone to show his displeasure.

Philip inhaled slowly. The so-called Phony War was wearing on all of them. After the declaration of war on September 3, there had been little action anywhere but on the Atlantic to indicate that there was a war going on. No one could tell if it was Hitler's way of trying to build pressure on the British to seek an armistice or if he was simply building up his strength for some kind of blow on one of his neighbors. Either way, nerves were frayed. Great Britain had lived under the cloud of uncertainty for nearly five months. Fortunately, the interlude was also giving British industry time to ramp up its production of war material so that when the fighting did start, they'd have a better chance.

There was a deep, sonorous sound from the ship's steam horn.

"Well, it looks like the final boarding." Philip gave Claire a big hug since she was going to accompany the children to Mesa to get them settled.

He'd be without her for three months or more, which was distressing. But the demands of his job had been keeping him away from home a great deal anyway, so he'd find plenty to occupy his time. The prime minister had asked him to keep up at least a partial schedule in the Lords so that no one would be suspicious of his other activities.

Turning to Grace, Philip said, "Good-bye, sweetheart—be happy over there, and know that you'll be in my prayers every single night." He gave her one of his legendary hugs. She returned it gratefully.

"Be safe, Papa."

"I promise to do everything possible to keep myself intact. When the war is over, perhaps we can go on a trip somewhere exciting—to the mainland or to some interesting place you've discovered in America." He smiled, but it was hard, and they both started crying. Finally, Grace followed her mother up the stairs, leaving Philip and Dominic at the bottom of the gangplank.

"It really isn't that I'm afraid."

"I know that, son."

"Michael thinks it is."

"Michael is off to the Navy, so it really doesn't matter what he thinks. All that I ask is that you take care of your sister and that you do your best to fit into the Daileys' schedule without upsetting things. It's kind of them to let you come." Dominic bristled as was to be expected, so before he could say anything, Philip continued. "It's just one of those foolish things parents say when they have to say good-bye and don't want to. You'll be fine in America. We trust you. Besides, you're the Honorable Dominic Carlyle, although I wouldn't insist on being called that at your school in Arizona." Philip smiled.

"Thank you," Dominic said without a smile. For a moment Philip saw that look in Dominic's eye that perhaps he wanted to say more. But then the look receded, and they hugged each other awkwardly. Then Dominic bolted up the ramp without looking back—at least not where Philip could see him turn and gaze.

With an almost deafening blast from the giant steam horn, the great ship started to swing away from the pier. Philip stood watching as three of the four people who mattered most to him in the world started a perilous journey across the Atlantic. In four days they'd be safe, and he could think of other things. Until then he would think about them every spare moment.

Chapter Three

HMS *HOOD*

London—May 1940

Michael had long dreamed of joining the British Navy. While his father had shown little interest in boating and sailing, Michael had loved boating with friends. The most memorable event of his life had been shortly after his family's arrival in England, when they had been invited onto the royal yacht as the guests of the Marquess Chartlain, one of his father's best friends in the Lords. They'd traveled by private railcar to Southampton, where they boarded the yacht for an English Channel crossing to Cherbourg. It had been a delightful day that reached its zenith when they were invited onto the bridge to meet the captain and the navigator. At nine years old, Michael had been allowed to stand on an upturned bucket to study the charts with all their depth markings. He smiled as he thought about how serious he must have looked as he pretended to understand what it all meant. The captain had taken him perfectly seriously, though, and treated him with great respect. It was probably at that moment that he had fostered the hope of one day serving on a ship.

However, joining the British Navy was difficult with Michael's American background—at least until his class was invited to sit for the prerequisite tests for entrance into the Royal Naval College at Greenwich. Michael had done well enough that the college was interested in him, particularly when they learned that he was heir to a British estate through his dual citizenship. So for the past four years he'd been in training as a naval officer, expecting to make it a lifetime career. With the outbreak of war, it was time to go to sea. With marks that put him toward the top of his class, he stood a good chance of getting a favorable first assignment, most likely a destroyer, but with any luck he might get a cruiser or even one of the new aircraft carriers.

Michael was at home for the weekend when a telegram was delivered to the door.

"Well?" Philip queried mischievously. "So is the wait about to end?"

Fumbling with the envelope, Michael gasped when he tore the telegram but quickly put the pieces together. At first he read with furrowed brow then burst into an astonished grin, accompanied by a deep intake of air. "This can't be true!"

"Well?"

"I can't believe it, Papa!"

"Hmm. Glad *you* get to enjoy it."

"What?" Then, looking up to see Philip's consternation, Michael said, "Oh, sorry. Here's what it says:

> *Sublieutenant Michael L. Carlyle,*
>
> *You are requested and required to report to HMS* Hood *at Liverpool on June 10, 1940. Contact the Admiralty for travel vouchers and instructions.*

"That's just two weeks!" Michael exclaimed.

"Well, this is what you've always wanted, Michael. Congratulations."

"Thank you," Michael said happily. "I can't believe I'm going to serve on the *Hood,* the British flagship!"

At 44,000 tons displacement, the *Hood* was the pride of the British Navy. Her long, sleek hull gave the ship a rakish appearance, and her incredible speed for a ship that large meant that she could outsteam any battleship in service. The concept of a battle cruiser was to build a ship with heavy armament equal to that of a battleship but with much lighter armor to improve speed. In a direct confrontation, the lighter armor made the ship vulnerable to enemy fire, but it was assumed that the cruiser could simply speed off to safety. Its real purpose was to move quickly on smaller ships, such as regular cruisers and destroyers, and blow them out of the water by firing its heavy guns from outside the smaller ships' range.

Having come into service in 1920, the *Hood* was fairly old, but continual updates had kept her in good trim. Since the outbreak of war, she'd been busy patrolling the Atlantic and escorting convoys to Gibraltar. She'd even successfully bottled up the German battleships *Gneisenau* and *Koln* during their attempt to break out of the North Sea, which was a tremendous relief to the convoys then en route from America.

At nineteen years old, Michael still looked young to Philip. In spite of his pride in Michael's willingness to serve, Philip felt a cold knot in his stomach as he pictured his boy actually going into active duty. The advantage of serving on the *Hood* was that the ship always traveled with the protection of a destroyer screen to chase off submarines and warn off larger ships in the area. The disadvantage was that it made an awfully large target for German guns and airplanes. Either way, Michael was going into harm's way, and the thought made Philip shudder.

"It's kind of scary, Father. I mean, I'm anxious to go, but things aren't going so well right now. We're likely to see action almost immediately."

Philip nodded slowly. That was an understatement. The previous six months had seen nothing but bad news for the British. German Kriegsmarine submarines were sending tens of thousands of tons of ships to the bottom of the ocean, and the Norwegian campaign of April was turning into a rout. Originally attempting to stop the flow of iron from Swedish mills to the Nazis, the British had planned to take over Norwegian ports to secure the raw materials for Britain, but the Germans had preempted the British plan with their own invasion, which was now seeing the Norwegians, French, and British being pushed northward by an ever-strengthening German invasion force, reinforced by Germany's growing command of the air over Norway. Once the Germans were fully entrenched, their planes would be able to fly into northern England at will from bases in Norway, which put the entire British fleet in danger. It was an ominous development. Fast on the heels of the invasion of Norway came the attack on northwestern Europe and the amazingly swift progress of the German Blitzkrieg toward Paris. Belgium had surrendered to the Nazis, and the British Expeditionary Force that had been sent to the Continent to reinforce France had barely escaped with the help of a ragtag armada of naval vessels, yachts, and fishing boats when they were cornered with their backs against the sea at the small French port of Dunkirk. The capitulation of France was imminent, which would leave Britain standing alone against the Nazi juggernaut.

"The only good news is the appointment of Churchill as prime minister," Philip said thoughtfully.

"What?"

"Oh, sorry. Your remark about things not going so well made me think. Really the only factor in our favor is that Churchill is finally in control. Hitler probably doesn't know it yet, but that development alone is likely to cost him everything."

"Is he really that great a leader?" Michael asked. "It seems like a lot of people didn't like him all that much before the war."

"He is, Michael. He is certainly the most effective orator I've ever heard. You should have heard him in the first cabinet meeting he presided over as prime minister. It was the day after the king went through the formality of requesting that he form a new government. Although Lord Salisbury was the king's first choice, Churchill is the only one who can bring us through without agreeing to an armistice with Germany as Salisbury prefers.

Salisbury was counting on Churchill to fail to rally the country so we could avoid war altogether—at the expense of abandoning all of Europe to the Nazi tyranny."

"But what happened? You tell me that Germany is still better prepared militarily, and it seems like a forced armistice is still a possibility. What happened to change all that?"

"What happened was a miracle. When the new cabinet met for the first time, all the talk in the room was about seeking an armistice. Even the most resolute of ministers seemed consigned to sue for peace. Finally someone asked Winston what our policy would be, at which point he stood in front of the group and changed the whole course of the conversation. In a matter of just two or three phrases, everyone in the room was electrified, and the decision was made to continue the fight."

Michael had never seen his father so animated. Picking up on his enthusiasm, he asked, "So what *did* he say?"

"I'll never forget what I felt, but I would do injustice to the words to try to paraphrase them." With that, Philip stood up and went over to his desk, where he fumbled about a bit. "Here it is. I asked his personal secretary for a copy of the text, which was recorded verbatim. I'll let you judge for yourself from this excerpt."

Michael took the typed sheet his father held out to him and read aloud:

> *You ask, 'What is our policy?' I will say: 'It is to wage war, by sea, land and air, with all our might and with all the strength that God can give us: to wage war against a monstrous tyranny, never surpassed in the dark lamentable catalogue of human crime. That is our policy.' You ask, 'What is our aim?' I can answer with one word: Victory—victory at all costs, victory in spite of all terror, victory however long and hard the road may be; for without victory there is no survival.*

"And then he said that he would never, ever, while there was life in his body, surrender to Adolph Hitler. The fire in his eyes was incredible, and when he was finished, everyone in the room leapt up into a standing ovation. It was the most thrilling moment of my life."

"Wow! And why were you there?"

Philip's face suddenly clouded in alarm. Hesitantly he replied, "Michael, I was there for a very specific reason. It's something you should never talk or speculate about. But let me just tell you that at that moment I believed the British Empire was saved. I don't know how we'll prevail, or how badly we'll suffer, but I know that God wants us to beat the Nazi scourge. With Churchill leading us, I think we'll make it."

Michael laughed. "I just can't believe this is happening. It feels like we're part of something really big—the fight of good versus evil. And we're both thick in it."

Philip couldn't help but laugh in return. "My young idealist." Before Michael could reply, Philip said, "And I think we need a lot of idealism right now to make up for the shortfall in supplies and airplanes." They laughed some more and stood and hugged. Then Michael dashed out the door to go over to the Admiralty to firm up his transfer plans.

* * *

Scapa Flow—June 1940

"If'n th' yung guntlemen'd care ter step inside the turret, we'll shew yer wot 'ellfire'll sound luk on judgmunt day." Michael grimaced at the strong cockney accent. Having spent his first nine years in America, he found it almost impossible to understand some of the stronger English dialects he'd encountered, and this one was a particular challenge. But he got the gist of it. Michael couldn't help but feel awe at the destructive power of the ship as he looked up at the massive barrels of the 15-inch guns that protruded menacingly from the front of one of the *Hood*'s half-a-million-pound turrets. Today they were going to do some target shooting, so he'd get to see and hear the guns in action for the first time.

"That's right, guntlemen; right now give your mince pies a mument ter adjust." Michael could tell that the gunnery officer giving the tour, Chief Coates, didn't think too highly of sublieutenants. And little wonder. The man had been in the service for more than twenty years, and now Michael and the others had shown up as commissioned officers who in a relatively short time would be placed in command of the turret crew. Everyone understood that the nonrated men would do the actual work of loading and firing the guns, while the officers got the credit when the firing was good. *We also get the blame when something goes wrong!* Michael thought to himself.

Inside the heavily armored turret, they were completely cut off from the outside world. It seemed strange to shoot at something you couldn't even see. But the actual siting of the guns would come from the gunnery control tower many decks above the turret, along with the order to shoot once the firing computers had made all the adjustments for the trajectory, roll of the ship, wind speed, speed of the enemy vessel, and other variables. It was incredible to think that a 2,000-pound, high-explosive shell could be fired some twenty miles with enough accuracy to destroy a ship. In some instances, with the new radar-controlled firing equipment, they would actually be shooting at targets beyond their visual range based on the ghostly images on the radar screen. At this point in the war, that was still rare, since accuracy increased with proximity, but the potential showed just how sophisticated these weapons were.

Michael was prone to letting his attention wander, and he had to force himself to concentrate with all the distractions of the gleaming brass and control panels calling for his attention. "As yer'll see, the loadin' mechernism combines an 'igh-speed elevatah that first lifts the perjectile from the forward magerzine, follered by two bags of cordite. The assistant gunnery mate 'ere's responsible fer controllin' th' openin' and closin' of th' breech-lock mechernism at the rear of the barrel, while Mr. Ranstrom'll control th' ram that shoves the projectile 'n' explosives inter th' barrel. We wivdror the ram, the bloomin' mechernism closes 'n' then seals the barrel, and we're ready ter shoot. Care fera demernstration?"

Everyone nodded, and Michael watched as the members of the gun crew slid into their places. Suddenly an alarm sounded, causing each of the young lieutenants to nearly jump out of his skin, and then in a motion that was almost too fast for the human eye to follow, the elevator came sliding into the view, cradling a highly polished armor-piercing shell. The gunner shifted into the clear, and a ram forced the projectile into the waiting breech of the gun. In a brief moment the elevator disappeared and then reappeared with a cloth bag that was also shoved in, followed by another. The breech was sealed, and the crew all stepped back and stood at attention. It was breathtaking to see the precision with which the gunnery crew handled their duties, and Michael's appreciation for the skill of the average Navy man increased dramatically.

"And that, guntlemen, is 'ow we load this 'ere gun!" There was a sound of triumph in the gunnery officer's voice. "Any questions?"

Of course there were questions. It had all happened so fast that it would have been impossible to have fully grasped it all, but no one was anxious to be the first to ask. "Right, now, one of yer must 'aff a question . . ."

Tentatively, one of the sublieutenants raised his hand. "It seems like there's a lot of exposed places where a man could get hurt when the mechanism goes into action."

"Right yer are. This is as dangerous an assignment as exists in th' Navy. Finks 'appen so quickly that if yer do anyfink outta strict protercol yer likely ter wind up in th' infirm'ry wonderin' wot 'appened ter yer arm. It's 'appened more thun once, I cun assure yer. Whenever yer workin' wiv explosives, right, there's danger of'n explosion from er stray spark 'r summat 'andlin' merstake." He said this with just the least hint of a smile, obviously pleased at the discomfort it produced in his young charges. "Anyfink else?"

"How do the shells get onto the elevator down below?" This was Michael.

"Well, o'course there's a 'oole crew dahn there, right, sortuv the opp'site of wot we do up 'ere. Ev'ryfink's done with mechernical assistance. Shells of this size simply weigh too much ter 'andle manually. When yer tour th' magerzine yer'll spot pneumatic tubes, hydraurlics, and electric motors all over th' bloomin' place ter quickly move th' shells 'n' explosives inter place." When everyone was quiet, he continued. "Yer've gotter remember that we'll spend monffs 'n' monffs where we don't spot 'ny action at'll, 'n' then when th' battle starts, ev'ryfink 'appens so fast that yer can't take time ter ffink about it. Th' life of th' ship depends on 'ow fast we cun fire, and it's up ter ffese 'ere crews ter see that we're faster 'n' more acc'rate than th' bloomin' Jerrys." Coates looked at his men and his weapons with obvious pride. Just then, another alarm sounded, startling Michael yet again.

"Right, then, now comes th' excitement. We're closin' position on our target. Gentlemen, yer'll want t' put these 'ere on." Lifting a pair of headphones to his head, Coates secured them over his ears. Michael and the others likewise pulled their headphones on. Then Coates motioned them to stand with their backs against the wall at the back of the turret. Michael felt the shiny, cold metal surface through his shirt and braced himself. A light flashed and then he saw, rather than heard, Coates shout, "FIRE!" Almost immediately Michael was hit with a concussion that knocked the wind out of him. It was as if he'd been hit in the stomach, and he winced from the pain. But that was only part of it. The sound of the blast was so overwhelming, in spite of the feeble protection of the headphones, that he was temporarily deaf. Unconsciously he staggered a bit as he tried to create equilibrium in his ears. Had he been outside, he would have seen a sheet of flame shoot out from the front of the barrels for more than thirty feet, accompanied by a massive black-and-white cloud of smoke filling the sky.

Before Michael could fully recover from the first blast, the second gun in the turret fired, and then the third. At this point Michael felt something on his face and reached up to find that a small amount of blood had come out of his nose, undoubtedly from the pressure of the explosions. More than anything, he simply wanted to shrink back into the wall and hope that it was over, but incredibly the gun crews had already opened and cleared the breech of the first gun, and the elevator was lifting another shell into position. Almost as if nothing had happened, the crew expertly rammed it into the barrel, followed by the cordite, then the sealing of the breech, then the word "FIRE!" and it all happened again. After the third shell was launched from each gun, the crew stood down, and Coates motioned for the sublieutenants to take off their headphones.

"Well, wotcher fink of that, guntlemen?"

"I'm speechless," one of them said, "and my mother said that would never happen in her lifetime. I hope she didn't die unexpectedly." This made even Coates laugh.

"Pretty excitin', ain't it?" Coates said as he smiled with relish.

"Not that I'm sorry we did, but why did we stop firing?"

"Heat. Th' barrels get so 'ot that acc'racy falls off quick affer th' fferd shot. In battle yer may 'ave ter try ter account fer it and keep firin', right, but there's no sense puttin' stress on th' barrels in target shootin'."

"How do we know how well we did?" someone else asked.

"Aye, that's alwuz the rub," Coates said. "First, a group of siters will determine which shells landed where, then they'll make a report ter the chief gunnery officer, right, 'oo'll report it ter the captain, 'oo'll report it ter the bridge crew, 'oo'll then give permission ter tell us. It's alwuz like that in the Navy—ffem wot does the bloomin' shootin' don't know a fink till the officers 're well 'n' ready ter tell 'em." Even though he made it sound bad, they could tell that it was mostly dramatics for their sake. Soon enough they'd be the officers. "We should know in about anuvver ten minutes 'r so. In the meantime, we should cop an order ter stand dahn, in which case we'll start maintenance on th' equipment. Yer cannever be too prepared."

* * *

The Western Mediterranean—July 1, 1940

The sight of the *Hood* from the outside was amazing. At 860 feet in length, she was two and half times as long as an American football field and more than thirty yards across at the beam. If the ship were turned vertically, she would be nearly three-quarters as tall as the Empire State Building, and with much the same grace and flowing lines. Little wonder that she was the pride of the British Navy.

Because of all the additional armor and equipment that had been added in the last twenty years, the *Hood* tended to ride low in the water, except for the bow, which swooped up in a graceful curve to add to the appearance of speed. The large superstructure, more than five stories above the waterline, bristled with the twelve big guns and all the other secondary armament that gave the *Hood* the appearance of the ultimate fighting weapon.

Inside was different. The actual function of a warship was to provide a mobile shooting platform for the guns. Nothing more than that. Of course, accomplishing their mobile mission required a great deal of complexity, ranging from the kitchens and cafeterias needed to feed 1,200 men on a regular basis to the massive steam turbines that powered the three screws at the stern of the ship. At maximum revolutions, the engines generated more than 150,000 horsepower. The ship had huge bunkers for oil storage, magazines to store explosives and shells, radio and radar rooms, the stores department where all the food and fresh water were stored, small showers for the men's personal hygiene, and hooks in the oddest of places where they could suspend hammocks when off duty. At night the mess hall turned into a dormitory.

In the course of his first month at sea, Michael got to explore every corner of the ship as part of his training. As far as he could tell, there wasn't a part of it that he didn't like, although the ubiquitous naval gray was boring.

"The part I wasn't ready for is the lack of windows," Michael said to Jamie Wilcox, one of the other lieutenants.

"No windows? What are you talking about? No warship could have windows—it would expose the whole interior to the blast of an enemy torpedo or shell!" He shook his head in disbelief.

"I know that—it's just that I'd never thought about it. The whole idea of going to sea is that, well, you'd get to see the ocean. But most of the time is spent indoors getting thrown around by the waves and bumping into a thousand other fellows you don't know."

Jamie laughed. "You're really something, Carlyle. Is that the American speaking in you?" Somehow it always came back to his being an American. Whenever he did anything the others considered odd, it was because he was an American. He couldn't tell if it was because they felt superior or envious. Maybe it was both.

"Well, it's different than I expected," Michael said stubbornly.

"Me too, actually. I didn't think it would be so boring. We've been out of port for nearly three weeks now, and there hasn't been a single call to action. We didn't even get off the ship in Gibraltar. Meanwhile, the whole of Europe has surrendered to Hitler, and the Royal Navy Volunteer Reserve barely managed to pull our men out of Dunkirk. That's where the action is—not here on this oversized bucket."

Michael smiled. He knew exactly how Jamie felt. Jamie had graduated in his same class at college, and while they had never been that friendly in school, out here they'd become good friends. As the lowest of the low on the ship, they needed to band together for mutual support. They found mutual ground in athletics. Jamie had been something of a tennis star, while Michael had favored soccer, although he wasn't nearly as notorious as Jamie. Jamie's father was a career naval officer, and it was apparent that Jamie felt the weight of family tradition.

"So if there wasn't a war on and you could choose whatever you wanted to do with your life, what would it be?" Michael loved to ask the British this question, because it always discomfited them.

"What? What kind of a question is that? I'm a Navy man. That's all." Sure enough, Michael had caused the consternation he'd hoped.

He responded. "I know you had to go into the Navy—just like I'll probably wind up in Parliament some day. But if it were up to you, what would you do?"

"Why do you ask questions like that, Carlyle? You serve where you're born. It does no good to speculate."

Michael laughed. "This time it *is* because I'm American. You see, over there you do whatever you want. No class structure—just people figuring out what they're interested in and then going after it. Sometimes I really miss their attitude, even though I was young when we left."

Jamie was thoughtful. It appeared Michael had actually piqued his interest. "Of course I'd like to pursue tennis . . . That's the only thing that really interests me," Jamie said with frankness. "A solicitor, I suppose. I like the law and think I'd be good at it." He looked up and frowned. "But a lot of good that does. The Wilcoxes are a seafaring family going back more than two hundred years. Far be it from me to spoil such a perfect record." He laughed, but Michael saw something of a wistful look in his eye. After a moment, Jamie caught himself and said, "Well?"

"Well, what?"

"What about you? Since you're now predestined to go into politics since you decided to be British, what would you do differently?"

Michael smiled. "That's the downside of freedom. I honestly don't know. I used to think I wanted to be in the British or U.S. Navy, but now I'm finding it's not everything I thought it would be. I'm not that great an athlete, so that's not going anywhere." He shrugged his shoulders. "I don't really know what I'm good for."

Before Jamie could press him further, they were interrupted by the sound of the Klaxon horn sounding overhead, calling them to battle stations.

"What's that, then?" Jamie asked anxiously as they started running to the forward gun turret where they'd been assigned.

"Maybe I don't want action, after all," Michael said, his heart pounding in his chest.

Once the ship had come to full readiness, there was a sustained silence as everyone waited for orders. The bosun pipe sounded through the loudspeaker system, and they heard the captain's voice say, "Attention all hands. This is the captain speaking. Vice Admiral Sir James Somerville wishes to address the crew."

Somerville had made the *Hood* his flagship just a few days earlier when they'd stopped briefly in Gibraltar. As the commander of Force H, he had the task of protecting the entrance to the Mediterranean for British shipping, as well as keeping the Germans out. He had a very commanding voice, even over the loudspeaker.

"As you know, our former ally France has capitulated to the Germans. Paris and the northeast section of the country will be placed under German occupation, while a separate and supposedly independent government will be established in the small southern French town of Vichy to manage the unoccupied precincts of the country. What all this has to do with us is that Mr. Churchill's government has been trying in vain to gain assurances from Vichy that the French Navy will not be turned over to the Germans to use against us. Unfortunately, the response has been tepid.

"Accordingly, our new orders are to proceed to Oran, North Africa, where I will offer the French four alternatives: Join with us and sail their ships to British harbors; turn their ships over to us with the assurance they'll be returned to the French at the end of hostilities; sail their ships to a French port in the West Indies in the Caribbean, where they'll be demilitarized; or watch while we sink their ships.

"Naturally, we hope they'll accept option one or two since it would be a tragedy if we had to turn on those who were our allies and friends less than a week ago.

"At this point our intentions are to remain top secret, so there will be no communications with home. It will take several days of sustained steaming to get there, and in the unlikely event of hostilities, it's imperative that our gunnery be accurate from the first shot. All gun crews will practice. I expect you will all do your duty in this action. Gentlemen, we shall prevail in this operation, code named 'Catapult.' Admiral out."

The bosun piped "stand down." Chatter began almost immediately in all quarters. While it was exciting to think of finally seeing battle, it was depressing to realize that they might have to destroy a fleet that until a few weeks earlier they had counted on to help them destroy the Germans. Without the French, they truly were alone against the seemingly indomitable Germans.

Chapter Four

A DISTURBING CONFRONTATION

London—July 1940

"What do you mean my minister can't gain access? He has the security clearance, you know!" The impeccably dressed man represented one of the most influential men in the government, but one who nonetheless was not on the cleared list.

"I'm sorry, sir, but he does not have security clearance for this facility. Twenty-two names appear on the list, that's all. Until you can persuade the prime minister to modify the register, neither you nor your minister can enter." The young staffer who was assigned to the security desk glanced up at Philip for reassurance because the other fellow seemed so certain. He was immediately reassured when Philip cleared his throat in such a menacing fashion that the older man was forced to look down for a moment. In that instant, the battle was settled.

But even so, he still stood there, as if by simply waiting long enough, he'd somehow win the point anyway. When the staffer failed to say anything, Philip stepped into the breach. "Well then, you've heard your answer. So be off and on your way, and do not attempt this again. If I need to speak to your minister, I will—but it will not be a pleasant conversation, I can assure you." Philip's voice was steady and calm, but there was absolutely no doubt what he meant.

At this, the fellow turned and huffed off down the hallway, muttering under his breath, "We'll see about this!"

Philip waited until he was out of sight and then turned to the young assistant. "Markus, you acted rightly, but you have to speak with absolute certainty so they don't think they can continue to challenge you."

"Yes, sir. I'll do better next time."

Philip smiled. "Of course you will. Just remember that you're the first line of defense to the very important work that goes on here. If you ever have any doubts whatsoever, you should immediately ring for your superior."

"I will. I'm very glad you were here."

Philip sighed. Markus was dependable, or Philip wouldn't have selected him for this detail. Markus had bad knees, which made him ineligible for military service, so Markus had found an administrative posting to help move the war effort along.

"Why don't you take a moment and go get some refreshment, Markus. I'll watch the desk for a few minutes."

"Oh, no, sir, I couldn't do that. You're a minister!"

Philip shook his head. "Not to worry. I know we ministers aren't up to much, but I'm quite sure I can cover for a few minutes at least."

"Oh, I didn't mean . . ." Markus started to stammer.

"I know what you meant. But believe me, this is not below my station. You have an amazingly important position, even though you may not fully understand it because of the confidential nature of it all. But it will do me good to get some frontline experience. So take a few moments to relax and stretch your legs."

"Thank you, sir. Thank you very much."

With that, Markus was off to the small staff lounge.

As Philip settled down in the chair behind the desk, he reflected on the fact that while only those with proper clearance knew exactly what was going on in the cabinet war rooms, there were a handful of people who were close enough to the center of power to see the comings and goings of enough important individuals to realize that they were being excluded from something very important. And it bothered them. But it was one of Philip's tasks to see that Civil Service acted properly to keep the facility secret and secure. In view of this encounter, he would request additional training on how to be assertive for each of those assigned to staff the desk. But he had to do it in a way that didn't reflect negatively on Markus, who after this encounter would undoubtedly act properly.

So quickly was he lost in thought that the sound of a seductive female voice startled him. "Excuse me, but am I to be denied entrance as well?"

The hair on the back of Philip's neck stood up. Claire's seductive voice always unnerved him, but more so at this moment because he hadn't expected her. In an instant, the tension of the day evaporated, and he looked up and smiled.

"Just how long have you been standing here?"

"Actually, I was standing over there where you fine gentlemen couldn't see me. I was there long enough to hear you put that man in his place. You're quite the harsh one. I'm afraid I may have to use hidden resources to get past you."

"Madam, we've been warned about enemy provocateurs who would try to use their feminine wiles to beguile us. Am I to presume I'm under such an assault on my integrity at this very moment?"

"Pure loyalty to Crown and country, I assure you, sir."

"But with that accent, it's clear you're a foreigner."

Claire laughed, and Philip stood and hugged his wife, who had been home for less than a week now. Having been a bachelor well into his thirties, Philip had never imagined how much he could miss someone—could miss her embrace. After such a long separation, her presence filled his heart with joy.

"I thought maybe you could slip away for lunch. Since I never know what hour of the day or night you'll come home, I want to make sure you see daylight for at least a few moments each day."

"That sounds delightful, my dear. How about we go over to the Travellers? I know it's your favorite pub." Philip stood up and stretched. "But you undoubtedly heard enough to know that I have to wait a few moments for the rightful occupant of this chair to return."

"I don't mind waiting—as long as it's legal."

Philip smiled again. "If you are arrested, I'll vouch for you. As soon as I can break away, of course." Now it was Claire who pursed her lips at this response.

But before she could offer a retort, they heard the sound of heavy footsteps on the marble floor. Glancing up, Philip was startled by a voice that he didn't wish to hear. "Carlyle! I say, Carlyle, hold your place!"

"Heaven help me," Philip said quietly to Claire. She turned to see the reason for his distress and saw the dark face of Lord Cook storming toward them, his perpetual scowl making the darkened corridor even more gloomy than usual. Cook was another of the landed Lords, but one who held no position in the government.

"How may I be of assistance, my lord?" Philip offered despite Cook's grimace.

Cook responded fiercely with, "I prefer not to do business at all with you, Carlyle. The only help I need from you is to find someone who can authorize my entrance to this facility."

Philip's throat tightened, but he resolved to keep his temper. Cook was known as a zealot and had been an endless source of trouble to Philip since his return to England from America. He would have preferred to simply dismiss Cook at this point but had to show proper courtesy if at all possible. So he said as evenly as he could, "It goes without saying that I regard your position in the Lords with the utmost respect, Lord Cook, and would do anything possible to accommodate you. However," and at this Philip's face hardened, "I am presently tasked with the responsibility of certifying credentials, and so you must work with me whether you prefer it or not. Now, how may I help you?"

"Listen to me, Carlyle. I have no patience with you as a member of the Lords or the government. It's a disgrace to you and your father that you emigrated to America and apostatized from the Established Church. That you would join an American cult and still have the presumption to sit with the peers is an insult. Based on what you have done, you should hold no office in this or any other government. So again I insist that you direct me to someone else."

Philip took a deep breath to steady himself. With as level a voice as he could muster, he replied, "You're wasting my time, George. There is no one else. If you choose not to talk with me, I'll be glad to have security escort you out."

Cook's face flushed. "Clearly this posting of yours is a matter that should be attended to!"

"Then deal with it on your own time, not mine. Good day, Lord Cook!"

Cook hesitated, clearly annoyed, yet painfully aware that Philip held the upper hand. Philip wondered whether he'd compromise and talk with him or surrender to his intransigence. Fortunately, he yielded. "You haven't heard the end of this, Carlyle. I promise you that!" And with that he turned to leave.

"By the way, George," Philip said levelly. "You're welcome to raise whatever questions you like about my government service, but this had better be the last time I ever hear you talk about my religious sensibilities. You know nothing about my beliefs, and they are irrelevant to my service in the government. I will not have you insulting both me and my church. Do I make myself clear?" The menacing tone had returned to Philip's voice, and Claire was startled to see the fire in his eyes.

Cook paused and turned with narrowed eyes. "As I say, Carlyle, you have not heard the end of this."

"Then let us end this little episode with my position perfectly clear. Any move on your part to limit my role in government will come at a dear cost to you, George. You are not a popular person in the Lords, and you are not in a position to tackle the friends that I have on my side. So I advise you to proceed with great caution, because I am not one to be easily cowed."

Claire moved to her husband and grasped his hand. When Cook dared to glance at her, she looked back defiantly, so much so that he quickly retreated and looked again at Philip.

"Talking with you is pointless. It's my time that has been wasted, and I'll not spend another second in useless debate." Cook gave up the fight for the moment and stormed off.

Philip leaned against the wall behind him and closed his eyes.

"Are you all right, Philip?" Claire asked softly, now trying to hold back tears.

Philip opened his eyes and reached out to pull her close to him. "I'm all right. I'm sorry you had to see that. Even George is usually more discreet. He must have been very angry about his lack of credentials. I've never seen him so rude."

"Is it like that often? Is this something you have to put up with regularly? I mean about the Church?"

"Thankfully it's hardly ever like this. Here in the ministries, people are far too busy to worry about such things. Even Parliament has its share of agnostics, Jews, and those who give lip service to the Anglican Church. So most are tolerant of a Mormon in their midst. But there are a few like Cook who have too much time on their hands." He tried to smile.

"You're usually so calm with people. It was surprising to see you come on so strong." Philip could sense the uncertainty in Claire's voice.

"It's my idealistic side. Usually idealists want peace and harmony in the world and will do almost anything to avoid a confrontation. But when crossed on a point of moral importance there's nothing quite so dangerous as a wounded idealist—we're all fangs and fury, I'm afraid." He smiled. "And today George crossed me on two counts—my role in the government and my feelings about the Church. I guess I went off like a double-barreled shotgun, didn't I?"

She slipped her arm through his. "You were actually quite magnificent, you know."

Philip shook his head. "I should have kept my temper."

"I mean it, Philip. You were eloquent and strong. I've never been so proud."

"Thank you, but in the long run it served no purpose—disagreements like this never do. I have no idea why he chose this moment to take me on. We've had confrontations in the past that went nowhere, and I thought he was finally ready to set them aside. But I must trigger some instinctual hatred in him." Philip was quiet for a moment. "The problem is I don't really know what the disagreement was about—the fact that he doesn't think I should be in the Lords because I'm a Mormon or whether that was simply a cover for whatever his real motive was in trying to get in here. He's arrogant enough that the thought of any facility being off-limits would irritate him. But to all outward appearances, this is no place of special importance. I don't understand why he'd want access." He let his mind wonder about Cook and then pulled his thoughts together and turned to Claire.

"I'll just never understand why people choose to argue over differences rather than find the common ground," Philip said as he squeezed her hand. "The problem is that such a confrontation simply invites hatred. No matter how effective I am, it still fuels hatred. With the nation in so much peril, you'd think we could be at peace with one another here."

"Good, my idealist is back trying to make peace again. But don't back down too quickly—ultimately you must stand up for what you believe, and you did that today."

They were interrupted as the staffer returned.

"Any problems while I was gone, sir?"

"Just one. Lord Cook tried to gain access, and I was forced to put him in his place rather sternly. I will see to it that the staff is on notice about him."

"Yes, sir. I'll be sure to note it. Anything else?"

"No, that was plenty."

"Thank you, then, for covering for me, sir."

Philip sighed and helped Claire through the door as they stepped out into the dampness of the London air. He was still trembling, and they walked in silence for a time until he was finally composed enough to speak again. "I shouldn't take this personally, Claire. People are under great stress these days—even Lord Cook. We should forgive him."

"Of course we should, Philip. And I'm sure you'll find a way to speak civilly with him again." Claire paused, then mischievously said, "But I'm still proud of the way you stood up to the old windbag."

Philip laughed and hugged her close as they strode into the public square. "Now I believe you promised me lunch," he said cheerfully, and the combination of fresh air and Claire's good nature helped him shake off the encounter with George Cook altogether.

Chapter Five

A NAVAL BATTLE
BETWEEN FRIENDS

Mers-el-Kébir, North Africa—July 3, 1940

Michael and Jamie stood silently on the same spot where they had spent the last five hours. The British fleet had arrived that morning at 0700 and had been waiting in increasing frustration ever since. At first it was assumed that an amicable accord would be reached, but by noon, everyone had watched with increasing anxiety as airplanes from the aircraft carrier *Ark Royal* had mined the entrance to the harbor to prevent any breakout by the French. That's also the time when Jamie and Michael came on duty, and they'd been there ever since.

It was almost comical to watch the destroyer *Foxhound* leave and return, leave and return, as Admiral Somerville's envoy, Captain Holland, had attempted to negotiate with the French commander, Admiral Gensoul. Although such things were meant to be confidential, word passed quickly in the Navy, and by now everyone had been made to understand that the admiral had been profoundly shocked that Somerville himself had not made the trip into the harbor to see him. The French were proud, and Gensoul reacted to this as an intentional snub, even though Holland had been selected because he spoke fluent French and had extensive contacts in the French Navy, which at the time was the fourth largest in the world. Accordingly, Gensoul initially refused to see Holland.

Eventually, though, Captain Holland had the dash and daring to simply force his way onto the admiral's flagship, the battle cruiser *Dunkerque,* where he had finally been given an audience. That was hours earlier, and still nothing seemed resolved.

"We're still at full steam," Jamie said quietly to Michael.

Michael looked up at the massive funnels and saw black smoke drifting into the hot afternoon air. It would take on a much darker cast if they started moving. Then he looked out across the water and replied, "The whole fleet is at full steam, as are the French."

It was actually one of the most impressive sights imaginable. The *Hood* was the largest ship in the British group, but the *Valiant, Resolution, Arethusa, Enterprise,* and eleven destroyers also waited nearby, poised to move in for the kill. Perhaps the deadliest ship in the fleet was the *Ark Royal* and its aircraft, which were massed and ready for action on the flight deck.

The French group was perhaps even more impressive. In addition to the *Dunkerque,* they had a second battle cruiser, the *Strasbourg,* and two great battleships, the *Provence* and *Bretagne.* These goliaths were supported by an aviation transport and six light cruisers and destroyers.

"How do you suppose we'll stack up against two battle cruisers and two battleships?" Michael asked, just a hint of anxiety in his voice.

"Oh, we'll do all right," Jamie replied as if he were an authority. "They don't have 15-inch guns like we do. Besides, they have no room to maneuver bottled up like that in the harbor. I hope it doesn't come to blows, not between allies!"

Michael happened to glance down at his watch. It was now 1700 hours. A runner came bounding up to Michael and Jamie, passing along the order for them to move into their respective turrets.

"Doesn't sound good," Jamie said. His anxiety seemed to be confirmed by the sight of the *Foxhound* steaming at full speed out of the harbor. "Good luck, Carlyle." Then, with a quick smile, Jamie said, "Bet you dessert that our shots fall truer than yours!"

"You're on," Michael shouted back, already on the run. Then he descended into the darkness of the gun turret, where he found everyone working in smooth precision to bring the shells into position for loading.

"It's stifling in here," he said breathlessly. Africa in July was breathtakingly hot, even on the deck, where the breeze provided some relief. But here inside the turret, the ventilator fans didn't stand a chance.

"You think it's hot now, Mr. Carlyle," one of the men said cheerfully, "Just wait till we start firing. You're going to be wishin' you were on the Iceland patrol before this is over."

Michael laughed.

As he moved into his assigned position, the interphone rang, and the man who answered it gestured for Michael to come take the handset. Michael's startled look brought a simple shrug from the seaman.

Picking up the phone, Michael stiffened, then replied curtly, "Yes, sir. Right away!"

"Wot is it, Mr. Carlyle?" Chief Coates asked him.

"I've been ordered to the bridge," Michael said, the shock of the order betrayed in his voice.

"Right, so yer get ter miss out on all th' action dahn 'ere?" Coates looked stern. "Too good ter be wiv the boys 'ere when the guns go a'flamin'?"

"I don't know why," Michael said haltingly. "I don't know what I might have done. I don't want to leave."

The chief softened. "Relax, Mr. Carlyle. It's likely that the senior officers spot potential in yer, right, and they're simply invitin' yer ter th' bridge ter view th' battle from a command point of view. It's a right great honor."

That shocked Michael even more than his initial thought that he was to be reprimanded. "Do you think?" No matter how hard he tried, he couldn't suppress the small smile that crept up on the corners of his mouth.

"Oh, fer the luv of—" Coates returned to his usual scowl. "Yes, Mr. Carlyle, I do. It's not like yer'd make a load o' diffrence dahn 'ere, now is it. They probably don't want yer junia officers interferin' wiv th' gun operation, so they might as well 'ave yer up there for the photos 'n' all."

"Thank you, Chief. Your sarcasm has brought me back to my senses." Michael pretended to return a scowl. "Now, I guess I shouldn't keep the captain waiting."

"No, sir, I spose not. And remember; if 'e gets killed in battle and yer take over command of the ship, just be sure ter order an extra tot of rum for the fellas dahn 'ere."

Michael tipped his head to the side. "I might just do that, Coates. Of course that depends on your shooting!"

"Git outta 'ere!" Coates yelled. "Before we load yer inta th' breech."

* * *

Bridge of HMS Hood—July 3, 1940

"Sublieutenant Carlyle, reporting as ordered, SIR!" *Darn, I made an American* R *sound on the end of "sir,"* Michael thought.

"At ease, Mr. Carlyle." The duty officer half led, half pushed him to an out-of-the-way spot toward the starboard side. "The captain wishes you to observe bridge action during battle. Do your best to stay out of the way."

"Yes, sir," Michael replied. Then, almost inaudibly and to himself he said, "I get to see the *Hood* go into action."

"It will be a first for all of us, Mr. Carlyle." Michael stiffened immediately as the captain came over. "Twenty years, and the *Hood* hasn't had to fire a single shot in anger. Now it looks like our first hot engagement will be against our friends. A tragedy."

"Yes, sir. Thank you, sir, for inviting me to the bridge."

"Knew your father in school. I'm glad the Carlyles have finally decided to support the Navy."

In spite of himself, Michael smiled. "Yes, sir—I feel the same way."

The captain acknowledged the smile, then turned to far more urgent matters.

At 1750 Michael overheard Admiral Somerville utter a mild curse—something to express his frustration that Admiral Gensoul had failed to accept any of their terms. On his own initiative, Somerville probably would have waited even longer to initiate the battle, but within the hour he'd received an order from Churchill to resolve the situation immediately.

"Well, then!" Somerville said with something of resignation in his voice. "That's the way it must be." Into the intercom he announced, "Open fire!"

Michael watched in fascination as the forward turrets swiveled on their mounts and the protruding barrels of the 15-inch guns raised their elevation to match the coordinates set in the fire control center one deck directly below the bridge. Subconsciously he steadied himself, as if he were in the turret. At precisely 1754 there was a great thwumping sound that shook the bridge, followed by a second and a third. The geyser of flame that shot out from each barrel was an awesome sight, followed by great billowing clouds of dark black smoke. A second volley followed in quick succession.

"Drat," Michael said to no one in particular. "Wilcox got the first shots." There was a pause in the shooting as the observers waited to see where the shots fell. They were shooting from the northwest of the harbor at maximum range of almost 16 kilometers. The launch from the *Foxhound* had remained in the harbor, and its crew radioed back that the initial volley from the *Hood* had fallen short.

After quick adjustments, a third volley was launched. The noise was tremendous, although not as bad as it was down in the gun turrets themselves. Michael had been handed a set of binoculars and had trained his gaze on the battleships when he saw a terrific explosion in the midst of the tightly packed French ships. A bright orange column of flame shot straight up into the air, forcing him to stifle his instinct to shout, "We got a hit!" He actually bit his lip to keep himself quiet, not only because it would violate protocol, but because it was totally unnecessary. The dark cloud rising up to nearly two hundred feet above the harbor quickly confirmed that at least one of their projectiles had found its quarry.

"It's the *Bretagne,* sir," one of the deck officers said in a forced flat voice. He had a headset on and was monitoring reports from the *Foxhound.*

"The battleship is blown to pieces!" one of the senior officers said. Before anyone could reply, there was a second, smaller explosion, making it clear that a destroyer had been hit as well.

In a matter of moments, the entire harbor was obscured by so much smoke that field glasses provided no additional insight. Even the aircraft from the *Ark Royal* flying above the scene couldn't penetrate the pall to give much information.

"Incoming shots," someone said. The *Strasbourg* and *Dunkerque* had opened fire. Michael watched everyone brace for a potential impact. Fortunately, nothing hit them or any of the neighboring ships, but they saw some waterspouts off to the port side.

By now, all the ships in Force H were engaging the enemy, and a simple glance around showed the fully relentless firepower of the British Navy in a full engagement. The guns were all firing in an even sequence that was positive testimony to the many drills the crews had conducted in the previous months at sea. As he saw three more rounds fired from his turret, Michael felt a twinge of guilt at not being down with his crew. He looked around and decided not to feel too guilty. *I'm watching the* Hood *control the greatest naval engagement since the Great War!* he thought as he felt his skin tingle at the sheer exhilaration of it all.

"Another hit!" This time it was harder for the officer to control his voice, since the tremendous sheet of flame that managed to brighten even the afternoon had by default declared another battle-ship hit.

Without realizing he'd been doing it, Michael mentally counted the number of rounds fired by primary armament. He paused to think, when he heard the guns fall silent. *Thirty-six rounds total. That's . . . let me see . . . 720,000 pounds of explosives we've dumped on the French.* He could tell by the look on the admiral's face that this was not a battle he had wanted.

"Port 180 degrees!" the captain commanded.

The admiral added, "All ships make smoke." The signals officer immediately sent the signal, and the various ships ignited the dark heavy oil in the smoke pots to create an obscuring smokescreen that quickly engulfed the ships in a heavy dark cloud that made it impossible for the enemy to visually sight in on their location.

By this point, the counterfire from the French ships had started to die down—obviously they had far greater problems to deal with. But the shore batteries were getting alarmingly close. In fact, as the British fleet started its turn, there was a small explosion on the port side of the ship near the base of the funnels. Damage control reported that there was no significant damage, but a shower of splinters had injured an officer and a seaman. Fortunately, the damage to the ship itself was superficial.

As the armada disappeared into the smoke bank, they received word that another French destroyer had been blown up while trying to escape through the entrance of the harbor. At this point, opposing fire dropped off completely, and the admiral ordered a cease-fire.

"We want to give them a chance to escape their ships and make it to land before they sink," he said to the captain.

Michael glanced down at his watch. It was now 1804. Without thinking, he let out a small whistle and said, "Ten minutes to destroy a fleet."

The officer closest to him turned to look at him, which caused Michael's face to turn red. But the fellow nodded to show that he shared his amazement.

They watched for a few moments as the smoky haze started to lift from the harbor. It was an incredible scene. The battle cruiser *Dunkerque* was dead in the water, the *Provence* and the *Commandant Teste* were on fire, and incredibly, the *Strasbourg* and two destroyers were under full steam trying to escape the harbor.

"Signal from the shore, sir."

"What is it?"

"Request you cease firing."

"That's confirmed by wireless transmission as well," another signals officer reported.

The admiral pursed his lips. He was clearly angry. "Reply, 'Unless I see your ships sinking, I shall open fire again.'"

No more signals were witnessed, and the ship remained on alert but refrained from firing for another few minutes until the enemies' intention could be determined. At 1820 an air report was handed to the commander, indicating that one of the ships had cleared the harbor and was now heading east.

"Missed our mines," one of the officers said quietly.

"Divert the Swordfish aircraft from our carrier *Ark Royal* to attack the *Strasbourg*. Initiate a pursuit to the east." With that simple command, the entire, largely undamaged, British strike force started after the two ships that had made it into the open waters of the Mediterranean. Perhaps twenty minutes later, the motor launch from the *Foxhound* was picked up, bearing Captain Holland, who had done his best to avert the unfortunate confrontation. It was disheartening to think that a significant loss had been inflicted on allies—and all because they insisted on pushing back against the legitimate demands of the British, who only wanted to prevent the French ships from falling under German control.

"Well, Mr. Carlyle, what do you think?" the captain asked Michael.

"I think I just witnessed something monumental. Congratulations, sir, on a successful engagement."

"I wish I could take pleasure in it. Now, then, I suspect you ought to get back to your gun crew. They'll have some stories to tell."

"Yes, sir. Thank you for this opportunity."

"And convey my personal commendation for a job well done. It appears that all our guns performed well."

"They'll be pleased by that, sir." And with that, Michael took his leave of the bridge.

* * *

"You have to agree that I deserve *your* dessert because at least *I* was engaged in the action, not drinking tea and watching it from the rarified view of the penthouse suite," Jamie argued to Michael at the mess hall after the battle.

"Ah, but I'm quite certain it was *my* turret that struck the first blow on the *Dunkerque.* The first volley clearly fell short. And *yours* was the first to fire."

"And this hit that you claim . . . you had *what* to do with that?"

"Training, of course. Train your crew how to do the job, and you really become a shadow after that. It's a weak leader who always has to personally supervise."

Jamie shook his head in disgust. "Can they really teach you Americans to be so self-confident in just nine years? Do they have classes on hubris?"

"Oh, ho!" Michael snorted. "A British aristocrat lecturing *me* on snobbishness? Now *there's* something to write in my journal." Then, before Jamie could retort, he added, "Still, I think you're entitled." He shoved his dessert across the table to Jamie.

"Good! But why are you giving in so easily?" Jamie said, looking suspicious.

"I just figure you need something to clear the taste of cordite out of your mouth. Rather more unpleasant down there than where I was, I suppose."

"Oh," Jamie said with a shake of his head. "I'll eat this with pleasure, you piker!"

"Just following orders. After all, they *needed* me on the bridge." When he saw Jamie getting ready for yet another volley, Michael decided it was time to end the repartee, so he leaned forward and asked earnestly, "So what was it like down there? I can't even begin to imagine firing that many rounds in such a short time. It must have been madness."

"I'll tell you, as long as you promise to give me every single detail of the battle from the bridge. It almost makes a person crazy going through all that commotion without any idea whatsoever about whether you're being effective or not."

Michael watched with some regret as Jamie stabbed a fork into Michael's prized pie, but it was a small price to pay for his experience on the bridge. Smiling, and in something of a conspiratorial overtone, he leaned forward and started retelling the battle from start to finish. The two friends spent the next hour reliving each and every detail of the ten-minute battle of Mers-el-Kébir, in which there were 1,297 French missing or dead and not a single British casualty. It was, perhaps, the most regrettable victory in Royal Navy history.

Chapter Six

THE BATTLE OF BRITAIN

The English Channel Ports—July 1940

"Quite a sight, isn't it?" Sir John Gaines asked Philip as the two of them rode in a car headed toward the harbor.

The sight of the naval dockyard in flames was sickening. Twisted wreckage smoldered on the piers, and as they were watching, a giant loading crane toppled to the ground in a sickening groan as the metal sagged, then crumpled, melting from the fierce heat of the incendiary bomb that had burned at its base at nearly 2,000 degrees Fahrenheit.

Having failed to win a British cease-fire with the surrender of France, Hitler had ordered the "softening up" of the British military by aerial bombardment prior to an imminent invasion of England. Hitler seemed to think it possible to extract a truce once the British felt the fearsome firepower of the Luftwaffe bombers.

"Well, the first blow on home shores has fallen," Philip finally replied. "And only the Royal Air Force and our prayers stand between us and an invasion force now."

Sir Gaines motioned for the driver to proceed toward the port, where they could conduct a brief tour so they could give a first hand account to those back at Whitehall. It was one thing to read the telegrams, but quite another to see the damage in person.

Stepping out of the car, Gaines and Philip showed their identification cards, and then Gaines headed toward one of the munitions fabrication plants that had been hit by German bombs. Philip, on the other hand, walked over to one of the ambulances, where a badly injured man was being carefully lifted onto a stretcher. As he came up to the man's side, Philip's stomach churned at the sight of his burned flesh. Half his face was an open, oozing wound, and it was clear that he was now blind in that eye. But not the other. The injured man looked up at Philip and attempted a small smile. In an instant, the years between the current war and the previous one disappeared, and Philip instinctively knelt at his side and reached down to take his uninjured hand. It was trembling. "Well, then, I see that you're one of the very first martyrs for our cause," he said in as confident a voice as he could muster. Having ministered as a chaplain to hundreds of injured men, he found that the best way to strike up a conversation was to acknowledge their wounds, but to do it in as lighthearted a fashion as possible to help them manage the inevitable fear that accompanied a debilitating injury.

"Aye, sir, Germany's claws 'r' shirp." The very act of speaking made the man wince in pain. "But yer see 'e didn't beat us. We're still 'n business, so ta speak. The British 'r' made of stronger stuff than that."

In spite of himself, Philip's eyes filled briefly with tears. "Indeed they are. At least you are." He glanced up at the medic, whose slight shake of the head indicated that the fellow wouldn't live through the night. "Can you tell me your name? I've been sent here by Mr. Churchill himself, and I'd like to mention you to him if you don't mind. He'd love a quote like the one you just spoke."

The man struggled for breath, but then he said, "The name is Chillsworth, sir. James Chillsworth—dock hand."

"Well, then, Mr. Chillsworth, I'll tell the prime minister that you personally stood up to Hermann Goering right here at the front of the war queue. He'll be proud, just as I am."

"Thank you, sir," Chillsworth said quietly. It was clear that he was drifting into unconsciousness, which would be a great blessing of relief. The morphine he'd been given was undoubtedly taking effect. Then, rallying, the man continued, "And tell him, 'God bless 'im fer wot 'e's doin'. He's the right man fer th' job, that's fer sure." Then his good eye fluttered and closed.

Philip stood as the stretcher was lifted into the ambulance, and he waited for its departure as a sign of respect. As he turned and looked around the dockyard, he realized that the medical teams were going to be very busy for the rest of that day and likely for many more to come.

* * *

The Cabinet War Rooms—September 1940

"Care to take a drive with me, Carlyle?"

"Of course," Philip said evenly. Although he and the prime minister had exchanged cursory greetings in the course of the past year, there had never been time for a serious conversation, so he looked forward to a chance to speak privately.

As they stepped out into the damp morning, the prime minister asked a few casual questions about Claire and the children and expressed his envy of Michael for serving on the *Hood*. "I'm an old Navy man, myself, you know. Navy and Army."

"Yes, sir."

"It's the Navy that gave us the Empire!" Churchill proudly claimed. Philip was well aware of Churchill's love of the British Empire, which extended to every quarter of the globe. Having been an ardent reader of Churchill's books and articles, he recognized the idealistic, almost romantic attachment the "old Navy man" felt for the Empire.

Without looking up, Churchill continued. "But it's airplanes that will save us now. Not capital ships nor soldiers in the field— our only hope is airplanes over the Channel."

"I'm afraid I'm so involved in my duties that I haven't kept track of how we're doing. It seems like the RAF must be stretched to its limits."

"If you only knew how thin," Churchill growled. "We're shooting their aircraft down at nearly a two-to-one ratio. Our pilots outmaneuver and outfight them in every battle, but they started the conflict with nearly twice as many aircraft as we have. No matter how fast we shoot them down, they just keep sending more. And with their control of the Low Countries and France, they can easily strike our production facilities while we're stretched to the limit to bomb theirs." They walked in silence for a few moments. "Our problem now is that we can't replace our pilots fast enough when they're killed. It's appalling . . . the punishment our brave lads are taking."

Philip simply nodded. There was nothing he could add to make the burden lighter.

Philip noticed they were almost to their destination—Fighter Command at Ipswich, where orders were given to dispatch the pilots in response to German excursions. He had heard about it, of course, but felt a thrill to think he would actually see the battles develop on the large map plots where all the information was tracked. Philip was surprised that Churchill hadn't asked him about the Lords or the operations of the war room. Churchill, apparently, had simply wanted some companionship—a brief chance to talk with someone who would not impose on him. *I'm content with that,* Philip thought.

"By the way, it seems that you have some powerful friends who are watching out for your interests."

Philip caught his breath and raised an eyebrow in curiosity. "Sir?"

"Apparently there was some ruckus created by one of the Lords about your posting. Now, who was it?" he furrowed his brow, trying to remember.

Philip's heart sunk. "Lord Cook, I expect . . ."

"Yes, that's it! Cook!"

"I had a row with him one day about access to some of the sensitive areas, and it turned rather personal," Philip started to explain.

"What? Oh, don't worry about that. Of course you did what was right. The interesting thing is that when he tried to stir things up, a number of the Lords rallied to your defense, including some of the Lords Spiritual, before the government even had to get involved. The report I got on it was that they spoke of your integrity and humanity. Even Cook was smart enough to know to drop the issue at that point."

Philip was so astonished that he didn't know what to say. Even the Lords Spiritual? They were the archbishops of the Church of England, entitled to sit in the Lords by virtue of their senior positions in the Established Church. To have their esteem meant a great deal to Philip, who had automatically left their circle when he joined the LDS Church. The truth was that he missed the association.

Just as they reached the steps, the prime minister stopped and turned to look directly at Philip. "It's lucky for his lordship that he did not press the issue further, because I hold you in exactly the same esteem as those who defended you. Although I think the abstemious habits of your church are dubious, you bring great credit to your faith. I thought you should know that."

Philip had to swallow before replying meekly, "Thank you, sir." Then Philip smiled at Churchill's dig about the abstemious Word of Wisdom. It was well known that Churchill relished a good glass of wine and a cigar and credited his longevity to his bad habits.

Churchill smiled mischievously. "Well, enough of that nonsense about Cook. Care to see where the real action takes place? You never know if this is the day that the Empire itself hangs in the balance."

"I can't imagine anything I'd like more." And with that they disappeared into the bowels of the great building.

Once inside the plot room, the prime minister moved forward and began engaging those in charge of the battle in pointed questions, frequently gesturing toward the map. Finally, he took a seat in the center of the room, where he started smoking one of his enormous cigars. Philip was offered a chair at the back of the room, in a darkened corner where he could observe the action without getting in the way. It was a fascinating place, much like the cabinet war rooms themselves, but with floor-to-ceiling maps of southern England covering the walls instead of the gigantic map of the entire world and its oceans. A bevy of clerks quietly scurried about carrying messages, updating the board to show which squadrons were engaged, which were in ready reserve, and which were in the act of refueling and maintenance. As the afternoon progressed, it seemed that more and more of the units were in battle, with a corresponding decrease in those that were available to take their place when fuel ran low or ammunition was expended.

"Blasted Huns are sending everything they've got," the prime minister cursed at one point.

Even though it was part of the British tradition to remain as impassive as possible in situations like this, Philip could see a growing look of concern on the faces of everyone in the room, which indicated to him that things were getting desperate. If the RAF was unable to fully engage the Germans at any point, there would be a German breakthrough that would bring massive destruction to the ports and factories in the vulnerable areas.

"There's a tipping point," he'd been told by one of the Air Force advisors earlier that week, "at which you suddenly begin to lose ground. When more of your aircraft are on the field for refueling, the Germans can focus their attack on that specific airfield to destroy the aircraft on the ground. Your ability to put up a defensive shield is compromised even further, and very soon your strength and vitality simply evaporate."

Philip imagined it to be like an arm-wrestling match in which two opponents are closely matched. As they struggle against each other with approximately equal strength, neither is particularly vulnerable until one gains a bit of ground at the other's expense, then a bit more, and then a bit more. The increasing advantage is so slight that it's hardly noticeable. But then, a certain point is reached in which a cascade of failure causes the match to end suddenly as the weaker of the two loses strength and finds his arm slammed to the table. Looking up at the board, on which more and more squadrons were engaged each hour, he couldn't help but wonder if today were the day. The thought made him shudder with horror.

By the afternoon, Philip was shifting uncomfortably in his seat as he watched more and more aircraft being removed from the board. The thought of the loss of human life made him want to weep, but of course he couldn't in that situation.

Finally, a point was reached at which every single squadron on the board was engaged, with no reserve units displayed. "What other resources do we have to back this up?" he heard the prime minister ask the air marshal. "None," was the simple reply. "We have no more reserves." At that the room went silent as all eyes watched the board to see what would happen. This was, indeed, the day when the fate of the Empire hung in the balance. *We have reached the tipping point!* Philip thought as another worker was removed from the board.

* * *

Driving home that night proved to be a nightmare. Philip had shared in the exhausted jubilation at Fighter Command when the number of British kills began to mount and one by one the German units had started to withdraw. In spite of the overwhelming number of aircraft the enemy had launched that day, the Royal Air Force had managed to turn them back. It was a superhuman effort—one conducted by so few for the good of so many.

After the battle was over, reports were received of pilots falling asleep while sitting in a chair having a drink because they were so exhausted from the multiple sorties they'd been forced to fly. And even now as Philip fought his way through the darkened streets of London, he could imagine the teams of mechanics frantically working to repair damaged fighters so they'd be ready for the expected onslaught the next day. It was a miracle of human endurance in the utmost extremity.

Unfortunately, Philip had his own problems to worry about. While the German fighter aircraft had withdrawn, the Wehrmacht had decided to follow up the daylight attacks with night bombing on the city. This was relatively unusual at this point in the war, and Philip felt a bit beleaguered that they'd decided to drop bombs on the one night he was out and about in a car. In spite of himself he laughed at the situation. Somehow he took it personally that the Nazis were trying to kill him—and doing a heck of a job at the exercise. As he made his way to the west side of the Thames, the bombing was in full fury, and driving through the maelstrom was proving a harrowing experience. Headlights were forbidden, and all the street lamps had been extinguished. Windows were covered in heavy blackout curtains, and Philip was forced to drive by the eerie glow of a small sliver of moonlight as he slowly worked his way back toward London. The greater problem was that the exploding bombs and ensuing fires lit up the night sky in brilliant flashes that ruined his night vision, forcing him to pull to the side of the road until he could see his way again.

If you'd had any common sense whatsoever, you would have stayed put at Fighter Command and slept on the floor, Philip scolded himself. But he'd wanted to get home to Claire so they could share a place in the cellar. Now he was a hazard to everyone coming out to fight the fires or maneuver the ambulances through the streets. Not only that, but he'd had a number of near hits that had shaken the car and left him feeling as if he might go deaf from the concussions. On one occasion, the blast had actually shattered the glass in the rear window. On another he'd been hit by a shockwave that forced him up and onto the sidewalk, where his car knocked off a fire hydrant, sending a geyser of water up into the night air. It made him feel guilty to know that he was denying water pressure to hydrants further down the line—hydrants that might be needed to save a home or a hospital or an entire block.

But the final blow came when a blast hit a parked truck just up the road from where he was creeping down a familiar street. The truck was launched into the air, and it landed on the trunk of his car. Although the car could still move, it was obvious that both rear tires had been flattened, and the growling of the gearbox told him that any movement he made from this point forward would do irreparable damage to what was left of the rear axle. With a sigh, he maneuvered his way to the side of the street, where he reluctantly turned the motor off. He was still several miles from home, and at first he decided that he would cautiously make his way to his house. But then a blockbuster bomb went off at the end of the street. He saw the flash, and it completely blinded him. Before he could even start counting down the seconds until it was safe to proceed, a blast of hot air picked him up and threw him into a collection of garbage cans nearly a third of the way to the corner from where he had been standing. The impact knocked him completely unconscious.

As he regained consciousness, Philip picked himself up out of the garbage cans, which had likely saved his life since the force of his body being hurled against them had been enough to crush several of the large metal garbage cans. By collapsing under the blow, the cans had absorbed enough force to save his life. Had he been blown into the side of the unyielding building instead, well, he wouldn't think about that.

The first thing he had to cope with as he came to was the sight before him. There were a number of bloodied bodies to either side of him. Houses further down the street had been torn to shreds. When he regained his wits, he crawled over to see if any of the people were alive, but there was no pulse as he put his trembling finger to their carotid arteries. Looking around, he realized that the entire block was aflame with great fingers of fire reaching up into the night sky from the apartment buildings just twenty feet away.

Dear Lord, please help me! Please help me to know what to do.

Before Philip could finish the thought, a firefighter came rushing up behind him and said, "You've got to get out of our way, man. You should be down in the Tube—what the blazes are you doing up here anyway?"

"I don't know where to find the nearest entrance to the Tube," he managed to squeak out. "I'm not from this neighborhood!"

"Oh, for the love of the saints!" The firefighter paused just long enough to physically turn Philip around and point him to the stairwell leading down into the Tube station. It wasn't more than fifty feet away, yet in the darkness Philip would have never spotted it on his own.

"Thank you . . ."

"Go. Just go!" And with that the firefighter was off and running down the street.

Half crawling, half running, Philip made his way across the now fully illuminated street, very much aware of a sharp pain in his left side. There was debris everywhere, and he had to carefully make his way past scalding hot pieces of metal that even now were still glowing red hot in the street. Suddenly he became aware of a terrible, overpowering sound—something he'd never heard before, something he'd not expected. The sound of oxygen being sucked up into the fires created a banshee shriek that was painful to his ears. Added to that were the sounds of fire sirens, water shooting under great pressure from the firemen's hoses, voices shouting orders above the cacophony . . . It all created a confusing and bewildering atmosphere that made it incredibly hard to think of even the simplest of tasks. All Philip had to do was make it to the stairwell, and yet it seemed to take him forever to pick his way across the street and down the many steps that held the hope of safety.

To fully escape the dangers of the bombs, Philip made his way down several levels before turning into the ramp area near the tracks. The sight that greeted him there was entirely different than the madness of the street above. Crowded into every conceivable spot of the platform were hundreds of people—families with crying children, older women who looked bewildered and confused, angry men who were struggling to maintain some bit of space where they could lie down and rest. It was clear that everyone was tired and frightened.

At first Philip despaired at finding a spot and figured that he'd have to rest inside the stairwell, where a direct blast would mean certain death. But eventually his eyes adjusted to the darkness, and he saw a spot over against a wall. The problem was that he'd have to step over forty or fifty people to get there, and he didn't relish the thought of raising their ire.

"Well, come on then, mate. We can all see where you need to get to."

Philip leaned forward and stared into the gloom.

"Yes, it's you we mean," the same woman's voice called out, and as soon as he spotted her he could tell that she was the unofficial leader for that spot of ground.

"Come on, we hope to get some sleep tonight if the blasted Germans will give us even a few minutes' respite."

"Thank you. I appreciate this very much," Philip said.

"Ah, a gentleman, is he! You have the manners and diction of a Lord or something!"

The woman kicked an old man in the side for not moving fast enough. "Out of the way, you blaggard. Can't you see we're being visited by someone important? He doesn't need to step over your sorry carcass." The man grumbled but moved quickly out of Philip's way.

As Philip finally reached her he paused and took her hand. "Thank you very much for helping me. I'm afraid this is my first visit to the Tube, and it's all a bit disconcerting."

"Don't that beat all," she said. "He really is a gentleman."

Philip smiled. "And right now I'm a gentleman in distress, and you're the heroine rescuing me."

Even in the dim light, he could see her face redden. "You'll do just fine. It's a bit stuffy and noisy down here, but it's safe. And you can rest without any worry. We'll watch over you."

Philip took that to mean that he wasn't in danger of being robbed or accosted. "You're very kind. For the first time all evening I do feel safe."

He started to pick his way over to the wall, where people had moved to provide him enough space to lie down comfortably.

"Excuse me, sir, but would you mind telling me who you are? We get visited by important people every once in a while, and it pleases me somehow to keep track of it." This was said by a young girl who had awakened at the sound of the conversation.

"Hush, child—you shouldn't ask!" the girl's mother scolded. "You know better than to interrupt a gentleman." Looking up, the mother said to Philip, "I'm very sorry, sir, for her impudence."

Philip knelt down and took the little girl's hands in his. "I don't mind being asked at all." He saw in her young eyes the fatigue that comes from interrupted sleep. But he also saw a simplicity and innocence that betrayed the horrors she must have endured. In the end, children always seemed to adapt to their circumstances—even such circumstances as this. It gave him hope.

"My name is Philip Carlyle. I'm a viscount who sits in Parliament. And tonight I find myself in your debt. Please tell me your name."

The girl turned, suddenly shy, so her mother told Philip that her daughter's name was Emily. By this point everyone in the area was listening in, of course, while Philip chatted with the little girl until he got her to smile.

Then, standing, Philip turned to the group. "I was on my way home from Ipswich, and I can report that our boys in the RAF held their own yet again. Hitler has thrown his very best at us, and yet he hasn't cowed us. Perhaps there is worse to come, but after this I believe we can endure whatever he has. Thank you."

Much to his surprise, the group broke into applause, and it struck him that perhaps a visit by someone in an official position was just what these people needed for morale. He was oddly grateful that fate had brought him to this place.

* * *

London—November 1940

"Claire, I plead with you to go out to the manor. I know you don't want to leave, but it's not safe here. Take the servants with you so they'll be safe too," Philip said, hoping to make Claire feel obligated to go for the servants' safety.

Just as on the first day of the war, the Carlyles were huddled in the cellar of their town house. But this time the alarm was anything but false. They could hear the sirens blaring, punctuated all too regularly by the deep concussion of bombs falling on London as the Germans increased the fury and intensity of their attacks. Having failed to subdue the RAF, Hitler had made the fateful decision to cancel the frontal attack on the RAF and to instead turn his fury on the British people themselves with indiscriminate bombing of London and other major cities.

After his tense experience at Fighter Command, Philip had fully expected the Germans to press their advantage and destroy the RAF. They could then invade England at their leisure. By changing the attack to civilian targets, however, Hitler had inadvertently given much-needed relief to the RAF, allowing them time to recuperate from their losses and rebuild their strength. It was an illogical decision on the Germans' part, but Hitler's angry and impetuous decision might well have been the thing that saved the British people.

"Philip, I want to be here with you," Claire said simply.

"And I want to be with you," he replied. He stroked her hand. "But the truth is that while I'm down there in the relative safety of the war rooms, I can't stop thinking about you and the danger you face up here. We're fooling ourselves to think this house will really provide any protection. You know what happened to the Smythes." His voice trailed off.

"Have they determined exactly what happened to the Smythes?" Claire asked tentatively. "I know Sister Smythe is still in a coma, and the children have been sent out to relatives in the north." Her voice trembled. She and Sister Smythe had worked together in the Relief Society.

"As near as they can tell, a five-hundred-pound bomb hit two doors away. It destroyed the house it hit, but the shockwave blew out all the glass in a fifty-foot radius, including at the Smythes' home. Apparently a shard was driven straight into Brother Smythe's heart. I'm sure he died instantly." Philip was thoughtful. "It's amazing that although his body was riddled with wounds from the glass, his wife sitting right next to him showed no sign of outward physical injury. The shockwave must have knocked her unconscious. It's all just speculation at this point, because how can you know for sure with a coma patient?"

"Why are they doing this? The daylight raids were bad enough, but now that they've switched to night bombing, it's terrifying!"

"Precisely. That's just what the Nazis want—to terrify the entire city so that no one gets any sleep. Eventually, people get short-tempered and jumpy, and soon morale collapses enough that mistakes are made." He turned and smiled at her. "At least that's what they hope."

"But it's not going to work, is it?" Claire said. "With the king and queen announcing their intention to stay in London at Buckingham Palace, the people are settling in for the duration."

Philip nodded thoughtfully. "The British people are patient . . . far more patient than the Nazis. Yes, I think we'll outlast them."

"Yet you want me to leave?"

Philip sighed. "Not permanently. We can still get together in the city whenever we need to . . ." His distress was evident.

"But what would I do out there? I think I'd go mad knowing there was so much suffering taking place here in London while I was hiding in your family palace in the country. I'd feel so useless."

Normally, Philip would have had a quick reply, but he felt that this was something Claire needed to think through for herself.

He'd said as much as he dared about how having her in the city made things worse for him, and he certainly didn't want to make her think he wanted to get rid of her.

"Perhaps," she said finally.

Philip waited a few moments. "Perhaps?" he prompted.

"Perhaps I could do something of value out there." She turned and looked at him. "What if we arranged for Sister Smythe to be moved out to Carlyle Manor? She and any other neighbors or members of the Church who are injured or in need of refuge would be welcome. We could probably accommodate upwards of thirty or forty people at a time. Of course, we'd have to establish ourselves as a recuperation site so that doctors and nurses could serve there." She looked at him earnestly. "Philip, would you object to turning the manor into a haven for those who need a safe place to recuperate? I'm sure it would place quite a strain on the old place."

Before he could reply, there was a terrific blast that must have been very near, because the ground under them trembled and dust and debris came floating down from the floorboards above them. Claire let out a little yelp, and Philip pulled her head close to his and did his best to shelter them. One of their young housemaids started crying until reprimanded by the cook—a no-nonsense sort of woman who was intolerant of such outbursts.

"I hope she doesn't yell at me," Claire whispered to Philip, and they both laughed. Moments later, the all clear sounded, which meant that the German aircraft had done their damage and left. There was no way of knowing whether another wave was on its way, but for the moment it seemed they were safe. Next came the ominous task of going upstairs to see what damage had been inflicted—on their own home or on the homes of their neighbors.

Crawling out from under the heavy oak table where they'd been sitting, Philip stood and helped Claire to her feet. She started toward the stairs, but he restrained her and turned her to look directly at him.

"Claire, I can think of nothing finer than to have Carlyle Manor be the kind of place you described," he said, faltering slightly. "You know the story of Dan O'Brian after the Great War. I honestly think he might have given up on life had it not been for the calming influence of the manor. It was there that he healed emotionally as well as physically. In my mind I think being in the old house somehow calmed his distress and helped him through the crisis."

Claire lifted her hands to his cheeks. "I think it was the man who befriended him that was the chief cause of his recovery." She smiled at her husband, who was always so serious these days. Of course he'd always been a fairly sober person—*kind* and *thoughtful* were the words most likely used to describe him, as opposed to *fun* or *carefree*. But the past year had exacted an unusual toll, and his dark brown hair had suddenly started to turn gray. While he never told her exactly what he did at Whitehall, she had the sense that he was in on some of the most serious decisions of the war, a war that so far was going in favor of Hitler and his thugs. England had not enjoyed a single real victory to that point, and Philip and those he worked with had to carry on in spite of relentless bad news.

"England's very lucky to have you," she said simply.

"What? What has that got to do with you starting a convalescent facility at Carlyle Manor?" Philip shook his head in genuine puzzlement. "You always seem to come up with these thoughts out of thin air, my dear."

She smiled mischievously. "They're connected in my mind."

Philip had to be content with that. After an awkward moment he asked, "So is this something you think you'll do? We can go to work on the necessary clearances and applications as soon as you're ready."

"Give me a few days to think about it, dear. You're always so impetuous—ready to start solving problems before they're even fully developed or explored. I need a little time."

"Of course. But just know that I think it's a fine idea if you determine it's something you'd like to do." He squeezed her hand affectionately. "Now, shall we go up and survey the damage?"

* * *

Philip unconsciously brushed a bit of debris off the antique partners desk that had occupied a prominent place in the study for as long as he could remember. Made of impeccably crafted cherrywood, the desk with its lacquered finish had always inspired him with its sheer masterwork. It was flawless, and he'd always been exceedingly careful to keep a leather writing pad over the work area so that the surface of the desk itself would remain unscratched and perfect. But all that had ended. Looking down, he realized that the debris he'd so casually brushed away had actually been a piece of shattered glass that had cut a long, slender scratch extending for more than six inches to the edge of the desk.

"Drat!"

"*Drat*. That's an interesting word. I love it when you talk English like that."

He looked up to see Claire smiling at him. She always managed to sneak up on him without his realizing it. "One more casualty of last night's bomb," he said dejectedly.

"Hardly the worst but probably the one that hurts you the most," she said sympathetically while glancing around the room. The only difference between their experience and the Smythes' was that Philip and Claire had had time to go to the cellar before the bomb hit. The damage to their home was otherwise quite similar, with small remnants of what had been their front windows still scattered in corners and crevices too tight to be reached by the brooms. Before nightfall, the openings would be boarded up, condemning the east wall of their home to perpetual darkness. The thought of that caused even Claire, an indefatigable optimist, to sigh.

"At least there was no significant structural damage," Philip said quietly. "We can be grateful for that."

"I always wonder if we're randomly lucky or blessed."

"I'm sure we're blessed, dear."

"Ah, but that's where it gets confusing. What about the Smythes? Why should they be any less blessed?"

Philip lowered his head. "Yes, and others of our friends die, both saints and sinners." He looked up and smiled weakly. "We simply have to trust God to sort it out."

"Well, I'm grateful that we made it one more time." She looked at him, knowing what she'd find in his eyes. Rather than force him to say it again, she continued. "But I have to admit you're right. I'll move to the country—if for no other reason than that you'll stop fussing at me."

She laughed at Philip's look of indignation and simply reached out with both her hands to grab his, and then kissed him. "We'll leave tomorrow if that's all right. I want one more night with you, even if it's in the dungeon."

"I love you," Philip said quietly, the conflicting emotions brought on by her decision betrayed in his voice.

"I know. And frankly it's the only thing that could persuade me to leave you." She reached out and wiped the tear on her husband's face. "Dark days, these," Claire said, yielding to his invitation to rest her head on his chest.

He held her close, feeling the sorrow of having her leave. As so often happens, one depressing thought led to another, and almost involuntarily he said, "And what to do about Dominic and Grace?"

Claire didn't move from his embrace, but she raised her eyes to glance at the letter on the desk. It was odd that in spite of the physical danger here in London, she actually felt greater anxiety from the contents of the letter from her sister than from the immediate threat of annihilation at the hands of the Germans.

Chapter Seven

PROBLEMS AT HOME
AND ABROAD

Carlyle Manor—January 1941

"How refreshing!" Philip stood in front of the plate glass windows in the conservatory, letting the sun warm his face. It had always been his favorite room in the house, with glass on three sides and a glass ceiling overhead. The panes allowed light in but refused to let the heat radiate back out, so the room was always warm and inviting on a sunny day. Here they were able to grow small trees and an abundant assortment of flowers and plants, even in the winter.

"I couldn't agree more," James Dimbly replied. Dimbly was another of Churchill's plants at Whitehall, and he and Philip had shared many a twenty-four-hour stint in the cellar of the war rooms as the Blitz had grown in intensity. The standing joke was to ask someone what time it was, and then to press the issue by asking whether it was AM or PM. Time disappeared in the perpetual artificial illumination of the place so that day and night lost their usual meaning.

As was often the case, Philip wasn't entirely aware of what James did at Whitehall—just that he had the proper credentials. When James's wife had died of a heart attack ten days earlier, undoubtedly caused by the strain of the bombing, Philip had invited him to spend the weekend at Carlyle Manor in hopes that some time in the country would help him deal with his pain. Philip really needed to spend his time at the manor helping Claire arrange things for her convalescent care. But this weekend it seemed more important to distract James and give him some support.

"I don't suppose you'd care to go riding?" Philip asked tentatively.

"No, I don't suppose so," James said quietly.

Philip waited a few moments. "I understand that you're quite an accomplished equestrian, which is certainly a claim I'm unable to make."

"What?" It was difficult to pull James out of the dark reveries he was prone to slip into. "Oh, equestrian. Yes, I suppose I do have some skill."

"I personally have an agreement with my horses that I won't trouble them with a lot of demands if they'll promise not to toss me on the ground."

James actually laughed. "An appeaser, eh? Not a good strategy from my point of view. I find they like direction—a firm hand, so to speak."

Philip was silent for a moment. Then, in as even a voice as he could muster, he asked, "Why don't we go riding, James? I could use the air."

James turned and looked directly at Philip for the first time, his eyes filling as he did. "I suppose it would do me some good too. It's certainly better than thinking of things."

* * *

Claire had been completely lost in thought, so she jumped at the sound of Philip's voice. He did his best to suppress a laugh but failed because of her dramatic reaction. But when he saw that his wife had what appeared to be tears in her eyes, he instantly regretted startling her and responded quietly, "I'm sorry, I didn't mean to startle you. Is something wrong?"

Instead of answering, Claire handed him a piece of paper. He started to read some very simple poetry, written in a juvenile hand:

Rocky Mountain ruggedness
The British suave and smooth
I am neither/nor of them
More like a dumb buffoon . . .

"Dominic?"

She nodded.

"How old was he when he wrote this?"

"Ten or eleven."

Philip shook his head. "That was a hard time for him."

"There's more. Some of it is quite eloquent." She handed him a sheaf of papers. "I found them while cleaning his room. They were hidden in his bottom drawer."

Philip leafed through the pile, settling occasionally on a poem to see how Dominic's ability had grown through the years.

Most rivers are wide and crossable . . . so safe and e'en
*   serene;*
A few run narrow, inscrutable . . . with dangers in
*   their deep.*
The first are the luckiest ones by far, with nothing to
*   hide or conceal,*
Not like the imposters who pose, yet yearn, and hide
*   when it's time to weep.*

Another was far more positive.

The grace of lilies marks the birth of spring and
*   springtime air,*
Reminding that the Lord was born in a season fine and
*   fair . . .*

"Oh, my. I had no idea he was a poet." Philip had an anguished look on his face. "He is always so contrary. Why can't he share these thoughts with us? Why does he keep himself hidden like his river?"

Claire bit her lip. "I don't know, Philip. I just don't know how to reach him—to help the beauty in his soul come out. I just don't know."

* * *

London—January 1941

The two men stood speechless as they gazed on the mass of destruction that had once been a prosperous West End neighborhood. Fires burned randomly as far as the eye could see in every direction. The skies were filled with an acrid smoke that you could taste in your mouth and wipe off your brow.

"How is this possible?" Philip's assistant, Jon Randall, asked. "The fires of hell can't be worse than this."

"Blood and horror are the coin of that realm, and there's an abundance of both in this godless assault," Philip replied as he surveyed the scene.

Philip's usual reaction to war was deep sorrow for all the suffering. This time, however, he thought, *How can the German people do this? The land of Beethoven and Goethe, home of the first university. How can they resort to such barbarism?* He had to check himself because the bile of revenge was coming up in his throat, and he realized how easy it would be to let his anger turn him into one of the people he now despised.

The air-raid siren sounded again for the fourth time that night. He waited for Jon to turn to go back down into the cellar, but his assistant didn't stir. If Jon felt the same dread that he did, then Philip understood why he hadn't retreated to the cellar. While it was dangerous up here, it still seemed better than going down into the artificial and cramped world below. Sometimes the cellar felt like a musty cave, and its inadequate ventilation created a sense of claustrophobia—so much so that he simply had to stay outside, even in circumstances like this.

"Four months, and still the nightly bombing continues," Philip said to Randall. "You wonder just how many bombs the Germans can manufacture before they run out."

The bombing was, indeed, relentless—some nights a handful of squadrons striking randomly, other nights wave after wave after endless wave of aircraft so that every precinct in the city was involved. Outside, Philip and Jon could feel the great concussion of bombs exploding, shaking the ground beneath their feet. If they had been close enough, the sound could have shattered their eardrums, and the shockwaves were strong enough even at a distance to make their noses bleed.

"Always a whistle and a boom," Jon said as they heard another bomb stabilizing midair and whistling all the way down until its explosion resounded. "I just don't know how long London can take this. People are showing great resolve, but how much can we take? And how can we continue to feed ourselves with the losses we're sustaining in the convoys? It's madness to think this can go on!"

"You could get arrested if you talked like that in Germany, Jon," Philip said, startled at Randall's outburst. "It smacks of defeatism." He didn't say it unkindly but meant it for a reminder that, as government officials, they had to be very cautious in what they said.

His mild rebuke actually had more than the intended effect, and Randall looked at him in alarm. "No, I'm not saying—"

"It's fine," Philip interrupted. "You haven't said anything that the rest of us haven't thought. We have to assume that they'll eventually grow tired of pounding us—particularly since we've now managed to land some blows on Berlin." He smiled. "You know how Goering promised the people in a well-publicized speech that if the British ever managed to bomb Berlin, he'd turn into a pastry?"

"No, I hadn't heard that," Jon said.

"Well, the old fool did, and now our informants in the Resistance tell us that the joke throughout Germany is that Goering is a Kaiser roll."

Jon laughed. "Well, even the invincible Nazis have their problems."

"They're not invincible, Jon. That's the whole point. They're a proud, inventive, and ruthlessly efficient people, but they're not invincible. And in this venture they are particularly vulnerable, because they are fighting without God's blessing. I believe with every fiber of my being that they are doomed because of their ambition and pride. Time will support us if we can only retain our humanity in this adversity."

Jon was silent. After a moment he said, "You're a man of deep conviction, aren't you, Lord Carlyle?"

"I was a chaplain in the Great War, you know. God has always been part of my life, and I believe He is with us now."

"He's certainly not making it easy on us." Jon's voice was strained as he reached up and touched his left sleeve—which Philip knew hid the wound that had taken Jon out of action.

"He didn't make it easy on His Only Begotten Son, Jon. It's not the purpose of our mortal life to have it easy—but rather to have integrity. That's the responsibility of the British people at this moment. To have the integrity to remain the defenders of the moral agency that is each man's birthright. No matter how many battles Hitler wins in the short run, he and his people will fail in the long run. I'm absolutely certain of that."

Jon Randall turned and smiled. "You're really very inspiring, sir. If you can find such certitude even on a night as appalling as this, then perhaps I can rely on your faith to bolster mine."

"You can," Philip said simply. "Because God will make it strong enough for both of us." Philip smiled, his own faith renewed. "In the short run, though, I think we should help Him out by going back into the cellar. The Germans have arrived overhead." The drone of the German bombers confirmed his assessment, and the two men quickly passed through the sandbagged entry and down into the comparative safety of the cellar.

* * *

Philip looked up from the menu and ordered the flounder. He wanted fish and chips but knew he'd suffer from all the grease later. He caught Claire grinning at his consternation.

"Yes," he replied, "I'm trying to be good, even in your absence." Claire had come into the city to drive an elderly widow out to Carlyle Manor. The widow's house had been destroyed the previous night. It was lucky that the poor woman's heart hadn't failed when she came up from the Tube and found a gaping hole in the ground where her house had stood for the previous sixty years.

Claire tried to maintain her smile, but Philip observed the look of concern that clouded her face as she quickly turned away. "Out with it!" he said sternly.

"Out with what?"

"There's something bothering you, and all the cheerful banter in the world can't conceal it. So just tell me what it is, and we'll deal with it."

She raised an eyebrow. "So you think you know me that well, do you?"

"I love my wife enough to know when something's wrong, but I'll admit I don't know what it is this time."

She reached into her purse and pulled out an onionskin letter postmarked in Arizona.

"Oh. Another letter from your sister." Philip felt a deep anxiety well up inside his chest, and his stomach muscles instinctively tightened. Reluctantly he reached across the table and took it from her.

Claire,

There are many good things I can share with you but none that offset the problem that I have to deal with, so perhaps it's best to simply get it out directly. I got a call from Dominic's school this week telling me that he's been suspended for cheating on an examination. He firmly denies it, claiming that the teacher misinterpreted an accident in which he knocked some of his papers to the floor, with an innocent glance at his neighbor's desk while straightening up. But the teacher, who is extremely well respected, stands by his assertion. Dominic is defiant, saying that he really doesn't belong in school and ought to get a job, anyway. That might be all right, except that he's making no effort to find one and so spends his days lying around the house listening to the radio. Tom is disgusted, and the two of them hardly speak anymore. It's a problem for our children to see him flouting house rules. So I don't know what to do.

Grace is doing better, of course, and seems almost to compensate for her brother by trying harder to be pleasant. But she, too, seems profoundly unhappy here. I remember her as a girl with a ready smile and wry sense of humor, but we don't see any of that. She's so solemn and solitary.

Now that I've unburdened myself, I feel guilty for even drawing it to your attention, because your situation is so much worse over there. We see the newsreels at the movies and can only imagine how horrible it must be. So in spite of these setbacks, you can rely on us to work things out.

Please forgive me, but I can deal only with the problems at hand, and for now these are at the top of my list. Perhaps you could come visit again sometime?

Love,

Karrie

Philip inhaled slowly. "Well." And then he could think of nothing more to say.

"You know that it must be awful for Karrie to write so directly," Claire said, the anxiety evident in her voice.

"I feel so guilty, as if we somehow failed him and now he is failing."

Claire stiffened. "There's no sense thinking that way, Philip, for a number of reasons. First, this isn't about you and whether you're succeeding or failing—it's about Dominic. Your feeling guilty for his actions won't help him solve his problems. It's just not as easy as that."

Philip felt appropriately chastened. He was the one with a doctorate in religion, yet it was Claire who could cut to the quick on personal spiritual matters. Still, he was angry at Dominic, and it was hard to suppress his natural, emotional reaction. He took a couple of deep breaths to gain control.

"All right. I'll stop. But that doesn't bring us closer to a solution. What do we do? It's not fair to Karrie and Tom."

"We should give it some time. Suppose we were dead and they were his legal guardians. Certainly they would find a solution—even if it meant moving him out of the house. I think we need to trust them on this." Then, as an afterthought, Claire said, "And we should leave Dominic to stew over his own problem."

Philip sat quietly. Claire was forming some kind of resolve, and it would be wrong to intervene at this point. His approach was always to step in and try to solve Dominic's problems, which often made things worse. This time he would yield to Claire's advice.

"Yes," she finally said, "I'm quite certain that's what we should do. I will send a cable to Karrie—if you can somehow help me get permission to send a cable—and I'll tell her that she and Tom have full authority to do whatever is necessary." Looking up at Philip with a look of resolve in her eyes, Claire said, "Then we must leave Dominic to his own devices, Philip. Even if it means that he suffers. You cannot send him money, no matter how much he implores you. He's old enough to live on his own if necessary. You have to withhold your support if he chooses to defy Tom and Karrie. Can you do that?"

For the second time Philip inhaled slowly. What she was asking of him was harder than almost anything. The thought of having his own flesh and blood living in extremity was both frightening and embarrassing when he had such wealth at his disposal. It just wasn't the way he'd been raised. When members of families in his class were troubled, they simply lived off their inherited wealth, even if it wrecked people's lives. He thought of his childhood friends who had become wastrels living off their parents' wealth. There were a lot of problems money couldn't solve, but it could certainly paper over them and postpone the day of reckoning.

"I'll do it," Philip asserted.

"Good!" Claire had a temporary look of triumph and hope, and then she started crying. She was strong, but at a great personal price. Philip felt himself growing angrier at Dominic for putting them through this. Then he caught himself. *But it's not about us! It's about Dominic.* His wife's wisdom calmed him, even now.

Chapter Eight

BREAKOUT OF THE *BISMARCK*

London—May 20, 1941

The First Lord of the Admiralty, A.V. Alexander, walked up to Philip before he'd even reached the war rooms. While not close friends, he and Philip were more than mere acquaintances because of the work they'd done together in Parliament. Alexander was the civilian chief of the Navy, while the First Sea Lord was the military leader.

"Lord Carlyle—have you heard the news?"

"News, sir?"

"Ah," the First Lord said quietly, "The Swedish cruiser *Gotland* has reported sighting the *Bismarck* passing between Denmark and Sweden on her way out to the North Sea! And just now I received confirmed sightings out of Norway from observers on the ground."

Philip wondered what else the Germans could throw at them. After nearly half a year of continued pounding, the Blitz continued unabated, and the German submarines continued to destroy tens of thousands of tons of British shipping. Now they hoped to add to that with surface ships.

"So Hitler has finally decided to let the wolf out among the lambs."

"Indeed he has." Alexander shook his head with something of a dejected look. "Fortunately, Admiral Lutjens is accompanied only by the cruiser *Prinz Eugen*. Intelligence tells us that the battleship

Scharnhorst is out of action for boiler repairs, and our Coastal Forces managed to damage the *Gneisenau* in April. Can you imagine having to contend with all three of those behemoths at the same time?" He shrugged in a way that made it clear that such an encounter would be the worst of all nightmares.

"So are we prepared to bottle *Bismarck* up before she breaks out of the North Sea?"

"We have no choice. The havoc that she could wreak on our convoys, to say nothing of morale, would be devastating. But even with the *Hood,* the *Prince of Wales,* and the *King George V* at Scapa Flow, the Germans still have many advantages. It's going to get dicey before long."

"The *Hood*?" A wave of panic swept over Philip.

"Yes, the good old *Hood.* It's our best hope against the *Bismarck.*"

In a very quiet voice Philip inquired, "If you don't mind my asking, sir, how well does the *Hood* match up to *Bismarck*?"

"On paper very well. The *Hood* displaces 48,400 tons; the *Bismarck* 50,900. Their top cruising speeds are similar, although the *Hood* has been slowed down by the additions made to her armament and weaponry in the past twenty years. They have the same main armament of 15-inch guns, although the *Bismarck*'s firing systems are far more modern, which allows for more rapid and accurate firing." He pursed his lips. "And the *Bismarck*'s secondary armament actually exceeds the *Hood*'s."

"But in a fair fight, *Hood* could hold her own?" Philip said hopefully.

"Of course either ship could prevail, but an honest assessment would give the advantage to the *Bismarck,* simply because it's a brand-new ship with the latest electronics and equipment, while the *Hood* is twenty years old. Since the *Hood* was built as a battle cruiser, she doesn't have as much protection in some of her vital areas as the *Bismarck*." He hesitated. "In fact, there are portions of the *Hood*'s deck that are just wood—no armament whatsoever."

At that Philip tipped his head back and gasped.

"Something wrong, Carlyle? You've gone quite pale."

Philip shook his head slowly as the reality of the situation sank in. "I have a son serving on the *Hood,* is all, sir. He's a junior officer in one of the 15-inch turrets."

"Oh, I see." Alexander was quiet for a few moments. "Yes, well, in spite of my candid assessment of their strengths and weaknesses, you shouldn't get too distressed. We have a great deal on our side as well. First, the *Bismarck* and the *Prinz Eugen* will have to pass within range of our land-based aircraft. It's possible that they can knock her out before she even reaches the Atlantic. Second, because they have to pass so close to Scapa Flow, we can bring out everything we have to track her. If worse comes to worst, we can even bring our other battleships up from the Mediterranean. The greatest advantage in a battle goes to the seamanship and skill of those who command the ship, and in that the British clearly have the advantage. The Navy is at the center of our world, while it's almost an afterthought for the Germans." He tried to smile in a way that would relieve Philip's anxiety.

"Those are significant assets," Philip said evenly. Sometimes it was very hard for him to maintain the impassive British reserve.

"Listen, Philip, I firmly believe this will be a moment of great honor for the British Navy. We'll stop and sink the pride of the Kriegsmarine, and your son will undoubtedly share in the honor." He laughed. "Who knows, perhaps it will be one of his shells that deals the fateful blow!"

Philip couldn't help but return the laugh. "I'd never hear the end of it if he did! Thank you, sir. I realize that I'm just one of thousands of parents who are in this situation. It just brings it a bit closer to home, if you know what I mean."

"I do." He was lost in thought for a moment. "Fourteen hundred serving on the *Hood,* twenty-two hundred on the *Bismarck,* and thousands more on the ships that support them. Parents on both sides will follow this battle with great anxiety."

He was thoughtful again. "Tell you what, Carlyle. When the time comes, why don't I get you clearance to come over to the Admiralty where you can track the battle with us. That way you'll know everything exactly when it happens. I find that's better than living in uncertainty."

A wave of gratitude swept over Philip—part of the ever-changing emotions he had felt in war. He was filled with appreciation that in the midst of everything else the First Lord had to think about, he would find a way to help out a friend.

"Thank you, A.V. Although I don't know much about the Navy, I'll take you up on your offer." Philip smiled and shook his friend's hand.

* * *

London—May 23, 1941

"A message from the Admiralty to you, sir." Philip reached out and thanked the young man, who saluted him smartly before turning and making his exit. He was a handsome fellow and, except for a missing left arm and some facial scarring, he appeared healthy in every regard. He'd undoubtedly been assigned to messenger duty here at Whitehall shortly after being wounded.

At first Philip had treated the note quite casually, setting it aside for a few minutes and moving along with the work he had to do. When he finally did open it, he stiffened and quickly rose from his chair.

"I have to leave immediately," he said to his secretary. "Will you please ring for Mr. Connors and let him know I'm leaving with my apology for missing our meeting?"

"Certainly, Lord Carlyle," she said. "Is everything all right, sir?"

In the act of gathering his papers, Philip didn't acknowledge the question for a moment. "What? Oh, yes, fine. I just have to go over to the Admiralty." He finished pulling on his raincoat and then added, "I don't know how long I'll be gone—it could be the rest of the day or even a few days, I suppose. Can you please adjust the schedule to cover my absence?"

"Of course. And my prayers are with you and your son, sir."

Philip stopped. By now everyone in the world knew that the *Bismarck* was out and about, as it had been reported by wireless and newspaper in every major capital of the world. It was only natural that his secretary would be sensitive to his distress.

"Thank you. I know that prayer is our best hope right now." He smiled and shook her hand. He quickly departed the building with some papers he had to work on, because even though word had been received that the *Suffolk* had discovered the *Bismarck* in the Denmark Strait just north of Scotland, it might still be many hours before the British could intercept the Germans and engage them in battle. The long wait began.

* * *

There were only two courses a German vessel could take when attempting to reach the Atlantic Ocean. Both required a trek through the lower Baltic up and around Denmark, but then the ship could turn to the right and go north through the North Sea or to the left and pass through the English Channel. The latter would have been pure madness for any German admiral, since British aircraft constantly patrolled the area and could concentrate their counterattack on a point of the Channel that was little more than twenty miles wide. The northern route allowed the Germans to pass close to the fjords of Norway, which were under German control at this point in the war, and to then choose from a number of routes out into the Atlantic. The northernmost would take them close to Iceland, well out of range of British land-based aircraft, but would also consume a great deal of precious fuel, while the lower route would take them through the Straits of Denmark with a more direct route into the North Atlantic. Through a combination of luck and skillful patrolling, HMS *Suffolk* had taken up position shadowing the German ships. Her report had created an instant sense of relief, since bad weather had kept all the available aircraft on the ground while the *Bismarck* sailed unseen for nearly two days. Assuming the *Suffolk* could keep up, shadowing with her radar, it was possible for the main fleet to steam northward on an intercepting course.

When he found his way to the proper room at the Admiralty, Philip was greeted by Lord Alexander. "I'm afraid you're really in for it now, Philip," he said. "The *Hood* sailed at 2000 hours and is plowing her way north at 27 knots. The sea is running rough, and she's had to pull away from her escort screen of destroyers, which have been taking a real beating trying to keep up with her. It will be one or two o'clock in the morning before they can possibly make contact, so you're welcome to go home and get some rest if you like. I called you over now just because I thought you'd like to know the chase is on."

"I'd like to stay, if it's all right, sir. I actually slept this afternoon on the expectation I'd have to work through the night anyway."

Alexander smiled. "I thought you might like to. We've set up a chair for you over in the corner. You can hear everything we hear as reports come in. I'm going to slip out for a while, but I'll be back in time for the fireworks. In the meantime, if you need any food or refreshment, my orderly will be glad to take care of you."

Philip thanked him and slipped into the comfortable chair that had been set aside for him. As he listened to the chatter in the room, it soon became clear that even though they knew the precise location of the *Bismarck,* it was still possible that the great ship and her powerful escort could slip away from the *Suffolk* in the night and perhaps get past the British fleet. Consequently, every report from *Suffolk* was greeted with a sense of relief.

Philip must have drifted off to sleep, because shortly after midnight he was awakened to a new sense of activity in the room. When he asked what had happened, he was told that the *Bismarck* had made an abrupt change of course in the direction of the *Suffolk,* which had required them to run for cover in a snowstorm. When they finally dared to venture back to their original course, the *Bismarck* had apparently not returned to its original course, which meant it was lost to the British on the open seas.

"So what will the *Hood* do now?" Philip asked the officer who was assigned to keep him briefed.

"Vice Admiral Holland has ordered a reduction of speed to 25 knots and has put the men on relaxed action stations, which allows them to sleep at their guns if they can. He's also changed their heading to 340 degrees north, which better positions them to catch the Germans regardless of which direction they may have turned."

Philip nodded as if he understood, but the astute officer saw the need to clarify his explanation a bit, so he added, "The danger is that if the *Bismarck* gets ahead of the *Hood,* they'll never catch her, since the 1.5-knot advantage she has at top speed is enough to gradually pull away from our force. The Atlantic is a big, open place, and once out there, the *Bismark* would be exceedingly difficult for us to track down." Then he added, "At least until we get reports of a convoy being attacked."

"I see." The mention of a snowstorm made Philip wonder what conditions were like on the *Hood* as it ploughed its way through the heavy seas. *At least Michael's in his turret, perhaps trying to get some sleep at this very moment.*

At 0247, word was received that *Suffolk* had regained radar contact at a position approximately 35 miles northwest of *Hood* and *Prince of Wales.* At that point Alexander was summoned, and he settled into a chair next to Philip's. Even though he was politically in charge of the Navy, this was a time to let the professionals do their job.

In the next two hours very little was said, which increased the anxiety in the room. As terrible as it must have been to be at sea, it seemed almost more nerve-racking to be bottled up in a room in London waiting to hear what happened.

* * *

The Denmark Strait—0537 Hours, May 24, 1941

"The *Prince of Wales* lookouts report two ships sighted," a yeoman announced.

Vice Admiral Holland took the news stoically. Throughout the night he had remained impassive, regardless of the news that had reached him. Now it was certain that they would be engaged in battle in just a matter of minutes, yet still he remained calm and unflappable.

"Order ships to turn forty degrees to starboard." His order was confirmed, and the two British ships turned in unison. While he had hoped to come out ahead of the Germans, their approach had been on a diverging path, and now he was forced to turn for a straight-on dash.

"Why is he heading directly toward them?" Jamie Wilcox asked no one in particular.

"Admirals aren't in the habit of telling me such things," his chief replied caustically. Sensing a teaching moment, the chief continued. "Perhaps it's because of our vulnerability to long-range plunging shells. Our weakest point is our deck armor. By closing range, I believe he hopes to shorten the distance and then turn at the last moment so we can bring our guns to bear on a flatter trajectory. That makes it harder for the *Bismarck* and easier for us."

At just about 0600, the *Hood* opened fire. Although the first shots were no different from all the others they'd fired in practice and in their shelling of the French fleet, there was an urgency about this action that made it unique. For the first time in this war, there were two other ships out there that were every bit as powerful, and they were completely devoted to the *Hood's* destruction.

"First shots fell forward of the target" was the report. There was cursing all around as the elevator quickly brought new shells up for loading.

"Change in bearing, get ready." They all grabbed hold of something while the turret started to swivel. "It seems we were sighting in on the wrong ship," Jamie reported to the gun crew. "The *Prinz Eugen* has taken the lead—not the *Bismarck.*"

"Well, there's a small fortune in munitions fired uselessly into the drink," the chief responded. "I wish they'd give me the money instead of wasting it. I'd be a wealthy man!"

In perhaps the shortest time ever, the barrel was reloaded and ready to fire. Once again the concussion slammed against Jamie's chest, feeling like a heart attack. The report came back on the salvo, indicating that they still hadn't properly sighted in on the *Bismarck,* which led to a new round of cursing.

"I wonder why *Bismarck* hasn't started firing," someone said. In fact, nearly two minutes—an eternity—had passed since the *Hood*'s first shots, with no response from either German ship.

But then they heard a dull sound in the distance, which indicated that they were now under fire, probably from both the *Prinz Eugen* and the *Bismarck.* It would be logical for the Germans to concentrate on the *Hood* first, and worry about the smaller *Prince of Wales* later.

Their third salvo rang out like thunder, and even though it was freezing outside, the men in the turret stripped off their shirts. The gun barrel was already glowing hot from the many tons of explosives that had been ignited in its long cylinder.

It was at that point that there was huge crashing sound behind the turret. "We've been hit!" someone shouted. They were grateful they were inside the turret when a sheet of flame illuminated the interior walls through the partially open doorway out onto the deck. Jamie ordered someone to close the door so that incendiary fluid couldn't seep into their cramped chamber. "It's going to get real hot in here now," he said. Surprisingly, there was a grin on his face. The excitement of battle had infected all of them, and they went about their work with an ever-increasing fury.

* * *

The Admiralty—0555 Hours, May 24, 1941

"The *Prince of Wales* reports that the *Hood*'s been hit on the shelter deck, and a large fire is burning. *Hood* continues to shoot, though."

Alexander almost leapt out of his chair, unable to contain himself any longer. "Still no reports of hits on the *Bismarck*?" he demanded.

"Nothing worthy of note," was the quiet reply.

Even Philip, with his limited understanding, figured out that things were now desperate. The *Bismarck* had found the *Hood*'s range and was in position to pound her with 15-inch shells.

"Vice Admiral Holland has ordered a turn to port so that the rear turrets can be brought into action."

"Good! We'll show them we can give as good as we get!" Word was received that one of the turrets had indeed fired.

Moments passed with no report. It was clearly the hottest part of the battle, and the observers on the *Suffolk* and the *Norfolk* were undoubtedly engaged in their own problems.

Alexander wiped his brow. "This is when it gets so aggravating," he said to Philip. "We can only imagine the battle inside the confines of our own minds, completely dependent on reports from outside. It's really quite maddening."

There was a burst of static, indicating that yet another message was being received. The protocol was that the message was quickly transcribed and then read to the group on an as-needed basis. But this message was different, and Philip could sense an immediate change in the staff as typewriters stopped clattering and the buzz in the part of the room where messages were decoded fell silent.

"Well?" Alexander was on his feet.

The young yeoman who had been assigned the task of reading messages had gone pale.

"Read it to us!" demanded Alexander.

In a trembling voice, the young man said, "It says only that the *Hood* is sunk!"

"Sunk?" Alexander said incredulously.

A stunned silence settled over the room.

"But that's not possible," someone said finally. "Perhaps it means that she's been hit."

The yeoman simply shrugged.

"But how is it possible?"

Suddenly all heads turned toward the teletype machine as it clattered into life. The next message was read instantly as each word was decoded.

"Reports indicate that a 15-inch shell fell on the *Hood* amidships and was followed by a tremendous explosion and a geyser of flame that split the ship in half. The stern twisted and sank in less than a minute, while the bow rose in the air and then slipped directly into the sea a few seconds later."

"Are there any reports of survivors?" Alexander asked quickly after a glance at Philip.

"Not yet, although it's feared that the concussion alone would have killed most of the men."

A dark silence hung over the room, as it did for a few moments at the battle scene. Even the *Bismarck* stopped firing on the *Prince of Wales* for a time as the horror of the sinking of the greatest ship in the British fleet settled into everyone's consciousness. Meanwhile, the two German ships were now free to break out into the North Atlantic.

Chapter Nine

A RIFT IN THE USA

Mesa, Arizona—May 24, 1941

"That's it! I've had enough. He has to go!"

"But Tom, where will he go?"

Tom groaned to express his disgust. "Back to England, for heaven's sake. He's old enough to take part in what's going on over there—why should he be exempt?"

"Please, Tom, he's an American—and Michael is already involved in the war. Claire wants to know that at least one of her sons is safe."

"Oh, he's safe, all right. He lives here doing nothing, going nowhere, and making a miserable example for our kids. Let him move to an apartment or back to Salt Lake. He keeps talking about all the friends he has there. The point is that he doesn't belong here. He hates our house rules and defies them. He doesn't do his part around the house, which is overloading you. He's got those terrible friends, and now he's trying to involve our children in his bad habits. It just isn't working."

Karrie was silent. She really had no answer to Tom's anger. She was the one who'd found Dominic out back showing their twelve-year-old son how to light a cigarette. She'd come down on both of them like a ton of bricks falling from several stories up. Dominic had displayed the good sense to act contrite, whether or not he was sincere, but it wasn't enough for Tom. *And frankly it's not enough for me,* she thought.

After a few moments of pondering, she finally sighed. "I suppose you're right. Perhaps it's time to tell him to find a place to live. Especially after this with John and the cigarettes."

The relief in Tom's bearing was immediate. "It will be better for him to be out on his own and responsible for himself." When Karrie's gaze hardened, he quickly retreated. "All right, maybe it won't be better for him—I'm just trying to give you support for an important decision."

"How will we tell him? How soon do we tell him?"

"I think we take him out to dinner so that he's away from the children."

Karrie shook her head. "You know how volatile his temper is. I'd hate to make a scene in a public place." Tom didn't respond, preferring to remain quiet so she could work out a solution. "Maybe we could take him for a walk by the lake."

"We're asking him to leave our house, not to write a poem."

Karrie glared. "This is hard enough, Tom, without you being sarcastic. I need to feel strong and supported."

Her husband raised an eyebrow. "So you plan to tell him? I'd assumed you'd want me to do that."

"No, I think there's too much bad blood between the two of you. It's probably wishful thinking, but I'd like to do this in a way that doesn't leave us enemies. He's a troubled boy, and this may come as a bigger blow to him emotionally than we think. He's already been forced to leave his home in Salt Lake City to go to England, then back to Arizona, and now he's being forced out yet again. He needs to hear this from someone who's not always angry at him." She heard Tom's intake of breath and quickly continued. "I'm not saying you've done anything wrong—it's just that the two of you tend to bring out the worst in each other. I think you'll agree with that."

Tom sighed. She was right. And even though he'd daydreamed about how satisfying it would be to show Dominic the door, he realized that even Dominic deserved better than that.

* * *

". . . So we think it would be better for everyone if you found your own place to live."

Dominic was his usual sullen self. Karrie's impulse was to say something to comfort him or to reach out and hug him, but that would simply have undone what she'd accomplished. So she waited in silence.

"Well, then," Dominic finally said, "I guess that's it. I make one mistake and I'm out. Tom didn't really want me in the first place. And now he's managed to convince you."

"Dominic, you know it's not like that!" Karrie found herself wavering but then recalled Tom's warning that he would try to divide them.

"It's not? I don't know how else you'd explain it. Your plan is to send me back to England, where I'll go into the military and get maimed or killed. I guess that's what family is all about, after all."

Karrie felt her face flush. Now he was trying to humiliate her into relenting. He was about to see a side of his aunt that he hadn't experienced before. With a hard, steady voice, she replied, "I won't try to explain it at all. This is simply the new reality of your situation. Whether you go back to England, find a place to live here in Arizona, or go somewhere else is entirely up to you. It's now your problem to solve."

He looked at her with eyes that were cold and angry—eyes that were unlike any she'd ever encountered. They frightened her. But she was determined to hold her resolve.

"And just how am I supposed to go to all these places? You know that I don't have any money."

Karrie shook her head and placed her tongue on the bottom of her upper teeth—a nervous habit of hers. "Your parents have given me two hundred dollars to cover some of our costs. You can have it. That's more than enough for a ticket back to England or five months rent or transportation to anyplace here in the United

States. It certainly should give you time to find a job so you can support yourself if that's what you decide to do."

"Fine," he said harshly. "When do I have to be out?"

She was glad that she and Tom had practiced this answer as well. "You have ten days. That's enough time for you to figure out an itinerary that will get you back to England if that's what you choose."

Dominic's eyes flashed. "Ten days? You've got to be joking! I can't possibly rearrange my entire life in ten days! Certainly you can't hate me that much!"

He's a professional—no doubt about that! Karrie thought. "I don't hate you a bit. I love you. But ten days it is, so you need to make some decisions quickly."

Now Dominic's eyes began to water—his most effective tool so far in managing his aunt. "You know I'm sorry for what I did with John—I told you that. Can't you forgive me, even though I don't deserve it?" Karrie detected the obvious manipulation, but at the same time the sincere fear in his eyes unnerved her. The mother in her wanted to reach out and comfort him.

"Dominic," she said softly. "I've already forgiven you. I want you to be happy, and that simply isn't going to happen here in my home. You know that as well as I do. So this is your chance to take control of your life and to feel good about yourself. At nineteen years old, you need some independence." She looked at him steadily, hoping to see some light of understanding. Instead she watched the shutters close. There really was no use in continuing.

In an instant he turned off the tears and adopted a cavalier voice. "I'll be ready in ten days, then. No, I'll be ready sooner. It's been a pain living here anyway, so I'll be glad for the change. Now, if you'll give me my money, I'll go to work on it."

She tried to take his hand, but he immediately withdrew it. "Where do you think you'll go?" she asked tentatively.

"Obviously, that's no concern of yours."

It sounded like he was going to say more, but they heard Grace come running down the sidewalk. There was a frantic quality to her gait, and as she drew near they could see tears streaming down her face. "The *Hood* has been sunk, the *Hood* has been sunk!"

Karrie stood up and rushed to her, taking Grace into her arms and allowing the poor girl to sob on her shoulder.

Helplessly, Karrie said, "Perhaps there were survivors."

"No!" Grace said, drawing away and looking at her aunt. "There were only three survivors—three out of fourteen hundred. And Michael's name isn't among them! He's been killed."

"Well," Dominic said. "Isn't this an interesting situation? I've just become the heir to a multimillion-dollar estate in England, and yet I'm standing here without a cent in Arizona. Fate plays a cruel game, doesn't it?"

"Dominic!" Grace shouted. "How can you talk like that when Michael's been killed?" When he simply shrugged, she shouted, "I hate being here, I just hate it! I have to go home!"

Never in her entire life had Karrie felt so disgusted, so sad, and so helpless all at the same time.

Chapter Ten

AN ORDINARY
NIGHT AT SEA

The English Channel—May 24, 1941

"You're awfully thoughtful," Eric Canfield commented to Michael on the deck of Michael's newly assigned ship—a motor torpedo boat patrolling the English Channel.

The two young sublieutenants stood gazing at the moon on the water—the moon that made any hope of sneaking up on a German Schnellboot, or "fast boat," virtually impossible.

"I was just thinking of how cruel life can be," Michael said.

"Cruel? I'd call this a very successful cruise since we didn't get blown to pieces by that German gunboat we stumbled across in the full glare of the moon. It's just lucky that we were faster than he was!" Canfield shivered as he said it. It really had been terrifying when the shells started falling. There had been no time to reply with a torpedo, and the British motor torpedo boat didn't have a surface gun to defend itself with the same range as the larger German craft.

"You're right. No, I was thinking about my decision to leave the *Hood*. After nine months of mostly empty oceans, it seemed like a good idea to accept the offer of a transfer to Coastal Command. I thought I'd like serving on a capital ship, but it was just so big and impersonal. Besides, I've always loved motoring in the English Channel."

"And how do you like your first luxury cruise on a motor torpedo boat?" Canfield asked ruefully.

Even on his first night out with this crew, Michael could see that Canfield loved to needle a person, which boded well for their friendship. Michael was perfectly suited to play the serious, boring one, while the other took advantage of his "ponderousness," as Jamie Wilcox had called it.

"Anyway, why are you regretting the decision to transfer now?"

Michael thought back on the experience, recalling the decidedly mixed emotions he'd felt as he walked down the long length of the wooden pier that eventually brought him to the small group of motor torpedo boats that were to be his new home. At 72 feet in length, a motor torpedo boat was a mere fraction of the size of the *Hood* and was often classified as a "small boat" along with other smaller craft in the British fleet. With a crew of thirteen, an MTB wasn't exactly a rowboat, and its speed and maneuverability meant that it could run circles around a battleship, reaching speeds of nearly 45 knots per hour compared to the *Hood*'s top speed of 31 kph. That was the advantage of the small boats—their incredible power and speed compared to size.

It was quite remarkable that he'd made the transition in the first place. Just as the *Hood* was about to pull out of port in Scapa, a commodore from Coastal Command came aboard and, with the admiral's assent, made an impassioned plea for some of the sublieutenants to join the flotilla of small boats being assembled to protect English shipping in the English Channel and hopefully to one day engage the enemy directly. "It will be a major adjustment," he said, "going from the largest ship in the fleet to the smallest. But you'll be promoted faster and can work into eventual command of your own boat." When even that didn't persuade any volunteers, he added, "We're quite desperate, you know. The Channel is our greatest vulnerability, and if England is to survive, we have to keep the shipping lines open." That appealed to Michael's idealism. He considered the commodore's plea for a moment, remembering how much he loved the fast boats from his childhood, and decided to raise his hand. A number of others, not including Jamie, raised theirs as well. With just a few moments to grab his gear, he raced toward the gangplank, forgetting to say good-bye, when Jamie raced up to wish him well.

"I think you're a bit daft leaving us for the plywood fleet," Jamie said. "But," he continued before Michael could protest, "I know you'll do well. Best wishes, mate." Michael gave him a quick hug and then disappeared down the gangplank.

Shortly after arriving at Dover, Michael had received word that the *Hood* was in pursuit of the *Bismarck*. It was all over the wireless, and he couldn't help but feel envious that he would miss the greatest sea battle of the war. Directly after that, his new boat had set out on an overnight mission to prowl along the coast of France in hopes of spotting an expected German sortie in the shipping lanes. But the blasted moon had blown their cover, and they were on their way back to port now with their tails tucked between their legs.

"Don't you see, Canfield—they've probably already sunk the *Bismarck*, with commendations to the entire crew. Why, it may have been my gun crew that fired the decisive shot!" He sighed. "No glory for me."

"Yeah, either that or the two ships passed each other in the thousand or so square miles of open ocean up there, and your crew is still bored out of their minds. That's the real Navy, you know."

"Jamie will lord it over me," Michael said darkly. "He'll regale me with tales of how exciting it was and how his crew was better than mine."

"If you don't mind my saying, Carlyle, there's no sense getting yourself worked up. We'll know soon enough." Just at that moment the morning sun illuminated the coastline, which was just emerging from the fog as they returned to port.

* * *

"I wonder what's going on?" Canfield asked cautiously. "I've never seen it like this."

Even the first officer, Sublieutenant Steadman, nodded his head. "It is strange. Usually somebody's out on deck to cheer our return, if for no other reason than that we *did* return."

Michael looked up and down the row of ships and boats moored to the Dover dockyard and could feel something ominous in the air. Sailors were standing around with their shoulders slumped. Finally, as they pulled into their pier, the captain called out to one of the dockyard hands. "What's going on—why is everything so quiet?"

When the dockyard worker looked up, the members of the crew standing on deck could hardly believe what they saw—there were tears in his eyes. "It's the *Hood,* sir! She was sunk by the *Bismarck* just five hours ago. Sunk in less than two minutes. Blown right out of the water!"

"Any survivors?" the boat's commanding officer, Lieutenant Will Prescott, called out.

"Apparently only three!"

There was a collective gasp from everyone on the boat. "Only three!" Prescott exclaimed. "That can't be true!"

The only response was silence—a silence that had already infected the rest of the harbor and which quickly settled over the crew of HMS *MTB-960.* After twenty years as the grand dame of the fleet, the *Hood* had become an icon. No one could fathom she was gone.

"Oh, no!" Canfield said. "Sublieutenant Carlyle!" And he raced down the stairs to try to find Michael in the small control room. He hoped to be able to quietly tell him the news before he heard it from somebody else. But when he slid down the stairs, he could see that it was too late. Michael had a tortured look on his face, which unnerved even Canfield.

"Are you all right, mate?" he asked quietly.

At the word *mate,* Michael simply groaned and slumped to a chair. *Mate* was the last word Jamie had used.

"He's dead. My best friend is dead!" He looked up defiantly. "And I should have been there with him and all the others!" Michael settled his chin on his hands and started to tremble.

"Belay that, Mr. Carlyle." Even in his distress, Michael recognized the voice of Lieutenant Prescott, the captain, and he quickly struggled to his feet.

"Yes, sir. I'm sorry, sir!"

"I don't need your apologies, Mr. Carlyle. We all feel the terrible weight of this news and recognize that it weighs far more heavily on you than on us. But it serves no purpose to question why you are here instead of there. That's just the way of the Navy. Guilt can ruin a man, so with all that you're feeling, don't let yourself feel guilty."

"Yes, sir." As he caught his breath and exhaled it slowly, Michael said, "Thank you, sir!"

Now the captain, a young man of about twenty-five or twenty-six, softened his voice. "I'm sorry I didn't get to know you earlier on the cruise, Mr. Carlyle, but I was tied up. Why don't we go over to the tender and find out the full story of what's happened. I'm sure that no matter how bad it is, it will be better to know all the details."

"Yes, sir. I should probably try to find some way to communicate with my friend's parents."

Prescott was about to reply that he thought that a good idea when Michael gasped. "Parents! I didn't have time to cable my parents that I was transferring off the *Hood*. They probably think I'm dead!"

This time the look of dread on his face was even more desperate, and Lieutenant Prescott quickly put his hand squarely on Michael's shoulder and forced him up the stairs. "Come on, Carlyle, we've got to get you to the wireless office so you can send out cables immediately." As they reached the gangplank, the captain shouted, "You're in command, Mr. Steadman!"

Michael fought a vigorous but losing battle to suppress the choking sensation he felt in his throat as they did their best to run up the cobblestone street without slipping on stones still damp from the morning dew.

Chapter Eleven

A TALE OF TWO TELEGRAMS

Carlyle Manor—May 24, 1941

Claire felt Philip trembling as he sat close to her on the sofa. It had only been a few minutes since he'd come charging into the manor in an attempt to be the first to tell her of the sinking of the *Hood*. She'd never seen him so frantic, and she'd had to shake him to give him the news that she'd just received a telegram from Michael, who was alive and well. At first the shock was so great that he acted as if he didn't believe her, but after reading the telegram, he started to tremble and shake, and she worried that he'd have a heart attack right on the spot. Fortunately, she'd been able to steer him to the couch, where he sat trembling without saying a word for what seemed the longest time.

"Are you all right, Philip? I know it's all a great shock . . ."

He turned and looked at her and acted as if he were going to say something, but even though he swallowed several times to clear his airway, it was obvious that he was too choked up to speak.

Tears formed in Claire's eyes, and she took his hands in hers. "I know how terrible it must have been for you to get the news and to think that Michael had been killed. I'm so sorry you had to make the trip all the way out here in such a state of mind. But the news is certainly better now, isn't it?"

Philip nodded and exhaled a deep sigh. "I just didn't know what else to do but to come here. I tried calling you as soon as the report came in, but all the lines were down, and I knew that you'd hear something on the wireless." He lost his voice again for a moment.

"And you were worried sick about what I'd do out here all by myself."

He nodded again.

Now Claire had trouble speaking. "It's so odd—the two telegrams actually arrived simultaneously. I asked the courier which to open first, and of course he didn't know. The one was from the Navy in London—the other from Dover. Hearing something from London didn't seem too unusual, but Dover piqued my curiosity so I decided to open that one first. It was the one from Michael. At first I couldn't understand why his tone seemed so urgent. Then I read the other telegram, which reported that the *Hood* had been sunk and that Michael was listed as missing in action, presumed dead. I know it was very early to arrive, but I suspect someone at the War Department thought you should have it straight away. It was only then that the meaning of Michael's telegram hit me, and I actually collapsed to the floor in terror of how close we came to losing him. Then a wave of gratitude washed over me when I realized that he was alive and that he'd had the presence of mind to send us the note." She choked up. "And then I thought about all the families who wouldn't get the second telegram." She squeezed Philip's hands to reassure him. They were cold and clammy, and she had the fleeting thought that he still might have a problem with his heart.

"Do you mind if I read the telegrams again?" he asked.

"Certainly you can." She handed them to Philip, who, in spite of the shaking in his hands, managed to open the one from Michael.

Am in Dover, not on Hood STOP Transferred at last moment to Coastal Command STOP Didn't have time to send word STOP Hope this arrived in time STOP Will contact you shortly STOP Sublieutenant Michael Carlyle RN

And then he reread the other telegram that started with those infamous words, "We Regret to Inform You . . ."

"Oh, my," Philip said. "I've never been so frantic in my life. When I thought we'd lost him . . ."

"I know. I felt the same way."

"It's just that he's so good and loyal and . . ."

"And he's your son, and you'd miss him desperately if he were gone."

Philip tried to smile. "He's also my friend. We see so many things the same way, and the future is so bright for him. It seemed it was all taken away in a moment. They say the ship sank in under two minutes. Imagine that! All those lives snuffed out in an instant."

"It's terrible. What a sad, dark day for England."

"I was beside myself worrying about you and feeling frantic about what would become of us without Michael. It was almost suffocating. A.V. Alexander was there beside me, and when he realized that we'd probably lost Michael, he was so kind to help me get organized. He tried to place the call to you, but he couldn't get through. That's when he insisted I come out to the manor, but I told him I didn't have a car since ours was damaged last week, and so he arranged official transportation in less time than it takes most people to get a drink of water."

Philip leaned back and closed his eyes, remembering all the details of the experience, struggling to regain his composure. Claire was surprised when he laughed. "You can't imagine the drive through the city. Alexander told the driver it was an emergency and to get me out here as fast as possible, and, boy, did the driver take that to heart! He turned on his light and siren, and we went careening through the streets of London like a drunken sailor on holiday. I had to close my eyes on more than one occasion for fear we were about to plough through a crowd of pedestrians and kill them all." He was quiet for a moment and then chuckled again.

"The closest thing to it is when we went to New York City on our honeymoon. Do you remember the cab drivers there?"

Claire laughed. "Remember? I thought we were going to be killed, roaring down the avenues. It was the most excitement I've ever had."

"That's exactly what it was like today. I thought I might be killed in a traffic accident. Wouldn't that be ironic after all the bombs?" He settled his head back on the cushion. "But it was worth it. I wanted more than anything in the world to be here with you when official word arrived. And then it turned out that in the darkest hour of my life, you had a brilliant ray of sunlight waiting to cheer me."

Claire was pleased to note that his trembling had stopped. Now he just seemed tired, deathly tired. "Did you get any sleep at all last night?"

"What?" he said groggily.

"Sleep—did you get any sleep?"

"No, I was up all night listening to the battle develop. It was maddening to be down there, helpless to do anything. The blasted Germans with their lucky shot."

He was quickly becoming incoherent, and his head slumped against Claire's shoulder. She got up and gently eased his head down onto a pillow, then lifted his feet up onto the couch and untied his shoes and slipped them off. He jerked awake, but she patted his hair, and he quickly dozed off again. She crossed the room and got a small afghan that one of the ladies had knitted while recuperating and spread it over him. She then motioned to the butler to draw the curtains.

"He needs sleep," she explained. "Not only is he deprived naturally, but he's had a tremendous shock." Their butler nodded knowingly.

As Claire sneaked out of the room, Philip jerked his eyes open and focused on her. She knew he wasn't really awake, but still he managed to call out, "He's alive after all."

"Yes he is, my love," she said quietly. *Yes he is, and for that I am eternally grateful. But how sad all those other families must be . . .*

* * *

Phoenix, Arizona—June 4, 1941

The sound of the train whistle indicated that it was time to say good-bye. With the bombing of Britain largely abated, Philip and Claire had consented for Grace to come home.

"Aunt Karrie, I have to say something."

"Yes, dear?" Karrie looked at Grace tenderly.

"I'm very sorry for what I said last week."

"What did you say?"

"When I told you that I hated it here, I didn't mean that I hated being with you and your family. You've been wonderful to us. It's just that I hated being away from my family—particularly when we thought Michael had been killed."

Karrie smiled at her niece. "I never thought a thing of it. You couldn't have been better behaved while you were here. We'll miss you terribly."

"But you can see that it's best for me to go home, right? Now that Mother's living out in the country taking care of all those people, she can use me. And I won't have to live in constant dread, wondering what's happening to them."

Karrie pulled Grace into a hug. "I agree completely. It's what I'd want if I were you." She stood back and faced Grace. "My, you are a beautiful young woman. Just two months short of your seventeenth birthday and you've had to go through all of this." Karrie did her best to smile. "You go with our prayers, you know."

The tremble in her voice was too much for Grace, who fell into Karrie's arms, crying.

"We'll think of you every day until this awful thing is over," Karrie said quietly.

"Thank you for everything. You've all been wonderful." Then Grace gave Tom and each of her cousins a hug, wiping a tear from the youngest one's cheek.

During this farewell, Dominic had been standing off to the side uncomfortably. He didn't have the defiant look that had characterized their earlier confrontation. Finally, as it was time to board, he stepped forward. "Listen, I know that I was unfair to all of you while I was here, and I said some awful things when I was angry." It was obviously difficult for him to talk this way, but both Karrie and Tom waited patiently. "You were extremely generous to let us come into your home." Finally, he mustered the strength to say what he really wanted to. "Yes, well, at any rate, I'm sorry that I was so unpleasant. Perhaps you can forgive me sometime . . ."

Karrie smiled at him. These words meant more to her than anything else he could have said. She stepped forward and gave Dominic an awkward hug. "As I told you earlier, I've already forgiven you. We very much want you to be happy and will keep you in our prayers as well." She smiled. "Perhaps you'll need them more in New York City than even Grace will back in England—I hear Manhattan's a big and ominous place."

Her wry turn of phrase was actually rewarded with a smile from her troubled nephew. "Oh, I think I'll be safer in New York than facing my father at the manor. Besides, my friend Geoffrey assures me that his apartment is in a good neighborhood. He's even lined up some work for me in one of the theaters in the Broadway district."

This was more talking than Dominic had done the entire time he'd been with them.

"You want to work in the theater?"

"Yes, I do. Geoffrey says there may be a chance to do some acting."

This astonished even Grace, to say nothing of Karrie and Tom. "But you've never talked about being an actor," Grace said. "What makes you think you'd like that?"

He grew serious. "I suppose because I like the thought of living other people's lives—having someone write a role for me." Almost under his breath, he said, "I don't seem to be able to write a very good script for my own life."

"Have you talked to your father about this?" Tom asked. Dominic had made several calls to England in the previous days arranging a transatlantic crossing for Grace without him.

Dominic dropped his head. "Not really. He's busy doing important things." He actually caught himself this time. "I know that sounds mean, but it isn't meant to be. He really is an important person, and lots of people depend on him. I know that he's very good at listening and helping people. But it's hard for the two of us to talk. I usually do something that makes him angry, and then I get uptight, and, well, we just don't talk very much."

The whistle on the large steam engine sounded its final warning.

"Well, I'm glad you can accompany your sister to New York and see her safely on the ship. Good luck, son." Tom stepped forward and awkwardly shook Dominic's hand. He regretted that they hadn't been able to connect like this earlier but recognized that sometimes it took extreme distress for a person to respond to life's challenges.

"Yes, well, thank you again." And with that, Dominic and Grace boarded the train.

Looking at them as they mounted the steps, both Karrie and Tom were filled with a sense of just how young and vulnerable they looked. "Perhaps there's a deeper side to the boy than I suspected," Tom mused.

"I hope so," Karrie replied.

Dominic and Grace looked like two young people made unexpectedly old by the war that had driven them from their home.

"Those poor children don't have much to go back to, with the way the war is going for England," Karrie said to Tom.

Tom turned to Karrie. "At least they tracked down the *Bismarck* and sank it on its way back to France." After the *Bismark* sank the *Hood*, the *Bismarck* had been chased by every capital ship in the Atlantic and those that steamed up from the Mediterranean until a torpedo dropped by a Swordfish bomber had managed to cripple her steering mechanism so that the great ship could only steam in a circle while the British *King George V* and others closed in for the kill. In the end, the *Bismarck* proved far more defiant than the *Hood*, enduring a pounding of 15-inch shells that left her a battered wreck without sinking. In ultimately took half a dozen torpedoes from the destroyers to finally send Germany's pride to the bottom of the ocean.

"It's all such a waste—such a huge and awful waste!" Tom said. "And it's not even close to being over."

"Will America be drawn in, do you think?" Karrie asked with a twinge of panic.

"I don't know. Certainly President Roosevelt is doing everything he can to support England. At some point Hitler may grow tired of our pretended neutrality. And then there's Japan."

Chapter Twelve

MTB 960

The English Channel Ports—June 1941

As Michael came around the bend, he spotted his boat, the *MTB-960*. He had been gone for a week on leave of absence to visit his parents. He'd felt bad leaving his new assignment so quickly after arriving, but after the fright his parents had received earlier, they needed his company, and he'd accrued the time off anyway. Still, it felt great to get back to the boat, and he walked confidently down the ramp leading to the edge of the deck. Compared to the mighty *Hood,* this thing was pathetic and small. Still, *MTB-960* had its own flare, and Michael decided he would be happy with his decision. He was alive, whether he deserved it or not, and now, more than ever, he had to make his life worth something.

To reach the boat he had to pass through a narrow alley that ran between two main thoroughfares. As he passed from sunlight into darkness, he was startled by a sound about midway between the two main streets, where he saw, off to the right side, two men huddled against a wall engaged in some kind of animated dialogue. Something about their demeanor, which suggested one was angry at the other, caused alarms to go off in his mind. Unfortunately, there was no way for him to get where he was going without passing by. So he crossed the street and started to walk quickly past. He could barely overhear their hushed voices, which only added to his anxiety. The words were familiar—so much so that he quickly pinned it down as German, which he spoke fluently. With his heart racing, he hoped to get by without being noticed, but he stumbled at that point, quickly drawing the men's attention. Clearly startled, they immediately broke apart, and one hurried off in the direction Michael had been heading while the other turned to go back in the direction from which he had come. It was such a narrow alley that Michael couldn't help but make eye contact with the fellow. He was fairly short and stocky and had something of a malevolent look in his eyes. As he passed Michael, he said hello in English with a clearly British accent. Although their passing was brief, Michael had the distinct impression that he'd seen the man before. He was older, so it wasn't likely he was a fellow student or anything. Perhaps a professor.

The thought nagged at him as he continued through the alley. The thing that concerned him most was that the two men had been speaking German. Replaying the scene in his mind, he concluded that he'd definitely heard the words *schnell* and *schlacht*—which both meant "battle." *German—why would they be speaking in German?* he thought. It left him extremely uneasy as he stepped out into the sunlight and once again came in sight of his boat. As he pondered the event, he considered whether he should report it to the captain. Perhaps one of the two unidentified men was using the word in connection with the German Schnellboots. Still, it was odd. Michael wished he'd listened more intently. His heart finally slowed down to a normal pace when he found himself back in the open air.

As Michael stepped up and onto the wooden deck of the little craft, it suddenly looked even smaller than from further up on the pier. The thought of having virtually no armor capable of standing up to the guns of a destroyer gave him momentary pause.

"Sublieutenant Michael Carlyle reporting—request permission to come aboard, sir!"

"Permission granted," replied the first officer, John Steadman.

"Thank you, sir!"

"We're a bit more informal here on a motor torpedo boat than you're used to on a capital ship, Mr. Carlyle. You don't really need the exclamation mark at the end of *sir.*"

Michael nodded, embarrassed by his own exuberance. "Thank you, Lieutenant Steadman." His mouth formed an involuntary smile. "Guess I'm still a bit nervous."

Steadman gave him a light salute and then turned back to his duties. Michael's first trip on the boat had been a last-minute sort of thing, with his boarding at dusk just as they were leaving port. No one had really taken the time to show him around. And then the *Hood* incident had further separated him from the crew. Steadman looked up and noted his confusion. "Ah, Mr. Carlyle. Now that it's daylight, Seaman Scofield will show you around the boat and give you a place to stow your mess kit."

"Thank you, sir." He purposefully left the *sir* unemphasized.

As Michael turned to follow Scofield, he bumped into the other sublieutenant, Eric Canfield, who'd been kind to him on their last voyage.

"I'd be glad to show Mr. Carlyle around, Scofield," Canfield said easily.

"Thank you, sir." Seaman Scofield, who was at least ten years older than either of the two sublieutenants did little to hide his contempt as he moved to the forecastle to help load stores into the crew's mess. "The war hasn't even really started yet, and they're sending us babies as officers," he whispered to one of the dock workers bringing supplies on board.

As he and Michael stepped past the twin .5-inch Vickers machine gun, Canfield said amiably, "So why did you sign up for MTBs—the frailest little craft in the King's Navy? They're made of nothing more than plywood, you know, in spite of the appearance of the chine hull."

"They told me it was the quickest way to glory," Michael replied.

"Ah, you want your parents to see your name in the *Times,* then?" This was a dark reference to the names of all those killed in action that were listed in the *Times of London.* The moment the words slipped out of Canfield's mouth, he caught himself. "Sorry, I forgot."

"It's okay," Michael said. "We all knew what we were in for when we enlisted." He tried to force thoughts of Jamie and the others out of his mind.

"Yes, well, still rather tactless of me."

Michael smiled. He instinctively liked Canfield, with his bright red hair and freckled face. He looked like an overgrown schoolboy, especially since his uniform hung too loosely on his scrawny frame. Hoping to continue the banter rather than think darker thoughts, Michael continued. "Actually, I'd heard that women can't resist a man in an officer's uniform and that this was the quickest way to a promotion."

"Now there's a good answer. You must be aristocracy or something to come up with that!" Michael suppressed a laugh, not wanting to draw attention to his actual status. Canfield put his hand on Michael's shoulder to guide him toward the narrow hatch that led into the wardroom. The HMS *MTB-960* wasn't even as long as the Carlyles' London home, and with a nineteen-foot beam at the widest point, it was a mere fraction of the size. Yet it was home to a crew of thirteen. Even with that foreknowledge, Michael found himself startled again to see just how cramped things were once he ducked below the deck. At six feet even, Michael was unusually tall, and the first thing that became obvious was that he'd spend the entire war stooping when not on deck.

"You can stow your duffel under the hammock over there," Canfield said casually. I know it doesn't look like much, but when you're out on patrol in the freezing squalls of the Channel or the North Sea, this place will look and feel like heaven itself when you get to come in from the weather." Instinctively, Michael shuddered at the thought. Moving through one of the sealed aft bulkheads, they went into the engine room. "All right, Mr. Carlyle, let's test your knowledge of the boat. What are we looking at here?"

Canfield was really milking his earlier arrival, since they both held the same rank.

"Three American-built Packard engines, 1400 horsepower each, as well as a 110-volt Ford electric engine for silent running."

"American built, you say?"

"Just like me," Michael replied playfully.

At that, a number of heads, including the chief's, turned in his direction. "A Yank—did I hear that correctly?" Canfield asked with genuine surprise.

"Yes, an American born in the high mountain desert of Utah in the wild, wild West."

"But how did you come to be in the Royal Navy?"

"My father is British and we've lived here the past ten years. Four years ago they accepted me at the Royal Naval College, and thanks to the Germans, I'm already assigned to active duty." That brought an appreciative laugh.

"Well, I thought there was something odd about that accent of yours," Canfield started to say. But before Michael could reply, all the men straightened up and saluted at a figure entering the engine compartment from behind him. Michael had the good sense to turn and salute his commanding officer.

"As you were," the captain said easily. "So you're back, Mr. Carlyle?"

"Yes, sir. Thank you for the leave to see my parents. It meant a great deal to them."

"The least we could do in view of the circumstances." There was an awkward silence, finally broken by Lieutenant Prescott. "Did I overhear that you're an American?"

"Yes, sir. But one who's lived most of his life in England."

"I guess I'm a bit confused. I thought you were the son of Lord Carlyle." Out of the corner of his eye, Michael saw Canfield's jaw drop.

"I am, sir. After the Great War, my father spent about ten years living in America, and I was born there."

"Ah, I see. My father knows him and thinks very highly of him. Your father actually ministered to him when he was wounded in France. You should be proud."

"Thank you, sir. I am."

"Well, then, I believe you were rehearsing the vital statistics about our little ship. Please continue."

Michael had to shake his head slightly to clear it from this rather surprising turn of events. "Yes, sir. As I was saying, three Packard engines capable of 39 knots at 2400 rpm, but 36 knots at 2200, our maximum continuous speed. We carry 2543 gallons of petrol and have a potential cruising range of 400 miles."

He hoped this was enough, but Prescott raised an eyebrow and quietly said, "Armament?"

"Yes, sir. Two 21-inch torpedo tubes, a single twin .5-inch Vickers machine gun, two single .303-inch Lewis machine guns, and two depth charges."

"Very good, Mr. Carlyle. You've done your homework. Now," Prescott said with something of a twinkle in his eye, "tell me how our sturdy little craft compares with the capital ships you've previously served on."

Michael's face flushed slightly. "Well, there is a bit of a difference from a capital ship. For one thing, you're a lot closer to the water."

Prescott laughed. "Indeed we are. Anything else?"

Michael didn't know exactly how to handle this gracefully. "Perhaps the biggest difference is that on a capital ship I wouldn't be standing in the engine compartment talking with the captain for another twenty years!" Michael thought it wise not to mention his trip to the bridge in North Africa.

"True enough, but you still haven't answered my question."

"Sorry, sir." Michael searched his mind for the answer the captain seemed determined to get at. Finally, he dared to say, "I guess I volunteered for this service because it seems like we can have a more immediate impact. Most of my time on the *Hood* was spent cruising in open ocean to scare off the Germans. Not much action in that. I just felt that doing this could help protect the convoys in the crucial home field."

That seemed to satisfy Prescott. "She does all right in a pinch. Your battle cruisers take miles to work up to their maximum speed, while we can get there in a matter of seconds—and we could outrun them if we had to!" He patted the side of one of the engines affectionately. His obvious delight in the ship was reassuring.

"Well, I've wasted enough of your time," Prescott said. "Carry on with your tour, Mr. Canfield."

"Thank you, sir!"

Lieutenant Prescott climbed up the thin rail ladder that led out onto the deck.

When he was out of sight, Michael's shoulders slumped noticeably. "I have no idea how I remembered all those statistics, but thank heavens I did."

"I should hate you for it," Canfield said ruefully. "I didn't do half as well." Just then they heard the sound of a dropped wrench, a clear signal from the chief that he wanted to get on with his work but couldn't while the two young officers were standing around.

"Ah, yes, sorry about that," Canfield said, his cheeks flushing slightly. "Mr. Carlyle, this is Henry Byrnes, chief mechanic."

Byrnes saluted. "Pleased to make your acquaintance, sir," he said, and he extended a greasy hand to Michael. Michael took it with no thought, which immediately proved a mistake. Byrnes seemed pleased when Michael grew flustered by all the grease that had transferred in the handshake. Michael couldn't really do anything to wipe it off, so he simply slipped his hand into a pocket.

Exiting the engine room, they quickly completed the tour and met most of the rest of the crew. Two of their gunners were on shore supervising the packing of their ammunition belts. Canfield received permission to take Michael over to the *Dorset,* an old

Great War–era supply ship that was permanently moored in port to take care of the crews of the motor torpedo boats and motor gunboats. When in port, many of the officers were billeted on the *Dorset,* where more spacious quarters allowed the men to relax while off duty. Having finished the tour, Michael and Eric were about to step off the boat when they were startled by the sound of a bosun whistle summoning everyone back on board.

After the crew quickly formed on the forecastle, Prescott announced that there was an inbound convoy that needed protection. At the simple command, "Make ready to launch," the crew dispersed to their action stations and prepared to cast off the boat's lines. There were none of the usual formalities associated with the departure of a large war ship, and before he even knew where to go, Michael heard the three engines rumble to life. He instinctively turned to see a cloud of dark smoke billow out from the stern.

"Join me on the bridge, Carlyle?" Prescott phrased it as a question but meant it as an order, and Michael immediately obeyed. "Stand to port near the flag locker." Much of the daylight communication between the MTBs on patrol was done by signal flag to maintain radio silence from the enemy. At night they either kept silent or used a signal lamp.

The little ship eased its way out into the Channel and made its way past the flotilla of military and civilian shipping still at their moors. In spite of the routine nature of their patrol, sailors and officers on the other ships either gave them a cheer or a salute. It was an important tradition, since even the most ordinary patrols could prove fatal. As the harbor opened up to the Channel, Lieutenant Prescott turned and said quietly, "I'd hold on if I were you." Michael almost missed grabbing the bulletproof plating that surrounded the bridge on three sides before he was deafened by the sound of the engines roaring to life below his feet. The acceleration was incredible and brought a thrill. The ship leapt forward, and in just a matter of seconds, the bow lifted up and out of the water, throwing an amazing wave on both sides of the bow as they easily worked up to maximum cruising speed. Michael leaned over the rail to watch the wave as the ship cut cleanly through the water. Prescott leaned over and yelled in his ear, "So do you like the bone in her teeth?"

"Yes, sir!" Michael shouted back, just as a tremendous spray washed up and over the bridge. He shuddered as he wiped the cold water from his face, but even that couldn't suppress the grin. They'd hit the first major swell out in the English Channel, and from that moment forward, the ride was something like trying to ride a bucking bronco. As Michael struggled to maintain his footing, he noticed that none of the others seemed to even notice. He hoped he'd soon get used to it.

"We should see them in approximately two hours or so. Then it will be four to six hours to get back. Care to take the wheel?"

Michael's heart faltered. "Me, sir?"

"All my officers have to be able to operate every single mechanical apparatus and weapon on the ship, including steering. You might as well get started." Turning to the coxswain, Prescott asked, "You don't mind, do you?" The young man simply smiled, relieved to get some time below decks. Michael moved behind the wheel and rather gingerly assumed control. It was easier than he had expected, particularly since all he had to do was keep a straight line.

After perhaps a minute or two, Lieutenant Prescott ordered him to reduce speed and practice some turning maneuvers. On his first turn, he nearly threw one of the gunners overboard. Face flushing, he said to Prescott, "Fairly responsive, isn't she, sir?"

Prescott laughed and stepped up to give him some help. Before long, Prescott pointed off to starboard, where Michael saw three lumbering merchant ships plowing through the water at perhaps 8 or 9 knots. At *MTB-960*'s arrival, an old destroyer peeled off and turned back into the Channel. The weather had come up a bit, and the sky was starting to darken as dusk approached. "I think that will do," Prescott said, and Michael stepped back to his spot by the flag locker while the coxswain moved back to the wheel.

As the ship slowed to match the speed of the convoy, Michael was very suddenly, and very unhappily, overtaken by a wave of nausea. As he felt his lunch come up into his throat, he willed it down and stood as still as possible, humiliated at the thought that he would get seasick. At this point, Prescott announced he was going below to be replaced by Steadman. As the second officer stepped forward, he turned to acknowledge Michael, giving him a quick glance and salute. He then did a quick double take and said, "For pity's sake, man, move down to the rail and let it go. You're no good to us if you're incapacitated."

Gratefully, Michael stepped out from the protection of the bridge and, holding onto a guy-wire, threw up in great series of convulsions that seemed to involve every muscle in his body. Once that was done, he weakly staggered back to the bridge.

"Sorry about that, sir," he said weakly.

"Happens to the best of us. You're free to go below if you like. Sometimes coffee or hot chocolate settles the stomach."

"Thank you, but I think I'll do better with some wind in my face."

"Have it as you like," Steadman said, then turned forward. Michael noticed him lean into the speaking tube, then face forward after yielding the wheel to one of the seamen.

Michael's thoughts started to torment him, adding to the physical misery that was unlike anything he'd ever experienced. Dominic used to get carsick regularly, which Michael had suspected was a ploy to get permission to sit in the front seat. *If car sickness is anything like this, I owe him a big apology,* Michael thought. He was so humiliated. He was sure all the other men would think him a sissy. Then he experienced a wave of fear that he might not ever get past seasickness. His stomach convulsed again, making him groan involuntarily.

Fortunately, at just that moment, the cook stepped up behind him and said, "Mr. Steadman says you might like some chocolate, sir." Michael was astonished, but he gratefully took the cup of hot cocoa and gingerly started sipping the steaming liquid. He had imagined it would simply give his body new fuel to lose but was surprised to find that his stomach almost immediately calmed down, and the warm vapors seemed to clear his head slightly.

"Thank you, Mr. Steadman," Michael said.

Steadman just smiled. "I really think you should go below. You've been out in this weather for nearly three hours. You'll be surprised how good a hammock feels." Michael was about to agree when the darkened sky was lit up by a brilliant flash off to port. He couldn't help but turn, and even though he hadn't consciously thought about it, he found himself counting the seconds until the sound of thunder struck. He'd automatically assumed that it was a lightning strike. Then a second flash lit up the sky, and the massive concussion that followed put his initial assumption to rest. One of the merchant ships had been blown up and out of the water in a great billowing inferno of fire and smoke. Michael watched, horrified, as the ship's back was broken while still in the air. The stern and the bow settled back into the water separately and almost immediately slipped beneath the waves. It was too much to comprehend in such a short time.

The sound of the Klaxon horn sounded, and the crew raced to battle stations. Prescott came bounding up and out onto the deck, yelling, "Full ahead!" The little boat turned sharply and headed straight toward the scene of the attack. Michael wanted to ask what had hit the ship but didn't want to interrupt anyone's concentration. It didn't take long to figure it out, though, as he saw the lean silhouette of a German S-boat heading straight for them through the pools of oil burning madly on the surface of the water. At nearly twice the size of a British MTB, the S-boat had a much longer cruising range, could carry heavier armament and weaponry, and yet had an advantage in speed because of its three 2000-horsepower Mercedes-Benz engines.

"Hard starboard!" Prescott shouted, and the boat turned quickly to avoid the S-boat's head-on course.

Michael realized that they were no match for the larger craft's surface gun and had little chance of hitting the S-boat head-on with a torpedo. Prescott was using the MTBs far greater maneuverability to angle the boat to where he could get a torpedo off.

The .303s started firing on the deck, and moments later he heard Lieutenant Prescott shout, "Fire!" There was a great whooshing sound in the long torpedo tube just under him, and he watched in grim fascination as the torpedo tore through the water, leaving a gleaming wake in the darkness. Unfortunately, the S-boat saw it coming and was able to evade it at just the last moment. To everyone's frustration, the torpedo passed harmlessly beneath its stern.

They'd drawn so close to the S-boat that Michael actually overheard an order shouted in German.

"Are we going to board them, sir?" Steadman asked the captain half in jest, since they were directly behind the Germans. Their machine gunners were feverishly exchanging fire with the German machine gunners.

"We're going to try our last shot. Even if we don't hit them, we'll chase them back to port!" And with that, Prescott ordered, "Fire two!" and Michael felt the boat lurch as the starboard torpedo burst out of its tube and into the water. Prescott immediately ordered, "All stop," so that the *960* would fall back from the German S-boat and avoid being hit by debris from its own torpedo if the attack were successful.

The German commander had seen the torpedo, though, and did his best to gauge its direction so he could turn out of its path. Since a ship loses relative speed in a turn, he had to make sure he chose correctly, or the entire profile of the boat would present a much fatter target. Everyone on the *960* watched in fascination as the torpedo gained on the S-boat.

With precise timing, the German commander ordered a neat turn to port just as the torpedo reached the boat. "A miss!" Steadman shouted.

But he was only partly correct. At the last instant, the torpedo nicked the corner of the S-boat with just enough impact to detonate the charge, sending a great column of water leaping up to the side of the boat. Michael watched in fascinated horror as two of the German gunners were thrown into the air, each completing a full summersault before smashing to the deck.

"We got them!" Eric Canfield shouted. "Sort of." It was still a great moment.

A short-lived one, however. In spite of their problems with the torpedo hit, the Germans weren't fully disabled, as evidenced by a shell that whizzed past the bridge of the *960* and landed in the water just a few feet behind the stern.

"Let's get out of here," Prescott ordered. Michael watched the German boat limp off toward the coast of France while the *960* turned its attention back to the convoy. Michael heard some cursing through the tube from the engine room. Their own hull had been damaged above the waterline by hostile machine-gun fire, but aside from that, it seemed they were still in good order.

"Order the convoy to re-form and head for port," Prescott said. While they had been chasing the Germans, the handful of survivors from the sunken merchant ship had been picked up and were now safely aboard the lead ship. The signalman conveyed the order to the lumbering ships by means of the signal lamp to avoid providing any radio signals that other Germans could tune into.

"Stand down battle stations," Lieutenant Prescott said quietly, and Michael watched in amazement as the crew swiftly disappeared into the bowels of the ship.

"So, Mr. Carlyle, what do you think of your first real action on a torpedo boat?"

Michael turned to Lieutenant Prescott and replied, "I think it would have been a lot worse for the sailors in that convoy if we hadn't been here, sir."

Prescott nodded. "Much worse indeed. Fatal for all of them, probably."

They stood silently on the bridge for a few minutes. Normally, Michael would have been nervous, but somehow this seemed quite natural.

"I'm going below. You have the bridge, Mr. Carlyle. Call me when we reach the outer buoy."

"Yes, sir," Michael said happily. He knew he'd found a home.

Chapter Thirteen

The Day Before

New York City—December 1941

As he walked down Broadway past the Rockefeller Center, Dominic was astonished to see the British coat of arms, with its distinctive rendering of the gold crown and lion, on a small plaque on the side of one of the buildings facing the street. It was unusual enough in this setting that he actually paused to make sure he'd seen it correctly.

"I hear the British government has some sort of secret operation going on here in New York. Maybe this is the place," Geoffrey Fox said in a conspiratorial tone.

"I'm sure it is," Dominic replied. "I know if I wanted to run a top secret mission, I'd be sure to emboss my name in bronze and display it prominently for anyone who happens to wander by. Makes perfect sense, really."

Geoffrey slugged him. "Nice sarcasm. Still, how do you explain this?" He pointed to the emblem.

"Probably an import company or something. England is buying so much stuff from America on credit that it could easily take the whole Rockefeller complex to keep track of what they owe."

As they moved on past the two-story statue of Atlas holding the world on his stainless steel shoulders, Dominic paused to look at the incredible beauty and symmetry of the main tower rising more than fifty stories above the ice-skating rink. He had to bend back almost to the point of falling over to see to the top of the magnificent art-deco building. It made him feel like the building, and the entire city, rose up forever into the clouds.

"New York really is the center of the world," he muttered under his breath. While London was of more ancient origin, New York's skyscrapers were clearly the wave of the future; Dominic was happy to be a part of it. Here he could blend in, with no one's expectations to burden him or interfere with the way he wanted to live his life.

"We're going to be late," Geoffrey said impatiently, and Dominic started moving again. The two worked their way south down the short blocks to 47th Street and then along the long blocks west leading to Broadway as it snaked its way between 7th and 8th Avenues, forming the unique triangular "squares" like Times Square, their ultimate destination.

Before the Rockefeller Center was completely out of view, Dominic cast one last glance at the huge Christmas tree that stood triumphantly behind the ice-skating rink and in front of the main entrance to the building. This was his favorite place in the city, particularly when he went for dancing and dining in the Rainbow Room at the top of the tower. The view to the south of the tower included the Empire State Building, the Chrysler Building, the New York Life tower, City Hall, and other specific buildings.

As they made their way through the rush of people, Dominic felt energized and looked forward expectantly to the evening performance. "I get to go on in the chorus tonight, you know."

"I guess I'd forgotten that," Geoffrey said amusingly. "Perhaps you should have mentioned it more than the twenty or thirty times you've already talked about it."

Now it was Dominic's turn to punch his friend. "I'm just okay at dancing, but the music director seems to like my singing, and tonight I get a small speaking part—'I beg your pardon,'" he said in a theatrical voice. "Think I can remember that?"

Geoffrey laughed. "Small, but crucial to the show, I'm sure. He probably likes your English accent."

"Good," Dominic said. "At least the ten years I lived there weren't a total waste of time."

Geoffrey had first gotten to know Dominic during a summer tour of Europe before the war broke out. They'd met at a reception following his group's performance in the West End, and they had made enough of an acquaintance that they'd exchanged a letter or two. Then Dominic had written Geoffrey to ask about coming to New York. Now, after only a short time, Dominic was making a good impression on the New York artistic scene.

"Come on!" Dominic shouted, turning to see how far Geoffrey had fallen behind.

"You're going to wear me out, you know!" Geoffrey said as he panted, trying to catch up.

"Oh, stop complaining. It's Saturday night and you can sleep in tomorrow."

"Sleep in? I better check my calendar. Let's see, Sunday morning, December 7, 1941," Geoffrey said as he pretended to look at an imaginary calendar. "I guess you're right. There's absolutely nothing scheduled for tomorrow. Should be a lazy day when I can *finally* get some rest."

Dominic smiled, happier than he'd ever been in his life.

Part Two

NO LONGER ALONE

Chapter Fourteen

I'D LIKE TO COME HOME

December 7, 1941—London

On the evening of Sunday, December 7, 1941, Winston Churchill was at Chequers, his country estate outside of London, when he and some of his advisors, including Averell Harriman, the American ambassador to Britain, listened in on a routine wireless news broadcast. The broadcast made brief mention of an attack by Japanese aircraft on American shipping near the Hawaiian Islands, but the story was delivered in such a low-key fashion that Churchill thought nothing of it. Harriman, however, took note and said, "There was something in there about America being attacked by Japan," which caused everyone to sit up and take notice. When his butler confirmed that he'd heard the same story on a different station, Churchill rose from his seat and left the room. By now, the anxiety in the room was high, so Churchill immediately placed a call to President Roosevelt.

Churchill related his understated conversation with Roosevelt to his company:

> *Mr. President, what's this about Japan?*
> *It's quite true. They have attacked us at Pearl Harbor. We are all in the same boat now.*

Harriman had taken the phone and talked with Roosevelt for a few moments, then he handed the receiver back to Churchill, who concluded the call with, "This certainly simplifies things. God be with you."

Churchill told his associates that there was neither sense of panic in the president's voice nor any description at all of the extent of the horrific damage the Japanese had inflicted. Rather, Churchill said, Roosevelt seemed relieved that at last he would have the political platform to provide the aid he had long desired to provide in this war.

A few days later Churchill shared a diary entry with Philip Carlyle. He had written it on the morning of December 8, one day before Britain declared war on Japan in accordance with its treaty with America and in response to the Japanese attack on British Singapore, which had quickly followed the attack on Pearl Harbor.

> *No American will think it wrong of me if I proclaim that to have the United States at our side was to me the greatest joy. I could not foretell the course of events. I do not pretend to have measured accurately the martial might of Japan, but now at this very moment I knew the United States was in the war, up to the neck and in to the death. So we had won after all! Yes, after Dunkirk; after the fall of France; after the horrible episode of Oran; after the threat of invasion, when, apart from the Air and the Navy, we were an almost unarmed people; after the deadly struggle of the U-boat war—the first Battle of the Atlantic, gained by a hand's-breadth; after seventeen months of lonely fighting and nineteen months of my responsibility in the dire stress, we had won the war. England would live; Britain would live; the Commonwealth of Nations and the Empire would live. How long the war would last or in what fashion it would end, no man could tell, nor did I at this moment care. Once again in our long Island history we should emerge, however mauled or*

mutilated, safe and victorious. We should not be wiped out. Our history would not come to an end. We might not even have to die as individuals. Hitler's fate was sealed. Mussolini's fate was sealed. As for the Japanese, they would be ground to powder. All the rest was merely the proper application of overwhelming force. The British Empire, the Soviet Union, and now the United States, bound together with every scrap of their life and strength, were, according to my lights, twice or even thrice the force of their antagonists. No doubt it would take a long time. I expected terrible forfeits in the East; but all this would be merely a passing phase. United we could subdue everybody else in the world. Many disasters, immeasurable cost and tribulation lay ahead, but there was no more doubt about the end.

Silly people—and there were many, not only in enemy countries—might discount the force of the United States. Some said they were soft, others that they would never be united. They would fool around at a distance. They would never come to grips. They would never stand blood-letting. Their democracy and system of recurrent elections would paralyze their war effort. They would be just a vague blur on the horizon to friend or foe. Now we should see the weakness of this numerous but remote, wealthy, and talkative people. But I had studied the American Civil War, fought out to the last desperate inch. American blood flowed in my veins. I thought of a remark which Edward Grey had made to me more than thirty years before—that the United States is like "a gigantic boiler. Once the fire is lighted under it there is no limit to the power it can generate." Being saturated and satiated with emotion and sensation, I went to bed and slept the sleep of the saved and thankful.[i]

"Philip, I know it sounds odd that I should sleep so peacefully, but you must remember that I didn't know the extent of the damage at Pearl Harbor at the time or I would have grieved for the slain. But even so, this was the day I had longed for. We had won. All that was left was to play the game out."

"I understand, sir. And you're right about America. They will prove a fierce and loyal ally. Sad as it is for them, this is a great day for our nation."

* * *

London—January 1942

Standing at the train station, Philip and Claire looked expectantly at the wave of people moving up the platform. In spite of the war, people still found reason to travel, and the British rail service remained as dependable as the gigantic clock in the Tower of Westminster Palace that housed the famous bell, Big Ben. You could set your watch by both with confidence.

"Is that them?" Claire asked excitedly, pointing to an older couple walking a bit slower than the rest of the crowd.

"I don't know," Philip replied, his eyes straining. "The fellow has gray hair instead of blond—but he's about as tall as Jonathon." They waved just in case, and were pleased when the couple saw them and waved back. Philip felt a surge of happiness at the thought of greeting his old friends from America. As Dan O'Brian's unofficial adoptive parents, Jonathon and Margaret Richards had welcomed Philip into their home in Salt Lake City when he first arrived there in 1920. He'd actually lived with them for a few months while investigating the Church until his courtship of Claire became serious enough to warrant renting a home of his own on 9th East in the Sugarhouse area of Salt Lake. As an expatriate Englishman, Jonathon had been able to share many memories of

England with Philip, and it had been helpful to have someone to guide him through the sometimes puzzling ways of American life. Now Jonathon was back with Margaret to serve as a special representative of the First Presidency in the London area during the war.

"Philip! Claire!" they heard Jonathon cry, and Philip instinctively rushed up to give Jonathon a hug.

Like most men his age, Jonathon had shrunk a bit, but he still had that confident air that had charmed so many people through the years.

"It's so good to see you two," Philip said as they released the embrace.

"Not nearly as good as it is to see you! After more than fifty years away, I find it a bit disconcerting to come back to England. I'm glad to have a friend in this madhouse."

Philip laughed. "Forgot what it was like to live in a metropolis?" At 8.6 million people, London was the most populated city in the world. Salt Lake City was a mere hamlet by comparison.

"It's unbelievable," Margaret said, looking around. "But it feels awfully good to be back. There's still a wonderful spirit about the place—I guess I didn't realize how much I missed it." The Richardses, particularly Margaret, loved the fine arts, and it made Philip smile to watch Margaret's face as the memories of London's amenities started coming back to her.

By this point they'd started walking through the terminal to where the Carlyles' driver was waiting for them. A separate truck would bring their luggage and steamer trunks directly to the town house where the Richardses would live for a time. As they stumbled through some rubble, Philip apologized for the inconvenience caused by the German bombings.

"Actually," Jonathon said, "I'm a bit surprised it isn't worse. From the newsreels we've watched at the movie theaters, I thought the whole city had been flattened."

"You haven't seen the East Side area," Claire said quietly. "They've taken the brunt of the bombing. The Nazis' hope is to bring the city to a halt by interfering with the docks and manufacturing areas by killing enough workers and terrorizing their families. At least that's how their reasoning seems to go."

"So it's pretty bad over there?" Margaret asked.

"Entire blocks flattened," Philip responded. "The incendiary bombs are the worst, with fires raging out of control all through the night and into the daylight hours. When a raid comes, people have to huddle down in the Tube or other shelters, which makes it hard for anyone to get enough sleep. In the worst days of the bombing, nearly everyone in the city suffers from the respiratory distress caused by all the toxic fumes that boil up into the sky. Fortunately, the worst is over, at least for the moment. Hitler's decision to attack Russia took a lot of pressure off London. The air raids are sporadic and unpredictable now—which causes its own unique sort of stress. Still, it's not nearly as bad as the relentless bombing we suffered last winter and spring."

They walked in silence for a while. The Russian campaign had been an unexpected surprise, given that Stalin and Hitler had signed a nonaggression treaty before the outbreak of the war. Breaking the treaty with Operation Barbarossa, Hitler showed that he had no principles whatsoever. While the Russian campaign diverted a lot of the American aid that had initially been directed toward Britain, the vastness of the Russian geography was more than enough to occupy the Luftwaffe for the time being.

"My goodness," Jonathon exclaimed as they reached the Carlyles' automobile, "I haven't seen a Bentley in I don't know how long. My father imported one twenty or thirty years ago just out of nostalgia, but a San Francisco newspaper man offered him nearly double what he paid for it, and father couldn't pass up the opportunity."

"I actually remember that," Philip laughed. "You were pretty upset at the time, arguing that there was more than enough money to go around, and people ought to hold on to some things for sentimental reasons."

"I was naive to say that," Jonathon replied in a suddenly subdued voice. "Money was easy until the Depression. After that . . ."

Philip was immediately sorry he'd said anything. He remembered some letters from Dan indicating that Jonathon had lost much of his wealth when the stock market crashed and that it had been very hard on the Richardses.

"Well, for us this car is a bit sentimental as well," Philip said as brightly as possible. "It's the last new car that we purchased, and it looks like it's going to be ours for a very long time before another is available. All the factories in England have shifted to war production, so we have to take good care of this one."

"Am I right in my understanding that Germany hasn't fully mobilized yet, even with the war being fought on three fronts?" Jonathon asked earnestly. "Are they really that confident?"

Philip was pleased that Jonathon had changed the subject. "That's what our reports tell us. Hitler doesn't want the general population to feel their lives are too disrupted by the war, because he doesn't want to lose any political capital, as if he has a problem with political capital. So far, everything he's done has worked to Germany's advantage. Until he had to call off the advance on Moscow last month, he'd been victorious in all his military escapades—essentially conquering the entire continent of Europe and most of Russia in less than two years. At this point, the only thing that's gotten in his way is the Russian winter. But come spring, who knows but that the Germans will be triumphant there as well."

"In other words, why mobilize when you can both win on the battlefield and keep normal working hours at home?" Jonathon replied.

"Exactly. At this point the German people should be satisfied with their leader—at least those who don't have a conscience," Philip said with evident bitterness.

"He hasn't won the Battle of Britain either," Claire said defiantly. "He keeps sending in his bombers, and we keep shooting them down. The RAF boys have been our most ardent defenders, and we haven't been beaten yet."

"And I don't believe we will be beaten," Philip said. "There's a lot of steel in the British people. Hitler may not know what kind of fight he's in for." After a moment he added, "We're certainly more likely to win now that America has come into the war. It feels great to have such a strong and good ally—even though it will be some time before they can make their presence felt in the war."

"That's another thing," Jonathon said. "What do you suppose possessed Hitler to declare war on America after the Japanese attack? Sentiment in the U.S. was very strong that we should focus only on Japan and ignore Germany. Then out of the blue Hitler declares war. Now he's facing Russia, England and her Commonwealth, and the United States. It seems almost insane."

"Insanity, or Providence," Philip quipped. "I think God interferes with Hitler's thinking at key moments to give us a chance to strengthen ourselves—like at Dunkirk and now by bringing America into the conflict."

"Well, you've got a thoroughly riled up American population. Roosevelt is moving to a full wartime footing in the States, and all American factories have been tasked with converting over to building vehicles for the Army and aircraft for the Navy and Air Corps. It will be a powerful force—America fully engaged."

As the car came to a stop, Claire said, "We've arrived. I hope you like what we've done with the windows." Jonathon and Margaret looked up at the boarded-over windows and didn't know whether to laugh or express the shock they felt. Before they could say anything, Claire added, "It's all the rage in London right now—even the king and queen have started using it on their windows ever since a Luftwaffe bomb hit Buckingham Palace."

"So they're staying in the capital, even though the bombs place them at such a risk?" Margaret asked.

"They are indeed," Philip said. "It's having a wonderful effect on morale. In fact, when the bomb hit the Palace, it was very close to where they were having dinner. Queen Mary's comment was, 'I'm glad because now we can hold up our heads with the East Enders.'"

"What a magnificent thing to say," Margaret replied.

* * *

February 1, 1942
New York
Dear Father,

I've just been notified by the Selective Service that I'm required to report to my draft board. Since I'll undoubtedly be classified as 1-A with no dependents, it's almost certain I'll be called into service. Even though it seems a perfectly wonderful excuse to me that I've been offered a permanent position in the show I'm performing in, I doubt the draft board will see it that way.

At any rate, I'm hopeful that you can find a place for me in the British services, perhaps some place where my theatrical talents can be put to use. I know you're well connected and all.

I'd like to come home. Please let me know what I should do.

Dominic

"Well," Philip said to Claire when he finished the letter, "so now he wants to be British." He winced at Claire's glare.

"I think he wants to be near us if he has to serve," she said. "I don't see that's such an unreasonable thing."

"I know. It's just that he's an American when it suits him and British when things change." Before she could chastise him further, he said, "I'm glad he's coming home. I'd sooner have him close as well. It's just that I don't know what I can arrange for him. There are military bands and such, but he's not well enough established to qualify. Besides, they usually use older volunteers who are not suited to combat."

"Perhaps he could work in the government?" Claire asked hopefully.

Philip shook his head. "Perhaps the Signal Corps. That may keep him close to home since he's apparently averse to combat." He had to work very hard to keep his voice steady while saying the last part of the phrase. Still, Claire understood exactly what he was saying.

"Listen, Philip, not everyone is like Michael. There are many ways to serve your country, and very few find their way to the front. So you shouldn't judge him."

"I suppose not." Philip was quiet for a time. Finally, he looked up and smiled at her. "It really will be good to have him home, although I'm sorry this new career of his has to be put on hold for a while. It sounds like something he's really interested in."

Philip could see Claire relax after he'd regained his control. "So you'll look into something, Philip?"

"I'll start tomorrow."

Chapter Fifteen

ATTACK ON THE GERMAN BATTLE CRUISERS

Dover—February 9, 1942

"Well, gentlemen, it looks like we get an interesting change of scenery," Prescott said.

The officers of HMS *MTB-960*, who were seated around the small wardroom table, looked at their commanding officer expectantly.

"It seems that air reconnaissance has picked up signs that the German battle cruisers at Brest are preparing to attempt a run through the Channel to return to Norwegian or German waters in the Baltic. We're to be given the chance to shove a few torpedoes into their bellies if possible. What do you think of that?"

"I think it's terrific," Eric Canfield said. "We're so little they can't drop their guns low enough to shoot at us."

"Always the optimist, Mr. Canfield," Prescott replied. "What about the flotilla of S-boats and R-boats that are likely to cover for them?"

Canfield's face fell but quickly brightened. "We'll just have to shoot them first!"

Prescott sighed. "And what about you, Mr. Carlyle? What do you think?"

"I think," Michael said evenly, "that there's nothing in the world that I'd like more than to shoot at those monsters."

As if to bring some reality to the scene, the chief said, "But why would the Germans risk bringing the *Gneisenau* and the

Scharnhorst through the English Channel? They'll be sitting ducks to our land-based bombers. They'd be daft to risk it!"

"The *Prinz Eugen* as well," Prescott corrected. "All signs point to them bringing all three ships through."

"Even more crazy," the chief interjected. "From what I understand, that leaves only the *Tirpitz* as the largest ship in their surface fleet. Do you suppose they've been faking all this just to tie up our resources when they really intend to leave the ships at Brest?"

"I think you think too much, chief. Adolf Hitler rules from emotion, not logic. He probably hates having his fleet all bottled up outside of German waters and wants to bring them home. From the way he behaved before the war started, he doesn't pay a lot of attention to his generals and admirals." Prescott smiled. "Because if he did, you all know that they wouldn't be trying this move."

"Well, all I know is that if we can't sink their ships when they pass right under our noses in the Dover Channel, then the Navy doesn't deserve another farthing of funding," the chief succinctly expressed himself.

"All we can worry about is our part, and with the expected German air cover, we'll be sitting ducks if they decide to take us on," Lieutenant Prescott said evenly. "Let's hope for the best."

* * *

Whitehall—February 10, 1942

"Is it appropriate for me to ask what all the excitement is about?" Philip asked Sir Hastings Ismay, deputy secretary. Ismay was responsible for implementing all cabinet decisions with the various chiefs of each of the military branches.

"We've got exciting yet disheartening news from our reconnaissance operations over France, Philip. It seems the Germans are preparing to bring their three battle cruisers through the Channel, perhaps as early as tomorrow."

Philip rocked back on his heels a bit. "Seems like quite a gamble on their part. They're certain to come under the range of our bombers. What do you suppose they're thinking?"

"Thinking? There's no thinking in this decision. This has Hitler written all over it. Our best intelligence indicates that he thinks we're going to launch a major military attack against Norway, and he wants to make certain he has his heavy ships in the area."

"Are we planning such an attack?" Philip asked.

"Of course not. We haven't enough ships to keep the sea lanes open right now, and the last thing we need is a major military engagement in Norway. Of course, it's not a bad thing to let him nurture his paranoia, since it keeps a goodly portion of his capital assets occupied there and poses virtually no military risk to us."

"So, I haven't heard the disheartening news yet."

Ismay turned and faced Philip with something of a look of contempt on his face. "The bad news is that we may not be able to stop the passage. All our capital ships are out of the area. With the sinking of the *Hood,* we're not particularly keen to have them in a direct engagement anyway. If the Germans get through, it will be a huge scandal in the press."

"But certainly you can bring bombers to bear. That's what eventually brought down the *Bismarck.*"

"We can try. But the Germans will have every fighter aircraft at their disposal in the air, to say nothing of covering fire from their destroyer and gunboats. It will be harder than you expect, even though the passage is barely more than twenty miles across."

"So if you don't mind my asking, what are your plans?"

"We'll start with the motor torpedo boats. It's doubtful whether they could get past the destroyer screen, but if they did, a well-placed torpedo could at least slow the passage, giving us more time to marshal our resources. It's something of a suicide mission for them, but they're all we've got at the moment. If that fails, we'll send in our aircraft, then deploy a group of destroyers, and finally lay mines. Even that's tricky since it reduces our maneuverability as well."

Philip nodded as though he had heard every word. The truth was that from the moment he heard that the MTBs would be engaged in the battle, his stomach had tightened and his thoughts had turned to Michael. While he didn't know for sure where Michael was serving, it seemed to him that Dover was a likely spot.

"This is, of course, still strictly classified," Ismay said.

"Yes, sir. I won't speak of it to anyone." *Particularly Claire,* Philip thought. Even if it hadn't been top secret, he didn't think he'd share it with her just yet.

* * *

Dover—February 12, 1942

Prescott acknowledged the signal from the despatch office, quickly signing their orders and returning them to the young ensign despatch rider.

"It's official. Mr. Canfield, prepare to take us out."

"Yes, sir!" At the appropriate signal, the engines roared to life in a great cloud of smoke, and the sleek craft quickly made its way out into the English Channel, where they idled their way toward the safe-speed buoy, after which they'd go to best-cruising speed. It was very unusual to be going out in daylight, and the entire crew seemed to relish the change. They went to full power at 1155 hours under the command of Lieutenant Commander Pumphrey in *MTB-221*.

"Excuse me, sir?" Michael said tentatively.

"Yes, Carlyle?" Prescott replied.

"I count only four other boats. Are we going to meet up with another flotilla as we get farther into the English Channel?"

Prescott shook his head in disgust. "No, Michael, you're looking at the entire British attack fleet. Five boats total. We shouldn't have too much to worry about. The latest reconnaissance report indicates that the Germans have just three battle cruisers, six destroyers, ten torpedo boats, and an undetermined number of S-boats and R-boats. So our odds are only five against twenty-five or so—all of them bigger than us. And that doesn't count the German aircraft that will be flying."

For the first time Michael felt real fear. If the Germans decided to take action against them, they wouldn't stand a chance.

Just as he was about to say something, Canfield called out, "Excuse me, sir, but the chief reports some kind of mechanical difficulty with engine number two."

Prescott simply shook his head in disbelief and quickly disappeared down the hatch to see what the problem was. Michael caught Eric's eye and mouthed the words, "Can you believe this?" to which Canfield replied with a simple shrug.

Whatever the problem with the engine was, it had slowed them only marginally, and Michael was surprised to see that they were easily keeping up with the other boats. He watched as the various crafts signaled to one another, and in what had to be a dark omen, it turned out that each boat in the group was suffering from some sort of mechanical difficulty. "Kind of unbelievable," Eric said.

"I think I'll check the torpedoes," Michael replied. The tension was great enough that he couldn't stand to be idle, so he called Scofield to join him and together they checked every valve and fitting, even though they both knew it was unnecessary.

* * *

"Have they gone into action yet?" Philip had slipped into the map room so quietly that he actually startled the officer in charge.

"Not yet. They should be joining the Germans in approximately ten minutes."

Philip looked at the five small pins the map showed moving out into the Channel between Calais and Gravelines. It took a moment for that fact to register.

"Pardon, but does each of those pins represent a flotilla?"

"No, not a flotilla," the officer said darkly. "Each one is a boat—a motor torpedo boat that's not a lot larger than the hallway outside this room."

Philip staggered a bit at the news, quickly counting the number of pins that represented the German boats. He thought of saying something smart to ease the tension, but there was nothing to say. He closed his eyes and tried to picture what it must look like to the men on those tiny wooden boats as the magnificent German battle cruisers came into view.

"David vs. Goliath," he said quietly.

"Except that these Goliaths have slings of their own."

Philip lapsed into the silence that characterized all the military officers in the room.

* * *

"I can hardly even see the *Scharnhorst*," Eric said testily. "Those blasted destroyers and gunboats won't give us even the slightest opening."

"It's true," Michael replied. "They have so many ships that they can form a solid line between us and the cruisers so we don't stand a chance of getting inside the screen."

It was maddeningly frustrating. There in the distance, perhaps three miles away, steamed the three German battle cruisers, making their best possible speed of nearly 30 knots. While the MTBs could normally travel at 45 knots, a hot bearing in engine number two had forced Prescott to go in at two-thirds power. The British boats were barely holding even with the convoy. The five little boats were attempting to slip through the destroyer screen, but each time they picked up speed, the destroyers matched it. When they slowed down, the Germans slowed down. Meanwhile, a nest of Messerschmitts flew overhead, the angry drone of their engines growing in intensity whenever one of the MTBs tried to move in.

"The good news is that no one's taken a shot at us. There are enough guns pointed our direction right now to send us all to heaven or Hades in less time than it takes to ask why the distinguished gentlemen at Whitehall have their heads in their—"

"That will be enough, Mr. Canfield!" Prescott said sharply.

"Yes, sir!" Eric said indignantly.

"Let me take the wheel," Prescott said irritably. He moved to the front of the bridge, where he made a quick cutting action that turned them directly into a gap between two of the destroyers while simultaneously signaling for full power. "That bearing can go to blazes," he said darkly.

The moment Prescott's intention became clear, the following destroyer made a move as if to turn in their direction, picking up speed to quickly close the gap.

Shaking his head in disgust, Prescott backed off on the speed and turned back to a parallel course with the Germans. At that the destroyer immediately returned to its position and steamed ahead without firing a single shot.

"Why don't they fire on us?" Canfield asked with disgust.

"We're not worth the shells," Prescott answered. "They expect to come under bombardment when they reach the narrows, and they want to save everything they've got. Why waste it on some puny torpedo boats they can fend off with no effort."

"Well, are we going to just trail them like this until we run out of fuel?"

"I don't know, Michael. I'm not in charge of the flotilla." Prescott was quiet for a few moments. "But I'd like to know what we do plan to do. Here, take the wheel!" He stepped away before Michael even had time to grab the wheel. At the speed they were traveling, you needed a hand on the wheel at all times, so the boat lurched to port a bit crazily until Michael regained control.

"Make a signal to *MTB-221:* 'What are your intentions?'"

Michael listened as the lamp furiously clicked the code. There were perhaps sixty seconds of waiting until he saw the semaphore start to blink again and Prescott started translating. "'Will attempt to break through the screen regardless of hazard. If that fails, will launch torpedoes from this distance and make a run for it.' Good man." Turning to his crew, Prescott said, "Men, prepare to watch *MTB-221* get blown out of the water—and then say your prayers because it will be our turn next."

* * *

Philip tapped his fingers nervously on the table. It took two irritated glances from one of the naval officers in the room before he realized what he was doing, and he quickly put his left hand on top of his right hand to stop it. He wanted to jump up and pace around the room, but it wasn't really his room. He was just one of the staff—not part of the military—and he really didn't have any good reason to be there anyway. So he had to make himself as invisible as possible.

Even though he had no way of being sure, Philip was confident that Michael was at that moment standing on the bridge of one of the small pins being moved on the huge wall map in front of him. Slowly but surely, the British pins had converged on the German pins, and they were now all moving east toward the narrowest part of the Dover passage. He could also see a new group of pins moving in the direction of the Channel, which represented British bombers.

* * *

"There he goes!" Eric Canfield shouted. Somehow Canfield could not help but state the obvious, as if his mouth were one of the "repeaters" that were used in large ships to send signals from the bridge to the engine room. Whatever was dialed on the bridge was immediately repeated down below. In this case, whatever Eric's brain thought, his mouth immediately repeated.

It was exciting. They watched the bow wave of *221* flare into a brilliant white foam as the ship roared ahead toward a small gap between two destroyers. For a moment, it looked like he was going to get through, and then suddenly the boat seemed to stall in the water.

"He's got engine trouble!" Prescott shouted, not caring that the men heard the curse that followed.

"He's fired his torpedoes!" Michael called.

"Quick! Hard to port and accelerate to full speed," Prescott ordered. The helmsman deftly implemented the order, and the *960* turned in the direction of the dark smokescreen that the German gunboats had started laying between the British boats and the German fleet. It was impossible to see anything now, so Prescott quickly calculated the last known position of the *Scharnhorst* and ordered up a firing solution. "Check my calculations," he ordered Michael, who quickly did the math in his head.

"Firing solution confirmed," Michael replied breathlessly.

"Then fire!" Prescott shouted.

Michael felt the ship shudder as the great whoosh of the torpedo exiting the tube was heard above the roar of the engines. Another lurch and they were free of their torpedoes.

"Now, hard to starboard to form up with the group!" Prescott ordered, and the ship turned away from the smokescreen. From where they were, it would be at least three minutes before they knew if they got a hit.

"Chances are very remote," Prescott said.

"But there is a chance," Michael replied.

"Yes, I suppose there is." Prescott burst into a grin. "What do you suppose the Germans are going to do with us now?"

They didn't have to wait long. As the five MTBs formed into a small group, ready to return to port, a German gunboat suddenly came tearing out of the smokescreen headed directly for them at top speed. Since the German's top speed was nearly 50 knots, while theirs was reduced to just 16 by the various engine failures, things were about to get ugly very fast.

"Pull out your oars and row!" Eric called to the deck hands. "We've got to get out of here!"

Michael winced as the first shot from the German gunboat fell approximately ten feet off their port side. He was nearly drowned by the cascade of water that came crashing down on the *960* from the explosion of the shell.

"It's going to get a little dicey now!" Prescott shouted, and then he ordered a hard turn to starboard to refuse the Germans a good firing solution.

* * *

"Air reconnaissance reports that torpedoes are running, sir."

This news was met with silence in the war room. Philip felt an immediate change in attitude as everyone silently hoped that somehow, miraculously, one of the torpedoes might hit a battle cruiser—any battle cruiser.

"How long is the run?" the commanding officer asked.

"Five minutes, at least."

"Five minutes." The officer bobbed his head up and down a time or two. Turning to Philip, he said, "Do you realize that at that distance, a change of two or three inches in the direction of fire can make the difference of two ships' length at maximum range? In other words, if they're off by three inches, they can miss an entire battle cruiser. What do you think the odds are of a hit?"

Philip didn't know if the officer was really asking a question or simply making conversation to pass the time. But when the fellow looked at him expectantly, Philip replied, "But there are up to ten torpedoes running, as I understand it, and three German battle cruisers. Certainly that increases the odds."

"It does indeed," the officer said, and he smiled. "I guess I'm glad to have an optimist in the room."

Unfortunately the optimism was misplaced. A spotting aircraft reported that while a number of torpedoes were running true and on course to hit both the *Gneisenau* and the *Scharnhorst*, at approximately three minutes into the torpedo run, both ships changed course, assuring that the British torpedoes would run until they were out of steam and were left bobbing in the middle of the open ocean.

The officer in charge cursed. Then he was handed another piece of paper, which caused him to curse again.

"The Germans have turned to attack our torpedo boats. Their motors are impaired and they're out of torpedoes. May God help them."

Yes, Lord, please help them, Philip thought. He felt as if he wanted to go shoot the Germans himself.

* * *

"All right men, prepare to abandon ship," Prescott said with urgency but with a coolness as well. "When one of those shells hits us, the Germans will turn to attack another, and it's very likely we can make it out alive by just staying in the water. The Germans will be anxious to rejoin their group and so will leave us here to be rescued. Be patient and don't panic!"

Michael tried to check the knots he was tying in his life vest, but his fingers were trembling so badly that it was hard to make them do what he wanted. There was another concussion, this time off the starboard bow, and he braced for the freezing shower of water that quickly drenched him. *We'll all freeze to death before they find us unless a rescue boat comes soon,* Michael thought in terror.

A third shot fell so close to the *960* that the boat was temporarily lifted up and out of the water, and Michael fully expected to feel the boat start to sink from under them. But the engines kept running, and they stayed on course. By now it was inevitable that the German gunners had calculated their position and were waiting for the next shot.

It didn't come. The time before the Germans fired should have been ten seconds, but Michael heard himself ticking off twenty, twenty-one, twenty-two, and then he heard a cheer go up from the men on the main deck. Looking up, he saw two British motor gun boats come tearing toward them with their own guns blazing in the afternoon sky.

"It's Stewart Gould on *MGB-43*!" Eric shouted. "They've come to save us!"

Sure enough, *MGB-43* and *MGB-41* charged right past the torpedo boat, all guns firing on the Germans, who even at this moment were making a furious turn to get out of the line of fire. In a matter of moments, the battle was over for the *MTB-960* and the other British boats. The German convoy hurried on its way undamaged, and the five little boats limped their way back home.

* * *

Philip breathed a sigh of relief as word was received that all five boats had survived the encounter.

"Am I right that your son was on one of those boats?" the officer asked kindly.

"I think so. He serves on the *MTB-960*."

"Then he was there. I'm glad for your sake that he made it out safely."

"Thank you, sir. What happens next?"

"Our aircraft are on their way, but they honestly don't have much chance of getting through the German fighters. So far things are going well for the Kriegsmarine."

Philip watched the officer clench and relax his fist a couple of times. "There's going to be a heavy price to pay for all this in the press," he said. "The prime minister will be furious."

* * *

Dover—February 13, 1942

"So it was RAF mines that hit them?" Canfield asked Prescott.

In spite of himself, Prescott smiled at his young officer's innocence. "It was the *Gneisenau* and *Scharnhorst* that hit the RAF
mines, Mr. Canfield. Mines don't actually move, you know."

Eric's face colored. "Yes, sir. Of course. But the point is that we
did end up damaging the ships?"

"We did indeed. But at the cost of six Swordfish bombers, all
of which were shot down attempting to launch torpedoes from the
air."

"I understand that Lieutenant Commander Esmonde, their
leader, has been recommended for a Distinguished Service Cross,"
Michael said.

"Posthumously. Not a lot of comfort in that, is there?" Prescott
retorted.

Michael didn't like it when Prescott became sullen like this. It
usually happened when he'd had too much to drink, which
certainly applied in this situation. They were at a tavern recounting
the great battle against the German capital ships—a battle that had
never stood much of a chance. In all, just five torpedo boats and a
handful of destroyers had made an attempt on them, in addition to
the pathetic raid of Swordfish bombers that was doomed from the
beginning. Only five men had been rescued. It seemed incredible
that it was all the British could put up against a target as tempting
as that, right in their own backyard. But that was the fact. The
Germans had made it to their home waters—damaged by mines,
but certainly not sunk—although there was hope they'd be out of
commission for a considerable time.

"The public is furious over this one," Eric said.

"Yes, I understand a board of inquiry is being set up to see why
more wasn't done."

Michael shook his head, and thought, *What will it take to slow
the Germans down?*

Chapter Sixteen

FACING THE STORM

Carlyle Manor—April 1942

"Can you tell me about your husband?" Philip asked gently. "I'm afraid I only knew him in his later years when he was retired. What was he like as a young man?"

The frail little lady rallied in her bed and brightened as the memories of her youth returned for a moment. "He was so handsome," she said brightly, "and strong—he was arm-wrestling champion at the local pub, you know."

"I didn't know!" Philip laughed.

"Oh, that was before we joined the Church," she hastened to add, her face coloring a bit.

"Of course it was. He still had a fine physique, even in his later years, didn't he?"

Sister Smythe smiled again. "Yes, he did," she said proudly. "He lifted weights every day, you know, to keep up his strength."

"You must miss him," Philip said quietly, in a way that invited further conversation.

Since coming out of her coma after the blast that had destroyed her home, Sister Smythe had been very withdrawn and depressed over her husband's recent death. The move to Carlyle Manor under Claire's direction had helped Sister Smythe, but she still languished. Her conversation with Philip was the most talking she'd done in months, and Claire marveled to see how skillfully her husband was able to draw Sister Smythe into a conversation. In a matter of moments, the dear lady was sobbing quietly as Philip held her close to him.

"He has a marvelous talent for helping people, doesn't he?" Margaret Richards commented.

Claire turned to Margaret, who was out at the manor visiting the members of the Relief Society who had taken up residence there.

It was Saturday, and Philip had taken the day off to relax. But instead of relaxing, he'd spent the entire morning talking with the fifteen residents who had been moved out of the city into the relative safety of the countryside.

"He gets so involved in his work in those government dungeons that it's easy to forget that people are his first love."

"Perhaps that's why the senior government ministers enjoy having him in their circle so much. He's one that you can talk to without fear of judgment. I know that Daniel O'Brian gives him credit for drawing him out of the dark shell he'd retreated into after his experiences in France."

Claire was thoughtful. The war had taken such a toll on everyone that it was easy to forget to savor the wonderful moments, like this, when her sweetheart, Philip, was doing something so unnoticed yet so immeasurably important for the injured souls who were in such desperate need of succor.

"You have similar skills, I believe," Claire said to Margaret. "I've watched you and Jonathon minister to the Saints here, and even after just a few months, you're making a great difference."

"That's a lot of rubbish. The need is so much greater than our abilities. Besides, it hardly compares with what you're doing here for these poor souls. It's very gratifying to offer whatever help we can, though."

Claire laughed easily. "Well, now that we've flattered each other, I should do something practical, like fix lunch. You'd be surprised how much these women can eat! We hardly get by even though we pool our ration cards."

* * *

Whitehall—April 1942

"What do you think about the new air circulation system?" Sir Edward Bridges asked Philip. Bridges held the nonmilitary position of cabinet secretary, the country's most senior civil servant. Traditionally the post had included responsibility for both military and nonmilitary activities, but the scope of the war was simply too great for one person, so the secretariat had been divided, with General Sir Hastings Ismay handling military affairs and Bridges presiding over all the civil servants. It was an awesome responsibility, requiring Bridges to attend all cabinet meetings, take minutes, and see that policy was implemented. What was sometimes forgotten by those outside England was that Churchill was not just the minister of defense, responsible for the prosecution of the war, but the prime minister as well. He had to oversee the day-to-day activities of the entire nation, including the operation of schools, maintenance of public facilities, distribution of food in a period of rationing, dividing precious fuel between civilian and military needs, and so forth. It was an awesome task that required the best and brightest minds of the nation. Philip had spent more than a year with Sir Bridges, and he'd come to admire the secretary immensely, and so he did everything possible to ease his duties with the cabinet war rooms.

Responding to his question about the air-conditioning, Philip replied, "Much needed relief for those in the cellar. I don't know how much longer they could have lived in the stifling conditions down there. I expect we'll see some genuine improvement in performance, as people can sleep more easily with a bit of fresh air."

"I certainly hope so. It's amazing how many people we crowd into this place." Bridges shuffled a bit.

"Was there anything else, sir?"

"What?" He looked at Philip searchingly, paused for a moment, and then said, "Actually, there is. I feel I've been remiss in checking in with you about security. You're the type of fellow one can quite easily overlook because things just seem to take care of themselves."

"If I may ask, is there some recent reason for concern?"

Bridges cleared his throat. "As you know, only cabinet ministers are allowed into the map room."

"Yes, sir."

"Well, I've received a number of questions recently about some of the staff taking in acquaintances when the room is otherwise unoccupied. Almost like a tour or something."

Philip's face flushed. "Ah."

"I realize that no one gains admittance to the facility that doesn't have top clearance, so it's not like any spying is going on."

"Of course not, sir. Please rest assured that credentials are strictly enforced. But the truth is I can't speak to the other issue as confidently as I'd like. We review the policy regularly with those who work in the map room. But as you know, there's a certain prestige associated with that particular room, and I can imagine that some might take advantage of it with others in their circle."

"You can see why that would be a concern."

"Of course, sir. Each additional set of eyes is a potential breach of security—even if unintentional. I'll deal with it directly. I think you can rest assured that there will be no further violations, if there have been some."

"It's just that you're a rather tolerant person."

That irritated Philip. It's true that he was good-natured. But that didn't mean he couldn't run a tight ship and enforce discipline. "Not so tolerant as you might think when it comes to the nation's security, sir," he said, tight-lipped.

"It was a compliment, Philip," Bridges said, seeming to have realized that he'd offended his friend, "not a criticism. I have full confidence in your ability to solve this. Believe me."

"Yes, sir. Thank you."

Bridges still wasn't convinced. "Philip, don't you be angry with me. At any given moment I've managed to irritate at least half of the hundreds of thousands of civil servants in the country. And when I try to make it right by them, I irritate the other half. There are plenty of people who are unhappy with me without it including a friend."

Philip smiled. "Well, then, the last thing you need is for me to be upset. So consider the matter settled. It's just that I really do try to keep problems off your plate, so I'm disappointed that one showed up."

"Personally, I'm glad. Who knows how long it would have been before we took time to talk with each other if it hadn't shown up." At that remark, Philip relaxed, and the two men sat down and chatted amiably about the affairs of state—from those of great gravity to the mundane—in what turned into nearly an hour of time together. With all that was going on in the world, it was a singular experience for Philip.

* * *

Carlyle Manor—April 1942

"So Dominic, I understand that you were starring in a show on Broadway. That's quite an accomplishment for one so young." Jonathon smiled at him warmly.

"Hardly starring," Dominic replied. "I was only there such a short time, but I did get a regular spot in the chorus and even had a small speaking part." Dominic had always taken to Jonathon Richards as a boy and seemed to enjoy chatting with him.

"I always loved going to the shows in New York City," Margaret said, "even though I've only been there a few times."

"Were you able to find a church to attend there?" Jonathon asked.

Dominic dropped his head. "No, sir, I-I didn't seem to have the time for it. The shows ran very late on Saturday night, and then I had to help clean up the set."

"It's all right," Jonathon replied. "I'm sure your heart was right."

"Actually," Dominic said, casting a glance at Philip, "I wasn't entirely sure I wanted to go to church. None of my friends did, and I'm just not sure it's for me."

Jonathon tilted his head back slightly. "Oh, well then, that's something interesting for you to consider. I'd be glad to talk to you about it if you like. But you have some very serious issues on your mind already."

"Yes, sir, in fact, I was going to speak to my father about it today."

Jonathon looked at Margaret, who immediately responded with, "I can only imagine how precious your time together is on Sundays. Jonathon and I really need to be going. I have to stop and visit some sisters on the way home, and Jonathon has agreed to accompany me." They stood and excused themselves, and Philip walked them to the door.

"I'm sorry Dominic was so forward," he told them.

"Not at all. It's obvious that something is bothering him, and this is a great time for the three of you to discuss it. So go spend an evening as a family."

"Thank you, Jonathon." Philip closed the door behind them.

Returning to the dining room, Philip sat down. "That was rather rude, Dominic. The Richardses were our guests."

"I'm sorry. It's just that I need to talk to you." Dominic dropped his gaze in an embarrassed silence.

"Let's talk, then. What's on your mind?" Philip wished he'd said it a little less brusquely.

Dominic cleared his throat. "So, Father, I'm under pressure from the Americans. Have you been able to find anything for me?"

This was the conversation Philip had been dreading yet desiring. Since Dominic had returned home two weeks earlier, they'd danced around it, with Dominic finding an excuse to leave whenever Philip tried to raise the topic of his service. Now, with a new piece of mail from the States, Dominic was ready to talk.

"Tell me again what you have in mind," Philip said, stalling for time.

Dominic was immediately exasperated. "Why, something in the government like I told you in my letter. Certainly there are many things I can do here in London." The tone of his voice irritated Philip, but he had promised himself he'd keep his composure.

"Please look at me, Dominic." The boy raised his face with that odd mixture of dread and obstinacy that had characterized so many of their conversations. "You've got to understand that the type of jobs you speak of are held by older men who have volunteered or by active servicemen who have been wounded in battle and are no longer fit to serve on the front. Young men your age are almost always called to serve in a forward position."

"So there's nothing you can do to help me?" Dominic asked with obvious irritation. Before Philip could respond, Dominic rushed on. "If all I'm going to do is go into the infantry or something, I might as well have stayed in America until the last possible moment. At least there I had something worthwhile to do while I waited."

"We were pleased to hear how much you enjoyed the theater," Claire said. "I'm sorry you didn't get to pursue it further. But after the war . . ."

"Yeah, after the war. If I'm still alive. Or not a cripple or something. You can't do a lot as a cripple."

"Dominic!" Philip said sharply, the image of young Dan O'Brian coming to his mind. A gas attack had destroyed Dan's singing career. Philip suspected that was exactly the image Dominic had intended.

"No offense," Dominic replied in his phony smooth voice. He lapsed into his familiar sullen slouch. "I know that for those pursuing a full-time military career, you know, those that bring honor and glory to the family, a good injury is like a badge of distinction. But for those of us with more mundane ambitions, it can be career ending."

"Dominic, please," Claire said.

Philip inhaled slowly. This was actually going worse than he'd feared. *Nice to know that Dominic can still surprise me,* he thought. Philip had been so hopeful when the positive letters from New York had hinted at a change of attitude.

Finally, with a sigh, Philip said, "Dominic, there is something I can do. I have some contacts in the Royal Corps of Signals. They serve in a supporting role, and perhaps you could find a place to serve there—perhaps with the interest of a senior officer."

"Signals?" Dominic actually seemed surprised. At first his voice was bright. But then it grew dark again. "Aren't they in combat along with the others—sending signals from ships and that sort of thing?"

"In some instances. But there are many roles to play, including electronics, flags, courier, and so forth. It's time mostly spent behind the front lines." Philip was slightly disgusted hearing himself talk this way. As a chaplain in the Great War, he'd prided himself on going out and mingling with troops at the very front of the battle. He felt it his duty to share their dangers if he was to give them counsel that had any meaning. They were the heroes, after all, facing their fears and defending their country anyway. Now he was trying to find ways for his own son to avoid that. *Still, he does have ambitions that require a whole and healthy body,* Philip considered.

"Well, perhaps that would be something. If there is some assurance—"

Philip bristled. "There are no assurances in war, Dominic. At some point you have to face your fear."

"Of course you do," Claire intervened. "I think Dominic understands that. But it seems like this is a good opportunity. Will you consider it, Dominic?"

"I suppose," Dominic mumbled, not trying to hide his disappointment.

There were lots of unspoken thoughts in the conversation. They sat quietly for a few moments.

"Do you mind if I'm excused?" Dominic said finally, breaking the silence. "I'd like to go for a walk and think."

After Dominic left, Claire and Philip were quiet for a time. Finally Claire turned to her husband. "I don't understand, Philip. I honestly don't understand."

"Understand what?" He didn't look up.

"I don't understand," she said very softly, "how it is that you, who are perhaps the most effective communicator I know, have such trouble with Dominic."

Philip shook his head and looked up. "I'm not an effective communicator. No matter how hard I try to control myself, I end up getting frustrated."

"And that's what's so puzzling. I've watched you with our friends, with the patients here, with members of the Church who are in deep distress. Goodness, I even watched you with George Cook. You held your patience better with him than you do with Dominic. Why should all these people matter more than your own son?"

"Perhaps that's the problem—they don't matter as much. I'm responsible for Dominic, and so his problems are mine. Yet he chooses to deal with them so entirely differently than I would. It's easy to give advice to the others—much harder when it's your own flesh and blood." He looked up just a bit defiantly. "And it's not all my fault—he seems to have a knack for saying things that provoke me."

Claire bit her lip. Philip braced, but he didn't need to; her reply was more a plea than a recrimination. "He does say things that he shouldn't. He's often exasperating. The point is, though, that he needs you. That's all. He needs your wisdom and support. I don't know why he's frightened, aside from the frightening times we live in, but his is an unusual fear. It would paralyze most people, but for Dominic it brings out a kind of bitterness that makes him belligerent.

We can argue about whether he should have such fear, but the truth is that our thoughts on the subject are irrelevant—he simply has it. Rather than feel your scorn, he should feel your love. What would you say to him if he were a soldier you found on the front lines while you were a chaplain? Would you bristle quite so quickly?"

"Dan O'Brian did his best to brush me off. He tried sarcasm, silence, and occasional hostility."

"But you were patient with him, weren't you?"

Philip looked at her. "I was. But his problems were different. He was brave but broken."

She shook her head in sudden recognition. "And Dominic is not brave. That's the basis of all this, isn't it?" Philip tried to avoid looking into her eyes. "I understand that he's lacking in this area and that it's difficult for you." She took his hands and forced him to look into her eyes, "But he is still broken, Philip. Can't you find a way to help him?"

"Oh, dear," Philip said in a desperate tone, "I'm frightened for him. The best thing ever to happen is that he started finding joy in what he was doing in New York City. If he could find a place like that, I'd be at rest with it, even if his lifestyle is different than ours. But the military services are not indulgent, and he has to be able to stand up to what is dealt him. I keep hoping that I can stiffen him somehow for what's coming. But it doesn't work. I'm all right with him getting angry at me if he will turn that anger into resolve. Instead he just sulks."

"Philip." It was amazing how much tenderness Claire could put in a single word. Fortunately for both of them, she was controlling her temper now and speaking out of love. "Philip, since it's obvious that your attempts at building his resolve by reacting to him aren't working, perhaps you can try it another way. Just tell him how you feel—whatever it is, even if it's unpleasant—but say it in love and gentleness. I believe he'll respond to that."

Philip turned his head, the lump in his throat making it hard to reply. "I'll try, Claire."

Chapter Seventeen

AN UNEXPECTED MISSION

Dover—May 1942

"Will there be time to catch up with the convoy, sir? It's almost 2100," Canfield asked.

Michael winced, knowing that the captain would not be pleased by his question. For the life of him, Michael couldn't figure out why Eric Canfield insisted on asking questions that were certain to annoy.

"There is no convoy, Mr. Canfield," Lieutenant Prescott replied.

Not so bad, Michael thought.

"So it would be very difficult to catch up with it, wouldn't you say?" Prescott asked in a deadpan tone.

Ah, sarcasm. That's more like it!

Fortunately, Eric didn't worry about such things. If he did he'd be a nervous wreck most of his life. He did, however, have the common sense not to ask any more questions. Michael watched Prescott check his watch yet again. It really was unusual for them to wait in port this long, especially since the other boats had sailed at sunset. In the year since he'd transferred from the *Hood,* a lot had happened. First Officer Steadman had been promoted and now had command of his own boat. Even though Canfield had been assigned to the *960* earlier than Michael, the nod had gone to Michael so that he was now second-in-command. At first Michael worried about the effect on Eric's morale, but Canfield simply had no guile. He'd sincerely congratulated Michael on the promotion and immediately started responding to his leadership. In time Michael decided that Eric probably preferred a supporting role.

For his part, Michael was surprised at how boring war was. Aside from a few spectacular scrimmages, most nights were spent trolling about in the English Channel, shepherding the merchant ships. The worst danger on most nights was falling asleep on shift, something Michael had never done—but a capital offense nonetheless and one that had to be resisted.

Michael heard the sound of voices on the dock and then saw a dark-coated figure step across the cowling onto the boat. There was some kind of discussion between the captain and the stranger. Suddenly, he heard his name being called.

"Yes, sir!" he replied crisply to the captain as he climbed down the few steps off the bridge.

"Mr. Carlyle, please meet Lieutenant Ellington. Mr. Ellington, our Lieutenant Carlyle."

"Michael?" The voice was familiar. And then recognition dawned for Michael.

"Jules? Is that you?"

"It is! Why, you old dog, what are you doing on one of these sleek little killers? I thought you'd be commanding a battleship by now!"

"Nope. I've got nothing better to do than pickup duty. What exactly is it you're doing here?"

Prescott cleared his throat and both men promptly stood at attention and stopped talking. "I take it you two know each other."

"Yes, sir," Michael replied. "Jules, that is, Lieutenant Ellington, and I went to public school together before I transferred to the Naval College. He was a tolerable cricket player."

"An endangered one—Lieutenant Carlyle tried to play rugby the way the Americans play their football. It nearly got me killed."

Michael and Jules laughed, happy to see each other. At a severe glance from Prescott, they both went quiet again.

"Well, that's all well and good, but it doesn't solve our problem. You're still missing your compatriot, Mr. Ellington. Do we scrub the mission?"

Ellington's face fell. "I suppose so, sir. There's no way I can carry it out since I don't speak German. I don't know what happened to him. Perhaps we could wait a few more minutes?"

"Not if we're going to make your rendezvous. We've got at least three hours at best speed, and as I understand it, you're supposed to be some two kilometers inland by 0230. Is that right?"

"Yes, sir."

Prescott sighed. "Well, can you get word to the French that we're calling it off?"

Before Ellington could reply, Michael interjected, "Do you mind if I ask what the problem is?"

Prescott nodded to Ellington, who began to fill Michael in. "I'm a commando trained to make raids inside enemy territory." Michael's eyes widened, since this was an elite group that was equipped to take on some of the most dangerous missions in the Navy. He hadn't ever thought of Jules in that kind of role, although it made sense given his superb physical conditioning and rather daring temperament. "At any rate, tonight I was scheduled to rendezvous with a small group of French Resistance fighters who have come into possession of some German codes. At this point, the Germans don't know they've been compromised, since substitute documents were placed on the German's dead body before his car 'drove' off the cliff, incinerating the corpse but leaving enough remnants to make them believe he'd still possessed the original documents."

Michael whistled slightly at this. "To make sure I understand, a dead German failed to properly control the car he was driving, resulting in a fiery crash. Now it's your job to collect the documents for use by our cryptographers in breaking the German code."

"Precisely," Jules said with a smile.

"But it takes two of you to make the connection?"

"We need to take some wireless equipment to the French to assist in their efforts. None of them speak English, so it would be difficult for me to debrief them about the codes. I don't know what happened to the fellow who was supposed to come tonight, but he's not here."

"I speak French—quite well, in fact." Now it was Ellington's and Prescott's turn to be surprised.

"I didn't know you spoke French," Prescott said a bit sharply.

"I suppose we've never had occasion to speak it together. My father is a firm believer that we should be familiar with the major continental languages, so I studied French extensively and even speak fluent German."

"German!" Ellington said with admiration. "Well, Michael Carlyle, you are a man of multiple talents. Any chance I might use him tonight, Lieutenant Prescott?"

"That's up to Mr. Carlyle. We're not really in the commando business." Michael couldn't tell from the tone of his response whether Prescott approved or not, but he had left the decision to him.

Michael nodded slightly while considering. After months at sea with very little action, this was extremely appealing. It was also extremely dangerous. The Germans would like nothing more than to capture British agents they could use as public examples of why not to cooperate with the enemy by executing them in the local town square, along with any collaborators who might be captured with them. On the other side of the argument, the value of the codes simply made it too important a mission to scrap.

"I'll do it," he said simply.

"Very good," Prescott replied. Turning to the bridge, he spoke in his official voice, "Mr. Canfield, please see to it that Lieutenant Ellington's baggage is loaded and stowed, then make ready for an immediate departure."

"Yes, sir!" came the crisp reply.

Of course, Eric would be dying of curiosity, but Michael noticed that from the moment he said he'd go, the captain had stopped treating him like a member of the crew. Apparently you were either assigned to the boat or to Special Forces.

After Prescott stepped up to the bridge, Michael invited Ellington below to his cramped little spot in the cabin. He looked for a place where they could be relatively alone. Once settled, he said quietly to Ellington, "So what have I gotten myself in for?"

"You'll be all right. This one's pretty easy from a physical point of view. Your captain will pull up as close to shore as possible on a quiet beach between Dunkirk and Calais. We'll take a skiff onto the shore and then work our way inland. Because of the swampy conditions, we have to travel approximately one kilometer inland. It's too dangerous for our French counterparts to be found any closer to shore, so we have to get to a secure location where their exposure is minimized. The primary reason we need to speak French to them is to try to verify their legitimacy—there's always the possibility of a double agent setting us up with false information or luring us into a trap after we're out of range of our wireless equipment. Once we feel good about it, we'll give them the equipment with some basic instructions on how to use it, I'll collect the codes in this waterproof pouch, and then we're out of there as quick as we can go. We'll have just ninety minutes from the time we reach shore until we have to be back to the boat. If we're not back, they have to leave, since twilight will be turning the sky pretty light by 0500. It would be crazy to put the crew at risk."

"And if we don't make it back in time but are still alive?"

"We'll lie in wait until the next night, when they'll attempt another rendezvous."

Michael had more questions, but the engines rumbled to life and the boat lurched as they pulled away from the dock. Normally they'd proceed quietly through the harbor, but it was clear that Lieutenant Prescott was worried about the time because they were slammed back against the wall as the boat roared to life the moment it was in the open Channel. Michael tried to speak, but the maneuvering threw them about so crazily that all they could do was laugh.

"Is it like this all the time?" Jules shouted.

"I don't know," Michael yelled back. "I've always been on deck. It's a lot better up there."

"What happens if I get sick?" Jules called back.

"I didn't think commandos were allowed to get sick!"

"They're not—but apparently my stomach didn't get the order. Either that, or it's insubordinate!"

"Come on, let's move out on deck—you'll feel better with some fresh air in your face!"

* * *

Standing off a Beach East of Calais—0130 Hours

"There's something I forgot to ask you," Michael said quietly.

"Ask away."

"What happens if it turns out they're double agents?"

"Then we shoot them—if they don't shoot us first."

"And what incentive do they have not to shoot us first, since we'll already be there with the equipment? Seems to me they can take it off our dead bodies as easily as our live ones."

Jules laughed. "You're a suspicious one, aren't you? Getting cold feet, Carlyle?"

"Not cold feet—I just like to know what I'm up against."

"Well, in this case, the equipment is incomplete. It turns out that there's a series of tumblers that have to be set to a specific sequence or the device is useless. They know that. They have to keep us alive at least long enough to convince us that they're trustworthy so that I enter the code."

"Ah! So it's really important that we make sure they're reliable."

"Very, and that's where you come in. I don't know French, so I couldn't tell if they were speaking it with a German accent or not. You've got to listen for any subtleties in their speech pattern that might indicate that they're other than what they appear. You should also listen for certain stress patterns when they respond to my questions."

Michael laughed indignantly. "I told you I speak French as a third language. You really expect to me to listen for subtleties in their reply?"

"Third language? I thought you said your French was better than your German," Jules said, sounding a bit alarmed by the revelation.

"German is my fourth language," Michael said, enjoying his chance to tease Jules. "Here's how my language skills shake out— American first, English second, French third, German fourth, and I could ask how to find a restroom in Spanish if I were desperate."

"Ah—American. Well, we might as well shoot ourselves. No subtlety in that language, is there?"

"It's like this everywhere I go here. Has it ever occurred to anyone in the British Isles that maybe the Americans have actually improved the language? After all, we do add more new words each year than the entire British Empire."

Jules tipped his head to the side in consideration of the question. "No—no, I'd have to say that that's never occurred to any of us. The mind automatically screens out preposterous things like that."

"Yes, well. I'm not promising that I can tell you how authentic your French speakers are. My father had some very good friends in Normandy where we've visited a number of times, so I'm pretty good at their dialect. We also went to Paris shopping quite regularly, so I'm familiar with that area as well. Outside of that, I'm not all that confident."

"But if they were foreigners?"

"If they're German foreigners, it will be a piece of cake."

"Piece of cake?"

"An American saying—it means it will be easy."

"Of course, why didn't I know that?"

"At any rate, the difference between spoken French and spoken German is immense. That two such incredibly different languages could share a geographical border is amazing. French is a beautiful Latin language with soft romantic sounds, while German sounds like a jackhammer smashing, even with the most delicate phrases. I'm very confident I could detect a German attempting French."

"That's all I need to know, Michael. You need to be sharp and decisive. If I smell a ruse I'll start shooting and expect you to join me without any hesitation." When Michael blanched, Jules asked, "Do you have any problem with that? If so, tell me now and we'll call it off."

"No, I don't have a problem. It's just that I've never had to do it before—not for real," Michael said, doing his best to hide his agitation and uncertainty.

Jules watched him for a few moments. "You'll be all right. I don't think we'll have to. But if we do, your training will help you do what's expected."

"Are you ready, gentlemen?" They turned at Prescott's voice.

Michael glanced down at the nondescript black clothing that Jules handed him. In just a few moments he was likely to get wet in the cold waters of the English Channel. *Guess I'm as ready as I'll ever be!* he thought briefly to himself.

He nodded to Jules, who called back, "We're ready, sir!"

"Then off with you. We're going to pull farther out from the shore to avoid detection, but we'll be back promptly at 0330. You'll have a fifteen-minute window, and then we'll be off. Understand?"

"Yes, sir!"

"Good luck to both of you, then." Prescott saluted and then reached out his hand to Michael. "And don't be late!"

"Not on your life," Michael said, as both Prescott and Jules gave him a funny look for his American idiom. And with that, Michael was down and over the side and into the small skiff. The wireless equipment had already been loaded.

Chapter Eighteen

ENEMY SOIL

The Coast of France—May 1942

"You didn't tell me this equipment weighed fifty pounds!"

"Navy boy having trouble walking on dry ground?"

"If only it were dry. There's water everywhere, and you've got my boots all muddy."

"We're almost there. Now's the time to be quiet, Michael. The Germans tend to patrol this area pretty carefully. If we come across a group, they'll probably shoot us on sight; but just in case, you should be prepared to use your German just long enough to give me a chance to shoot them first."

"With my accent, they'll probably be disabled by laughter, so no need to worry."

Michael never fully understood his own tendency to attempt humor when he was nervous, but right now he needed it more than ever, having gone past nervous to downright scared.

Ellington signaled for him to stop, and the two of them knelt in some bushes, listening for what Michael didn't know exactly. "Okay, Michael, here's what you should say to them in French: 'The moon is beautiful over the English Channel tonight.'"

"And the correct reply?" Michael asked.

"'But the clouds often obscure the stars, don't you think?'"

Michael nodded, quietly repeating the phrase as he started to make the appropriate translation. He heard a distinct clicking sound in the bushes. It had a repeating pattern to it, indicating human origin. Michael noticed he was holding his breath. He had to force himself to release it very slowly so that he wouldn't make a sound. Ellington was cautious, waiting for the sound a second time. Then he made a clicking noise in reply. There was nothing for a moment, and then the slight rustling of leaves. Although Michael's eyes had long since adapted to the darkness, he was still taken by surprise as three dark forms emerged from the brush. Ellington nodded at him to proceed.

"La lune est très belle au dessus de la Manche ce soir."

Immediately one of the fellows responded with, *"Mais les nuages obscurcissent souvent les étoiles, non?"*

"They gave the correct greeting," Michael said to Ellington.

"Ask them to describe their code names, location, and purpose of the rendezvous." Michael started to challenge them but Ellington interrupted with, "And listen to their accent, for heaven's sake."

Michael scowled. *As if I need to be reminded!* In as confident a voice as he could muster, he recited, *"Mon collègue souhaite que je vous demande vos noms de code, votre position géographique, et l'objectif de ce rendezvous."*

The fellow scowled for a moment and then replied, *"Nous sommes membres de la résistance de Calais. Notre nom de code est bon vivant et nous sommes ici pour vous procurer les messages codés allemands. Nous attendons que vous assemblez et modifiez l'équipement de transmission la plus rapidement que possible. Et nous, comment pouvons nous être sûrs que vous êtes bien ce que vous dîtes être?"*

Now it was Michael's turn to scowl.

"What is it?" Ellington asked urgently.

"He provided the correct answer but then asked how they can know that we're legitimate. Who else would be here?"

"Are they legitimate?" Ellington asked.

"There was no German accent from what I could tell."

"Just to make sure," Ellington said, "ask some questions about Paris."

The French responded easily and then repeated their challenge.

Michael was about to improvise an answer when one of the Frenchmen startled them both by saying in perfect English, "And what city in America is the capital of Texas?"

"What?" Michael asked.

"Apparently my initial question was too difficult, so I came up with one of my own. Your French is obviously spoken with an American accent. So what is the capital of your largest state?"

Michael smiled. "The capital of Texas is Austin."

"So why am I being addressed by an American?" the Frenchman asked.

"It's too complicated to explain, but you are correct," Ellington said. "My comrade here grew up in the western United States, although his father is British. It's difficult for us to understand him as well."

That pleased the Frenchman and brought an appreciative humph from Michael. After that, they settled down in the bushes to transact their business. Jules had decided that the men were trustworthy.

After carefully unpacking one of the electronic components, Jules removed two screws from the back and lifted off the protective cover. Michael could see a maze of vacuum tubes and wires inside. With great dexterity, Jules reached inside and pulled out a small block that was connected by wires between the tuner and the amplifier. He dialed the tumblers into position, then secured it with a locking mechanism.

"Should this ever be about to fall into German hands before you have time to destroy it, simply slip this locking mechanism out of place and randomly switch the tumblers. That will render the device useless."

"Very good," a Frenchman replied.

The French quickly repacked the device, and their leader indicated that the two men who had accompanied him should start out with it. As they moved through the bush, he pulled out a sheaf of papers and quickly explained their significance and what he knew about the codes themselves. From what they could determine, the codes were used in local communication to redeploy coastal defenses up and down the coastline. In the right circumstances, the information intercepted could prove of inestimable worth for the ultimate Allied invasion of the mainland.

"These were obtained at a heavy price," the French leader explained. "Two of our men lost their lives, and our entire operation was nearly compromised. As it is, we believe the codes are secure and the Germans suspect nothing. So treat them with respect." He paused for a moment. "One of the men who lost his life was my brother. I hope his sacrifice has meaning."

"We'll see that they make their way into the proper hands. Thank you." With that, the three men shook hands, and the remaining French leader started to move out toward the west as Jules and Michael prepared to work their way north back to the coast. They were on schedule to arrive by 0330 as promised.

"By the way," Michael said, causing the Frenchman to turn and look at him, "how is it that you know so much about America?"

"I went to Princeton for four years. Imagine English being spoken with both a French and New Jersey accent! That's a nightmare, to be sure."

Michael laughed and wished him well.

* * *

"Half a kilometer to go." Even Jules, cool commando, sounded excited.

As they started to move across the marsh, Jules suddenly pulled up and froze in position, and Michael followed suit. Why they hadn't heard it earlier was hard to imagine—perhaps it was because they had been slouching their way into the wind. Up ahead and directly between them and the beach was the distinct sound of bored German voices. Motioning with his hands for Michael to get down, Jules lay down beside him and crawled up to where he could put his mouth directly next to Michael's ear.

"Can you tell what they're saying?"

Michael strained to hear their voices, but they were too far away. He was pretty sure it was just idle chat—certainly there was nothing in the sound to indicate that they were suspicious or out looking for something. He whispered his impression to Jules, who nodded.

Jules motioned in the direction that would take them down-wind from the Germans and started to crawl his way through the fetid waters of the tide pools that lay between them and their boat. There was a slight rise in the land that had sheltered the boat from the Germans' line of sight, which had probably kept the Germans from sounding an alarm.

Michael was startled to discover that the path Jules was following took them almost directly toward the Germans, not around them as he had imagined it would. Confused, he finally tapped Jules's leg and made his concerns known by hand signals. There was just the hint of light in the sky now so that that they could see each other better. Jules motioned him to scoot forward and then whispered in his ear, "We have to kill them, Michael. When the MTB arrives, they'll certainly hear it and sound the alarm. Even if we get away, they'll know that there's been contact between the British and the Resistance, and they'll immediately invalidate all of their codes. In other words, all of this will have been in vain."

"But if we kill them, won't that sound the alarm?"

"Not if they disappear. The Germans will have to assume the Resistance killed them and buried them somewhere nearby. There'll be no reason to associate it with the British."

Michael's stomach lurched, but he indicated that he understood. Slowly they started forward, doing their very best not to make a sound as they moved across the sand and weeds. As they drew near, Jules pulled two lengths of wire out of his pocket and silently handed one to Michael. Jules motioned in such a way to indicate that they were to strangle the Germans. Michael's heart started pounding in his chest, but he moved quietly to within just a few feet of the German, ready to spring at a sign from Jules. Jules held up five fingers, then began counting down on is hand. When the countdown reached one, Michael took a deep breath and lurched forward, grabbing the German from behind and slipping the deadly cord around his neck. The poor fellow was so startled that he didn't even resist at first, then he started twisting to get out from the trap while desperately clawing at Michael's hands to get him to release his grip. But Michael just held tighter. It was a horrifying event, but it had become a life-or-death struggle because the German had managed to turn to where he could grasp Michael's head and was now doing his best to pull it forward in an attempt to break his neck. The pain was terrible, and Michael felt a crack in his neck, but still he struggled to hold his grip. After what seemed an eternity, he felt the German start to slump and his resistance falter. Then he heard a gurgling sound, and the fellow went limp. Michael was so frightened that he held the cable for another moment, too upset to release it. In spite of himself, he felt his hands trembling at the same moment he felt tears trickle down both cheeks.

Just as he finally released the grip, he was startled by the crack of pistol, fired just a few feet away. Turning wildly, he saw that the German had managed to shoot Jules, who had fallen back and was twisting on the ground. The German rose to a sitting position and took aim to finish Jules off. Before he could even process what was happening, Michael felt the retort of his own gun as he shot the German in the back. His aim was good, and the German fell forward with a moan.

"Oh, what have I done?" he said to no one. "Dear God, what have I done?" He instinctively dropped the gun and backed away from the two bodies that lay in front of him.

"You saved my life," he heard Jules say faintly. "You've done just what you were supposed to do."

"Jules?" Michael's head was spinning, and he knew that he was going into shock. *But there isn't time for that. You've got to do something,* he thought. "Jules, what should I do?" He scooted over to his friend, whose shirt was soaked in blood.

"I'm afraid I made a mess of things," Jules said weakly. "I failed to immobilize his arms and he was able to reach a hidden weapon. He brought it up and shot me before I noticed what was happening."

Acting on instinct, Michael tore Jules's shirt open. The wound was oozing blood, but it didn't look like it had hit anything vital. Tearing a piece of his own shirt, Michael quickly applied pressure to the wound to try to staunch the bleeding.

"Michael . . . Michael, you've got to get out of here. There are undoubtedly other patrols nearby, and they will have heard the gunshots. You've got to leave."

"But I have to get you to safety."

"No, you don't. You need to leave me. I can feel that I'm slipping away. You can still make it out with the code. That's all that matters."

"But the Germans will find you, and then they'll know we were here. You said that would cause them to change the codes. So it makes no sense to leave you."

"Ah, but it does. I have French papers in my pockets. They'll think I'm a member of the Resistance."

"What? You didn't tell me about that. Why don't I have papers like that?"

"Because they are on the person who was supposed to assist me. Now please, get to the boat."

Michael sat down for a moment and listened to hear if there were any Germans nearby. There was quite a wind blowing, which meant it was possible that between the sound of the surf and the blowing wind, no one had heard the shot.

"Get going—that's an order!"

"We're both lieutenants—you can't order me around."

"It's my mission. I'm in command."

"You're incapacitated, so you can't make me do anything."

"Carlyle—get your sorry self out of here. Now!"

Michael still didn't move. A thought came to him. He knew that Jules would be furious, but he also knew that Jules was likely to lose consciousness shortly, so it wouldn't matter. Standing into a crouching position, he said, "This is going to hurt you more than it hurts me." He reached down and pulled Jules up and over his shoulders in the fireman's carry he'd learned as a Boy Scout in Salt Lake City a decade earlier.

"What are you doing?" Jules demanded. "Trying to kill me?" Michael knew the pain must be incredible, although it couldn't have been much worse than what he was experiencing himself. The German had clearly injured his neck, and the pain of hoisting Jules up was excruciating. But Michael was convinced he could get Jules to the boat, then come back for the two Germans. They could still pull the mission off and stand a chance at saving Jules.

"Carlyle—" Jules said before his voice cut off. In some ways, Jules's silence was even worse than being yelled at, because now Michael realized he was alone. Who could tell when a German patrol might overtake him?

You can't think about that. You've got to get to the boat, Michael thought. He gritted his teeth and started the painful task of carrying his friend through the difficult terrain to their boat.

* * *

By 0345 Michael was exhausted. After dumping the last German into the boat, he simply fell in on top of the others. The thought of falling on a dead body would normally have been far too creepy to even consider, but now it didn't mean anything. He had heard the sound of the *960* nearly ten minutes earlier and knew that if he didn't make himself known, they would shortly take off without him. Finally, pulling himself to a kneeling position, Michael reached inside his jacket and pulled out a flashlight, which he used to signal the boat. He was gratified to hear the sound of the motor moving closer. With what remaining strength Michael had, he started to paddle toward the sound. The tide was rising, which meant the *960* could get a lot closer to make the pickup, but it also meant he was fighting the incoming current.

After what seemed like an eternity, Michael heard Prescott call out in a stage whisper, "What the blazes is going on? Why is it taking you two so long to pull out to us?"

"I've got a wounded man here, sir. I need help." He hadn't meant for his voice to sound desperate, but it did. He was particularly irritated when an involuntary sob forced its way up and out of his throat.

"Quick, throw him a line, Canfield, and then pull them in." In a matter of moments Michael felt a rope slap across his shoulders, and he quickly anchored it to the skiff. He was relieved more than words could express to feel the tether being pulled in by strong arms.

As Michael reached the side of the *960*, Prescott peered down and asked, "What's this?"

"The Germans were between us and the boat. They would have heard your approach, so we had to kill them. One of them shot Jules." The lump in Michael's throat made it difficult to talk, but he did his best to give his report in as steady a voice as possible.

"Help them in, then get those German bodies on board." There was a flurry of activity, and Michael winced in pain as he was lifted up into the boat. His neck felt like it was on fire, but he felt grateful to be on the deck.

"Heave in the boat," Prescott said firmly, "and prepare to make way."

Michael lay back on the deck to take some pressure off his neck. Then he sat straight up.

"We've got to go back, sir!"

"What? Are you crazy? It's already starting to show light in the east."

"We left Lieutenant Ellington's gun back there, sir. I couldn't manage it with him. I first had to drag the lieutenant to the boat, then go back for each of the Germans. I was so frantic to make it back in time that I must have left it."

"Well, we have to leave it, or we're likely to come under shore fire when they spot us."

"But, sir, that would ruin the whole mission. If they find a British weapon and two missing Germans, they'll know we were here. That will cause them to change the codes, which means all of this will have been for nothing. It might also lead to recriminations against the local population."

Prescott stooped down next to Michael. "Carlyle, you're in no shape to go back. The tide is coming in and will wipe out all traces of your being here anyway."

"But the gun. They might discover the gun. Please, sir, I don't want all this to have been for nothing."

Lieutenant Prescott's face looked perplexed, although he wasn't one to stew over a decision. "Fine, you've got thirty minutes—no more. Take Seaman Scofield with you—he's our coolest head. Find the gun and get back here. I simply *have* to leave in thirty minutes, and you'll have to hide for another day. I don't think you're in any shape to do that. Do you understand?"

"Yes, sir."

"Quick, Scofield, help Lieutenant Carlyle into the boat, and pull like you've never pulled in your life."

"Yes, sir." Scofield was nothing if not efficient. He picked Michael up with ease and dropped him unceremoniously into the boat. As they started to pull away, Michael looked up to see Eric Canfield mouth the words, "Good luck!" For his part, Michael was beyond luck. He simply wanted to either pass out or die.

* * *

"Where should we look, sir?" Scofield asked urgently.

It was very hard for Michael to concentrate, and the land looked different with the tide coming up. Finally, after studying the scene carefully, he pointed to a small hill, then moved his finger to a point just to the right of it. "Over there—I'm sure this time."

"I hope so," Scofield said. "We're down to about two minutes until we've gone past halfway."

Michael's neck ached so badly it was almost the only thing he could think about. He started to move stiffly in the direction of his skirmish, but Scofield motioned for him to stay put. In what appeared to be lightning time, Scofield had closed to the spot, spent several moments fishing around, then triumphantly raised the pistol. Michael gave him a thumbs up and started moving back toward the *960*. He knew that Scofield would catch him shortly.

Michael thought he was moving rather well, at least until Scofield came up and nearly lifted him off his feet. "Come on, sir, let me help you. We've got no time to lose."

It was at that point that they heard, very distantly, some German voices. Michael strained to hear what they were saying. Finally, he was able to make out a German phrase.

"What are they saying, sir?" Scofield asked, moving even faster. By now Michael was only half walking, half running, with most of his weight being supported by Scofield, who had draped Michael's arm over his shoulder.

"They're calling out to their dead friends. They're telling them it's time to come in from patrol. Hopefully, the tide will wash away the evidence of our struggle before they get there."

"Not to worry about that, sir. I found the gun in nearly six inches of water already. Our biggest problem is that we may well be drowned before we reach our skiff."

Michael struggled to do even better, and they sloshed their way through the water to the point where they'd tied up their dinghy.

"Where is it?" Scofield asked desperately.

Michael looked around in all directions, trying to make out the difference between the brush and the lighter color of their skiff.

"Is that it?" he asked, pointing to the east.

"It is, sir!"

Scofield dragged Michael to the dinghy and dumped him in, then started rowing feverishly toward the rendezvous point. With only seconds to spare, Scofield flashed the recognition signal.

Michael could hear Prescott mutter, "Thank heavens."

In no time they were being dragged on board.

"What can you tell me?" Prescott asked urgently.

"We got the gun, and the tide should have covered our tracks. But there are German patrols out there looking for the men we killed. They might have heard our retreat, so it was all for nothing after all." The fatigue and sorrow in Michael's voice made him sound heartbroken.

"Not if I can help it," Prescott said firmly. "Please implement our plan, Mr. Canfield."

"Yes, sir."

"Meanwhile, it's down into the galley for you, Michael. You need some food and some hot liquid. You look awful."

"It's my neck, sir. The German tried to break it. From the way it feels, he may have succeeded."

Prescott gently felt Michael's neck, which made Michael wince and cry out in such pain that he fainted. Turning to Scofield, Prescott said, "Take him below, but be gentle about it. Our Mr. Carlyle may be in serious trouble."

* * *

Had Michael been awake, he would have been puzzled not to hear the engines come to life. The only sound was of the surf and the quiet purr of the electric motor. Prescott was very slowly backing them out to sea without any engines. It increased the risk of being overtaken by German aircraft in the daylight, because they would certainly be late getting back to port at this point. But it dramatically increased the odds of pulling off the theft of the German codes. Prescott had concluded it was a risk worth taking.

When they finally made it out far enough that it was okay to use the engines, Prescott ordered full speed ahead then slipped below decks to check on his landing party.

"How are they doing?" he asked the chief, who doubled as their medic.

"Not so good, sir. Lieutenant Ellington has lost so much blood I don't know if he'll ever regain consciousness. I've tried to force liquid, but he simply gags on it. I've managed to stop the bleeding, so that may be a good sign."

"What about Lieutenant Carlyle?"

"He's sleeping, but if his neck is as bad as he says, who knows?"

"To think that he was hurt like that, yet still brought Ellington to safety and then returned to drag each of the two Germans. You talk about foolhardy."

The chief, who was not one for sentimentality, said quietly, "You can talk about brave if you like, sir, but I for one wouldn't say foolish."

Prescott turned and looked at him gravely. The chief was at least ten years older than him, perhaps even more. Some would consider his comment out of line when spoken to a commanding officer. Prescott thought it remarkable.

"Very brave indeed, chief. I didn't know Mr. Carlyle was made of such stuff."

"It's likely he didn't know either, sir."

Prescott nodded. "I just hope his efforts don't result in a permanent disability." The two men stood looking at Michael for a few moments, then Prescott straightened up.

"Well, the best thing for him now is rest. Try to keep an eye on him. Hopefully the engines won't trouble us on the way back."

"Aye, sir. I'll watch both of them."

Chapter Nineteen

THE ROYAL CORPS
OF SIGNALS

An Army Training Center outside of London—May 1942

"This is so humiliating," Dominic muttered under his breath, doing his best to make sure the sound was virtually inaudible to avoid incurring the wrath of the sergeant major. Standing in line with twenty other recruits who had no clothes on simply accentuated how skinny he was. At six feet even, Dominic was taller than most of the men, but when it came to bulk and muscle, he didn't even begin to compare.

"All right then, get dressed and move on to get sheared. We'll reassemble at 1500!"

"Yes, sir!" he found himself shouting along with the others. The sound of his own voice submitting like that startled him. By the time 1500 arrived, his humiliation was complete, his thick dark hair lying on the floor along with that of a hundred other inductees, and his expensive clothes tucked neatly into a bag that he could either send home or contribute to the poor. He chose to make the contribution, since after the war he'd need a good shopping trip to shake off the doldrums his new uniform invited.

The next six weeks of fundamental training was an ordeal—not so much because of the physical demands but because of the constant harassment designed to break the recruits' spirits. Dominic found that he was able to run with the best of them, and his weight, or lack of it, actually proved an advantage when running obstacle courses, doing calisthenics, or drilling on the parade ground. The challenges came in different ways, such as during drills in the countryside when he had to carry a fully laden field pack as heavy as he was. He ended the first such exercise so thoroughly exhausted that he could hardly lift his arms. Which was why he was outraged when, upon returning to camp, the sergeant major ordered them all to clean the barracks yet again because some of the bedding hadn't been properly creased. While the other men simply groaned and got to it, Dominic seethed inside.

"It's always worse for those of us from the upper class," his lower bunkmate, Frederick Tippins, whispered as he saw Dominic furiously unmaking his bed to start over. "So if I were you, I'd just hold my tongue until it passes. We'll be out and into our individual assignments soon enough."

Like Dominic, Freddie was from an influential family, though not as high in rank as the Carlyles. But unlike Dominic, Freddie didn't have the misfortune of being American born. The double curse often made things even more miserable for Dominic since at least some of the instructors felt it their duty to demand near perfection from the "young gentleman," while others ridiculed his American-tinged accent. Tradition held that those of the upper class were somehow supposed to be naturally suited to the military, which Dominic clearly was not.

"It's just so stupid!" he whispered back to Freddie. "There was nothing wrong here, so why do we have to plough through all this, this . . ." He was so angry he couldn't find the words to complete his thought.

"I don't see how this can be too aggravating, assuming you went to a school," Freddie replied. "I've certainly suffered much worse at the hands of some of the housemasters there."

Dominic relented and sighed. "Oh, I've been to more than one school. More of them than you can imagine. And I got thrown out of them for resisting things like this."

Freddie turned very serious. "Well, the difference between schools and this place is that they couldn't shoot you there. Here they can."

"A problem here, Mr. Carlyle?"

Dominic jerked at the sound of the sergeant's voice.

"No, sir, sergeant major, sir!" He braced for the sarcastic remark that was sure to follow, but his real concern was that the entire company would be punished for whatever his offense had been. That was the worst, when the silent glares and resentment for some mistake left him isolated and alone.

Instead of punishing him, the sergeant simply said, "You missed a corner there," pointing to the top of the bed where Dominic hadn't completed his final tuck.

"Thank you, sergeant major!" he replied crisply, with the open palm salute common in the British Army. He was unbelievably relieved to see the sergeant move down the row of bunks, ultimately declaring that all was in order and the men were dismissed to go to dinner.

"I thought you were in for it there," Freddie said with the same surprised sound in his voice that Dominic felt.

"Me too. I wonder what saved me."

Freddie, who had been the only one to extend any sort of friendship thus far, looked earnestly at Dominic and said, "Perhaps it shows that a person doesn't automatically lose his humanity when he serves his country. Perhaps you should stop fighting things so much and learn to simply comply."

It irritated Dominic to be lectured, but he could see that Freddie was sincere and knew that he had his best interest in mind. "Maybe it does." Not wanting to spoil the moment by showing how doubtful he really felt about what Freddie had said, he quickly added, "I don't know about you, but I'm starved. Care to join me?"

* * *

"Watch your cables, Mr. Carlyle!" Dominic turned to see with dismay that the telephone cables he'd laid so carefully across the fifty yards of scrub brush had become tangled yet again.

"Sorry, sir!" he said dejectedly and went back to try to untangle the mess. He glanced from side to side and saw the other men's rows still lined up perfectly.

"The problem is that in spite of your best efforts, you continue to apply uneven pressure to the two cables, which means they inevitably work themselves together." Dominic looked up at Sergeant Weems, the instructor, who had not said this unkindly. He felt rather desperate inside, since so far none of the tests he'd taken had turned out well.

"Permission to speak freely, sir?"

"Permission granted."

Dominic rolled back on his haunches, then brought himself gracefully into a standing position. "I'm sure you're right, sir, but I really was concentrating hard to avoid that very thing. I simply don't seem to have a knack for it. Or for anything, for that matter."

Sergeant Weems looked at him with something almost like sympathy. He was from the Royal Corps of Signals, rather than basic Army, and so was here to help the men who had volunteered for this specific branch of the service. For the past three days Weems had been putting each of the men through a series of trials to test their aptitude for the various tasks performed by the Signal Corps. It was a venerable service responsible for maintaining communications all around the world so that vital information could be shared quickly between those in command and the men in the field. It included flag semaphore messaging for silent daylight communication, Morse code signal lamps for use at sea or across large distances at night, and also electronic communication via radio and telephone.

"Listen, Carlyle," Weems started to say, and then his face brightened. "Hold on, I've just had a thought. How comfortable are you with extended periods of solitude?"

Dominic was surprised at the unexpected turn in the conversation.

"Solitude? I'm quite good at it. In fact, I like being alone." Without consciously doing it, he dropped his gaze and continued. "It tends to keep me out of trouble. Why do you ask?"

"I have a second question. It seems to me that you have good reflexes and muscle control."

Dominic smiled at this, viewing it as the first compliment he'd received since joining the Army.

"Yes, sir, I believe I do." He wanted to tell Sergeant Weems about his experiences in New York, but knew that it was superfluous to the conversation.

"Here's what I'm thinking. The most basic of Signals responsibility is despatch riding—physically carrying a message from one point to another. In prior days it was done on foot or by horse, but now the messages are carried by motorcycle. There are times that wireless or telephonics are unavailable or the message is too important to transmit." He looked at Dominic to gauge how he reacted to this.

"Motorcycles?" When thinking about the Army before, he'd always picture heavy equipment like armored cars and tanks—nothing so graceful and quick as a motorcycle. He couldn't suppress the grin that forced its way onto his face. "I love motorcycles!" he said quickly. "I've ridden them on our family estate since I was twelve. I used to scare my mother almost to death, but it was the one thing my father and I seemed to have in common. He loved to go riding with me." Dominic smiled at the memories then caught himself and quickly came back to a more proper military bearing. He hadn't talked so freely to an officer since this whole ordeal had begun.

"Well, then, I suggest you coil up your cables and plan to join me in three days for a trip out to Catterick Camp in North Yorkshire to test yourself on the moors. Perhaps there's a place for you there."

Dominic shook his head in unbelief. For the first time since New York City he actually felt hopeful. "Thank you, Sergeant Weems. Thank you!" He bounded back to the starting point of the infernal phone lines, where he quickly began to coil them into an acceptable bundle so that he could leave them behind, hopefully forever.

* * *

Having spent a lifetime being the odd man out at sports—seldom selected early in the draft because of his lack of skill and interest—Dominic found it exhilarating to participate in the motorcycle trials at Catterick Camp. He'd arrived the previous day after a three-day leave of absence in London, where he and his father had actually spent some enjoyable time together. With most of the normal activities of the city shut down because of the nightly blackout, Philip had somehow managed to find a small theater in the West End where they had a contemporary dance revue, and the two of them had enjoyed a marvelous evening dining out and then going to the theater. Philip had whispered questions to Dominic about the various dance moves, many of which were somewhat provocative for someone as conservative as his father. Dominic had been surprised that he'd taken it all in stride and had seemed interested in it. That night after getting home, they'd talked for perhaps another full hour before retiring. The next day Philip had taken Dominic to the Houses of Parliament and his private club, pleased to introduce him to the peers and his other influential friends. It was obvious that his military service was pleasing to his father, even though he hadn't belabored the point. At the end they'd hugged without the awkwardness that was so often the case.

"Carlyle—you're up next!" said Freddie Tippins, who had also decided to try out for a posting to despatch rider.

"What?"

"Pay attention—you're always daydreaming," Freddie hissed back.

Fortunately, there was enough fussing around with the comings and goings of the motorcycles that his potential mistake went unnoticed, and he stepped forward smartly.

"Private Dominic Carlyle reporting as ordered, sir!"

"Very good, Carlyle," the officer said distractedly. "Have you had any experience with the 499 cc Norton 16H?"

"No, sir. I mostly used a Douglas and lately a Triumph." In Dominic's opinion, both these motorcycles were superior to the Norton, but there was no sense provoking a reaction with an editorial comment.

"Right, then. Yates here will give you a briefing, and then I want you to go out onto the course and demonstrate basic handling techniques like those the other riders have been displaying."

"Yes, sir!" Dominic felt a strange sense of anticipation—fear, to be sure, mostly that he might make a mistake and wash out. But this fear was different than most, an excited sort of fear that got his adrenaline up. Somehow he felt equal to the challenge.

As he moved to the assigned vehicle, the young man Yates asked him, "Which Triumph did you ride?" It was obvious from his trim, muscular build that Yates was an experienced athlete.

"The 350 Sidevalve—Coventry's best," Dominic said with as much modesty as he could muster. This motorcycle had been widely recognized as one of the best in the world, and Dominic was happy to chat about it as Yates showed him the basic shifting, clutch, and other controls of the Norton.

"The Norton has a great deal of power but is heavier than the Triumph. You'll notice it most in the boggy soil where it's likely to feel a bit clumsy. It's very easy to get it stuck, particularly if you feel yourself slipping and apply too much power trying to get out. The greater chance is that you'll simply dig in and sink down to the oil pan." Yates searched Dominic's face for understanding and saw that he was paying attention. "Remember that they're judging you on speed only secondarily. The main task of a despatch rider is to get the message through, and sometimes the hotshots make a mess of it. So just be steady and you'll do fine."

"Thank you." Somehow this fellow's kindness actually increased his sense of anxiety. If this was the way all despatch riders acted, then he felt he'd really like to be part of it.

Mounting the motorcycle, Dominic waited for the signal, then kick-started the engine. For a moment he panicked, thinking that he'd flooded the blasted thing by giving it too much gas, but with a puff of bluish smoke the motor sputtered to life, and he had it running smoothly in just a few moments. He cast a glance to the left and right to see the other two riders going through the course with him. He was relieved that Freddie wasn't one of them, since he really didn't want to be in competition with his friend.

The starting flag waved, and the three were off with a roar. At first it was a piece of cake as they drove down a hard-packed road, the peat of the moors well compacted by several thousand previous runs. Dominic thrilled at the power of the Norton and momentarily regretted his earlier defense of the Triumph, but then they hit the first turn and he struggled to maintain control as the sheer mass of the monster did its best to fight him through the turn and he actually felt the wheels slipping under him. He quickly stabilized the turn and thought, *This is going to be harder than I imagined.* He redoubled his concentration as they left all semblance of a trail and started working their way into the sandy mound of the leading edge of the moor.

The bike started to bog down immediately as it hit the soft mud. It was then that Dominic realized that all his riding on the estate, in far different conditions than these, was going to provide him little help.

Take it easy! he told himself. But as he backed off on the throttle, he seemed to bog down even further and came danger-ously close to stalling. He noticed the other riders speed up. Suddenly the meaning of what Yates had told him became clear. He hadn't been telling him to go slow in the mud but rather to be gentle only if he got stuck. He needed to stay ahead of this. By this point he'd managed to make it to the crest of a molehill, and the richly colored rolling hills came into view. Even in the midst of his problems, he couldn't help but appreciate the beauty of the scene.

Advancing the throttle very slowly, he felt the wheels bite into the muck but not sink, so he gave it a bit more and then a bit more. To his great relief, the motorcycle responded well to this, and in short order he was flying down the path with much greater control.

His two competitors had developed a commanding lead while he'd been busy figuring out how to maneuver in his new environment. He advanced the throttle until he felt like he was on the absolute edge of his ability to control the motorcycle, but even this didn't seem to shorten the distance. He was tempted to throw caution to the wind and go full throttle, but at that moment he hit a particularly wet spot and nearly lost control of the vehicle, so he slowed down again. It was frustrating to be stuck in such a position. Unfortunately, he didn't have long before the next turn, where they'd pull onto a different kind of surface, and he was worried that he might never catch up.

This area was marshy except for a small ridgeline that had some treacherous rocks on it. Dominic realized there might be a chance to get a somewhat harder surface if he moved in closer to the ridge.

He eased the motorcycle out of the usual track and onto the narrow shoulder, where the peat yielded to rockier ground. The difference in the behavior of the bike was immediate, and he almost snapped his neck as the powerful Norton surged ahead on the better surface.

Although he was being bounced around a great deal more, he knew that he could handle this. In some ways it reminded him of riding in the Arizona desert after a rainstorm had compacted the sand into something of a cement. He leaned forward as low on the tank as possible to reduce wind drag and to give him greater control at the faster speed. Occasionally he'd slip as he hit a spot of mud, but he just laughed as he licked away the mud that was thrown up onto his upper lip.

Fortunately the other riders thought it prudent to follow the more well-traveled course, and so he was able to quickly shorten the distance between them, pulling ahead for just a few moments before they reached the flags that indicated their final turn for the last leg of their course.

The moment he hit the dusty surface, he was pelted with clods of congealed mud, and for a moment he thought he'd lose his balance as he inevitably flinched. The bike started to slide out from under him, but acting on sheer instinct, Dominic corrected the slide and used his leg to regain his balance.

Successfully making the turn, he found himself perhaps ten yards behind the others as they got into the scrub brush of the moors. At first it was disconcerting to hit the vegetation straight on, which jolted him quite roughly at the speed he was traveling, but once he adjusted, he decided he liked it much more than straddling the gap between the mud and the edge of the hills. Gaining confidence, he advanced the throttle again and, deciding he'd had enough of the others' dust cloud, pushed it all the way. As he advanced slowly on his competitors, he felt like he was being battered about like a rag doll shaken by a dog, but he held tight and maintained his speed. After perhaps three minutes, he pulled even with the second, and then the first rider. This fellow attempted to block him, but Dominic had had more than enough experience with that sort of thing and simply pulled back and maneuvered to his other side, taking the inside edge of the turn that brought them back on a heading toward the starting point. It had been a slick little trick, and he was now in the lead.

The only problem was that they were once again on soft ground, and any unexpected cuts in the marshy soil posed the potential for launching a rider from his motorcycle. At one point he hit a small hill that was steep enough that on the following edge he was actually airborne—a feeling he found exhilarating.

It was also at that point that he sensed a dark shape coming up at the extreme edge of his peripheral vision. With a quick glance in that direction, he saw that the fellow from whom he'd stolen the lead was making an attempt to blast past him. Gunning the bike for a moment, Dominic managed to match his speed but at the cost of control. At this point they were going so fast that any bump or rise lifted the front wheel off the ground, which meant he had little control when it landed.

He decided to give up the glory of first place and backed off on his accelerator till he had the ideal combination of control and speed once again. The other rider surged out ahead of him, quickly increasing the distance between them.

Even though he felt he'd made the right decision, it still galled him to come in second. He'd done that so many times in his life . . . He'd hoped just this once to get the prize—even though there wasn't really a prize. As his anger flared, he felt his speed creeping up again.

When he saw the third rider start to pull even with him, he had this unaccountable fear that if he came in third, he really would wash out, so he advanced the throttle yet again and felt the pickup in speed. It was okay, but the ground here was frightfully uneven, and the bike was so heavy that the springs couldn't absorb all the shock, which meant that his control was greatly diminished.

He reluctantly yielded speed again. Surprisingly, he noticed the other fellow back off. Turning to look at him, Dominic saw the guy smile and nod in an implied understanding that Dominic's was the best decision. Somehow Dominic knew that they would come in as a tie, and he felt buoyed by that.

As they drew within fifty yards of the ending point, the first rider, who was just about to cross over the line, hit what must have been a massive hole. The effect was that both the rider and his motorcycle flipped up into the air, where the rider somersaulted perhaps two or three times before slamming into the ground. The bike flipped over twice and then crashed into a group of onlookers, knocking some of them over.

It had been lucky that there was as much distance between the lead rider and the other two, because it gave Dominic time to pull back on his speed considerably and to give wide berth to the hole that had tripped up the first rider. Going a fraction of their previous speed, Dominic and the third rider crossed the line together and then quickly pulled up and dismounted to see what had happened to the other man in their group.

As he and the third man started toward the ejected rider, an officer called out, "Hold tight!" In spite of an overwhelming urge to continue, Dominic stopped short and snapped to attention. The other fellow formed up beside him as they waited for the Signals officer to come up.

"There's nothing you two can do. He was a blasted idiot to drive at that speed on this terrain and got what he deserved."

"But how is he? Is he badly injured?" Dominic asked tentatively.

"Injured? You've got to be joking!" When the officer seemed to figure out that he wasn't joking, he said, "He's dead. The fool broke his neck. The only place left for him is the mortuary." Dominic could hear the siren of an ambulance approaching in the distance.

Dominic felt sick to his stomach and wondered if he'd retch. The thought that he'd been near someone who died was entirely new in his experience. Even though he didn't know the fellow at all, he somehow felt that they had been kin—future despatch riders. Now he was dead. *And you'd have hit the same hole if you'd been racing him!* Dominic thought.

"So what does this mean, if I may ask, sir?" the other young rider asked.

"What? Oh, about you two? You both did fine. That was a nice piece of driving, Carlyle. You brought yourself to greater control, which allowed you to increase speed safely. Then you had the common sense not to push it too hard here in the rough. Out in the field, such thinking can make the difference between life and death, you know."

"So we're in the DR group?"

It was clear that this particular officer was not as shaken by events as his two young charges, but even he finally relented and said in an exasperated voice, "For glory's sake, yes, you're in. That is, if you can pass the written exam, show that you know how to repair a tire in the middle of nowhere, fix a leaking crankcase well enough to make it back to base, and read a map in strange territory with enough competence to find your way home—if you can do those minor sorts of things, then you're in."

Dominic couldn't help but smile. "Well, if that's all it takes, sir, then all that's left at the present is for you to tell us where to order our new uniforms."

"Very clever, Mr. Carlyle. Now, if you'll leave the entertainment to the division's brass band, you can take your leave and report at headquarters to 0600 tomorrow morning. In the meantime, I suggest you both get something to eat along with some sleep. You're in for a rather grueling six weeks!"

"Thank you, sir!" And with that Dominic and his new friend started the long walk over to the next group of prospective riders to share whatever they'd learned about the course.

"By the way, my name's Carlyle—Dominic Carlyle."

"James Mitchell. From Newcastle. And you're from?"

"London, I suppose."

"You suppose? Do you mean you don't know?"

Dominic laughed. "It's all rather complicated. I could as easily say I'm from Arizona in the United States, our place out in the English countryside, or New York City." He paused for a moment and shook his head. "Yes, that's it. I'm from New York City. Dominic Carlyle from New York."

Mitchell laughed. "You really are daft enough to be a Yank. Well, at any rate, you did some marvelous driving for a New Yorker."

Dominic returned the laugh. Then the conversation went into a lull.

"Kind of hard to know what to feel, isn't it?" Dominic asked.

"You mean should we be excited or somber because of that other rider's death?'

"Exactly."

"I don't know how it's possible, but I feel both," Mitchell said as they walked on quietly. "I guess, more excited. I don't know why I want this so badly." After a pause, he continued. "That's not entirely true. What I really want is to one day join up with a stunt rider group, and this would be the best possible recommendation I could get. I mean, we need to do something after the war." James's face flushed.

"Don't be embarrassed," Dominic said. "I hope to go into theater, so we're both sort of in the entertainment field."

"I hadn't thought of it like that . . ."

Their chat was interrupted by the anxious voice of Freddie. "What on earth happened out there?"

Dominic smiled at Freddie. "Nothing you can't handle, Freddie. Not if you keep your wits about you."

For the second time in his life, Dominic felt as if he'd found a place where he fit in, and it was wonderful.

Chapter Twenty

AM I DREAMING?

Naval Hospital at Folkestone—May 1942

As Michael drifted in that hazy state between dreams and waking, he suddenly had an image of being strangled, and his body involuntarily jerked as he imagined that he felt his neck and throat being pulled and constricted. The jerk caused an excruciating pain in his neck, which convinced him instantly that it wasn't a dream.

"Help!" he tried to gurgle as his eyes flew open. "Someone help me!" But the pressure on his chin increased with each word he tried to say.

"It's all right, lieutenant! Lie still or you'll hurt yourself." At the touch of a soft hand on his cheek, he instinctively relaxed and turned his eyes upward, realizing that he was in bed.

Looking back on it later, he realized just how foolish the next thing he said must have sounded, and his face colored just to think of it. In that wild moment of frantic struggling, he'd opened his eyes to look on perhaps the most beautiful young woman he'd ever seen. She had short blonde hair, soft blue eyes, and a smile that could have melted a polar ice cap. She was wearing a white tunic, and, with the afternoon sun behind her, his eyes had trouble focusing on her because of the intensity of the light. Altogether, the scene created an otherworldly sort of feeling that led to his saying, "Have I died—are you an angel?" His face reddened again.

The girl had laughed. "It's not as if I haven't heard that before, you know."

Even in his confused state, he was embarrassed. "I—I mean, where am I?" Then, with a genuine sense of urgency, he asked, "And why is my neck so constricted?"

"Unfortunately, I've heard that question before, as well," she said softly while taking his hand. She stroked it for just a moment, which had the most miraculous calming effect. "You're in a naval hospital, and your neck is in traction to stretch the vertebrae that were injured in your recent action. It's nothing to worry about, although I know it's uncomfortable."

On hearing this, Michael used his eyes to glance from side to side, where at the extreme range of his peripheral vision he could see the triangular shape of white fabric coming together on each side of his face, perhaps four inches out. There was a bandage strapped under his chin exerting pressure on his neck and back. In his mind he could picture the assembly of pulleys attached to a set of weights at the back of his bed so gravity could do the work of gently stretching his bones—except that it didn't feel so gentle.

"Is my neck—is it broken or something?" The scenes of his encounter with the German soldier replayed in his mind, and he knew that the chance of a serious injury had been much greater than he'd acknowledged at the time. He also remembered reporting to Lieutenant Prescott after getting everyone on board, but that's where the memories ended. He had no concept of how he'd wound up here.

Bringing him back to the present moment, the nurse replied, "I think it would be better if the doctor talked with you about that." It was hard to stop the feeling of panic he had in his stomach until he saw the nurse give him a wink before stepping aside for the doctor.

"How long have I been here?" Michael blurted out. "How long have I been unconscious?" It deeply disturbed Michael to think that an indefinite period of time had passed without his having had any awareness of it all. He'd never considered the possibility that the world could go on completely independent of him, and it left him shaken.

"Your neck isn't broken, although there was some damage to the vertebrae," the doctor replied.

"Will I be paralyzed or . . ." Michael's voice trailed off at the enormity of the question.

It was at that point that the doctor poked Michael's left toe with what felt like the sharp edge of a scalpel, although the doctor claimed it was simply the back side of a pair of scissors. In the second most embarrassing moment of the day, Michael shouted out in pain, wincing at the unexpected prick.

"Seems as if that foot isn't paralyzed. Let's try the other one."

"No!" Michael shouted, but he wasn't in control, and the same thing happened to his right toe. He obliged everyone with a second, "Ouch! Stop that!"

"If you think that's bad, then you're really going to be angry with me for what comes next—but I promise it won't sting," the doctor said cheerfully. And then in the greatest indignity of all, he ran the metal up the center of Michael's foot, which tickled him and caused him to giggle—a sound that no naval officer would willingly choose in any circumstance, but more particularly in the presence of such a beautiful girl. But the doctor was relentless, going up and down each foot, up his legs, and ultimately down his arms.

"Are you quite finished?" Michael said with as much dignity as he could muster.

"I'd think you'd be happy with the outcome," the doctor replied. "Your reactions mean that you aren't paralyzed—nor does it appear that your nerves are impaired in any fashion. We didn't think there was permanent damage, but we couldn't be sure until you woke up. Your neck was quite swollen when you arrived, and it was urgent that we take the pressure off the nerves before something bad did happen."

To complete the day's embarrassment, Michael felt tears of relief trickle down his cheek. They were warm tears that belied the anxiety he felt as all of this had unfolded. He reached up to brush them away, but the nurse intercepted his hand and then used a soft towel to dab his cheeks.

"I'm very glad for you, Lieutenant Carlyle. Now you should relax, since too much movement can undo all the good things we've accomplished so far."

Michael caught movement out of the corner of his eye and rotated his eyes as much as possible to see the doctor filling a syringe. They were going to give him morphine or something to make him sleep. Although he didn't like getting a shot, he didn't resist, and in just a matter of moments, he felt his eyes start to burn and grow heavy. And then he started dreaming again.

* * *

"Jules? What happened to Jules!" Michael jerked as he awoke, which caused the traction assembly to hold his head firmly in place while his body moved. Stabbing pain shot down the center of his neck. In spite of the anxiety aroused by the question, he forced himself to relax and lie still.

"Welcome back again, lieutenant. How are you feeling?"

Michael smiled ruefully. "I'd probably be all right if I could learn to wake up slowly instead of with a start."

"You shouldn't be too hard on yourself. It's difficult to do when you have drugs in your system. Besides, we have you strapped in well enough that you can't really injure yourself—just cause some temporary pain, perhaps."

Once again his nurse's voice calmed him.

"Do you think I might have some pillows under my knees? Lying flat like this is making my lower back hurt."

"Of course!" she said brightly. In a matter of moments his legs were propped up, which felt wonderful to his aching back.

He'd never felt so helpless. Having his head immobilized took almost all control away. He didn't even dare think about what had been required to keep his body functioning, although he was embarrassed to think about who had been responsible for keeping him clean. There was nothing he could do about it, so he simply had to accept it.

"But about Jules? I mean Lieutenant Ellington. Do you know anything about my friend?"

"I know that he's incorrigible," the nurse replied.

Michael surprised himself by laughing. "So he's okay? He's alive?"

"Oh, he's very much alive. I'm doing my best not to hold it against you." Michael loved her smile. "He's quite a flirt, you know."

"We never had occasion to talk about it, but I can imagine that he is." Michael smiled happily as he realized the effort that had put him in this place had been worth it.

Just at that moment they heard from the man himself when in a booming voice he said, "Are you trying to make time with my girl, Carlyle? Do I need to throttle you?"

In spite of himself, Michael laughed again, which of course caused him to grimace in pain. Apparently Jules had seen this, because he continued with, "Good! I hope it hurts. Nothing like a guilty conscience to make you do the right thing."

"I am not your girl, lieutenant. Apparently you suffered some brain damage along with your wound. Now if you'll excuse me, I have some needy patients to look after."

Michael felt an enormous sense of relief to hear her brush Jules off. For just a moment he entertained the thought that perhaps he had indeed been trying to steal Jules's "girl." It was certainly something to think about.

"Wait!" Michael called out. "I don't even know your name."

"See!" Jules rejoined instantly. "You *are* trying to gain her affection."

Michael was embarrassed by this and foolishly tried to explain. "No, it's just that I don't know what to call her—I mean you . . ."

"It's all right, Lieutenant Carlyle. Not everyone is as pushy as your friend here. My name is Nurse Chandler."

"Thank you, Nurse Chandler. Thank you for being so kind to me." The sincerity in Michael's voice made her blush, and she brushed his cheek before moving off again.

"And it's Michael," he said quietly to himself. But she didn't hear. He closed his eyes, lost in the moment.

"Oh, that was smooth," Jules said. "All that sincerity stuff really gets to them. I keep telling myself I should try it sometime."

Michael opened one eye. "Unfortunately, you have to *be* sincere for it to work."

"Ah, that would be a problem, then."

Michael tried to turn to look at Jules, but he couldn't, so he used his hand to indicate that he should move into range. Jules came closer, and Michael could see that his left arm had been immobilized with a sling.

"So you didn't bleed to death after all? That's what everybody on the *960* seemed to be predicting before I lost consciousness."

"So it seems. I'm in the same boat you are—forgive the pun—but I don't remember anything after giving you a direct order to leave me where I was and get yourself back to the boat."

"Yes, well, you seem to have fainted after I picked you up and put you over my shoulder. I asked you what I should do, but when you failed to answer, I assumed you'd surrendered command to me, so I used my best judgment and just kept dragging your lifeless carcass until we reached the rendezvous point."

"I should put you up before a court martial! You disobeyed a direct order!"

Michael smiled. In a rare moment of triumph he actually had a witty reply. "Well, actually, it would be highly embarrassing if you did that, Jules. You see, in a trial I'd have to explain how you went a bit mad out there, ranting and raving how you were indispensable to the war effort. You said that I better rescue you no matter what the cost because you are so important. Of course I'd have to tell the court how you were making so much noise that I finally had to knock your sorry brain unconscious so that we wouldn't be discovered and the entire mission scrubbed."

"I did no such thing, and you know it! How dare you. This is insubordination!"

"Yes, well, who are they going to believe—a blood-soaked lieutenant who came in unconscious, or the selfless hero who saved him?"

"Why you . . ." Jules started, then gave in to a laugh. "You really are a blaggard, aren't you, as to this hero stuff."

"Just kidding. I was way too frightened to be a hero. The real reason I did what I did is that I just couldn't stand the chance that the whole thing would be a failure. The codes were too important. And I didn't want to have to face your parents and tell them how you'd died while in a patriotic frenzy and such. Women would have swooned, and you'd have been enshrined on the family wall as one of those tragic figures that everyone here in Britain is so proud of. I'm afraid I'd have gagged, and think of what a scandal that would be. So in the end it was easier to just haul your sorry skin down to the beach."

Michael was startled when Jules came back at him in a very serious tone, rather than responding to his banter. "Four trips you made. Me and two dead Germans, plus a trip back to retrieve my weapon, as I understand it."

"Well—"

"No, you can say what you like, but it was clearly way beyond your duty, particularly in view of your neck and all. At any rate, I'm very grateful."

Michael was surprised to feel his face burn. "I guess the real truth is," he said with something of a choking sound, "I didn't want to be out there alone. And I didn't want to lose another friend to the Germans." The image of Jamie Wilcox came to his mind, and he felt the sorrow and anger rise simultaneously in his throat.

Jules was quiet for a moment. "Well, at any rate, what you did really was heroic. I tried to put you in for a medal or something, but I found out I was too late."

"Too late? What do you mean, too late?"

"Lieutenant Prescott beat me to it. Apparently he's already written up the recommendation and submitted it. Now the bureaucrats will have to fight over it and decide just how important it was. But at least it's on the record."

"But I don't want a medal. I'm not a hero, and I certainly don't want any attention drawn to this mission."

"It's not up to you," Jules interrupted. "Besides, you're going to need every possible advantage if you really are serious about getting into a tussle with me over Nurse Chandler!"

At the mention of her name, Michael brightened, which caused Jules to swell up again. "So you *do* have designs on her. What a scoundrel!"

It was at times like this that Michael desperately wished he could offer a quick retort. But he couldn't, so he simply suffered in silence.

* * *

Philip's grasp on Michael's hand tightened as they spoke with the doctor. His father was a reassuring presence to Michael. His parents had stayed away nearly the whole first week of his hospital stay, even though he knew it had been agonizing for them, but he was grateful that they allowed normal protocol to be followed. Somehow whenever a viscount showed up, everybody started acting funny, with some becoming overly obsequious as they tried to win his favor while others turned resentful. By now enough time had elapsed that Michael was simply "Lieutenant Carlyle" and would be judged for himself.

Still he'd missed his family, particularly when his neck tingled or when he became distressed at not being able to turn his body in the bed. At times like that nearly everyone wanted their mother, and he was very pleased to have her there.

At this point the doctor had barely introduced himself to Michael's parents and was busy studying his chart. The silence finally got to Michael, and he said, "So if you're right that there's no permanent damage, why am I still in this device?"

The doctor took another moment to finish his reading and then looked up. "It honestly isn't to torture you, although I'm sure that's how it seems. The fact is that while you've had no disabling neurological damage, you've still suffered a major trauma. It's vital that we give your neck time to heal so that you can resume as close to a normal life as possible."

Michael was glad that his mother's gasp was loud enough to mask his own. "What do you mean, 'as normal as possible'?" she asked.

The doctor was surprised by her reaction. Raising an eyebrow, he said, "Poor choice of words. Don't worry, your son will be fine. It's just that with injuries of this type, there may be recurring pain and an increased sensitivity to stress. It's something he'll have to watch and protect against."

"How do I do that?" Michael asked, wanting to be spoken to directly.

"First, we'll keep you in traction for at least another twenty-four hours. Then we'll ease it off and see how you do. Chances are that you'll feel a great sense of relief at first, followed by what seems to be a terrible relapse. But that's to be expected as your nerves resettle themselves inside the neck in the absence of the external pressure. That will go away after another day. Then if all is well, I'd like you to spend at least two weeks on a medical leave of absence so you can get used to supporting your neck in everyday situations. You can either go to a rehabilitation hospital or to your home. Of course, you will need some attention so it might be easier at the hospital."

"We're well equipped to care for him at home," Philip said quietly. "And if we need any help, we'll acquire whatever resources are necessary."

When the doctor realized who he was talking to, he quickly said, "Of course. That will obviously be the easiest course."

"So when can I return to duty?"

"Well, with the collar it shouldn't be more than three or four weeks."

"Collar?"

"Yes, I thought I'd told you already. We'll give you a leather neck brace that you can put on when you feel your neck getting tired or stressed. It will hold it in position and help support your head, which should provide relief when you need it."

"What will other people think?" Michael could only imagine the effect on the crew of seeing one of their officers wearing a neck brace.

"What they'll think," the doctor said, "is exactly what they'd think if you'd injured your arm and wore it in a sling. They'd think that you received a war injury that needs remediation. And if they want to make something of it, you can refer them to me!"

Michael laughed. "No need to get worked up, sir. It's just that the Navy isn't always tolerant."

"The Navy doesn't have to put all the mangled bodies back together that we do, so they'd better not give you any trouble."

"Thank you, sir. I'm very glad you've been able to put me back together."

"And we're grateful too, doctor," Philip said.

Chapter Twenty-One

REST, REHABILITATION, AND ROMANCE

Naval Hospital at Folkestone—June 1942

"It's definitely time for you to be discharged."

"What do you mean?" Michael asked defensively.

"Perfectly normal, really. As soon as men start to get better, they get a bit grumpy and sullen like they can't possibly wait to get out of here. For a day or two they're miserable, and everybody can't wait to see them go."

Michael didn't like the thought that he'd been grumpy, but as he thought back on the past few days, he realized it was probably true. "Then what happens?"

Nurse Chandler smiled. "Then when the day arrives, they get all melancholy and sentimental and want to make up for their bad behavior with kind words and expressions of gratitude."

Michael's face flushed. He had just about been ready to tell her how much he'd appreciated everything she'd done.

Marissa Chandler laughed. "Don't worry. We like it. In fact it's the best part. Collecting bedpans and soiled sheets isn't the most glamorous work in the world. Seeing someone get better makes it all worthwhile. So go ahead and say what you were planning."

"It's going to sound so trite now."

"Oh, for heaven's sake, are you really that easily intimidated, lieutenant? Your obnoxious friend told me I could expect this from you."

Michael sighed. Jules had obviously already made his play, and apparently with some success.

She sat down on his bed. "I'm sorry. Now I've embarrassed you. The truth is that you've been a model patient and a favorite of everyone on the floor."

He looked up with sad eyes, which surprised her.

"What is it then?" she asked. "This really is a happy day, you know. You get to go home."

"It's just . . ." Michael said, considering carefully if he wanted to finish the sentence, "that I'll miss you."

"Of course you will!" She tried to say it cavalierly. This sort of emotional dependence was quite natural on the part of a recovering sailor. Emotional trauma always accompanied the physical injuries that brought them to the hospital in the first place.

Michael fell into silence. He sensed his hopes wouldn't be realized, and he didn't have the emotional reserve to banter his way out of the conversation. He busied himself with the task of sitting up, which was still something of a challenge with his neck immobilized by his leather neck brace. The simple task of buttoning a shirt when you couldn't look down was surprisingly difficult. In a previous burst of energy he had pulled on his pants. He turned his attention to his socks and shoes. They were the hardest because it was so difficult to bend while wearing the contraption.

For her part, Nurse Chandler scurried about gathering his things until she saw that he was fully clothed and ready. She didn't offer to help with the shoes.

"Well, Lieutenant Carlyle, we'd better get you into a wheelchair. Your parents should be downstairs any minute, and we don't want to make them wait."

He obediently swung his legs to the side of the bed and then awkwardly stepped off onto his feet. After weeks in hospital, he was a bit unsteady, even though he'd been going for walks the past few days to get ready for discharge. He settled into the chair heavily and then accepted the bundle of his belongings, which he folded into his lap.

"Lieutenant, are you really going to do all this without saying good-bye?"

He looked up at her. "My name is Michael. Just once I'd like to hear you call me Michael. It's all I've really wanted since I've been here."

Now it was his turn to be surprised as suddenly her face clouded up. Looking at her made him crazy. Never in his life had he felt such a physical attraction. More than anything in the world he wanted to rest his head against her body and feel the touch of her hand on his face again. He wanted to smell the light perfume she wore and take her into his arms and feel her embrace. He wanted to tell her how much he loved talking with her, and how the sound of her voice was the most welcome sound in the world to him, always so pleasant and upbeat and soothing.

But in the same moment that he wanted to say these things, he also felt foolish. There was no question but that every man who had been helped by her must feel the same. How could they not? And what did she feel for them? *Pity? Probably. Sympathy? Certainly. Affection? How could she? She can't love them all, so she doesn't love any of them. What right do I have to think I'm any different?*

"All right, then," she said softly. "Are you going to say good-bye to me, Michael?"

At the sound of her voice saying his name, he felt as if a great dam that had been restraining his emotions suddenly gave way, and he was powerless to stop himself from gushing what had been growing inside him over the last days and weeks. "It's just that I don't want to say good-bye to you. I don't want to leave—or at least I don't want to leave you. I want to get to know you better." Looking up for the briefest of moments, he asked, "Can't you see how I feel?" He then dropped his eyes, embarrassed and frightened for what would come next.

"Michael," she said very softly. "Are you asking me out on a date?"

Okay, that's a surprise! He hadn't entirely thought of it that way, but that's exactly what he wanted to do.

"Because if you are, I'm not sure it's such a good idea. Aside from this place, we have nothing in common."

"How can we know that for certain if we never make an attempt to discuss it?" He didn't dare look up at her for fear that he might mist up.

She was quiet for a long time.

"It's against policy . . ."

Now he did look up. "It isn't like it has to be a formal date or anything. We could simply meet sometime to have dinner together or something. You could check on my progress." As he thought about that tack, he liked it. "Certainly no one can object to a nurse checking up on a patient, and we all have to eat, don't we?" Whether he was convincing her or not, he was certainly talking himself into the idea.

She hesitated for a moment, but then her basic nature seemed to assert itself. "All right, as long as it's a simple thing in a pub or somewhere. I don't want to go to a fancy restaurant. And you need to agree in advance not to attach any real significance to it. We'll just chatter for a bit and then be done with it. Can you agree to those terms?"

Michael took two or three big gasps of air, definitely risking hyperventilation. He looked up tentatively to see if she was serious. But the serious look on his face amused her, and she burst out laughing. It was a beautiful sound, a joyous sound, and quickly he found himself laughing with her.

"Oh, for heaven's sake, you're so serious, Lieutenant Carlyle." She turned to the night table and scrawled something on a piece of paper. Handing it to him, she said, "There, you have my phone number. When you're far enough along in your recovery to be really bored, you can give me a call."

"Like tomorrow?"

She shook her head firmly. "Don't you become incorrigible like Lieutenant Ellington."

Michael quieted down immediately. Just hearing her talk of Jules made him uneasy. "No, I wouldn't want to become like that." They were silent for a few moments. He had no experience at this sort of thing and didn't know what to say exactly. Finally his face lit up. "If we're actually going out for a non-date, I should at least know your first name, shouldn't I?"

Her face softened. "Asking me to break yet another rule." She looked down at him for a moment, and Michael saw her eyes soften. "Oh, all right then, it's Marissa."

"Marissa!" Michael said it in an awed tone. "Of course it would be. It fits you perfectly."

Marissa shook her head. "Oh, lieutenant, you are a dear one, aren't you?"

* * *

"We can move the ladies out of your room, if you like," his mother said tentatively. "I know Dominic's been quite put out to have so many 'strangers,' as he calls them, living at the manor, even though he knows most of them from church. We want your recovery to go as smoothly as possible, so please tell us what you want and we'll do it."

Michael looked out the window at the incredible green countryside. Having spent his early years in the high mountain desert of Utah, he was always astonished at how green the English countryside was, even when it wasn't summer.

"I'll be fine wherever you want to put me." He looked up and smiled at his mother to reassure her. "Just think of me as another one of your little old ladies who's in need of tending, and I'm sure you'll know what to do. Besides, Grace has told me over and over how she really runs the place—particularly when you're in the city."

Claire laughed and relaxed. "While some of the nurses might take exception, the truth is that she has been remarkable. For such a young person, she digs right in and helps the patients with everything from reading magazines to them to helping them to the water closet. Nothing is too trivial or unimportant for her to tend to. I honestly don't know how we'd get along without her."

"Good for Grace," Michael said quietly. "The war has made all of us grow up a bit faster, hasn't it?" Then he lapsed into silence.

Claire shuffled a bit uncomfortably for a moment before saying, as brightly as possible, "We've been thinking of converting your father's study into a temporary bedroom. It's right next to a bathroom, so it will be convenient for you, and I thought it might be easier if you didn't have to come down the stairs when it's time to eat."

Michael recognized her attempt to cheer him up and affectionately reached up and took his mother's hand. "That would be great, Mom," he said reassuringly.

As his father walked in the room, Michael added, "I think I'll actually love being in the study since I'll have lots of books to read—as long as my arms hold out."

"Your arms?" Philip asked.

Michael laughed. "Yes, sir. You see, with my brace on I can't possibly bend my head forward to read, so I'll have to hold the books straight out in front of me." He demonstrated awkwardly. "Seems like my arms will give out eventually."

* * *

It was on his third day home that Michael broached the subject. "I was wondering if I might go into town to visit a friend of mine."

"Of course, dear, if you think you're up to it," Claire said absentmindedly. "One of your friends from the Navy?"

"Someone I met at the hospital, actually," he said. "I was hoping you could lend me your car and driver since I'm not sure I'm up to driving yet, and I'll need to pick her up and get there myself."

That was enough to get Philip to lower his newspaper, and his mother to put down the spoon she'd been using to stir the ladies' soup.

"Is it permissible for us to ask about this 'her' person?" Claire asked.

Michael tried to sound nonchalant. "She's just one of the nurses that cared for me. I told her I'd like to get together and chat with her over a light meal."

"And she was all right with that?" Clair asked indignantly. "It's not very professional, you know."

"She was a bit uncomfortable," Michael replied defensively. "But I assured her it was just two friends getting together— nothing more than that—and then she was fine with it."

"It's all right, dear. I was just asking."

"It wouldn't be that lovely young woman who brought you out in the wheelchair, would it?" Philip intervened.

Michael's blush answered the question. Rather than torture or tease him, Philip picked his paper back up. "Just give Charles the address, and he'll be glad to take you anytime. I have to go into town tomorrow, but I can drive the Aston Martin if needed." Then he looked up and smiled behind the paper where Michael couldn't see, but Claire could. "Of course, only if it's all right with your mother."

"Oh, it's all right with me. Frankly I could use the break. Besides, if she turns out to be a very good friend, perhaps we'll put her to work with some of our ladies. We could always use another nurse on hand."

"Mother!" Michael said indignantly.

"Oh, for heaven's sake, Michael, I'm teasing. You're always so serious. You should learn to relax."

Michael sighed. "Funny, but that's exactly what she says."

* * *

"Oh, dear," Marissa said.

"What is it?" Michael said in alarm.

"It's just that I've never been picked up in a Rolls-Royce. I'm afraid this will cause quite a stir with my neighbors, and some of them work at the hospital."

Darn! I knew I should have brought a simpler car. Michael had struggled with every detail of the evening. On the one hand he wanted to impress her, and yet he'd developed a nagging feeling from the tone of her chatter with others at the hospital that she wasn't someone impressed by wealth and status.

"Well, I would have brought my Ford, but I thought that was way too pretentious, so I settled for this old thing. It's actually the oldest car we own."

She laughed, which reduced his anxiety a bit. Just to have her sitting next to him was intoxicating, and he felt as if he might kiss her then and there when her perfume wafted over him. So pleasant was the feeling that he didn't notice the rather uncomfortable silence that seemed to settle over Marissa.

"So how is your recovery coming? This is supposed to be a professional visit, you know," she said with mock seriousness.

Michael smiled. "I'm feeling a lot better right now. My nurse out at the manor is about eighty years old, and I usually have to help her in and out of a chair rather than the other way around. So this is a nice break."

She laughed. "From the looks of it, you could afford to hire anyone you wanted. Why do you have her?"

Michael darkened a bit. "It's my mother's doing. She heard that this woman, who is really only in her fifties or something, was out of work and so she took her in. My mother is always doing things like that."

Marissa was very quiet—so different from how she'd been in the hospital. There she'd chattered away, cheering people and teasing them. But ever since his arrival, she'd had an obtuse look on her face. Michael couldn't tell if she was frightened or put off.

"You're very quiet," he said solemnly. "Have I done something to upset you?" The moment he said it, he regretted it. He'd wanted so desperately to make a good impression, and drawing attention to his shortcomings hadn't been the way to do it.

"Of course not," she said. "It's wonderful to see you again. It's just that . . ."

"Just what?"

"It's just that I had no idea your family was so wealthy—a driver, nurses and servants, expensive cars. I can only imagine your house! Or is it a mansion?"

"We do have a manor house in the country, but Mother's turned it into a rehabilitation center for people injured in the war. And we do most of our living in a small town house here in London." He tried not to sound defensive, but she had knocked him off balance a bit.

"And what should I call you—the Duke of Carlyle or something?" she said with a distinct edge to her voice.

Michael laughed nervously. "I'm not a duke. I'm not anything, really. My father is a viscount, but he's not at all pretentious about it. He didn't even want to come back to England from America, but his mother sort of forced him into it."

"What did he do in America? I've never understood how you can be both English and American, even though I heard you talking about it with Lieutenant Ellington."

There's his name again! Michael thought almost angrily.

"It's something of a complicated story. Years ago my father had a falling out with my grandfather after my father accompanied a sick friend to his home in America. Father ended up staying there for about ten years and married my mother." He decided not to bring up his father's religious conversion at that point. "All three of us were born in America, and my father was quite happy living the life of a poor college professor. All the years that I was a boy, we lived in very ordinary circumstances, and that's how I think of myself today. All of this aristocracy stuff is still uncomfortable for me. Please don't be put off by it. I'm really much more like you than you might think. You do understand, don't you?"

She took a very long moment to respond. "It's just that people from your class don't really mix socially with people from . . ."

"From your class?"

"Precisely. It's fine that we liked each other in hospital because you needed me. But I don't really belong in a Rolls-Royce." Her face hardened. "Perhaps this wasn't such a good idea." She tried to sound cheerful, but he could tell that she was really quite distressed.

Here he was with one of the most beautiful women he'd ever seen—someone whose very voice lifted his spirits—and she was trying to brush him off. So he took a deep breath and then reached out with both his hands and took hers. "Marissa, I told you I was raised in America. There is no such thing as class over there, so it makes no difference whatsoever to me. We're taught that a person's place in the world is determined by the good they do, not by an inherited title or wealth. On that measure, you're definitely in the very highest class of all." He smiled, trying to reassure her.

The window that separated the driver from the passenger compartment growled to life. "Pardon me, sir, but we've arrived."

Michael looked up, startled. "Thank you, Charles." Turning to Marissa, he said, "*I'm* sure it was a good idea to see each other tonight. So can you try to relax and enjoy a nice dinner?"

As they stepped out of the car, Charles holding the door, Marissa gasped. "But this is Galbraith Tavern!"

"You told me you wanted something simple like a pub?"

She turned and looked at him in astonishment. "But not the most exclusive pub in London! Oh, Michael. I'm not sure I can do this."

He did his best to maintain his mental balance. "I promise it will be all right. They're very nice people in there, and they'll all be envious to see a young officer accompanied by such a stunning young lady." He smiled and tried to act cavalier. Yet she stood there, essentially frozen in place. "Really, it will be fine, Marissa. Please trust me."

He felt bad to see the anxiety in her eyes but decided to press ahead. He would gladly go somewhere else if it made her feel better, but the problem was he didn't have a lot of experience with pubs and didn't know where else to go.

"Michael," she said breathlessly, "it will be a miracle if I live through this night!"

"Then we'll pray for a miracle." Taking her arm, Michael led her through the doors of the most fashionable club in London.

Chapter Twenty-Two

ASSIGNMENT: NORTH AFRICA

With the British Eighth Army near El Alamein—August 1942

"I need a despatch rider—now!" said the brigadier general over Dominic's camp.

"Yes, sir!" said Captain Riggins, turning to Dominic. "You heard the general, Corporal Carlyle. Step forward and receive your orders."

Dominic suddenly felt sick to his stomach. It was hard to believe that with barely four months of training he was about to go into action. He was glad he'd practiced so much as a boy in the sand of Arizona since the boggy moors of Camp Catterick bore no resemblance whatsoever to his current surroundings. The North African desert was nothing but sand, and it would take a great deal of control to make his way in this hostile environment. An endless sea of white burning sand extended as far as the eye could see in all directions, with very little vegetation able to endure the mid-August temperatures in the low hundreds. *This place almost makes Arizona seem temperate,* he thought. Except that in Arizona there was color to the landscape, the muddy purple hues of the mountains contrasting with the cream-colored valley floors. Here it was nothing but white shimmering sand in the afternoon sun. On arrival the riders had been warned to always wear their colored goggles or risk being blinded by the sun and sand.

"Carlyle! Did you hear me?"

"Yes, sir!" Dominic lurched as he was startled from his thoughts, and he almost stumbled as he approached the brigadier general.

"What in the word *now* is difficult for you to understand, corporal?" the general said in a cold, steady voice.

"Sorry, sir!" was the best Dominic could muster.

The general didn't respond but simply continued to scratch furiously on a number of sheets of paper. *What's the need for a blasted rebuke if he isn't even ready when I show up?* Dominic felt the anger rise in his throat but kept his tongue.

"There!" The general snapped a sheaf of papers into a protective leather pouch, secured its strap, and then thrust it toward Dominic, who quickly slipped it into his over-the-shoulder satchel. "This has to reach Lieutenant Colonel Dougherty at his camp before 1600 or there's risk that a German reconnaissance group will get through our lines where they can measure our strength. Do you understand the urgency?"

"Yes, sir. I do."

Sensing Dominic's uncertainty, the general added, "You've been there, I assume? You've got less than two hours."

"No, sir."

The general shook his head. "Just how much experience do you have, corporal?"

Dominic dropped his gaze. "This is my first day, sir. I've never carried a dispatch—at least not in the war zone."

"Oh, for the love of—Riggins, I need another man. Someone with experience."

Captain Riggins stepped forward. "Sorry, sir, but everyone's out. Corporal Carlyle is all I've got."

"Well, is he reliable?"

Dominic hated being talked about in the third person, as if he wasn't there. He wanted to tell this general where he could get off, but of course that would be the very worst thing he could do—particularly on his first day in this theater of war.

"All my men are reliable," Riggins replied evenly. "Carlyle received excellent ratings and was noted for his proficiency in finding directions. I've personally drilled him on all the outposts we're responsible to cover, and I'm confident of his abilities." From the tone of Riggins's voice, Dominic suspected that Captain Riggins had tangled with this general before and that he didn't particularly like him.

"Of course you'd say that. Well, if he's all we've got, I guess he'll have to do." Turning to Dominic, the general added, "Men's lives are in your hands, so I hope you don't make a mess of it."

There were a lot of things Dominic would have liked to have said in reply, but instead he saluted smartly, perhaps with somewhat exaggerated form, and moved off toward his motorcycle.

As he was doing a quick check of his vehicle to make sure he had enough petrol, and scanning the engine block to see that there were no obvious oil leaks or other signs of trouble, he heard Captain Riggins come up behind him. "You are comfortable with how to do this, aren't you, Carlyle?"

"Yes, sir, I am." Dominic was now thoroughly irritated at having his competence questioned. He'd graduated at the top of his class, hadn't he? Back in England they'd treated him with great regard, particularly after he'd cut the best previous time on the map-reading exercise by more than twenty minutes—a record not likely to be broken for some time.

"Listen, Carlyle. You're not likely to encounter any Germans along the way, although there's always a possibility that a reconnaissance team may have slipped through our lines. If they see a despatch rider, they're going to try to snipe you so that they can get at the orders you're carrying. Neither of us knows what is in those orders, but chances are high that they would give material aid to the enemy and perhaps cost many British lives if discovered. So you have to be watchful the entire way. Do you understand?"

"Yes, sir." Dominic looked at Captain Riggins with something of exasperation.

"I'm sure you think you understand, but you've got to understand that it's different here in Africa. I know you did well back in England, but you weren't under enemy fire then. There's enough variety to the terrain there that you can mentally reconnoiter a scene. Here it all looks the same, so you have to follow your compass no matter what your mind tells you. And . . ." Riggins paused for effect. "If they should shoot you and you survive the attack, your first task is to destroy those papers. You do have your cigarette lighter handy?"

Instinctively Michael put his hand up to his breast pocket and felt the device through the material.

"Yes, sir."

"Good." Riggins smiled. "You'll do fine, Carlyle. And when you get back tonight, I'll introduce you properly to the other men to celebrate your arrival. Now good luck and be off with you."

"Thank you, sir." And with that, Dominic kicked the starter and roared off into the dazzling sand.

He had the sickening realization that he'd started off without pulling his goggles over his eyes—an obvious mistake that would certainly have been noticed by Captain Riggins and perhaps many others. He was so furious that he pulled his goggles down and gunned the motorcycle, streaking down the hard-packed surface of what passed as a road in those parts. It was a foolish thing to do when the distance to be covered would nearly consume his entire petrol supply at a normal rate of consumption. At full throttle, he was likely to run out before he reached the Dougherty camp.

* * *

"I should be there," Dominic said to himself as he glanced down at his watch and felt his stomach muscles tighten when he saw it was already 1530.

A wave of panic swept over him. Finding a small rise up ahead, he idled to the east side of it where there was a spot of shade, then he reached down and turned off the ignition. Before dismounting he shook the gas tank and was dismayed by the sound. *Besides—it really is a gas tank, not a stupid petrol tank like the British always want to call it!* When frightened or angry, Dominic often changed his nationality to put down whoever it was who had made him angry. Right now he wanted to be an American.

Sitting down in the sand, he took off his leather gloves and set them carefully at his side, then he reached up to his face to slip his goggles up on his forehead. He was startled to feel the skin on his face, which was rough and coarse from all the sand that had been blown into his face by his forward momentum. "This place stinks!" he shouted, heedless of any German patrols that might be nearby. At that thought he burst out laughing.

Dominic carefully retraced each leg in the journey, verifying that he'd followed each twist and turn precisely. "Blast you!" he said suddenly. Looking at the map he saw his mistake immediately. At signpost three he was supposed to bear left, but had gone right instead. With a funny weakness in his legs, he quickly calculated how far off course that had taken him, and he realized that while it was a major mistake, it was close enough to the end that he could still make it by 1600 if he went at near top speed. He quickly penciled in the shortest correcting course and started fumbling to get his things back together. When he touched his gloves, which had been sitting outside the shade, he let out a yelp of pain. They were so hot they burned his hands. He slid them under his thighs to absorb the excess heat over a broader surface, then pulled them on in spite of the pain it caused. He quickly mounted the motorcycle and kicked it into life. As he pulled back on the throttle, he felt his hands trembling because he realized just how serious this was and how difficult it would be for him to cover the required distance even in the best of circumstances. He simply didn't want to fail in this effort—not when he'd done so well back in England. *Please, God, please help me. I need to get this packet through!* He tore off through the sand.

* * *

"Ten more minutes—stay with me, darling!" Dominic said to his motorcycle. Riding in temperatures this high was murder on a machine, particularly since a light breeze was kicking up the ultrafine sand grains. As the carburetor sucked in the thin hot air, the filter had to absorb all the dust and sand to protect the piston from being ground into powder. Fortunately, the heat made the engine run more efficiently, which provided a vital edge needed for his fuel consumption.

"Nine minutes—just nine minutes to go."

At eight minutes estimated travel time, it was twelve minutes before 1600. *Four minutes to spare! That will be just good enough that I won't be ridiculed.*

He resisted the urge to advance the throttle even further. He was in a desperate game of conserving fuel while maximizing speed, and he had to make compromises on both sides if he was going to make it to his destination.

There it is! Off in the distance, perhaps four miles, he saw the British flag flying above a set of tents. *You've done it—you've blooming done it!* He'd never felt so relieved in his life. He realized just how frightened he'd been, out there all alone in the desert. But he'd proven himself, and he was now within sight of his destination.

It was at that moment that he was struck by the most unbearable pain in his right shoulder. The force of it twisted him on his seat, causing the motorcycle to wrench out from underneath him, and both rider and motorcycle went tumbling out of control into the scorching sand. It was soft enough that the motorcycle came to an abrupt stop, but Dominic rolled two or three times, crying out in pain with each twist as his shoulder hit the ground.

"What's happening?" he cried out desperately. His shoulder felt like it was on fire, and all the tumbles left him a bit dazed. Turning to look at his right arm, he saw that he was bleeding profusely, and he let out a yelp of terror. "I've been shot—oh, dear heaven—I've been shot!" The shock of it was almost more than his mind could process, and without thinking he started crawling toward his motorcycle.

As he moved toward the machine, there were a number of distinct pinging sounds in the sand next to him, and he instinctively flattened himself to the earth. He'd never felt a terror like this and found himself whimpering in the sand as he crawled crab-style toward his bike. As he thought about what he was doing, it was clear that it made no sense. Whoever was shooting at him had his range, and he couldn't possibly get his motorcycle up and going without being killed immediately. Still, he couldn't help but feel that it would be more comforting to be near something familiar than to lie there exposed in the open desert.

Ping! Ping! Little clouds of sand popped up all around him, and he finally settled right where he was.

That's when Captain Riggins's voice came into his mind. *"You've got to destroy the orders, Carlyle. You've got to destroy them. You can't let them fall into German hands—you just can't!"* He winced as he pulled off his gloves, because his hands were immediately seared by the sand. He fumbled in his shirt pocket and found the lighter. Painfully pulling the leather satchel out in front of him, he reached in and pulled out the general's case and started fumbling to get it open.

Ping, ping, ping!

"So you don't want me to destroy them, you ruddy blaggards!" He was furious to think the Germans might kill him before he could do this last thing. He glanced to the side to see if they were upon him, but he still couldn't see anything. Reaching in, he found the papers and, his hands trembling, started to pull them out.

Ping, ping, ping! One of the shells hit the satchel, tearing it from his hands.

"Oh, no you don't," he said, and he climbed up on his haunches to reach for the satchel.

"Ow!" Dominic screamed as a bullet grazed his upper buttock, and he lunged for the satchel. Off to his right he heard noise and realized that the Germans were coming over the rise. He desperately prayed that he could get to the papers and burn them before they got there. As he felt a shadow come over him, he looked up and saw a young German soldier point a rifle directly at him. Although it would do no good whatsoever, he still put his arm up in front of his face to protect it.

He wanted to shout, "Go ahead and shoot me, you jerk," but instead heard himself saying, "Please don't shoot—please don't shoot me!" and he was disgusted at the words coming out of his own mouth. He drew back as the German raised his gun, and then just as quickly he moved forward toward the satchel, determined to defy the enemy rather than shrink in cowardice. He fully expected to be killed, thinking that it would be all right to die that way, when suddenly he heard a rifle retort from his left side. He recoiled in horror as blood splattered on him. The German fell backward, his face blown into a bloody mess.

"Are you all right, mate?" he heard someone call.

This unexpected turn of events was almost too much to process.

"I asked are you all right, corporal!"

Dominic rolled to his side, wincing in pain as his shoulder touched the ground. There, coming up to him, were two British privates.

"You've been shot into a bloody mess," one of them said.

"But the guy who shot you got it a lot worse!" the other one said.

"Where did you guys come from?" Dominic said, unable to think of anything more profound to say than that.

"We've been watching that bloke for some time. He's doing some kind of reconnaissance, and we wanted to let him get close enough that we could kill him without the rest of his team knowing. Then you came on the scene, and we could see he was going to get you so we started forward. You were riding along so highly focused that you didn't even see us waving you away from him."

"I was up against the clock—I have to get some orders to Colonel Dougherty by 1600. It's urgent!" At that Dominic tried to pull himself into a standing position. "I may be able to make it." But as he tried to stand up he collapsed.

The one fellow laughed. "You made it, corporal. You made it." There was the sound of a motor truck approaching. "The colonel's come out to see you himself."

As the colonel descended, the two men quickly explained what had happened, and Dougherty immediately moved over to pick up Dominic's satchel. Glancing at the communications inside, he quickly issued a set of orders to his driver, who moved over to a wireless set in the back of the colonel's vehicle and started transmitting the message.

"Looks like you've been hit pretty hard, corporal. Let's get you back to camp so our medics can fix you up." Dougherty was nothing like the general. He had a kind tone to his voice and conveyed a sense of calm competence that set Dominic at ease.

"Thank you, sir." Dominic tried to stand again but found he couldn't. The colonel himself put his arm under Dominic's left shoulder and helped him to his feet.

"You did very well to get your message here. We could see that you were attempting to destroy it even when the German was pointing his weapon directly at you. That was exactly what you should have done. Well done."

"Thank you," Dominic said weakly. By this point they were helping him into the back of Dougherty's open convertible truck.

As Dominic lay back on the seat, he felt his eyes growing heavy. He no longer felt frightened. In fact, he felt quite good. As the driver started the engine, he suddenly opened his eyes.

"Excuse me, sir. Can you tell me what time it is?"

"What?"

"The time, sir? What time is it?"

Dougherty looked down at his watch. "It's 1600 straight up. Why is that important?"

Dominic smiled. "Oh, it's not really. I just needed to know."

Chapter Twenty-Three

U-BOAT ATTACK

A Post Office near Dover—August 1942

My Dear Marissa,

I have been given a weekend pass and plan to return to London STOP Since we survived Galbraith's I thought you might try again STOP Would love to take you to the Servicemen's Dance at the Old Armory on Saturday STOP If I promise to pick you up in the Ford will you come STOP Please say yes STOP

Michael

* * *

Lieutenant Carlyle,

Telegrams expensive STOP Armory more my style STOP Yes STOP 8:00 PM STOP

Marissa

* * *

The English Channel Ports near Dover—August 1942

"I wish these blasted cows would get themselves into proper formation," Eric Canfield said with disgust. As the officer of the deck,
he'd been on the bridge for fully three hours in the moonless night
nervously patrolling in and around a small convoy of merchant
ships laden with manufactured goods and foodstuffs from the
United States. Their manifest included such mundane items as
flashlights, kerosene cook stoves, and canvas field tents. Nothing
particularly impressive but vital nonetheless.

Turning to Michael, who was just coming on watch, Canfield
said, "It's that ugly troglodyte in the center of the pack that gives
me the most heartburn."

"Our ammunition ship, is it?" He looked at the giant hulk
lumbering through the night, making the sky even darker with the
billowing clouds of coal dust belching from its two funnels.
During daylight they backed off on the amount being burned so as
to not be quite as easily spotted from the air, but at night they
poured on all the coal the boilers would handle to take advantage
of the darkness that masked their voyage across the long miles
between the old and new worlds.

"Can you imagine what it must be like to serve on that thing?"
Eric asked. "I mean just think about putting yourself on a tub that
can't make anything better than 10 knots per hour and that's filled
to the brim with machine gun shells just waiting to explode. I have
no idea how they can live with the uncertainty."

"I don't know that we're in a lot better position guarding it,"
Michael replied. "If they get torpedoed or fired on by a German
gunboat, can you imagine all that ammo exploding and flying off
in every direction—it would be like watching firecrackers on the
Fourth of July, except with a lethal casing. Odds are that any
number of them might pepper our boat as they go flying off in
every direction."

"Why would anyone set firecrackers off on the fourth of July?"

Michael laughed. "Ah, Independence Day in America. We'd light fireworks and other small explosives to celebrate our independence from the onerous rule of Britain way back in 1776."

"Oh, I see," Eric said with a wry grin. "So your true loyalties remain over there where you have a great holiday at our expense."

"It's really the perfect day for a holiday. We have hot dogs and hamburgers at outdoor picnics. And cotton candy and parades and marching bands. It's quite a show. Might even tempt you to celebrate."

"We have nothing against your crazy holiday. Good riddance, as far as we Brits are concerned. You can have all your mountains of gold and copper and endless plains of grain. Who needs 'em? We've still got king and country after all, and what does America have to compete with that?"

Before Michael could reply, Eric added, "But I do envy your California. The palm trees and beaches and perpetual warmth sound pretty inviting right now. Perhaps you're right to keep your heart there."

"But it isn't. I choose to live here. I'd think by now it's clear that I've thrown my lot in with all of you. Besides," Michael continued, "I've done my part for Britain. I think I deserve my multiple citizenship after getting shot at and strangled and such."

"I'm sure you do, and in gratitude for your service to the Crown, I might point out that you stand to inherit a vast fortune as well as houses and lands and the ability to treat those of us from the lower classes like dirt. Isn't that gratitude enough from a grateful nation?"

Michael slugged him. "I believe it's time for you to go below. Frankly, I'll be quite relieved to only have to worry about exploding ammunition ships rather than listening to you carry on."

Canfield smiled and then said devilishly, "You're in an awfully good mood for such a miserable night. What's up with you?"

Instinctively, Michael put his hand on his pocket, where Marissa's telegram was hidden.

"You've heard from your nurse, haven't you?"

"It's none of your business who I've heard from." He instantly regretted this mistake—he shouldn't have referred to hearing from anyone.

"That confirms it, then. She's sending you notes."

"I thought you were tired, Mr. Canfield. Now unless you'd care to stand a double watch, you're dismissed." Eric smiled broadly and then ducked below for something warm.

"Sorry you had to hear all that," he said to the helmsman.

"Actually, it's quite enjoyable, sir. It gets awfully boring here night after night."

"Captain on deck!"

Michael stepped aside so that Prescott could step to the fore. He was now Commander Prescott, in recognition that he was in command of three of the motor torpedo boats that patrolled together, even though he still held the military rank of lieutenant.

"Anything to report, Michael?"

"No sir. Everything has been quiet so far. Sublieutenant Canfield is nervous about the ammunition ship and keeps urging the others to maintain their formation so that they'll be struck first in the event of an attack and thus protect the ammunition ship."

Prescott chuckled. "That's got to be a bit galling, don't you think? Take up position so that you get killed first. Who would want to obey that order?" He shook his head. "Still, I suppose that the ammunition will do a lot more to end the war than a general's field tent."

They stood in silence for a while. Michael had come to enjoy the brief chats he occasionally had with Prescott but had learned that it was better to wait for him to initiate a conversation than to start it himself.

"By the way, how is your friend Ellington? I didn't hear about him after the two of you were taken off to the hospital."

"He's out of hospital and back doing whatever secret agent thing he does. Apparently he made a full recovery."

"Not like you, who paid the greater price."

Michael felt the leather collar around his neck. He'd tried to avoid wearing it, but the jarring of the boat as it worked its way up to full revolutions proved extremely painful as they crashed through the swells of the open ocean. The collar provided a great measure of relief, even though it meant he had to turn his whole torso when he wished to see something or to face a speaker directly in conversation.

"It was a small price to pay," Michael said quietly. "Hopefully those codes have already saved some British lives."

"That's the great challenge of it, isn't it? We'll never know if they proved valuable or not."

"What do you mean?" Michael asked incredulously. "I assumed they were already being put to good use."

"They may well be. It's just that we can't ever know. You see, if we used the intelligence we pick up to directly thwart some German plan, or to intercept one of their hunting packs, they'd figure out pretty quickly that we were able to read their messages, and they'd change the codes instantly. So the cryptographers have to use whatever intelligence they gain very subtly so as to not raise suspicions."

"In other words, they may be able to prevent an attack or warn a group like ours, but they don't?" Michael said in a distressed tone.

"You shouldn't fret, Michael. You'd be amazed what those fellows can do with just a little misinformation. For example, they can shift a convoy just enough to make it difficult for the Germans to intercept them before daylight without making it look like they had any knowledge that they'd be in the neighborhood. Or they can use it to send out their own false signals to send the Germans on a wild goose chase. The possibilities are endless."

"Well, all I know is that you'd have to be pretty coldhearted to possess knowledge that could save someone's life yet withhold it from them to protect a code."

"My brother is a cryptographer at Bletchley, and he's anything but coldhearted."

Michael instantly regretted having said it and started to stammer out an apology.

"Not to worry. It does call for some very steady nerves. From what I gather, we've already scored some real victories in the clandestine war of codes and ciphers. So you should be proud of what you accomplished."

Michael didn't know if he should feel proud or betrayed. It had never occurred to him that the work of gathering the codes might not be put to any direct use. If so, what was the purpose of it all, anyway?

"Another hour and we ought to see a little light on the horizon. Radar hasn't picked up anything in the way of German S-boats, so perhaps we're going to get off easy tonight." Michael could hear the strain in Prescott's voice. Perhaps the hardest thing about commanding in a situation like this was to keep morale up when the vast majority of time was spent idly going up and down the Channel in darkness with nothing at all to do, yet having to keep the ship and its company in good fighting trim in case something happened.

It was at that moment that the night sky was punctuated by a series of bright flashes from a convoy boat off to their port side.

"Can you read it, Michael?" Prescott asked while their signalman was quickly writing down the official transcript of the message. Everyone knew that Michael had proved a very quick study in reading the coded semaphore messages that were flashed from one ship to another. To make sure the light wasn't detected by a hostile force, it was used only when the exact location of each ship was known, and then the messages were always short and succinct. While there was still danger, it was less dangerous than using the radio.

Suddenly, as quickly as it started, the message ended. "That's easy enough," Michael said in a serious voice. "Just two words— 'Possible U-boat.'"

"Ahead full," Prescott ordered without directly acknowledging what Michael had told him. "Take us directly through the convoy to that ship, being sure to keep their profile between us and the open sea so our bow wave isn't obvious."

The helmsman acknowledged the order and calculated the appropriate course.

"I need to know what they've seen," Prescott said. Calling the signalman on deck, the commander handed him the small lamp used for very close communication and started to dictate a message. Then he hesitated. "Belay that. If there is a U-boat out there, we're in a direct line for them to see a message. We'll just have to go outside the perimeter of the convoy and take a look ourselves."

Michael waited for the call to go to general quarters, but Prescott left things as they were. When he caught Michael's curious stare, he said simply, "No need to raise everyone's hopes."

Michael laughed. It was part of the craziness of war that people actually got so bored that they looked forward to action—any kind of action—even if it meant a life-or-death struggle.

"Pull up under his stern!" Prescott ordered, and the helmsman deftly swung the *960* up to the side of the old steamer that had sent them the initial message. He was immediately angry when a brief flash of light revealed to the whole world that someone on the bridge had opened the door and come out to speak with them.

"Can't you keep your infernal lights off!" he shouted.

The captain of the ship ignored him and said urgently, "We can't be sure, but two different men spotted what appeared to be a feather in the water at the extreme range of their vision. It appeared twice."

"How long ago?" Prescott asked.

"Perhaps five minutes."

Prescott stroked his chin with his right hand. It was a nervous habit he displayed at times like this, and Michael was quite certain that he was totally unaware of it. For their part, the crew was glad he didn't know it since it gave them an indication of what he was feeling. Otherwise, he was completely inscrutable.

"All right, I want to sound general quarters and order all ships in the convoy to start zigzagging, being sure to keep the ammo ship in the center of the group. We'll order all MTBs to go to full speed, circling and watching for the submarine or torpedoes. Please sound the alarm, Mr. Carlyle!"

"Yes, sir!" Michael hit the button for the Klaxon horn, which sounded like a banshee rooster shattering the night air. Simultaneously the signalman sent off a radio message to all other ships in the convoy to alert them to the danger and to give direction to their next step.

"At this point there's no sense maintaining silence. If there is a submarine out there, they're on to us anyway, and if not, we're too close to port for any S-boats to catch up to us. If there's going to be a battle, I want to have as much control of the situation as possible."

"Yes, sir," Michael acknowledged. For just a moment, he wondered why Prescott was sharing his thoughts with him. Then the thought struck him: *He's teaching me how to command. He wants me to know his thought process as he goes into battle.* That was at once flattering and frightening. It meant that Prescott was aware of his own mortality and that Michael might one day have to succeed him in the midst of a battle, and it also meant that he was trying to mentor him for his own command someday. In spite of the flurry of activity that was going on all around him, Michael paused for a moment to enjoy the thought that his commanding officer had that kind of confidence in him.

"Signal from the lead ship, sir! 'Torpedoes running'!"

"Ahead full and swing us to starboard!" It was undoubtedly too late to save the ship, but Prescott wanted to be in position to see the track of the torpedoes so he could estimate the point from which they were fired. That would give him some chance to calculate an attack pattern with the few depth charges they were able to carry on board.

"Of course that assumes they're even the least bit wary of us. They might not think a torpedo boat much of a challenge," Prescott had said to himself without noticing that everyone on the bridge had heard it.

Just as they swung clear of all the other ships, they saw the trail of bubbles left by the compressed air of the torpedo as it tore through the water in a direct line for the lead ship. They were close enough that they could see that the captain of the freighter was doing his very best to turn away from them, but it was also clear that he wasn't going to make it.

"Cover your eyes!" Prescott shouted, and Michael and the others reacted against their natural instincts and turned away from the ship, quickly covering their eyes with their hands—just in the nick of time, since there was a brilliant flash that managed to show through Michael's fingers, followed by a terrific concussion that almost deafened him, and finally by a searing wave of heat. Staggering, he took his hands down for just a moment to steady himself when a second flash illuminated the night sky off to their starboard.

"Drat!" Michael said, his night vision completely gone. As he looked out toward the horizon to try to spy the point of origin, all he could see was a big, white circle of light where the blast of the second torpedo had left its image on his retina. It would be minutes before he could offer any substantive help in the search.

Fortunately, Commander Prescott had not suffered the same fate. "I've got a general bearing," he said quickly. "Join me at the plot table to try to figure out their most likely position now."

Michael stumbled down the stairs and over to the table where they could run a simple plot. The red overhead lights gave an eerie glow to the room, but red was at the long end of the light spectrum, which meant it wouldn't interfere with their night vision. Even now Michael was starting to see again.

"Here's where the torpedoes came from," Prescott said quietly, drawing a line out into the open sea. "If you figure a three- to five-minute run, they would have time to move forward to here, reverse course to here, or take evasive action by moving either closer to or further from the convoy." Michael watched as the lieutenant plotted each of these points on a grid, then drew a circle to indicate the area where the U-boat still had to be.

It was an unfortunate circle, because with only two depth charges they couldn't possibly cover the entire area—particularly since the U-boat could keep moving while they were setting up the attack. In other words, the circle grew larger with each passing moment.

"I don't know why we even bother to carry the depth charges," Michael said under his breath.

"They are a great way to catch fish if you get hungry," Prescott said wryly. By that he meant that each time a charge went off at a depth and location where there were fish, you were likely to see a couple hundred dead ones float to the surface, killed by the force of the concussion under water. The problem was that U-boats usually went a lot deeper than fish.

Michael laughed at the joke. "Well, sir, with all due respect, what do we do next?"

"We get the other ships away from the dying one as fast as possible. All that light from the burning ship is certain to illuminate them in profile. Send an immediate message to that effect, reminding them to continue zigzagging, but in a tighter pattern that lets them make faster progress away from the cripple."

Michael raced upstairs and made the appropriate order. He was quickly joined by Prescott. "We don't really have any chance with depth charges other than to make them keep their heads down." Turning to Michael he added, "That's why we carry our little supply of two. The chance of a kill is slim, but it gives us the opportunity to scare them a bit, which may just give some of our ships a chance to get out of their way." When Michael still looked dubious, Prescott said, "A small chance, perhaps, but a chance still the same."

Prescott spoke in a louder voice so that everyone on the deck could hear him. "Now, unless they've run out of torpedoes, you can be certain that they're going to try for another ship. With all the light of the burning fuel, there's a good chance he's spotted some of our other cows. If he's really good, he's figured out that the big prize is in the middle. So you've all got to keep your eyes peeled for another torpedo track. Shout it out the moment you see it. Does everyone understand?"

All the men acknowledged. Turning to Michael, Prescott added, "As soon as we see the run, I plan to follow the trail right up into his throat. I want you to be prepared to take the wheel and to give it everything we've got. Is your neck up to it?"

"Yes, sir, it is. I'll be ready." Michael immediately moved to the helm, relieving the young seaman to take up post at one of the machine guns.

"Off to port, sir!" one of the men shouted out triumphantly. All eyes immediately swung in that direction, and sure enough, way out in the distance they could see a thin white line growing in the inky darkness of the sea as it streaked across the horizon.

"Quick, signal its intended target, and tell them to take evasive action. It's coming from far enough out that they stand a chance if they handle the ship correctly." This order was quickly followed by a dispatch to the other MTBs to tighten up the convoy and continue to move it out of range while checking for other U-boats in the area. "They sometimes fight in pairs," Prescott said evenly.

Once the convoy's needs were tended to, Prescott shouted to Michael, "Turn to port, and follow that line right back to its point of origin. I want to see how fast this boat can go. All ahead full!"

"Yes, sir!" Michael replied, thrilled at the thought of a high-speed chase. The boat surged ahead with a full-throated roar, the bow wave rising in intensity as the boat started to plane and fly across the wave. The MTB had been designed to travel nearly as fast as a torpedo, so by following back on the track, they would arrive at the firing point before the submarine had much time to take evasive action. By careful placement of their depth charges, they might be able to do some damage, or at the very least force the sub to break off the attack before it went after other ships in the convoy.

As they sped through the water, the captain made some slight course corrections to continually plot the shortest route to the

firing point. Approximately four minutes after spotting the
torpedo, all eyes focused on the intended target. They were far
enough out that they didn't have to worry so much about their
eyes, and the anxiety of waiting for the explosion and corresponding waterspout made it impossible not to look.

"It should have hit by now," Michael said. Prescott didn't say
anything but kept glancing at his watch. At five minutes it was
fairly clear that with their warning, the ship had managed to take
evasive action.

"Well, that's one piece of good luck," Prescott said simply.
"Perhaps we can do even better at this end." By this time they were
approaching the point where the trail of oxygenated water started,
and Prescott ordered, "Slow ahead." The ship immediately lost
way, and they started a search pattern for anything that might indicate the present position of the sub. It was submerged and had
probably seen their approach, so Prescott and Michael quickly
calculated where it was likely to be. They had to be careful, because
even at this moment the German commander might be plotting
his own attack on the *960,* either by surfacing and firing or by
chancing a shot with a torpedo.

"We have two probabilities that make this a bit easier," Prescott
said. "The first is that they're probably not very worried about our
approach, knowing that we only have two depth charges. Second,
having tasted blood once and then missed, they're going to be even
more obsessed to get another shot off before the convoy gets away.
Which means," he said with a smile, "that this is their likely plot,"
and he sketched a series of dotted lines on the makeshift map they
were working from.

Michael reviewed each step in Prescott's thinking, did the mental
mathematics of how far the Germans would have progressed, and
then drew his own spot on the map to indicate where he thought
they'd be. The two were close to each other but not identical.

"Good," Prescott said. "So we have an informed guess of their
position. Now what about depth?"

"They're not likely to go deep because they'll need to stay at periscope range to set up a new firing solution."

"You don't think our presence will force them down for a while?"

"We're a very small boat, sir."

Prescott laughed. "Let's make ourselves a little larger! We may be off by a mile, but at least they'll know we're here, and if the German commander is smart, he will have figured out that we have other ships in the area that can pick up the attack if we miss. Let's make him keep his head down!" They tore off on an approach to Prescott's mark on the paper.

"Shoot!" Michael commanded, and the two seamen assigned to the depth charge rack pulled the firing mechanism, which launched the steel drum containing the explosive up and over the side of the ship to splash into the black water of the English Channel.

"All ahead full!" Prescott immediately ordered, moving them quickly to Michael's spot on the map.

"Shoot!" Michael ordered the moment they reached it, and up went the second canister. Michael had set this one a bit deeper on the chance that they had started to dive when they heard the first can in the water.

At just that moment a distinct whomping sound reverberated through the ship, and then an enormous waterspout appeared in their wake, illuminated by the burning oil from their own ship that had been hit in the first attack and by the growing light on the horizon.

"Ease us out of the way," Prescott said sternly to Michael, who had been so transfixed watching the first attack that he'd left them dangerously close to the second depth charge. The boat moved to starboard just as the second "whomp" hit them with two or three times the force of the first one. The boat shuddered in the water, and it almost seemed like the spray from the displaced water would cascade on their boat, although they were far enough away that there was no danger of that.

"All hands watch for any signs of debris or oil. Or a very large and angry submarine surfacing to take its revenge on us." Everybody laughed. The joke broke the tension and seemed to help the crew think more clearly.

"Oil on the port side!" a seaman shouted. There was just enough color to the water by this point that the dark oil stain stood out as a dark splotch on the surface.

"Drat!" Prescott said. "It was your shot that seems to have done it, Mr. Carlyle. I owe you a drink when we get back to port."

"Thank you, sir," Michael said without showing any sign of emotion. Inside he was thrilled at the compliment and gratified that he'd been the one to find the sub.

"Uh-oh! Better get ready!" Eric Canfield called from the deck below. "I hear noise, and it doesn't sound good!"

Sure enough, there was a huge gurgling sound as a hundred thousand air bubbles forced their way to the surface. The sound was unmistakably that of a surfacing submarine.

"Michael, I want you to go down on the deck and personally supervise the firing of the torpedoes. The Germans may well try to fire on us. Their only chance is to launch a broad enough pattern that no matter which way we turn, we can't get out of the way. Otherwise our superior maneuverability makes it nigh impossible for them to get us that way. Their most likely course of action is to use their gun to try to blow us out of the water. Our gun can fire back, but it will be relatively harmless compared with theirs. That's why I've got to make sure the torpedoes run true as soon as I give you a firing solution. Any questions?"

"No, sir!" was Michael's crisp reply, and in an instant he was down on the forward deck relaying the captain's orders to the crew, while the seaman moved back to the helm.

"There she is, sir!" Canfield shouted out and sure enough, off the port quarter of their stern the night sky was broken up by a large black shape in the water.

"Torpedoes in the water!" the helmsman shouted.

"He's good," Prescott muttered. "All ahead full!" and he grabbed the wheel himself to indicate where he wanted the helmsman to take them.

Just as the captain had predicted, there were four torpedoes running on a very wide course. It was going to be a very close call to see if they could get out of the way in time to avoid being hit.

"If you've got anything in reserve down there, chief, now's the time to give it to me!" Prescott shouted into the communication tube.

"I've got some oily rags I'll throw in, sir!" was the reply, and Prescott was impressed to feel a slight increase in speed, even though he'd thought they were at full throttle already.

Once the track of the torpedoes became clear, Prescott could see that it was impossible for them to get outside the outer track in time. They were going to get hit. Thinking as fast as he could, he considered turning to run with the torpedo to see if he could pull away, but the torpedo was faster.

"What about back to the center?" Michael shouted from the deck below.

"What?"

"They're on a diverging spread," Michael explained, "which means the center is growing larger the further we are from them!"

"Quick, give me the wheel," Prescott ordered as he shoved the young helmsman aside. Deftly, Prescott turned the boat so that it was heading away from the sub at top speed, and with barely seconds to spare, he turned back toward their original position, which put them in the middle of the growing V that had two lines on each side of it as the torpedo spread followed its original trajectory. The German captain had counted on them trying to escape outside the V, but that would have increased the chance of a German hit. The real chance for their success was to hide in the middle.

With seconds to spare, they recrossed the inner line of the V to the safety of the center. Their only hope was that the torpedo had been sent to run true and not programmed to curve back in. As the torpedo passed them in the water, they noticed it start to curve, but by then it was too late.

The shrewdness of the German commander became evident. Apparently he'd anticipated the possibility of the *960* returning to the center, because at just that moment the deck of the *960* was illuminated by a flash as one of the shells from the submarine's surface gun crashed into the stern machine gun. There was a shriek of agony as the gunner was thrown up and back onto the deck, where he lay writhing in pain. Eric Canfield rushed to help him, but in the seconds it took him to get there, the young man had perished.

"That's enough," Prescott cursed under his breath. The boat roared to life again as he swung the bow around and headed off to the port side of the submarine at full speed. His zigzag pattern made it almost impossible for the Germans to site in on them. Shells fell right where the ship had been a moment earlier or directly in the spot where they'd be in a moment. It took all his concentration to keep moving forward through the gauntlet while positioning himself for a counterattack.

The German captain knew what he was doing and did his best to turn his submarine so that he was always bow forward to the MTB, maintaining the smallest possible shooting profile, but it was obvious that the badly damaged submarine couldn't submerge, and a submarine on the surface was simply no match in speed or maneuverability for a torpedo boat.

"Mr. Carlyle! You can see the ship. I'm kind of busy up here, so you come up with the firing solution and send our calling card from the two forward tubes!"

"Aye, sir!" Michael shouted back. It took him just a moment to make the calculations. "Shoot one!" he shouted. "Shoot two!" There was the great whooshing sound of the torpedoes being fired by compressed air from their tubes and then the splash of the great monsters landing in the water. It was easy to follow their track as they headed directly for the submarine. The *960* was so close that there was no chance of missing, and even in the relative darkness, they could see men jumping frantically over the side. With his field glasses pressed to his eyes, Prescott could make out the captain of the ship standing on his bridge, awaiting his inevitable destruction. And then he had to look away, because through the darkness he saw the German captain salute him. Two seconds later, a great explosion lit up the night sky, and then a second. Surprisingly, there was a third that dwarfed the first two. Undoubtedly they had hit some fuel or munitions, and the submarine was lifted up and out of the water. Silhouetted in the light, the submarine broke in half at the apogee of its lift, and the two pieces quickly settled in the water. In a matter of moments, both the stern and bow slipped noisily beneath the surface, and then the *960* was alone in the water. Great pools of burning fuel filled the night air with crimson flames.

"Wow!" Eric Canfield said. A great cheer went up from all hands on the boat. "Three hurrahs for the commander!" Eric shouted jubilantly and was quickly joined by everyone in celebrating this, their first major victory against a German submarine.

Prescott said quietly, "Prepare to pick up survivors. I want everyone to have a sidearm. If anyone looks even the least bit suspicious, like they have a weapon, shoot them. Otherwise, bring them on board and keep them on the main deck back by the stern where we can keep them under guard."

The ship moved in the direction of the churning water that indicated the continued escaping air from the doomed submarine. In the course of the next ten minutes ten survivors were taken on board— dirty, terrified men who had just had their ship shot out from under them. Only ten out of a submarine crew of probably fifty.

Having identified two officers, Prescott asked Michael to speak to them to find out the relevant information about their ship. Michael used his German to ask the question, only to be startled when the first officer of the German ship replied in near perfect English.

"I went to Oxford, so I know what you want from me." The German then proceeded to provide the bare minimum of what was required of him.

After receiving the German's warrant that his men would make no attempt to escape, the more seriously wounded were taken below decks for medical attention. Michael escorted the German officer to the small bridge, where he presented him to the captain.

"Well, it looks like the war is over for you," Prescott said.

"That assumes a British prison can hold me. Yours is a remarkably open society."

Prescott didn't smile. "More than likely it's off to the United States with you. That leaves the whole of the Atlantic Ocean between you and 'the Fatherland.'"

Prescott and Michael were pleased to see the arrogant German officer blanch for the first time.

Chapter Twenty-Four

POWERLESS TO ACT

Tobruk, North Africa—Early September 1942

North Africa was an odd place for the major European powers to be fighting, but at the present it was the most hotly contested battlefield between Germany and England. It also had the distinction of being a place where the Nazis had not wanted to be involved. In fact, Hitler had been furious when he'd learned that his earnest but somewhat inept ally Benito Mussolini had attacked the British in Egypt. He was even more upset when some 35,000 British, half of which were not military, managed to fend off an attack by more than 200,000 Italians. To complete the indignity of that first battle, the vastly inferior British force had counterattacked, driving the Italians back from the battle scene.

In just a matter of weeks, it was clear that the Italians were going to be soundly defeated, which forced Hitler's hand. Rather than gaining control of the British colonies in North Africa, which was Mussolini's original hope, both Germany and Italy risked losing their own possessions on the African continent. Hitler had sent General Erwin Rommel to North Africa along with a large German contingent, and in just a matter of weeks he had taken control of the battlefield, pushing the British back to their original position. In the intervening two years, the battles had gone back and forth, with Germany extending its reach under Rommel's brilliant leadership, only to have to yield somewhat when the British counterattacked.

But now it seemed that the dynamics of the battlefield had finally changed. The arrival of Bernard Montgomery, the brilliant and vain British general who had won a particularly meaningful victory at the Second Battle of El Alamein in August, proved to be the difference. Rommel had been unable to withstand Montgomery's assault and had had to abandon that key position.

The Americans had landed in western Africa, establishing a base in the Vichy-dominated French colonies, which further complicated Rommel's difficulties. While the French had initially put up a spirited defense, the Allies had quickly subdued them and won rights to their territories and ports. This put Rommel squarely in the middle of the British possessions in Egypt and the American position in the west, which left him vulnerable to a pincer movement from both sides. And the brash American general George Patton was showing amazing skill in deploying his own tanks to fight the German panzers.

Rommel had to keep his supply lines open between Germany and the battle zone, but with increasing Allied air power, the Axis shipping across the Mediterranean was now being harassed almost daily by the British Navy. Finally, with a major German offensive taking place in Russia, the much-needed reinforcements and supplies that Rommel kept pleading for simply were not arriving. For the first time since the war broke out in September 1939, it seemed the British had something to cheer about.

For his part, Dominic had found that the wound to his shoulder was not as serious as it first appeared. Only the flesh had been torn, but no bones broken. And the gash across his backside was purely superficial. While his recovery was painful, there was never any question of it ending his ability to reenter combat, and after a two-week recovery, he'd been posted back to his unit, where he'd done light work for the past week transcribing coded messages and such while he regained mobility in his arm.

"Ready for a real assignment, Carlyle?"

Dominic looked up from the table where he'd been working. "Yes, sir, Captain Riggins," he said tentatively. That he'd been treated with great regard for his performance on the previous assignment was satisfying, even though there had been a few uncomfortable moments when his commanding officer had asked about the time of his arrival. Rather than disclose his mistake in navigation, Dominic had ascribed it to motor difficulty from the sand. His response prompted a curious, perhaps skeptical look, but no further inquiry was made. The troubling part of it all was that he'd had nightmares during his recovery that reminded him of the terror he'd felt when the bullets had whipped up the sand near him. He wasn't entirely sure that he wanted to face that again, but there was really no graceful way to avoid it.

"Good. We have a milk run, as the Americans like to say. The division time cards need to be taken back to Eighth Army headquarters so that the lads can get their pay. You'll be traveling well within our lines and on a clearly marked road." Riggins flashed a quick smile. "The perfect place to get your wits about you again after your last escapade."

"Thank you, sir." Dominic was actually quite buoyed by this and looked forward to getting out by himself on his motorcycle. The advantage of what he'd been doing for nearly a month was that he'd been well out of harm's way. The disadvantage was that he'd never had a private moment the whole time he was there, and he craved privacy. Rising from the table, he excused himself and went over to the supply truck, where he retrieved a new pair of goggles, a leather helmet, and other riding gear. He was sad that his own motorcycle had been bashed beyond repair in his encounter with the German but was pleased with the new bike they had given him.

Completing a final check, he threw his leg up and over the bike and was reaching painfully for the throttle when Riggins came bounding up to him. "Don't want to forget this, do you?"

Dominic blushed as he realized that he'd almost taken off without the despatches.

"No, sir. That would be a fine waste of petrol and time, wouldn't it? Thank you." Dominic diverted his gaze but knew he shouldn't leave until dismissed.

Riggins was quiet for a few moments. Very quietly he said, "You'll do fine, Carlyle. There's no hurry on this, so take your time. I expect you'll probably want to spend the night there, so we'll see you tomorrow sometime around noon. You've checked your main and auxiliary fuel?"

Instinctively Dominic turned to look at the extra canisters of fuel that he'd need on this long trip. *Of course I checked them.* But before he completed the thought, he scolded himself for getting angry. It was obvious that his commanding officer was going out of his way to help him, and he should be grateful. To follow through he gave each of the petrol cans a shake to verify that they were full.

"Very good. Well, good luck then. See you tomorrow!"

"Tomorrow." Then Dominic started the engine and advanced the throttle so that he moved quickly out of the staging area and onto the hardpack.

It didn't take long before his arm started to hurt, but he also felt a rise in his spirits as he cleared the edge of the camp and started out into the open wilderness, all alone with his thoughts. With all the tank tracks that had passed over the ground, it was pocked with bumps and small moguls in what his American cousins had called a "washboard effect," and he found the jarring quite painful. He decided the arbitrary 1600 arrival set by that jerk of a general was in part the reason for his poor performance on the previous journey. He spent at least half a dozen miles thinking of all the ways he'd like to get even with the cocky leader. But in time he tired of the exercise and let his spirits rise again as he cruised along in the autumn sun. Even a month had made a noticeable difference in the temperature, and now it was at least bearable.

Soon enough the true character of his job revealed itself, and he faced extended periods of boredom. Because this was a milk run, there was very little to hold his interest and surprisingly light traffic at that. He had only two major turns to make, and they were easily identifiable, so there was little risk of his getting lost. To pass the time, he started singing the songs from the Broadway show he'd worked in, mentally practiced the scene changes, and even tried to see how many of the leading character's lines he could recall. That was good for at least an hour, but there were still two more to go, so he started singing all the other songs he could think of, including, to his surprise, a Primary song from church. Church had never really been that interesting to him, and he had little in common with the young people there. Still, the children's songs reminded him of his mother, and that was a good thing. So he started singing his way through children's songs, sometimes at the top of his lungs as if he were performing in Carnegie Hall.

Somewhat beyond the halfway point, he pulled over to the side and got off to stretch his legs and to eat the small snack he'd brought along. He then topped the fuel in his tank, put in nearly a quart of oil, and checked all his linkages. The chain needed tightening, so he did that before climbing back on his mount for the next leg in the journey.

Half an hour later he was daydreaming when he was pleased to see a group of trees off in the distance. This was an oasis that he'd been looking forward to seeing almost since starting out. The other riders spoke of it affectionately as a place to take a break and to soak your feet in a small pool where the animals watered. As dry and dusty as his mouth felt, he could only imagine what his poor feet were suffering in this heat.

It was in this frame of mind that Dominic's incredibly consistent string of bad luck asserted itself. While humming the tune of one of Cole Porter's more recent hits, he was startled out of his skin by the unexpected roar of an engine overhead that was quickly followed by the shadow of a low-flying aircraft. Instinctively he winced but managed to keep control of his motorcycle. Glancing to his left, he saw the infernal thing disappear over the horizon.

Probably some cockeyed RAF pilot having his fun with me! At the indignity of it, Dominic cursed. *I hope his pay chits are in here. If I knew who he was I'd accidentally lose his here in the desert. He'd like that, I'm sure!"* The thought of the fellow pleading for his pay made him smile.

A bit more alert now, Dominic periodically scanned the horizon to both sides just in case another one tried the same thing. While he couldn't stop them, at least he wouldn't give them the pleasure of seeing him jump the next time.

Which is why, a few moments later, he wasn't particularly concerned when he saw an aircraft coming from his right. *Probably the same guy!* This time he was resolved to indicate his displeasure in a more obvious way. As the aircraft approached, Dominic got ready to shake his fist at him. Then he saw bright little flashes on the outer edge of each of the wings. Before he could fully understand what was happening, he felt his back tire explode, and he was thrown forward against the handlebars as the vehicle immediately lost speed. He very nearly lost his balance but struggled to bring the bike to a controlled stop as the aircraft roared overhead. This time he took a moment to look up as it passed overhead, and he clearly saw the black swastika painted on the underside.

An overwhelming sense of panic overtook him, and he decided he had to make a run for it. He gunned the motorcycle as it labored forward on the now completely flat rear tire.

What am I going to do? he thought desperately. He spied the trees of the oasis and left the road to head directly for their protective cover. The motorcycle was almost impossible to control, and his speed had been cut by at least two-thirds. But he was still able to make progress, and so he pushed the throttle to its maximum and held on with all his might as he and his motorcycle wobbled to the protection of the trees.

Almost there. His shoulder was throbbing at this point, in part because he had tensed every muscle in his body as if to help the motorcycle make its way faster. Suddenly he sensed something off to his right, knowing even before he looked that it was the German coming back for another shot.

Why me? Why in the whole of North Africa do you have to chase me! He was terrified beyond words and so angry that he couldn't think rationally. Pure instinct drove him forward as he braced for yet another attack. Flying past him at a speed too fast to register, the Nazi plane hadn't fired on him this time. He didn't stop to ponder this bit of good luck as he continued to crawl toward the oasis. A second shadow passed overhead, and he realized that the German was being pursued by a British fighter. "Good for you!" he shouted, sorry now that he'd thought ill of the RAF earlier. As he neared the protection of the trees, he saw the German and the British aircraft off in the distance, coming back in his direction. At first he was puzzled, trying to figure out which was which, but then he realized with some horror that their positions had been reversed so that the German was now pursuing the British pilot. Even to an amateur, it was obvious that the British aircraft was in trouble from the increasingly wild maneuvers he was making in an attempt to get out of the line of fire.

"Leave him alone!" Dominic shouted. But apparently the German wasn't listening, because as they got within perhaps a hundred yards of Dominic the British airplane suddenly burst into smoke.

"NO!" Dominic yelled, but no matter how much he wished it wouldn't happen, he saw the lead aircraft break up and come crashing down—straight for him. With his damaged tire, there was no time for him to take evasive action, and so he laid the motor-cycle down on its side and slid off, quickly covering his head as great pieces of wreckage came flying over him. He felt a wave of heat as the remnants of the main fuselage came shuddering to a stop just fifty or sixty feet from where he'd been. Dominic looked up and saw the pilot trying to climb free of the aircraft, but apparently he was tangled up in his belts or something because he couldn't get out of the cockpit, even though it was turned so that it was right against the ground.

"Help him! Somebody help him!" Dominic heard himself shouting. But of course there was no one to help—except Dominic himself. And so he ordered himself to stand up and run toward the plane. But his legs refused to move. They were shaking too hard.

Please, help me to get up. I've got to do something. For a moment he
flattered himself that he could actually overcome his fear and get up
to help the poor fellow, but in his heart he knew he wouldn't. *You've
got to do something! He's hanging there because he tried to save your
life! You can't just let him die.* He couldn't or wouldn't move. After
perhaps thirty seconds, he dared to look up and saw the pilot
hanging there. Apparently he'd been injured, or had simply given
up in despair. Dominic resolved to try one more time and actually
started to lift himself when he heard the sound of an aircraft overhead. Just as in the earlier episode, he felt the ground being churned
up as the German pilot first fired on Dominic, missing him by a
matter of a few feet. Then Dominic watched in horror as the shells
of the German aircraft tore into the fuselage of the British plane. If
the pilot were still alive before that attack, he certainly wasn't afterward as the entire superstructure was torn into shreds.

Dominic finally found the strength to stand up, and he found
himself cursing the sky where the German had disappeared. In the
distance, he saw the German circle and start back again. That's
when he started to run. It was sheer luck that he ran in the direction of the trees because he had no idea where he was going. He
just ran as fast as he could, heedless of anything but getting away.
As he dove behind one of the taller trees, he felt the wash of the
German aircraft as it swooped down low and to the side of him. In
his imagination, he heard the pilot laughing at him. That's when
he lay prostrate and started sobbing.

* * *

When Dominic came to, he had no idea where he was. Somehow
he was vaguely aware that he must be in Africa—or was it Arizona?
The smell of the desert was unmistakable, and in the blackness of
the night it was freezing cold. As his mind started to sort things
out, he was first aware of a throbbing in his shoulder. That's when
he sat up with a start.

"My motorcycle! Where's my motorcycle?" Feeling a tree behind his back, he slid up against it so he could have some point of reference as he tried to get his bearings. Slowly, his mind replayed the events of the previous afternoon. He had no idea how long he'd lain under the tree crying before sleep overcame him, but it was obvious that it had now been many hours since the attack by the German airplane. As he thought about it, he felt himself trembling but couldn't tell if it was out of fear or from the cold temperature. Either way he wished it would stop.

As his eyes adjusted, he saw that though there was no moon to give light, there were more stars in the sky than he had ever seen in his life, and together they cast an eerie grayish-blue aura on everything around him, giving him enough light to sort out at least some of the details of his surroundings. Before long he was able to discern the direction of his abandoned motorcycle. Rising to his feet, he tentatively took a step forward but found that his limbs felt like jelly, and before he could stop it, he'd slumped to the ground again.

After a second attempt, he gave up and started crawling toward his motorcycle. In time he gained enough strength to stand up and walk. It wasn't long before he reached his bike. With his eyes fully adjusted now, he did a quick inspection and determined that the only damage was to the tire, which had been shredded.

The prudent thing would have been to reconnoiter the entire area first to make sure he was safe, but Dominic couldn't bring himself to look in the direction of the downed British aircraft. He was quite certain that someone would come looking for it in the morning so that even if he couldn't travel on his own, at least he'd be discovered and rescued.

So what are you going to tell them tomorrow? Are you going to tell them that you saw the fellow struggling but you did nothing to help him? Or are you going to tell them that he was obviously dead and that the German returned before you could take any action? Dominic decided that the advantage of telling them the truth was that at least they'd know who he really was and he wouldn't have to keep it all inside anymore. He also decided that telling them the full truth was likely to wind him in jail or in an infantry unit where somebody could watch his every move. The one thing he was sure of was that the British Army would not coddle him. There was only one course he could take—the one he always took. He'd have to tell them what they wanted to hear and hope that he might do better next time. *Except that I never do.* Being disgusted with himself was perhaps the greatest punishment of all, and by this point in his life he was exquisitely suited to it.

* * *

Philip pondered the letter he was about to seal, rereading the last paragraph one more time to make certain it reflected his feelings.

> *I'm sorry things aren't going as well as you'd like, Dominic. I promise I'll ask about a transfer out of the war zone. But to be honest, it's quite doubtful in our current situation. Still, I will try. Your mother and I love you, and you're in our prayers.*

He sighed, his heart aching for his son's distress.

Chapter Twenty-Five

CAUSES FOR ANXIETY

The Old Armory, London—September 1942

Even if he'd he wanted to, Michael couldn't take his eyes off of Marissa. She was wearing a light blue chiffon dress that emphasized her shapely figure. Her blonde hair, sparkling blue eyes, and the sharp features of her face simply made her the most beautiful woman in the room.

The Old Armory had abeen converted into a dance club for servicemen when it was retired from active service at the beginning of the war. Now it hosted live dance bands nearly every night and provided a relaxed atmosphere where members of each of the branches of service could come to meet young women for a casual evening of dancing. In most regards it was the British equivalent of an American USO club, with its strict rules on behavior enforced by numerous uniformed military police who broke up the inevitable fights that accompanied young men who'd been drinking. Perhaps that's why Michael had only come here once before. It wasn't exactly the type of atmosphere he enjoyed.

His intuition was correct that it was exactly the kind of place Marissa liked. She had brightened immediately when they entered and had been chatting cheerfully ever since with nearly everyone they came in contact with. He had no idea how many friends she had, both male and female, and his hope for an evening together was frustrated as she accepted invitations to dance from numerous fellows. He eventually found himself sitting rather forlornly with one of Marissa's friends from the hospital—Karen—a young woman not quite as attractive as Marissa. At least she'd talk with him.

"I'm pleased to see that you're quite recovered, lieutenant."

"Thank you," Michael said, clearly distracted as he watched a soldier cut in on the Navy chap that Marissa had been dancing with.

"She's very beautiful, isn't she?" Karen said in a subdued tone.

"What?" Turning to look at her, Michael replied, "Yes, she is."

"You're lucky she'd come with you. She doesn't usually accept dates with patients."

Michael's mood darkened. "But she does date frequently?"

Karen laughed. "Not as much as you might think. Most men are intimidated by her. She's so beautiful that they assume she's already taken. I'm sure everyone here thinks it's an honor that she would come with you." She hastened to add, "Even though you're every bit as handsome in your own right."

Michael blushed at her compliment but failed to have his spirits lifted by it. "A hollow honor since I've had only two dances all night."

"Yes, that's a problem, isn't it?" she said as they lapsed into silence since the only topic they had in common had just started dancing with another fellow.

"She gets like this when she's been drinking. I wouldn't take it personally. She just loves a crowd and can't really help herself."

Michael had been uncomfortable at how many drinks she'd asked him for. Not that he minded paying for them, but more because she'd poked fun at him when he explained that he didn't drink.

"My, but you are a little boy, aren't you?" she had said. As he thought of the words, his face flushed in embarrassment. At least he attributed it to embarrassment since he wasn't yet ready to admit that he could be angry at her. His infatuation still left him blind to some things.

When the music stopped, he stood up and moved toward Marissa. She came running over to him, laughing cheerfully. "Michael. This is a lovely evening. And since you're dry as a desert, you can make sure I get home safely. Will you dance this next one with me?"

"Of course!" His irritation vanished and he was delighted by her attention.

As the music started, Michael was pleased that it was a slow dance. Moving closer to her he felt her body sway to the beat of the music. The touch of her skin against his felt right, and he quickly found himself lost in the moment. Instead of striking up conversation, Marissa was quietly singing the words of the song, and it pleased him to hear her voice. She wasn't a great singer, but the way she lost herself in the music was enchanting. Michael sighed and pulled her even closer— a move that she readily accepted. It was precisely at this moment that two thoughts collided in his mind—the first that perhaps she really did like him; the second more disturbing thought was that perhaps she only danced closely because she was a bit tipsy. He fiercely tried to rationalize the first and reject the second. He finally gave up and decided instead to enjoy the dance, whatever her motivation.

As he closed his eyes and whirled in a small flourish, she instantly adapted. It was obvious that she loved dancing and was very good at it. The dance instruction Michael had involuntarily endured when he first moved to England was paying off.

Just as he hoped the moment would never end, he was startled by a light tap on the shoulder. Pulling him instantly from his reverie was a ruddy-looking fellow who had previously danced two or three times with Marissa. He was smiling a big toothy grin when he asked, "Mind if I cut in?" *Of course I mind, you idiot.* But that wasn't polite. When he looked at Marissa it was obvious that she was pleased by the prospect, so he wordlessly stepped aside.

He half stumbled back to his table, where he sat down heavily.

"At least you got a moment or two," Karen said as though nothing had changed since Michael was last at the table.

Michael turned and looked at Marissa's friend. He found it amazing that she was able to set aside what must be her own disappointment at not being asked to dance by anyone and still try to cheer him up. As he studied her face, she became self-conscious, but he didn't turn away.

"You know, Karen, you're a really kind person."

She blushed. "*Kind* is certainly an encouraging word in a setting like this," she said, apparently as a tease.

Michael realized that he'd embarrassed her in a negative way. Being compared to Marissa on looks would be a challenge for Karen. People probably always spoke of her temperament and good nature.

"But it shows in your face. And that really does make you lovely."

"Please don't . . ."

Michael stood up with a flair. "Karen, would you do me the honor of a dance? Since we're both on the sidelines, perhaps you'd condescend to share the dance floor with me."

Karen looked at him for a few moments as if to see if he were sincere or simply reciprocating her sympathy. She must have decided he was sincere when she said, "Thank you. I'd like that a lot."

Michael was not prepared for what came next. As the band struck up a lively tune, he discovered that the girl he'd been looking past all evening was actually a terrific dancer. Before he could fully process what was happening, the two of them were doing dance moves that he'd been too reserved to try before. Although she allowed him to lead, Karen managed enough subtle hints that he felt his inhibitions slipping away, and soon they were the center of attention. Michael was laughing as the dance came to an end, surprised beyond measure at how well he had done. It was even more surprising when those around them applauded. Michael and Karen took a small bow.

"Wow, that was fun!" he said, out of breath.

"You didn't expect it from me, did you?" she said as an accusation, although it wasn't delivered unkindly.

He stopped and looked at her directly. "I'm afraid it was a surprise. And I'm sorry that it was. You're delightful. Perhaps I could buy you a drink—and then we could try our luck again?"

"Thank you. But I'm afraid I'm a teetotaler, too."

He tipped his head to the side and smiled. "Even better. Maybe a Shirley Temple would suit you—7-Up with grenadine?"

She smiled. "That would do very nicely."

Just as they reached the bar, Marissa came sliding up. "I saw you two out there. Just remember, Karen, that he came with me," she said without malice, but Karen still blushed. For his part, Michael was flattered and yet vaguely uneasy about it. If Marissa had come with him, why was she so content to spend the night with others?

When they had finished their soft drink, Michael escorted Karen back to the dance floor where they danced the next three songs to their hearts' content.

* * *

"Michael, do you have a cigarette?"

It was now 0200, and Michael was driving his Ford sedan carefully through the neighborhood where Marissa lived. It was extraordinarily difficult to find his way through the streets without any headlights, and so he had to use all his concentration not to hit something. The strain of both the dancing and the tension he felt at driving was making his neck ache something awful.

"Michael! I asked if you have a cigarette."

"No!" he snapped. "I don't smoke."

"Oh," she said. "Sorry to inconvenience you."

He instantly felt guilty. "I'm sorry, Marissa. It's hard driving in the dark. I didn't mean to snap at you."

"I don't like it when you're mean to me, Michael." She looked at him with pouting eyes, which made him feel even more miserable.

"I really am sorry, but I just don't have any."

"It's okay" she said thickly. "I know I've got one in here someplace." She lapsed into silence as she emptied her purse onto her lap. She was moving so clumsily that most of the contents fell onto the seat and the floor. At that she let out a mild curse and started fumbling even more to try to recover everything.

They had reached her flat, and Michael pulled the car over and started to help her. As he did, they brushed against each other, and Michael caught her eyes in a brief glance.

Sitting up, Marissa said, "Would you like to come up to my apartment for a while—to visit?"

Michael got out of the car to come around and open her door. He'd never been invited to a woman's flat before.

As Marissa stepped out, she said, "You don't need to worry, Michael. I have roommates," as though sensing he was weighing whether it was proper for him to take her invitation.

Michael's heart warred within him. He very much wanted to get closer to Marissa, and this was innocent enough. But for some reason, alarms were resounding in his mind. He wished they wouldn't. A part of him wished that he could simply ignore them. "You know, I have to drive out to our place in the country, and it's already so late . . ."

She stiffened. "I thought you'd say that. Well, then, you can say good night to me here at the door."

"Please . . . can I see you again?"

Michael hated that he sounded so desperate. But at least it was honest begging.

As she fumbled with the key, he finally steadied her hand at the lock and the door opened.

"Well, good night, then, *lieutenant.*"

He held her hand for a moment, perhaps wondering if he shouldn't go upstairs after all. Instead he said, "Can I call you again?"

She looked at him for a few moments. At first it was clear she wished to punish him, but when he smiled weakly, she relented. "Oh, fine. But you really need to learn to loosen up and have some fun."

He relaxed. "Thanks. We'll have more fun next time. I promise."

* * *

"Can I talk to you privately, Michael?"

"Yes, sir, of course." They moved off to the stern deck.

"We have a special assignment tonight—one that could get pretty dicey. It seems that there's a high-speed troop transport coming through that has to make its way to London."

"You've got to be kidding!" Michael blurted out. "Why would they risk bringing troops through the Channel?" Then he was embarrassed to think that he'd interrupted his commanding officer. "I'm sorry, sir."

"No, don't be. I asked the same question in about the same way. It seems that it's a group of American commandos that need to go into some kind of special assignment at an exact combination of tide, so they can't follow the usual routing. To meet their scheduling deadline, they have to chance the hazards of running the Channel."

Michael whistled softly and shook his head.

"The point is that we're sending out the whole flotilla to try to guard them. Normally we wouldn't want to do anything to draw attention, but have you noticed how many times the S-boats have been right on us lately?"

Michael furrowed his brow as he thought about it. "Now that you mention it, it does seem kind of uncanny, doesn't it? Just when we get to the most difficult spots to defend, the S-boats show up. Do you suspect something?"

"It could just be good luck on their part. Or it could be that they've broken our code."

"But lately we've been running without wireless communications, and they still seem to find us."

Prescott responded in a dark tone. "That's the problem, isn't it? The only other answer is espionage. It may be that we've been infiltrated and word of our plans is getting through."

"Espionage? I thought that we were the only ones who got to do that."

Prescott smiled at this attempted joke. But both he and Michael knew that this was deadly serious.

"Well, the point is we don't know. But if the enemy comes out in strength tonight, it could be a massacre on the high seas. So we've got to do whatever is necessary to protect the Americans."

"Is there anything special planned?"

"Just me. That's all that's planned. I'm in charge of the torpedo boats. The transport itself has a destroyer escort, so we're not entirely alone. Our best hope is that there are no U-boats in the area." Prescott glanced from side to side. It was a huge responsibility the Navy had put on such a relatively young man, and it was clear he felt the weight of it. The transport, even if it was a small one, would carry nearly a thousand men. It was very sobering to think that they could make the difference between life and death for so many people.

For his part, Michael was surprised to find that their American nationality also seemed to matter to him. He'd come to think of himself as British, particularly with so much experience in the war now, but the thought of his compatriots at risk somehow made it even more urgent that they do a good job that night. He felt loyalty to both countries, and the kinship increased his anxiety.

"Listen, Michael. The reason I'm telling you all this is that when we get out there I want to turn the boat over to you. I'll have my hands full just trying to keep on top of the whole situation and directing the other boats, so I don't want to worry about what we're doing. Are you fine with that?"

"Yes, sir. Of course." Michael was flattered to be taken into Prescott's confidence and even more so to be trusted with his boat. The *960* meant the world to Prescott.

"Good. You're more than capable of it. By now you should have a command of your own anyway, but there just haven't been any openings, and we're not getting any new boats for a bit. So tonight you're in control of the *960*," Prescott said, obviously pleased that Michael didn't hesitate. "Now, let's go brief the other captains. Watch what you say to anyone else. If there is a problem with espionage, we have to be doubly careful."

"I still find it hard to believe," Michael started to say, but the words trailed off as the pieces of the puzzle started forming in his mind. He had to fight the temptation to suspect everyone. A boat, no matter how small or large, ran on trust. Otherwise paralysis set in. But the reality was there: somewhere a spy was lurking.

Chapter Twenty-Six

ENTERTAINING GUESTS

Carlyle Manor—September 1942

Michael wasn't accustomed to seeing Marissa Chandler nervous. It was amazing that a nurse who could supervise an entire hospital wing would get so nervous over a dinner with the Carlyles. This was the first time they'd seen each other since their awkward parting after the Armory dance. He couldn't tell if Marissa was embarrassed that she'd gotten so inebriated or if she was angry at him for making her feel embarrassed. Either way, the ride out from London would have been excruciating if Marissa hadn't insisted that Karen Demming come along with them. Karen had probably sensed the tension but had managed to keep the conversation going until they reached the manor.

When they drove onto the manor grounds, Marissa exclaimed, to Michael's dismay, that she had no business being at a place like this and that she should never have agreed to come. Michael had entreated her until she finally agreed to come in. It was uncomfortable, though. He was worried that his parents might say something to embarrass Marissa, since she smoked and drank. He was angry that he had to explain himself to Marissa and his parents about this, which was why he'd avoided talking to his parents in advance.

His worries were in vain, however, since his parents seemed to adjust to her very quickly and did nothing that put her on the spot. When Grace started to say something that could have headed in the wrong direction, Michael touched her leg under the table, and she was smart enough to figure it out and quickly change the subject. By using glares, coughs, and suggested topics, Michael had managed to keep the dinner conversation superficial and meaningless, which was to his suiting with Marissa there.

As they finished dessert, Marissa turned to Claire. "I really do admire what you're doing to help people here. Perhaps you wouldn't mind showing me around a bit, Lady Carlyle?"

"I'd be glad to. Would you care to join us, Karen?"

Before Karen could respond, Marissa said, "Oh, she works in administrative matters—she's not a nurse. I'm sure she'd find this all rather tedious. Would you mind entertaining her, Michael?"

Claire and Philip exchanged a quick glance.

"Of course not," Michael said, disappointed that he didn't get to go on the tour with Marissa. As he reflected on it, though, he was glad that his mother would get a chance to spend some time with her. Claire Carlyle had a great way with people and could undoubtedly work a bit of magic on Marissa.

After the two had departed, Michael turned to Karen. "Well, then, since we find ourselves together again, what would you like to do?"

Karen was obviously still uncomfortable at being tossed aside by Marissa. And yet she was gracious enough to do her best to help Michael feel at ease. "Perhaps you wouldn't mind showing me the gardens? I noticed them as we were driving in."

Michael nodded appreciatively. "The gardens are my favorite. I'd be glad to give you the tour." They exited the study, and he took her out onto the patio that overlooked the small lake that had been built behind the house to provide a reflecting pool for the stately columns in the back. They chatted amiably as they wandered through the rows of well-tended shrubs and flowers. Michael was surprised that Karen seemed to know the names of all of them, and she was happy to share why they worked together to form a perfect English garden.

"It's different in America," Michael said. "Over there, flowers tend to be grouped by type, where we like the natural look—even though it takes more work."

Karen smiled. "You're very lucky, Michael. Others might take this for granted, but you enjoy it."

Michael returned the smile. "I do love it. When we first moved from America, I was so intimidated by everything that my father had inherited. My brother and sister and I grew up in relative poverty in America, although we never wanted for anything. When I first got here, I hated having servants around me all the time and I found myself craving privacy. Maybe that's why I spent a lot of time outdoors, both here in the gardens and in the surrounding woods."

Again they lapsed into silence, but this time it was a comfortable silence. Karen finally broke it. "I've never had anything like this to enjoy, but when I was a teenager I used to dress in my very finest dress and take a bus to the Queen Anne section of town, where I'd walk up and down the streets enjoying the flowers in front of the homes. Then I'd walk through the park to the Houses of Parliament and go to the public gardens there. I would pass entire afternoons that way."

Michael laughed easily. "We live in that neighborhood—in a town house just a few blocks from Westminster. Who knows, maybe we've walked past each other and didn't even notice."

Karen's eyes grew wide at this revelation. "You have a house there as well?"

"Oh, no," Michael said. "I've intimidated you, haven't I?"

She looked at him cautiously.

"Just remember what I told you—I spent much of my life outside of this world. So I hope you won't be put off by all of this."

Hesitantly she answered, "It's all a bit much—a lord and all. But your family certainly is pleasant and gracious." She smiled. "I'm not put off. I'm just grateful I had a chance to see all this," she said, making a grand gesture with her hand toward the garden and the manor.

Michael bumped her hand then and pulled his back quickly, hoping she hadn't noticed.

Very shortly Marissa came running up to them. "Michael, your mother is truly amazing. She's doing a great work here."

Michael smiled and said, "I hoped you'd like her."

After briefly showing Marissa the flowers, the three walked back to the manor.

* * *

Later that evening after Charles had taken the women back to the city, Michael joined his parents for a board game in the breakfast room.

"So what did you think of her?"

"Think of who, dear?" Claire said, keeping a straight face.

"Marissa! What did you think of Marissa?" Michael thought he saw her smirk, and he shook his head.

"I think she's a lovely young woman. I can see why she had such an effect on you during your recovery."

"The one I like is her friend Karen," Grace said.

"What do you mean?" Michael asked.

"Oh, she's just a lot more like us than Marissa, I think," Grace said frankly.

"I don't know what you mean by that," Michael said peevishly. "Marissa's a perfectly wonderful girl."

"Of course she is," Claire said, apparently trying to soften Michael's reaction. "But Karen seemed more interested in the things that you enjoy. At least I heard you talking with her more over dinner than you did with Marissa."

"And after dinner," Philip chimed in. Claire turned to look at her husband to confirm her suspicion that he was totally unaware of what was going on.

"Oh, I see. So you all like Karen more than Marissa. You don't approve of my interest in her."

"It's nothing like that—"

Before Claire could finish, Michael stood up and excused himself abruptly, knocking over a chair as he went.

"Well," Philip said, finally looking up. "What was that all about?"

Claire shook her head in wonder and shrugged.

Chapter Twenty-Seven

FROM THE SHADOWS

The Cabinet War Rooms, London—September 1942

Philip was working at his desk, deep in concentration in spite of the myriad sounds that filled the underground bunker. In spite of all that, something broke through his thoughts and caused him to look up.

"Excuse me," Philip said to his secretary, "but did you hear that?"

She looked up, startled. Not that that was out of the ordinary—she often was taken by surprise.

"I didn't hear anything, sir, but I'll listen more closely if you like."

Philip laughed. "Not to worry. I thought I heard something in the map room. Why don't you go back to your office and find the Rutgers file." He handed her a note card, and she headed down the hall.

Curiosity got he best of Philip, and he walked over toward the darkened map room. The door was open a crack, a strict violation of protocol, but when Philip pushed it open so that some light filtered in, he noted that everything was as it should have been. He attempted to find the light switch but couldn't easily locate it. He opened the door to its full extension and stepped inside.

He heard a thud against the floor, along with something he recognized as a well-known German swear word. "Who's in here?" he called out to the darkness. Silence. "I heard something. Come out into the light, or I'll call the guards!" Philip was overwhelmed with a sudden sense of dread. The door behind him slammed shut, and he whirled in the darkness. He was blinded as the lights overhead flared to life.

"Who's there?" Philip yelled.

"Philip Carlyle. I thought it was you," a malevolent male voice said.

Even though he recognized it, Philip put his hands up to shield his eyes so he could match the face to the sound, and turned to the door.

"George? George Cook! What are you doing in here?"

"What I've been doing for a while. What you tried initially to prevent me from doing."

Philip did his very best to calm himself so that he could talk with a level voice.

"George . . . you shouldn't be here, and you know it. I insist that you leave at once."

"Oh, Carlyle, you are so naive. It took me more than a year to gain access to this place—what makes you think I'd leave it now?"

"But . . . how? How did you gain access?"

"You're not the only one who can provide clearance, you know." Cook smiled.

Philip didn't smile, but responded with, "Yes, George. It's part of my portfolio to oversee who has access to this facility. That's the whole point!" Philip made a move toward the door, but George blocked it.

Philip surveyed the scene to see how he could sound the alert. He decided the only thing he could do was yell, but the problem was that the door was soundproofed so that no one could overhear the conversations that took place inside. Even if he shouted at the top of his lungs, he wouldn't likely be heard unless someone happened to be passing directly by the door by at the moment he yelled.

Stalling for time, he said, "Well, let's set that aside for a moment. Why don't you tell me why you're here?"

"You wouldn't like it and wouldn't understand. So why bother?"

"George—you're in the middle of an underground bunker, surrounded by hundreds of people with the highest level of security, and there are guards in every corridor. This is no time for you to be coy with me. Whatever the reason you're here, you're in deep trouble, and I suggest you start cooperating to limit your exposure. If you plan to beat me up or something, there's absolutely no way you can get out."

George simply laughed. "And why wouldn't they let me out?" He reached in his pocket and flashed his official credentials booklet to Philip. "After all, your signature appears on my papers—why should anyone doubt the authority of a properly credentialed member of the Lords to come in here? I've been using your authority to get information for the Nazis for quite a few months now."

"What are you talking about . . ." Philip started to say, stepping forward to look at the papers that George was holding out to him. "I didn't sign anything of the kind."

As Philip stepped forward, George Cook suddenly lunged toward him, grabbing his outstretched hand and pulling him close. As he did, Philip gasped in excruciating pain as he felt a knife blade slip into his side, probably very near his liver.

"Actually, it just looks like your signature," Cook said as Philip sank to the floor. "It's a forgery of course, but a very good one." He watched as Philip writhed on the floor in agony. "It should be. I paid some good money for it."

"But why? Why are you doing this, George?" Philip could barely get his breath, and as he pushed his hand against the wound, he felt the warm blood coursing onto his jacket and the floor.

"Why? You ask why? Because Europe has become a cesspool that needs to be cleaned up. The Christian nations live in slavery to the Jewish-driven capitalism that wreaks havoc on the world. We sell our independence to the gods of greed and lust. What's needed is someone strong, someone who can exert control and order over the nations. England lost its will years ago, but not Germany. Not Hitler. He rules his people with an iron hand—one that won't tolerate deviants, Jews, or infidels! Germany is the rightful ruler, and it's time to yield to her leadership."

"You're a traitor, George? I can't believe that."

"It won't be betrayal when Germany wins the war. It will be patriotism." Cook said this with relish. "I'm just helping expedite things."

Philip was in too much pain to try to debate him. "George, I have no sympathy whatsoever for what you're talking about, but we're old colleagues, and you've got to help me. I'll die without aid. Please . . . help me."

Cook scoffed at his plea. "You wouldn't understand, of course. You went off to America, you joined your obscure little sect, you toddy to Churchill, and all the while you've missed the bigger picture. Why can't you understand that the Jews have got to be brought to heel if we're ever to put things right? Hitler has started to clean up the stench, and yet England resists him. He invited us to join him in the crusade, but we spurned him. Now I have to make things right."

"George, please."

"You've ruined it for me, of course. They'll find you dead and lock this place up again with new credentials required. You've *ruined* my chance to help the right way prevail. After all this time that I've been keeping Germany informed—you had to *spoil* it! That's just my sort of bad luck. But at least you've paid dearly for it, and I've silenced one more of the voices who stand in the way of progress." He turned to leave. "By the way, at least my efforts won't have been in vain. Can you imagine how pleased the Germans have been with the secrets I've been giving them? They'll build a statue to me after winning the war."

"George, you can't do that. This is *your* country!"

"Not only that, but I'll silence two Carlyles before this day is ended. The current Lord Carlyle *and* his heir apparent!"

In spite of his rapidly deteriorating condition, Philip looked up in even greater alarm at this new terror. "What do you mean? Cook!"

"Your son—he's going out on a special mission tonight." Cook held up a piece of paper that he'd found in the map room. "But with this information he'll find a welcoming committee that will send him to join you in whatever hell it is you people go to. I've been targeting him for some time now with contacts I've made at the Navy. But somehow he's always eluded my grasp. Not tonight—tonight will be his end." And with that, George Cook turned off the light and slipped out the door.

Chapter Twenty-Eight

TANGLING WITH A GERMAN SCHNELLBOOT

The English Channel—October 1942

"So far, so good." Michael leaned his elbows on the shield at the front of the small bridge.

"They certainly missed their best opportunity an hour ago when we were in the deepest part of the Channel and at maximum distance from the shore," Prescott replied. "Perhaps their intelligence failed them this time."

"It's been kind of *boring*, actually."

Prescott laughed. "And isn't boring a wonderful thing?"

Michael stepped back onto the bridge and stretched his legs, putting his hands behind his neck and twisting from side to side.

"This infernal waiting and watching is enough to give a man ulcers." He put his left hand on the railing and lifted himself onto his tiptoes several times. "I can't wait to get back and take a quick shower, then go to bed."

"I thought you'd want to see your nurse again," Prescott said mischievously.

"What do you know about that?" Michael asked in astonishment.

Prescott burst out laughing. "What doesn't everyone know about it? You find reasons to sneak away every time we're in port to go up to London. You never used to do that."

"Well, people should learn to mind their own business— present company excepted, of course."

"It's just that we need something to gossip about, and what better subject than romance—with a nurse, no less!"

Michael sighed. "It's romance on my side of the ledger, but I'm not sure she's all that interested. She seems to like my company, but whenever I try to turn talk about how we feel about each other, she stiffens up and makes some wisecrack about my needing to 'loosen up.'"

Prescott nodded with a smile. "I can see that it would be a problem for her."

"Why is it such a problem? Who got to decide who's upper class and lower class in the first place? We're all just people!"

"Yes, but we're not all Americans."

"And what does that mean?" Michael said defensively.

"It just means that in spite of the years you've lived here, you still have no concept of how our society is organized. People are born to a station, and they find comfort in that. They know what to expect from life, who they will associate with, and what role they'll play in society. It's very upsetting when someone disregards all that."

Michael sighed again. "Well, it makes no sense to me. If you're competent at something, you deserve respect. If you're not, then you earn no deference. And when it comes to love, it should be left to the heart, not to your position. It all seems ludicrous."

Prescott began to interrupt Michael to argue his point, but he was brought up short by a tremendous explosion off to their port side. Fortunately they hadn't been looking in that direction or both of them would have been temporarily blinded. The reflection off the water was enough to tell them that something major had been hit, and Prescott immediately ordered everyone to battle stations.

"It's the destroyer, sir. It must have been a direct hit by a torpedo," Canfield yelled.

"Thank you, Mr. Canfield. Please order the transport to change its zigzag pattern and head directly for the coast. I'm moving to the wireless to set up a battle plan with the others. Michael, you're in command. Take us off to the beam of the troop ship. If another torpedo is launched, I want us to take the blow rather than them. That transport must get through!"

"Yes, sir." Michael ordered full speed ahead and provided directions to the young seaman at the helm.

"And find out what we're up against—a submarine or S-boats," Prescott ordered. "Send word as quickly as you can to all the ships in the convoy to identify the enemy."

"Yes, sir," Michael said. After Prescott disappeared down the stairs for the second time, he turned to the helmsman. "That is one angry lieutenant commander."

"Yes, sir!" the young man said.

"Somebody's let down on their job. If it's anything other than a submarine, then someone should have spotted it before the torpedoes found their mark." They reached the point of impact and were distressed to see that there were no survivors in the water. Chances were high that the torpedo had hit the ship right in its main magazine, increasing the force of the explosion at least tenfold. The odds that anyone survived were small since the shockwave would have killed even those not directly impacted by the explosion.

Pulling up alongside the troop transport, Michael acknowledged their bridge with a signal and then started scanning the horizon for enemy ships.

"There, sir! Off to port!"

"What do you see—I can't make anything out!"

"A dark spot against the horizon—it looks like an S-boat, sir!" Michael strained in the direction he'd been pointing to, focusing his eyes against the darkness. Just when he was about to admit that he couldn't see a thing, he saw what appeared to be a movement at the extreme range of his vision.

Lifting the interphone, he rang up Lieutenant Prescott. "It appears the attack was initiated by an S-boat, sir. So far just one spotted at extreme range."

"Watch for torpedo trails, and signal the transport so they know what we're up against. It's doubtful there's just one of them, and we have to be on guard for torpedoes and surface fire."

Michael acknowledged the order and relayed it to the signalman. "Tell the transport not to acknowledge our signal." When the fellow raised a curious eyebrow, Michael explained, "We're signaling away from the S-boat so they're not likely to see us, but a response would be in their direction and would reveal the transport's position for sure—not that the Germans might not already know, but just in case."

"Yes, sir!" In moments their lamp was flashing quick signal bursts.

Although it seemed impossible, Michael perceived that the transport picked up even more speed. It had to be traveling at more than full speed, probably with all emergency valves on the boilers lashed down to keep the pressure beyond maximum on the gauge. *Risky business, but the best defense against a torpedo, to be sure.*

At this point, a second MTB came up on their port side and started closing in on the S-boat, which was now obviously coming straight for them. The combined speeds of the MTBs and the S-boat had them approaching one another at more than eighty miles per hour, closing the distance quickly. Michael guessed that Prescott had ordered the other boat to attempt to get a torpedo off while the *960* provided cover for the transport. As the two ships drew closer, there were quick flashes of light on both of them, indicating they'd opened fire with surface guns.

"Do they really think they can get a torpedo into an S-boat?" the helmsman asked.

"They hope they can, but the real reason for this attack is that while the S-boat is tied up fighting with our boat, it can't get a good shooting solution on the transport. Our job is to watch for other S-boats that may be coming up from behind or another direction, and then we'll go off to intercept them. The whole point is to keep their course erratic so the transport has a chance to get away. As we get closer to the shore, it's more dangerous for the Germans because they don't know what other resources we can bring into the battle."

"May I ask what resources are available?" the new helmsman asked.

"We don't have any. Nearly all our destroyers are at sea protecting convoys like this one, and it's so unusual to have a transport come in by this route that the Navy didn't bother to send anyone down to support us. It's really just the five of us against whatever the Germans have."

"But an S-boat is much larger than our torpedo boats, isn't it?"

"It is indeed. And faster." He threw in the second part just to add to the helmsman's anxiety. "But don't worry—there are two torpedo boats and three gunboats, and among us we have a lot of firepower. Being smaller and more maneuverable can mean a great deal in these close-order battles. It's a lot more exciting on our small boats than on a capital ship, where they oftentimes don't even see their intended target—you all just hunker down and wait for whatever the enemy is sending your way. At least in the Coastal Service you get to see who you're fighting." From the look on the helmsman's face, he wasn't sure this was comforting.

"It's getting pretty intense, sir!"

Michael turned and saw that a British gunboat had joined the fight and was now firing on the Germans. From Michael's distance, it looked like a series of firecrackers going off, with an occasional blast when one of the projectiles hit home. He counted at least two or three hits on the German but an equal number on the two British boats.

"Mr. Carlyle, let's see what we're up against." Michael turned at the sound of Prescott's voice. "Fire a star shell so we can see who's out there."

Michael acknowledged the order, and shortly there was a loud pop. They followed the arc of the star shell as it went up and above the three boats that were engaging each other. With a huge explosion, the star shell illuminated the entire night sky as it hung there, seemingly suspended from one of the stars. The whole scene took on a ghostly white appearance, but they could see clearly for perhaps a mile or more.

"There's a second one coming up!" the helmsman shouted. "And a third one over there." Michael and Prescott did their best to follow his pointing.

"Okay, then, our boats on the starboard side of the transport haven't reported anything yet, so I'm bringing one across. It looks to me like that fellow at the nine o'clock position is getting ready to make a torpedo run on the ship, so let's see if we can't put one in him first. Mr. Carlyle, bring us into a firing position."

Like a knife slicing through frosting on a cake, the *960* veered to the left, leaving a great white arc of foam as it pulled away from the transport and onto a new course to bring them head-to-head with the second German boat.

Glancing off to his right side, Michael saw the fourth British boat come around the bow of the transport as it moved out to engage the third German boat.

"Hold your course, helmsman," Michael said calmly. Heading straight toward the enemy at high speed, Michael had a natural inclination to deviate to avoid a collision. But he couldn't yet. If he was going to get a firing solution, he'd have to hold this course for at least another twenty seconds, then turn sharply to port followed by a heel to starboard so they could expose the full length of the enemy's hull.

"Prepare to fire torpedoes one and two!" he shouted and was gratified to see the men on the deck responding to the order. "Now!" he shouted to the helmsman, who quickly executed their prearranged maneuver. The force of the two countervailing turns was almost enough to knock some of the men off balance, but in quick order they were presented with the full broadside of the German ship. Michael took advantage of the good firing opportunity with the order to "Shoot one! Shoot two!" as well as "Open fire!" and every gun on the *960* and the German ship flared into life. They were so close that it was difficult to break away, and Michael was knocked from his feet by the force of a concussion off the bow. Pulling himself quickly to his feet, Michael saw that the young helmsman had been blown into a bloody mess at the back of the bridge. Although he wanted to run to offer help, he realized the helmsman couldn't have survived, so he turned his attention to the ship.

What did survive, miraculously, was the wheel. The armor plating had deflected the force of the blast up and over the shield, which is what had killed the seaman. Pulling himself up to the wheel and quickly surveying his own body for injuries, he was surprised that even though he'd been standing less than two feet away from the helmsman, he wasn't hurt. The first order of business was to survey the damage and determine if they were still seaworthy. In the panic of trying to figure out if they were sinking, Michael neglected to see if the torpedoes had found their target. At least one had, because there was a terrific explosion. Although he should have averted his glance immediately, Michael was transfixed by the spectacle of the German Schnellboot flying out of the water while breaking in half midships. In less than ten minutes, two ships had been sunk by these deadly missiles, and Michael marveled that he was the one who had ordered this destruction.

"Damage report!" Prescott demanded from the stern. That brought Michael to his senses quickly enough.

"Yes, sir!" Quickly scrambling to take in the scene, Michael registered that the shell that had hit them must have been fired on a very level trajectory, because the force of its blast had blown up and over the bridge, rather than arcing down and through the stern. While there was certainly a lot of twisted metal down there, including the ruined remains of their forward gun, the ship itself seemed to have survived the blow without any irreparable damage. "It appears that we're seaworthy, commander."

"Good, then kindly get us the blazes out of here and move against that third German ship. The gunboat isn't having much success deterring them from firing on the transport!"

Michael took control of the wheel and ordered full speed ahead. The three engines roared to life with a reassuring throb, and they lunged through the wreckage of the German boat as great pools of fuel burned on the surface. Michael was aware that there were German survivors in the water, and it chilled him to have to move his boat through them without offering assistance—perhaps even running over some of them—but right now he had more than a thousand men to protect, and two unharmed German boats were still in the area.

As they passed the line of the first German boat, which was still being engaged by the MTB and MGB, two things happened simultaneously. First, the other MTB was hit by a shell that sent up a great shower of splinters from its stern. Michael quickly saw that it was out of action and that, in fact, it was sinking quickly—perhaps too quickly for the men down in the engine room to get out alive. *Assuming they are alive.* At the same time, a direct hit on the British gunboat engaging the third S-boat in front of them sent another shower of splinters and debris high into the air, completely destroying the craft and undoubtedly killing all on board. The S-boat now had unrestricted access to the transport. In spite of the transport's best efforts, it still hadn't put enough distance between the Germans and itself to avoid a torpedo run should the Germans get some off.

"Give me everything you've got!" Michael shouted into the tube, and somehow the engineer managed to coax a bit more power out of the engines. They were now certainly going as fast as an MTB was capable of going.

"Fire a torpedo ahead of them, Michael, to force them to turn away from the transport!"

Michael immediately grasped the brilliance of this tactic and ordered his men to shoot one of their last two torpedoes. Its track was very obvious in the nighttime, the trail of bubbles forming a white line just ahead of where the Germans were lining up to shoot.

"He's not turning, sir!" Michael shouted.

"I can see that," Prescott said calmly at his side. Michael was so worked up that he'd acted as if the commander were still on the stern deck.

"What do we do? He's going to get a torpedo off anyway—even if it means taking a hit himself."

"I think it will be fine. He's got to have a nervous crew right now, and the transport has enough distance that they might be able to take evasive action. Have your men stand by to send a signal. Go ahead and use the wireless and the lamp since at least half the coast of England must be watching this by now."

Michael gave the orders and watched with great as anxiety as a torpedo slipped out of the deck tube of the S-boat and into the water. He quickly did the calculations on its course and then shouted the information into the interphone so that the signalman could warn the transport.

"He's turning now, Michael, though I'm not sure it's in time."

They continued to close on the S-boat at top speed while watching in fascination as the path of their third torpedo and the German boat closed on a single point.

"I think we're going to hit them, sir. I don't think they can turn away in time."

"Let's hope so—any damage is better than none." Somehow Prescott still managed to retain that infuriating level voice that seemed the birthright of every ship captain, but which Michael could never fully master.

"Should hit or miss right *now!*" There was a blast at the bow of the S-boat, which caused a cheer to go up from the men of the *MTB-960,* followed by a deafening concussion that seemed totally out of proportion to the blast wave they should have felt from the hit on the S-boat. It took one or two seconds for Michael to realize they'd been hit again by a shell from the S-boat in reciprocation. Even in the act of launching their torpedo and turning to take evasive action, the S-boat's gun crew had managed to sight in on the *960* and get a shot off at them.

"I'll try to get a damage report, sir," Michael said, turning to where Prescott had been standing. To his horror the lieutenant commander was no longer there. Because of all the blasts, it was difficult for Michael's eyes to focus. He dropped to his knees and felt on the deck. When his hands came in contact with fabric, he shouted out, "Lieutenant Prescott, is that you? Are you okay?"

He managed to find Prescott's face. It was still warm, and he could sense that he was still alive. "Lieutenant, are you all right?" He felt the face roll in his hands. Then he did something he'd never done to that point.

"Will, it's Michael. Are you okay? Please tell me you can hear me."

"Michael?" he said weakly. "Michael, we've been hit. How bad?"

"I don't know yet. It doesn't feel like we're sinking, but we're dead in the water."

"You should've called me Will a long time ago. You know as much as I do now and are every bit as suited to command."

"That's not true—but if it sounds good for you to hear, then I'll call you whatever you like."

Gaining some measure of strength, Prescott tried to rise up to a sitting position. Michael did his best to help him. "Here's the thing, Michael. You've got to figure out some way to protect that troop ship. There's a dozen of us and a thousand of them. I can't do anything, so you're in command. You direct the battle in my name."

"But I'm not in charge of the rest of the flotilla." *Or what's left of it.*

"You know that and I know that, but they don't know that. Just transmit your orders and they'll obey."

"But—"

"Listen," Prescott said savagely. "You're the best I've got—even better than the men commanding the other boats. Just do what I tell you and figure out how to save this mess." With his strength spent, Prescott slumped against the bulkhead.

Michael started to feel lightheaded and began hyperventilating. Forcing himself to slow his breathing, he took a couple of long, moderate breaths, and then stood up.

"What do we do now, sir?" one of the seamen asked him.

"First, you need to give me a damage report. Meanwhile, get me the signalman if he can be found."

"Yes, sir!" the seaman said before darting off.

Moving to the front of the bridge, Michael could see that the bow was a mangled wreck and that their remaining torpedo tube had been wrenched from its fittings. The next thing he did was to turn and look at the transport. The lone torpedo fired by the Germans should have already struck by then, but it was obvious that the transport was still making good speed. He glanced at his watch, where he'd been counting the seconds, and felt an enormous sense of relief that the time had more than elapsed. The transport's captain had obviously figured out an evasive action that left the torpedo running impotently in the open water.

The last thing on his list was to look to where the third German had been, and he was startled to see that in spite of taking a hit by their torpedo, it was still afloat and actually seemed to be gathering itself together to put on speed.

"That's impossible—we hit their bow. They must be sinking!" He said this to no one in particular but realized that everyone was listening.

"It was a glancing blow, sir. Just like that other one we hit in the tail. It was enough to set off the torpedo, but the force of the blast was directed into the open air. We probably punched a few holes in it, but they're obviously figuring out some way to get going."

"What's the status of our other boats?"

This time it was Eric Canfield who replied. He had by default become the first officer. "The MTB is still shadowing the transport. The other one was pretty much battered to pieces by that second German. But they've managed to stop their S-boat."

"So the only risk is that these fellows will get their boat turned in time to launch another round of torpedoes." He mentally did the math on the position of the transport and realized that it was still within range of the German boat, if barely.

"Do we have any weapons capable of firing, Eric?"

Canfield shook his head. "No, sir. We're dead in the water."

"Dead as in unarmed or dead in that we have no engines?"

Canfield shook his head. "I'm afraid I don't know the answer, sir. Let me check with the chief." Finding that the interphone had been shattered, he raced down the back stairs.

The thirty seconds or so that it took him to return were like an eternity to Michael, who continued to watch in anxiety as the captain of the S-boat maneuvered slowly into position to shoot a round of torpedoes. "You're a determined fellow, aren't you?" he muttered. He wanted to curse.

"Chief Byrnes reports that the electric is still working, and we can probably get some power out of one of the Packards. But it's doubtful that we have enough fuel to get back to port."

Michael motioned for Canfield to come close. "It's not port that I'm interested in, Eric. It's that German. Here's what I want you to do. Take Commander Prescott and all the other men into our lifeboat. All I want on board is Byrnes and me. I'm going to ram that blaggard so he can't shoot those torpedoes."

"But that's crazy!" Eric said. "You'll get yourself killed—sir."

"I won't—but even if I do, that's my business. I have no time to talk about this. Get moving right now, Mr. Canfield. That's an order!"

Eric paused for just a moment, intently searching Michael's face. Then with just the slightest hint of a sigh, he said, "Yes, sir!" Eric called out to the men to abandon ship and then raced down the stairs to tell Byrnes what was up. Byrnes agreed to stay, as Michael knew he would. It took slightly more than ninety seconds for the crew to get the life raft in the water and to gently move Prescott into the soft bottom. To save time, they all jumped into the water and pulled themselves into the boat from there.

Michael turned to Byrnes, who had come up for orders, and quickly shared his plan. "You stay below giving me all the power you can for exactly two minutes. I figure that's how long it will take for us to build up a head of speed sufficient to deflect their boat. Then you come up and jump overboard with your life vest on. I'll stay on board till the last possible moment to make sure I hit them near their damaged bow so that I can disable their torpedo tubes.

"It's going to get very dicey for you, sir. They're going to start firing on us the moment they figure out what you're up to."

"You worry about the engines and let me worry about the boat." Byrnes acknowledged him and started to move away. "But thanks for the warning, chief. You're a good man."

Byrnes turned and saluted Michael—something he was hardly ever known to do with an officer—then disappeared downstairs.

Realizing the urgency of their task—after all, once the Germans launched their torpedoes it didn't matter whether the MTB crashed into them or not—Byrnes fired up the sole remaining engine while engaging the electric motor, pushing the boat to accelerate as rapidly as possible.

On the bridge, Michael pulled on his helmet and steered a course straight for the Germans. There was enough activity on the S-boat that no one noticed at first. After all, the hit that the *960* had taken was more than enough to disable a boat that size, so it made sense that the Germans weren't even paying attention to them. The Germans' inattention bought Michael nearly sixty seconds out of the two minutes he needed. As he mentally counted off the seconds, he was relieved to hear Byrnes call out, "Best of luck, sir. Don't wait too long to jump!" Michael turned and waved and heard a splash as Byrnes leapt into the water.

By that point, they were so close to the S-boat that the Germans wouldn't be able to bring any of their heavy guns to bear, but when one of the deckhands looked up and saw the British boat gaining speed as it headed straight for them, Michael could hear his frantic cries to the bridge. It seemed like everything moved in slow motion from that point forward. Soon every German who had a gun started firing at Michael. There was also an increase in their frantic activity as they attempted to launch their torpedoes. Because of the heavy fire, there was no way for Michael to make an escape, so he simply hunkered down behind the metal screen, wincing each time a shell ricocheted off the thin metal skin. He felt one of the shells strike and dent the metal with enough force to bruise his arm.

Counting down the seconds, he raised his head to make sure he was still on course and was relieved to find that the stern of the German boat was right where it was supposed to be. He laughed at the mental image of the two boats shaking hands. Except that with the speed Byrnes had built up, it was not likely to be a gentle greeting. Ducking, then looking, ducking, then looking, Michael saw the men on the torpedo tube pull the lever to launch the torpedo at precisely the same moment that the *960* crashed into the hull of the S-boat.

There was no question about the success of his steering as Michael crashed against the screen to the tune of the sickening screech and groaning of metal against metal as the two ships collided. Collecting his wits, he rose above the screen to view the effect just in time to be knocked senseless by a terrific explosion that sent him reeling backwards. It happened so fast that he couldn't really figure out what was going on, but he had the oddest sensation of flying through the air. As he futilely waved his arms, trying to gain control, he flailed head over heels for what seemed an eternity. And then he felt a crushing blow that knocked the wind out of his lungs as he crashed into the open waters of the ocean. The force of the explosion plunged him far under the water, even with his life vest on.

The water was freezing cold, and his initial instinct was to gasp for air, but he managed to scream to his own brain, *DON'T INHALE!* At this point it was hard to get his brain to do anything, but fortunately he managed to implement this one vital directive. Otherwise, he undoubtedly would have drowned.

It seemed like it took forever to bob back up to the surface, but eventually he popped through and took a great gasp of wonderful but smoky air. After a couple of quick breaths, he quickly scanned the horizon to try to figure out what had happened to him. What he saw was astonishing. By whatever means, he had been blown approximately twenty-five feet from what was left of the *960*. There wasn't much—just a mass of debris that was bubbling and churning off to his right, accompanied by burning petrol that flared on the surface. There was more of the German S-boat, but not a lot. The bow had been blown away completely, and as the German boat took on water, the stern was pulling up and out of the water, and the handful of men who survived the blast were doing their best to jump into the sea without crashing into the wreckage and flames.

As he continued to try to make sense of things, Michael could feel that his face had been burned, but not nearly as badly as he would have imagined, given the force of whatever it was that had hit him. Still, the saltwater stung his face, so he did his best to keep his head above the surface.

As he calmed down and collected his wits, he was finally able to ask himself what happened to cause the explosion. Thinking about it, he realized that it wasn't likely that the fuel tanks on the *960* had exploded, at least initially, because they weren't involved in the collision. And the Germans used diesel fuel, which wasn't prone to explosion.

Then it struck him. The Germans had fired a torpedo simultaneously with the impact. It must have hit the *960* just as it left the tube! He mulled that over for a moment and realized it was the only possible explanation. The Germans had blown themselves up along with the old *960*.

The mystery solved, he rocked back in his life jacket and let his legs float out in front of him. Replaying the scene in his mind, he decided that the shockwave in front of the superheated air of the torpedo explosion had blown him free of the boat. He'd been something like a human cannonball, minus the cannon. The reason he hadn't been incinerated was that the explosion's displaced air must have lifted him up by the crest of the shockwave that hadn't yet been heated by the blast. When the heated air had passed over him, he was under the water doing his best not to drown.

As the light of the fires started to die down, he rested in the water. Only then did it dawn on him that he was floating in the waters of the English Channel not very far from the German sailors whose boat he'd just destroyed. Depending on who won the battle of the second German S-boat and the other British torpedo boat, he could wind up a hero or a prisoner of war. *Or dead.* That thought prompted a whole new set of anxieties. Forcing himself to control his breathing, he started to reassure himself. *I can't worry about that right now. My only job now is to stay alive. It's going to work out.*

As the last remnants of his boat and the S-boat sank, the ocean suddenly became very quiet. He could hear some German voices perhaps twenty or thirty yards away, but no one was swimming toward him. *They have problems of their own and probably have no idea that I'm alive.*

At first he expected something to happen immediately, but as the minutes ticked past he felt his body temperature dropping. *Gotta keep moving!* He started churning his legs and arms, which brought some relief from the cold. It also made it obvious how much his neck hurt.

That's when he heard the sound of a boat off in the distance. He strained his ears to hear. "A boat!" he wanted to shout but decided he ought to wait until he knew more about the sound. After all, why alert the nearby Germans until absolutely necessary?

The big question was whether the engine sounded German or British. He listened intently during the four or five minutes it took for the sound to draw closer.

As the sound started to resolve itself, he thought it sounded like the enemy. But after another moment, he could hear the very distinctive sound of the American Packard engine.

Once he was confident it was British, he yelled, "Hey!" at the top of his lungs. "Hey! I'm over here!" It was futile to yell—there was no way in the world they could hear him or see him. Flailing in the water, he brushed across his calf. When his hand hit something hard, he burst out laughing. "A flashlight!" He pulled the flashlight out of the lower pocket of his trousers. When Prescott had ordered him to be prepared to signal, he'd slipped it into his pocket just in case he needed to alert friendly forces from a distance. Pulling the light above the surface of the water, he started flashing it in the direction of the boat. While not one hundred percent certain it was the British, he was absolutely certain that he wanted to be rescued—by the Germans or the British.

At first there was no change in the sound of the engines, but then, just when his heart was starting to pound in his chest, he heard a distinct change in the pitch, indicating that the boat had turned and was on a new heading. As the sound grew louder, moving toward him, Michael finally rested his head in the water, his feet out in front of him again. It felt great to take the pressure off of his neck and just relax. It was in that pose that they found him, pondering the events of the most remarkable night of his life.

Chapter Twenty-Nine

TO CATCH A THIEF

The Cabinet War Rooms—September 1942

"Lord Carlyle! Lord Carlyle! Are you in here?"

Though it was difficult to concentrate, Philip vaguely heard his name being called, and he struggled to respond to whoever was inquiring after him. But as he tried to rise, he found he simply had no strength. Lying back on the floor, he did his best to say, "I'm here, I'm—" and then he realized that he didn't even know where he was.

"Lord Carlyle? Oh, dear mercy of heaven! HELP, SOMEONE HELP! Call a medic immediately! Lord Carlyle's been hurt!" Elizabeth, his secretary, belted at the top of her lungs.

He felt a warm sense of relief and gratitude as she kneeled down and lifted his head into her lap. Then the alarm went off in his head. *Michael—Cook's going to betray Michael!* "Elizabeth," he tried to say, but he found it difficult to articulate the warning.

"You just lie there, and we'll have help in a moment." She patted his hand and made shushing sounds.

Seconds later he heard some of the men of his staff come crashing into the room and as Elizabeth stood up, Philip blurted out as strongly as he could, "George Cook—you've got to stop him. He's stolen plans—" and then the room started to fade.

Philip could feel them lifting him onto a stretcher and then experienced the odd sensation of being wheeled through hallways on a gurney. At one point in his fading in and out of consciousness, he rallied enough to croak out, "Cook?" and was able to relax when it registered with him that Jon Randall, his primary aide, had leaned down and whispered, "It's okay, Philip—we've got him. The alarm was sounded, locking all the doors, and it was only a matter of time before we found him cowering in a corner. He's not going anywhere."

"So Michael's safe."

Randall turned to one of the other assistants with a puzzled look and then said to Philip, "As safe as an officer can be on a wooden torpedo boat." At some level of consciousness, Philip heard this remark and even thought it rather clever. But that was the last thing he remembered.

* * *

Perhaps the most disconcerting thing about surgery was the complete lack of personal awareness that accompanied the anesthetic. Winston Churchill firmly believed that consciousness ended with death and that the soul entered into what he called "black velvet," a state of nothingness in which there is no sense of loss, sorrow, or happiness. The person simply ceased to exist and had no more responsibility for the cares of the world.

Philip had always disagreed with him. But on finding himself being awakened and in a hospital bed, he was startled to realize that for some unknown period of time he had had absolutely no awareness. For the first time in his life, he understood Churchill's view of things. He focused on the sound of the doctor's voice, resolved to not say something stupid, but such were the effects of the anesthetic that he muttered, "Where—where am I?" He felt foolish the moment he said it, but he seemed powerless to stop himself from uttering the next line. "What happened?" The fact was that everything was a blur.

"You're in a hospital, Philip. You had serious internal damage, but the doctors have sewn you back together, and it looks like you're going to be fine."

At first Philip was surprised to think the doctor was a woman, but then he recognized that it was no doctor talking and he turned affectionately toward the direction of his wife's voice.

"Claire . . ." he said, struggling to focus his thinking. "Is Michael okay? Something bad was going to happen to Michael."

"Why don't you ask him yourself?" she replied.

"What?" he said groggily. "Michael, are you here?"

As he turned his head toward the foot of the bed, a blue shape came into view, and he tried to lift his hands to rub his eyes but found that his arms were somehow restrained. "It's all right, Father. It's me. I'm here and in good shape."

Philip allowed his neck to relax and felt his head slump into the pillow. "Thank God," he said. *Thank you, dear God, for protecting my boy!* He could feel tears form and drip down his cheek.

Claire wiped them away. "You lost a lot of blood and would probably have died had Elizabeth not found you when she did."

"Elizabeth?" It was frustrating to act so stupidly, but his only consolation was that he could do nothing about it.

"Yes, she found you and was able to get medical attention in time to staunch the bleeding. But that vile man had stabbed you right in the side near your vital organs so that they've had to give you transfusions until your body could start to heal itself."

It registered with Philip that all of this must have taken a great deal of time. To already be mending meant that he'd been out of it a very long time. And so he asked the third in his series of profoundly intelligent questions. "What day is it?" When told that it was Thursday, he realized that he'd been out for nearly three days. All he could do was shake his head in disbelief.

Fortunately, at this point his head had cleared enough that he was starting to focus on shapes, and he saw one that was a bit shorter than the others. "Grace, is that you?"

"Yes, Papa, it's me," Grace said as she came up and gave his face a small hug with her cheek. "You scared me almost to death, you know. I don't know what I would do if you really left us."

He smiled. "I'm sorry I scared you. It was my own fault, of course, so I'm the one to blame."

"What do you mean?" Claire asked defensively. The she-tiger was ready to protect her brood, including keeping Philip from impugning himself if necessary.

Philip sighed. "Somehow George Cook gained access to our facility and was stealing military secrets." He turned to Michael. "And apparently he'd been targeting you because of his hatred for me."

Michael nodded his head and said, "So that's what's been happening."

"Dear, perhaps you shouldn't talk about these things out here in the open. There are many ears."

Phillip felt his pulse accelerate. With the drugs in his system, he seemed incapable of restraining himself. "Then help me, because it just seems like the words are going to tumble out whether I want them to or not. So divert my attention somehow." He managed to smile. "It shouldn't be too hard to do, as daft as I'm acting."

"Well, perhaps you'd like to hear about Michael's exploits. It seems that he's found his way into the London *Times*."

Philip turned and looked at his son. "And what great thing have you done to gain such distinction?"

"Mother—I wish you wouldn't do that. It's embarrassing." Turning to Philip he said, "She's been telling everyone and even has the neighbors clipping the article. It's humiliating."

"You can ignore your own son's accomplishments when you're a father, Michael, but I plan to relish yours." Claire's smug look made Philip laugh—something that he instantly wished he hadn't done as he gasped in pain and tried to decide which hurt worse— the muscles stretching against the torn flesh under the skin or the bandage pulling on the skin itself.

"Now see what you've done, Mother. You've hurt him with your attempt at wit. You've injured both of us."

Claire simply turned her head away from Michael with an imperious look.

"Well," Philip said, "what did happen?"

"We were protecting a transport ship, and the *960* saw some action that took out two S-boats. Lieutenant Commander Prescott was responsible for most of the action."

Claire looked at him expectantly, but when she figured out that he didn't plan to say anything more, she huffed and said, "That's hardly a fair description of the matter, Michael, and you know it!" And with that, she proceeded to tell Philip everything that had been declassified for the newspaper. Then, leaning down very closely to his ear, she said, "What they couldn't say in the paper is that the transport he was protecting was filled with more than 1000 American boys who would surely have been killed had Michael not rammed his boat into one of the German S-boats. He's quite a hero in the Navy from what everyone tells me."

Michael shook his head in disgust. "What you don't understand, Mother, is that every time you brag about me, I get teased back at the barracks. It's humiliating."

"Well, I'll try to restrain myself, then, but you can't fault me for being glad that you're alive in spite of all that."

"You can fault me for putting him at risk," Philip said quietly.

"You keep saying that, Philip, but it wasn't you who betrayed him."

"No, but it was part of my responsibility to oversee security, and somehow Cook got past us. It's a major breach." Philip sounded miserable, and everyone in the family wished they could comfort him, but they didn't know what to say.

The doctor did, however, and he ordered them all out so that Philip could get some rest. When Michael leaned down to give him a hug, Philip said quietly, "I'm with your mother on this one, Michael. I'm a very proud father. Well done!"

"Thanks, Father—just don't go blabbing about it to everyone."

Philip smiled and squeezed his hand.

After Grace and Claire kissed him good-bye, Philip's little family promised to return whenever the doctor allowed them.

Once they were gone, the doctor said, "Now you need rest, Lord Carlyle. You've suffered a life-threatening trauma."

He was about to leave when Philip motioned him over. "Doctor, I will rest, I promise. But it is a matter of great urgency to the state that I speak with my associate, Jon Randall. I simply won't be able to rest until I talk with him, so would you make an exception and try to find him?"

"I'm not inclined to make an exception, but it's easy enough to find him. He's been waiting outside since morning."

Of course, Philip thought.

"I'll let him in, but you have to promise me that you won't talk any longer than is absolutely necessary."

"I promise, doctor. Thank you."

The doctor left, closing the door firmly behind him, and then it opened a few moments later as the bright face of Jon Randall peeked round the corner.

"I'm so glad to see you've rejoined us, Lord Carlyle."

"Jon, you have to tell me what happened after Lord Cook stabbed me. Did you apprehend him?"

"We did. Miss Hawkes had been worried about you when you failed to come back to your office, so she went back toward the map room to find you. As she was rounding a corner, she heard a door slam and then saw the figure of what proved to be Cook scurrying down the corridor. She knew something was wrong, which is when she burst in on you. Fortunately, you told her to stop Cook, and she shrieked down the corridor after him. I heard the ruckus and had the presence of mind to shut the automatic doors. After that, it was just a matter of time until security found him."

"Where is he now?"

"We have him locked up at Whitehall, strangely enough. The prime minister decided it was too great a security risk to put him in a prison, where he might talk to others. The secret of the war rooms has to be kept."

Philip groaned. "I've been so stupid—imagine someone breaking into the cabinet war rooms themselves. The prime minister has undoubtedly decided to sack me."

Randall replied reassuringly, "Quite the contrary. He's been telling people how remarkable it is that even after being stabbed, you were able to apprehend your man."

Philip didn't smile. "That's kind of him, but the fact is that I failed. Do you have any idea how this could have happened?"

Randall cleared his throat and then paused for a very long time—long enough that Philip turned to face him directly. "What is it, Jon?"

"It was me, sir. I'm the one that caused the breakdown. The reason that the prime minister isn't angry at you is because it was my fault."

"What do you mean? I don't understand."

"I saw you talking with Cook in the corridor one day and assumed that it was official business. Later, when you weren't there, he asked for me specifically and presented a very authentic looking set of papers with your signature, so I cleared him for entrance and told the guards to grant him access. It was well beyond the scope of my authority, but it seemed fine in view of your signature along with the appropriate civil service clearances."

Philip was horrified. "But Jon, we have a standing order that the chief of security is to review all credentials, no matter whose signature appears on the papers. The staff contacts each signatory directly to make certain the credentials are valid. How could you have overlooked that?"

Jon shifted very uncomfortably on his feet. Before he could respond, Philip said, "Has this happened with anyone else?"

"No! Absolutely not!" Jon spoke with more force than was needed, but it was obvious that he wanted to limit his humiliation as much as possible. "It was just that he said he'd already cleared it with you and he needed entrance that night. And I had seen you talking with him."

Philip could see that Jon was miserable.

"Oh, Jon. This is a serious breach." His voice trailed off. "But somehow we'll get through it. George is a crafty one, knowing who to attract with honey and who to boil in oil."

"I'm very sorry, sir. I'm fully prepared to resign over it."

"I hope it doesn't come to that. I'll do my best to protect you. Of course, we'll have to conduct a formal investigation to make certain we build an even more rigid structure around this process. Hopefully, they'll take mercy on us."

"I've already told everyone in the chain of command what I just told you, including the prime minister. I'm sure that's why they're not holding you responsible."

Philip took this heavily. He'd come to think of Jon almost as a son—one who was disabled in a military action that cost him his left arm and severe disfigurement to his face. The last thing he wanted was for this good young man to suffer any more trauma.

There was no use pursuing the topic at the present, so Philip changed the subject. "Well, at least the thief has been apprehended. I'm not sure how they'll convene a court to try him. We can't really admit to having someone breaking into a top-secret facility, as it wouldn't be secret anymore, and the press would have us all hanging from the yardarms for such a breach."

"I think his trial has already been held, sir. He's to be hanged at dawn as a traitor. They're actually taking a detail from our group to do it, rather than risk having him blurt something out in front of those who don't have clearance."

Philip struggled to absorb this new turn of events. "Already tried, but how?" Then he realized it didn't matter. Cook was a very dangerous man, and he was guilty. They would probably never know how many people had lost their lives to his treachery. "Ah, George," he said wistfully as he envisioned Cook's face. "Zealotry and hate claim another victim, and Satan rejoices."

Jon had stood by silently as Philip thought. "So you did know him then, sir?"

Philip turned and looked at Jon. There was an innocence about him that made him the perfect target for a man like Cook. As one who had never contemplated doing evil himself, it must have been impossible for Jon to suspect what had been in the other man's mind.

"Yes, I knew him. We grew up together."

"But why would he betray us? Why would he turn on his own country?"

"George was always a jealous and bitter fellow, blaming others for his mistakes, making excuses for his failures, and treating with contempt those who were not in his social circle. I should have picked up on his intent the day he came in. What you didn't understand when you saw me talking to him in the corridor is that we were not having a business conversation at all—I had denied him entrance. It was his sympathy toward the nationalist, unified Third Reich that drew George to Hitler in the first place. Only after he stabbed me did I come to understand that. Only when I saw him gloating over Germany unifying Europe." Philip paused and furrowed his brow as he relived the moments in the map room with Cook. "I'm sorry that I couldn't have helped him."

"You're not angry at him?!"

Philip shook his head. "I'll probably find enough energy to be angry someday. But right now I'm just sorry for him—sorry that he brought his life to such an ignominious end. It's a tragedy and one I take no satisfaction in."

"If only I'd have known you two were arguing that day . . ."

Philip was getting very tired. He was relieved that Cook's damage had been contained, and he felt drained thinking about Cook's fate. His eyelids fluttered and finally shut.

Chapter Thirty

PANZER ATTACK

North Africa— Late October 1942

In the nearly three months that had passed since his ill-fated adventure with the payroll, Dominic had completed at least a dozen other long-distance missions and countless short runs, all without being overwhelmed by the panic that had left him power-less at the oasis. He flattered himself that it had just been a momentary lapse of courage and that it would have been foolish to try to help the British pilot anyway. While it still sat uneasily on his conscience, he'd made a kind of peace with it, and each successful mission tended to build his confidence and salve over the raw feelings.

Perhaps that's why when he was asked to carry a top-secret dispatch nearly a fifth the length of Egypt, he was pleased to accept. It was a rather prestigious assignment, since it would require a brief meeting with General Montgomery himself— "Monty," as the troops called him. Dominic had also come to look forward to the long trips by himself with no one to report to or interact with. Solitude was definitely his friend, even in this hostile terrain, and the thought of nearly a week away from his problems was enticing.

"I know it's late," Captain Riggins said. "But if you leave now, you can probably get in sixty or seventy kilometers before it's too dark to travel. You can sleep with one of the infantry units posted along the way, as we'll send a coded wireless transmission so they'll expect you. We'd send all of this by wireless, but it's got maps and other valuable information that are too complex to transmit. You'll be traveling behind our lines most of the way, but certainly you know the hazards of an airplane or other unexpected threat, so be on guard. We've loaded the pack with an explosive charge in case you need to destroy it in a hurry. Any questions?"

"No, sir!" Dominic replied crisply.

"Good. We're fitting a couple of extra fuel tanks, plus an emergency rations kit, as well as a small transmitter you can use to send a basic Morse-code message if you get in trouble and need backup. The codes for that are in the bag as well."

"Thank you, sir. I should be fine." Dominic was now anxious to get on his way, having learned by now that the best way to tackle an anxious moment was to simply plow forward.

"Oh, one more thing, Carlyle. Be sure to send us your position by wireless whenever you stop along the way with a British unit." Riggins passed him yet another piece of paper with instructions and codes on how to do that.

"Is that all then, sir?" Dominic asked, getting fidgety and annoyed with being delayed.

"That's all—good luck, Carlyle," Riggins said, dismissing Dominic.

With that done, Dominic made his way over to the mechanical shop, where he noticed his motorcycle being topped off with petrol and loaded with supplies.

"You might want to be careful, Mr. Carlyle," the chief mechanic said. "The weatherman tells us that a storm may be brewing."

"It's okay. I've got a rain slicker, and it would actually feel good to get some cool air." Even in October the temperatures were still stifling.

"I don't think you understand, sir. A desert storm is unlike anything you'll experience anywhere in the world. Sandstorms have winds that can throw you right off your motorcycle. If you get any inkling that a storm's brewing, try to find shelter as quickly as possible."

"Thanks, chief. I'll keep that in mind."

* * *

The meeting with General Montgomery had gone even better than Dominic had hoped. After three days of rather aggravating travel, including a fierce dust devil that seemed to search him out specifically and knock him off his motorcycle, he'd reached Army HQ looking rather like a ghost, with fine white sand dust that covered him from head to toe. When he took his goggles off, the flesh-colored rim around his eyes made him look like some kind of alien creature descended from the stars to deliver a message to the planet.

As ordered, he'd gone straight to the general's tent. The satchel had been secured to his person by a locked chain that only Montgomery's staff had a key to. The original key was safely back at Dominic's camp.

Montgomery laughed when he saw him, and on finding out that he was a Carlyle, he invited him to join the general's staff for dinner after he had a chance to clean up. Once it was known that he was slated for dinner, the heavens were opened, and before he knew it, he had that rarest of desert luxuries afforded him—a nice lukewarm shower and a cot to rest on while his clothes were laundered. When he presented himself at 2000 that evening, Montgomery's preferred time for dining, Dominic felt as if he'd stepped into a gentleman's club ready for an evening of dinner and theater. He loved it.

At first he was a bit worried about the conversation, but after a few brief anecdotes about his passage across the desert, including the dust devil, he quickly figured out that all you had to do to sound brilliant in Montgomery's company was to listen and occasionally nod. The general did the rest. He was every bit as vain as it was rumored, but he also had some tremendous stories to tell, and in no time at all, he'd completely won Dominic over. Dominic later remarked to one of the orderlies that with Montgomery in charge, it was impossible for Britain to lose North Africa, to which the orderly, a man in his sixties, had silently nodded. Dominic had the distinct feeling that he'd heard that before—probably from Montgomery himself.

Even though they'd spent little more than an hour together, Dominic had a new objective—to find a place on Montgomery's staff. While the general often took risks that went far beyond what was safe, his staff was always tucked safely behind the front, keeping track of the thousands of details that were necessary to guide an Army into battle. Dominic could certainly manage that sort of thing.

I'll send a letter off to Father asking him to help. With his connections with the prime minister and Lord Ismay, it ought to be a cinch for him to secure an appointment. Dominic was ecstatic at the thought of it.

He spent the night at headquarters, had a marvelous breakfast, and then started back for his own post. As he thought about his dingy quarters and the grimy men who maintained his motorcycle, it now seemed quite beneath him, and he quickly fell into a mild depression at the thought of going back.

It was in that vein of thought that Dominic completely failed to see the onset of a horrible sandstorm. Although he was close to a British airbase, where Quonset huts protected the men from the ravages of sandstorms, he was too late to make for it.

He hadn't noticed the storm until it tore the bandana right off his neck and sent it whirling into oblivion. After bringing the motorcycle to an abrupt stop, he turned and looked in the direction of the storm. The sight that greeted him made his blood run chill—a dark bank of clouds and sand as high as the eye could see was rolling across the desert. He could measure the progress of the front by watching the telephone poles he'd been following disappear one by one—some snapped off and torn into thousands of splinters that were driven through the air as lethal projectiles that could tear the flesh off an animal or person who happened to be in their way, others simply disappearing into the impenetrable cloud of sand that was rapidly moving toward him.

Dominic panicked as the seriousness of the situation dawned on him. He had approximately ninety seconds to decide what to do before the storm hit him. At first he thought he'd hunker down behind his motorcycle, but when he saw the remnants of an Army jeep flying through the air at the front of the storm, he quickly abandoned that idea. He knew he'd be buried alive if he stayed. Scrambling up and down the packed roadway, he spied an abandoned tank about twenty yards ahead. Desperately, he started running for it. With his slight body frame, it was tough to stay on his feet, even though the main front hadn't yet hit. Fortunately, he still had his goggles on, so his eyes were protected, but it was getting more and more difficult to breathe as the sand around him was torn up into eddies and swirls of dust that left him choking and gasping for air. Reaching the tank, Dominic quickly scrambled up on top and found the hatch was closed.

"NO!" he shouted into the fury of the storm. Finding it difficult to hold onto the hatch, Dominic felt his feet slip out from under him. He was being held in place by the ring of the hatch, his feet and legs flying horizontally in the wind behind him. Luckily, the wind changed direction briefly, and he was able to reel himself in and turn the cumbersome latch. The wind caught the top of the hatch, almost tearing it from its steel hinges, but it gave Dominic enough time to scramble headfirst into the tank. It was totally dark inside, and he hated the thought of cutting himself off from the outside world, but the sand was already pouring in, so he climbed up and pulled the hatch closed. Twisting the ring, he felt the threads grab, although there was enough sand in the mechanism that he couldn't get a complete seal.

For the next two hours he crouched inside the darkened interior of the tank, where the remnants of diesel fuel gave him a headache. The air was stale and sweltering, and soon he was bathed in sweat. His escape had been so sudden that he'd neglected to bring his canteen, and soon he was frantically thirsty. After nearly three hours, he decided to feel around the tank once more for anything that might provide him something to drink, and as he crawled around on all fours, he eventually felt a canteen under a seat in the back corner. Greedily tearing the lid off, he found that there was some very stale hot water, but even though it was old, it tasted so good to his parched throat that he drank great gulps until he'd consumed nearly half the contents of the canteen. He took another couple of gulps before finally pulling it away from his face and securing the lid for later use.

The groaning sounds of the storm outside were wraithlike to Dominic—like a banshee's call. He remembered crossing an old bridge with his brother during a storm when they were younger. The water was running high and fast, and the bridge shuddered as a branch or other piece of debris hit it, making the same kind of sound that he heard now. He'd been terrified then, even more so after the storm when they went back and found that the bridge had been swept off its footings by the flood and lay in a pile of wreckage downstream. Now in this awful storm he felt that same terror, only amplified by Michael's not being there to reassure him.

In exhaustion, he finally curled up in one of the corners, closed his eyes, and covered his ears. Although it didn't seem possible, he eventually fell asleep.

* * *

No—leave me alone! Dominic jerked awake. He'd been dreaming that he was trapped in a suffocating oven that was being stoked by demons. Their laughter was terrifying, and the flames were getting closer and closer, which is what finally woke him.

As he gathered his wits and figured out where he was, it dawned on him that he really was trapped in a suffocating oven. The only difference was that there were no flames in this oven— just darkness. At first he started flailing about in the darkness, desperate to get fresh air and feeling as if he were trapped in a coffin.

After calming himself, Dominic realized that it was quiet outside. The storm was over. Slowly, he rose to his feet and crawled to the hatch. He twisted the ring and found it very difficult to turn. He started to panic again, but he managed to get a grip on his feelings and crawl back down and pick up a pipe he'd discovered earlier. He used it as a lever, and slowly the handle creaked its way open. He pushed on the hatch and was rewarded with a cascade of sand in his face that left him sputtering and temporarily blind. Shaking his head, he did his best to clear his eyes, but there was hardly enough moisture to work up a tear. Eventually, he turned his head down and pushed on the hatch again, but it refused to open.

He imagined himself buried alive, with twenty feet of sand on top of the tank. He frantically pawed at the hatch and shouted at the top of his lungs for help.

Finally, he pushed the pipe out through the crack of the slightly open hatch, and pushing it to its full length, he was rewarded by a small shaft of light coming through the pipe and shining on the floor of the tank. It also had the effect of creating an immediate draft as the hot air in the tank was sucked up and out.

He did a little dance in the darkness and decided that his morbid thoughts hadn't been legitimate after all. He was glad to be alive. The only question was how to get out of the tank. He could hardly get the hatch to budge, let alone open it enough to pass through. And if he did get it open, the sand would come cascading in.

The image of the sand coursing in caused him to burst out laughing. He remembered an old story where a mule had fallen into a well and couldn't get out. Thinking he would die in there, the mule started pawing at the side of the well only to have dirt fall in. At first he feared that he'd be buried, but in time the mule figured out that he just needed to keep bringing enough dirt in and patting it down with his hooves until he could fill the well and get out. So that's what the mule did, and he'd eventually escaped.

Even though he'd never been so terrified in his life, Dominic got a grip on himself and used the pipe to pry the hatch ever wider as more and more sand poured in around his feet. Eventually he was able to reach out and pull some of the sand in with his hands, which in turn gave him more room to force the hatch open, and after several minutes he had it nearly vertical. At that point a huge final inrush of what must have equaled a small sand dune poured in, and then he was able to scramble up and out of the tank with his canteen.

It was twilight when he crawled out on top of the drift that covered his sanctuary. A number of stars were starting to shine in the evening sky. It was beautiful—the indigo sky punctuated with pinpoints of light representing hundreds of thousands of stars.

After perhaps half an hour of just lying in the sand and breathing in the fresh air, Dominic finally decided he ought to start figuring out what to do. Taking a quick inventory, he discovered that he had perhaps a quart of water, no food, a compass, a flashlight, and nothing to communicate with. *A Signals man with no way to communicate!* He laughed.

Eventually he decided that the best course of action was to sleep again and to get his bearings in the morning. He could make out the general outlines of the tank in the sand below him, and he was able to retrace in his mind the course that the road had followed past the tank before the sand had wiped out all traces of where he'd been. With his compass he could pretty well find the direction he'd need to travel to get back to the British base he'd gone past while lost in thought. He settled back in the sand for the night.

* * *

The next morning found a very disgruntled young corporal trudging through the sand, frequently checking his compass and making small calculations in the sand. The sun scorched him with every step. He took some consolation in how bad people would feel when they found his lifeless body. He thought about how Michael would feel. How his father would feel.

After a couple of hours of walking and after becoming more and more certain that he was off course, he finally saw what appeared to be movement in the distance. He first thought it was a mirage. But in time he became quite convinced that he was indeed seeing some kind of human activity—probably a small convoy or something.

Waving his arms would do no good—he was too small against the horizon. Shouting would have even less effect, particularly since he was so hoarse at this point that he could hardly hear himself speak. He thought about his flashlight, but of course that was foolish as well since it was the middle of the day.

Pulling out the flashlight anyway, he was startled when the sun glinted brightly off the polished reflector behind the light bulb, hurting his eye as it did. Quickly unscrewing the cap, he pulled the reflector out and started aiming into the sun at the proper angle to catch the attention of the little convoy. A flashing mirror in the middle of the desert couldn't be mistaken for a mirage, so there was at least a slight hope that he would be seen.

Unfortunately, the convoy kept moving until it was almost out of the angle where he could flash a signal. He repeatedly sent an SOS signal with the mirror. Just when he was about to give up, thinking that he'd have to try to walk over to the line they were traveling on, he saw the lead vehicle suddenly turn and head in his direction. Jumping up, he continued to flash at the group until he saw a mirror flashing in return. To his great surprise, it was flashing a Morse signal as well. "On our way!"

"I've been saved!" he shouted.

* * *

By the time the Jeeps arrived at the spot where Dominic was, they found him mostly incoherent and dehydrated. When they offered him water, he grabbed for the canteen so greedily that they had to restrain him. Too much water too quickly could make him violently ill at that point, so they forced him to take small sips even though he pleaded for more. When they arrived at their base, a message was sent ahead, indicating that he'd been found and was in need of transport. His motorcycle had been buried in the storm. Eventually word was given that he should join a small troop convoy that was being sent from HQ to his forward position at the front. By the time he arrived three days later, he looked little worse for the wear, although Riggins noticed that he was even more jumpy than usual. Unlike his previous escapes, he didn't talk much about this one except to answer direct questions.

Riggins decided that the best antidote to whatever was bothering Carlyle was to keep him active, so at the earliest opportunity, he gave Dominic his next assignment. Dominic and two other riders were to carry identical sets of papers to a position off to the right flank of the Germans' main position. The reason for three sets was the high probability of at least one of the riders not making it through alive. The self-detonating satchels assured that if one was separated from the rider by any means, the satchel would explode, destroying the papers. The satchel itself was attached by a cable to the rider that could only be unlocked by the field commander it was assigned to using a specially designed key.

After reviewing the various message routes, Captain Riggins asked if there were any questions. Dominic raised his hand.

"Yes, Corporal Carlyle?"

"Could I see you a moment afterward, sir?"

"You can ask me anything right here," Riggins said not unkindly, but he was also no-nonsense.

"It's private, sir."

Riggins got a suspicious look on his face, but he agreed. "Well then, dismissed. You all leave in an hour. We're sending a small infantry group out with you to the point where your routes diverge. From that spot on, you'll be safer on your own since you'll be harder to spot. Good luck!"

When the other riders had left the room, Captain Riggins turned to Dominic. "What is it, Carlyle?"

"Well, sir," the words caught in Dominic's throat, "It's just that it was quite—"

"It's just that what was quite?" Riggins asked. "I don't have time for chitchat."

"It's just that it was quite distressing out there in the sand-storm," Dominic said defiantly. "I'm just not sure I'm ready to go out again."

Riggins shook his head in disgust. "Are you telling me that you're afraid to accept this assignment?"

Dominic looked down at his feet. "Not afraid, sir, just not quite ready. I'm not really sure I can do it—at least not yet."

"Look at me, Carlyle." Reluctantly Dominic looked up. "This is all a bunch of rubbish. I know that you had a hard time of it out there. But with the time spent at the other camp waiting for a lift, the time in transit, and the idle time here, it's been more than a week. And in spite of everything you've been through, you've been given time to recuperate. So it's time to get back out there and do your job."

"But—"

"But nothing," said Riggins, irritated that the young man wouldn't look at him. "Listen, Carlyle, you've had some very bad luck since you've been here, except that I'm not entirely certain it's all attributable to luck. I think you tend to let your attention wander, and so you find yourself in trouble. If you'd learn to concentrate, you'd do much better. As to this unwillingness to serve because you think you've suffered too much, all I can tell you is that you've faced nothing compared with what those poor blokes in the infantry or in the tank corps have, or even compared to some of our other riders. Your request is denied. Do I make myself clear?"

Dominic shook his head but gave a crisp, "Yes, sir!"

"Then you're dismissed, corporal. Now go get ready for your assignment."

Dominic turned on his heel and exited the tent. Riggins shook his head in disgust—but not unmitigated by a sense of distress. Riggins was a good man—a public school headmaster in his professional life—so he hated to be hard on a young man like this, even when it was for his own good. He cursed the war for putting them in this spot and then turned to the hundred other concerns that clamored for his attention.

* * *

As the couriers and infantry approached the junction where they would take time for lunch and then split up to go their separate ways, Dominic started feeling nauseated. It was something like how he felt when he had to play rugby in high school. He had been scared of being hurt. But this feeling was a hundred times worse. It hadn't been so bad up to this point because they'd been riding together as a group and had enjoyed the additional protection of an armored car full of heavily armed soldiers. But in just a few minutes, he'd be expected to strike out on his own, and then he'd have at least another three to four hours without any protection whatsoever. The armored car carried excess petrol for them to refuel before breaking out on their own, so there was no way to plead out of the assignment for lack of petrol. He tried to think of other reasons—like why it wasn't fair that this assignment had been given to him instead of one of the other men, but he thought of each of them in turn and had to acknowledge that most had seen at least as much action as he had.

They pulled off to an intersection in the road. At the cross-roads, there were three routes to the southeast that the riders would go on, another to the northwest that led to some obscure Arab village that was hardly big enough to even note on their maps, and the road behind them that led back to their main posting.

Dismounting from their motorcycles, Dominic and the others did a quick check of the bikes to make sure they hadn't developed any mechanical difficulties. Dominic was disappointed to find that his new Triumph was doing just fine. In fact, it had been quite pleasant to ride, and he might have enjoyed it had the circumstances been different.

Six soldiers dismounted from their truck and broke out a wooden case that contained a lunch of canned meats, relatively fresh bread, and tins of jelly. They used the tailgate of the armored car as a table, and soon the riders were all happily eating their last meal before they switched to the infamous canned rations that they'd have to rely on until getting back to the rendezvous point. There was cheerful banter, and the group got Dominic to laugh a time or two with some of their jokes. But the reality of the trip before him was ever present in his mind.

Too soon the lunch was ended, and the soldiers started cleaning things up while the riders strapped the extra petrol tanks onto the wire baskets mounted on either side of their bikes' rear tires. Dominic looked up to confirm his direction of travel just in time to see the armored car explode in a sheet of yellow flame. He let out a scream along with the others, then went into shock when he looked down and saw himself splattered in the blood of one of the soldiers who had been eating with him just a few moments earlier. A second explosion hit off to his left side, and he instinctively dove to the ground. As he was going down, he looked up ahead to see two German tanks off in the distance. A bright flash at the muzzle indicated that another round had been fired, and before he could even start a mental count, a third shell plunged into the camp, hitting one of the other motorcycles. The rider had just finished strapping his petrol on it, which magnified the force of the explosion. Dominic watched in horror as the motorcycle was torn into flying shrapnel that sliced through the rider, even as he was trying to run for cover.

A fourth, fifth, and sixth shell soon leveled the camp, and Dominic was left covering his head with his hands while crying in fear. His fear became worse when he felt the ground tremble as the huge panzers came rumbling up to check out their handiwork. The monsters ground to a halt just twenty feet short of where Dominic lay prostrate on the ground. He heard the clank of the hatches as they swung open and managed to raise his right eye just enough to see a German tentatively poke his head up and over the side. When no one fired on him, the soldier stood up a bit further. Surveying the flaming wreckage of the British armored car and the dead bodies lying around, he actually started laughing and called down to his comrades in German. Dominic couldn't understand what they were saying, but he was pretty confident they were glorying in what they had done.

Next, a couple of them came out and stood on the deck of their tank with machine guns. Dominic did his best not to flinch when they started firing at everything in the camp. The bullets plinked into the sand next to him, and he grimaced in pain as one struck his leg. By now tears were running down his cheeks, but he knew he had to play dead or he really would be. The Germans were about to get off the tank when there was a shout from inside. The men hesitated, obviously disappointed that they wouldn't be able to collect any booty from the dead bodies, but they obeyed whatever order had been given, and with what sounded like cursing, the two quickly climbed back down and slammed the hatch closed. There was a great puff of smoke as the tank engines fired to life, and in less than twenty seconds the tanks seemed to pivot around without any forward movement and then started to move away with incredible speed for vehicles of their size and weight.

Dominic didn't dare move for about two or three minutes. He was afraid of the tanks coming back and even more afraid of what he'd find when he got up. He finally realized he couldn't lie there any longer, so he picked himself up. He felt his leg and found that he'd only been grazed, but it hurt tremendously. There wasn't enough bleeding to worry about, so he started to move over toward his motorcycle, where he was relieved to see that at least it hadn't received a direct hit. On closer inspection it appeared that it was totally undamaged, even though it was lying on its side, knocked over by the concussion of the blasts.

Dominic leaned down to pick it up when he suddenly fell back in horror at the sight of a body lying just a few feet away. That's when he started sobbing uncontrollably. Without consciously thinking about it, he pulled the motorcycle to its upright position and quickly mounted it. He looked at the map to figure out which way he should go.

As he kicked the starter, he was alarmed to hear what sounded like a human voice very quietly saying, "Help me." It was very weak and probably represented the last breaths of a dying man.

His heart started racing. *I can't—I can't help you! I've got to get out of here!* And with that, he pulled back on the accelerator and started toward his assigned course of travel. Even though that's where he intended to go, he suddenly felt himself turning his motorcycle to the northwest—not toward the battlefield, but directly away from it. *Don't do this, Dominic!—You mustn't do this!* But he seemed powerless to stop himself. *I tried to tell them. I tried . . .* The tears on his cheeks poured down as his feelings of self-contempt grew with the heat of the sun.

Chapter Thirty-One

ABSENT WITHOUT LEAVE

North Africa—November 1942

"Tell me again where you found him."

"We found him in El Adere, sir. He attempted to hide, but we had the cooperation of the locals, who told us a British soldier had been staying there for the previous three days."

"I was hiding, sir. But I was trying to find my papers so I could provide proper identification when I reported."

"Quiet, corporal. You'll have your chance in a moment."

"And what did he say was his reason for being there?"

"He said he was lost—that he got disoriented after being fired on by German panzers."

"Well, the part about the Germans is true. The whole group had been reported killed." Captain Riggins sighed. "All right, sergeant, thank you for your report. Dismissed."

The sergeant and the two privates who had accompanied him looked at Dominic with contempt as they exited the tent.

"Well, Mr. Carlyle, what am I to do with you?"

Dominic had the good sense not to reply.

"You're the lone survivor of the group, you turn up missing in action for three days, and then they find you at an African village apparently unharmed. Now you're here expecting me to believe that you got 'disoriented.'"

"But I did, sir. The attack happened at noon, my compass was destroyed, and the sun gave no direction. The road led in three directions, and I chose the one I thought most likely to get me through. No one else had survived, so I felt I had to go forward. It was hours later that I found myself at the village. At that point my motorcycle had a damaged piston ring, and I was losing so much oil that I couldn't go any further. So I decided to wait for the next British group to come through. I don't know what other course I could have followed."

Riggins reflected on this. "And how is it that the Germans didn't come down and attempt to take our despatches?"

"I don't know why they didn't, sir. They got out on their tank and fired machine-gun bursts. That's how I got wounded. But just as they were about to dismount, they were ordered back inside and took off lickety-split. I couldn't account for it at the time, and I can't now. I just know it saved my life."

This part of the story sounds authentic, Riggins thought. He wanted to hear more. While there was nothing to contradict Carlyle's story, all Riggins's senses told him that Dominic wasn't telling the truth—or at least not all of it. The oil ring looked suspicious, as if it might have been tampered with, but there was no proof.

"Well, Carlyle, in the absence of any other information, I have no choice but to believe you. Of course, this proves that you have both the worst luck and the best luck of anyone I've ever met." He didn't intend it as a joke. Shaking his head, he finally said, "You can go get some dinner."

"Thank you, sir."

Riggins tried to detect any sign of guile in his voice, but it was flat and unemotional.

It was time for Riggins to go to supper as well, but he found he'd lost his appetite. Perhaps it was the letters he'd just finished writing to the parents of the two young riders who'd been killed in the attack.

* * *

"May I ask why I've been summoned back, sir?"

Dominic had stood at attention in Riggins's tent for at least two minutes while the captain had conferred with a medical corpsman.

"You'll speak when spoken to, corporal, and not before!"

Dominic burned furiously but refrained from saying anything.

Finally, after what seemed an eternity, Riggins looked up. "Do you recognize this man, corporal?"

"No, sir. I don't believe I've ever seen him."

"He's a medical corpsman who was called on to treat the survivors of the attack on your company."

"Survivors?" Dominic said in alarm. "There were no survivors. At least no one responded when I checked on them." His mind raced. "I went around and made certain."

"Quiet, Mr. Carlyle. You dishonor the dead with this prattle. The corpsman treated one of the other Signals riders, Corporal Williams. Before he died a rather horrid death, he managed to give his account of the attack. Everything matches what you told us up to a point—the point at which he called out for help, and you turned and looked directly at him and then drove off."

"Sir, it wasn't like that at all."

"I told you to be quiet!" The fury in Riggins's voice was barely suppressed.

"And then you took off in the correct direction to reach the front, deliberately paused, and then turned and headed to the north."

"Sir, the man was mistaken."

"Corpsman, was Corporal Williams mistaken?"

"He was in deep distress when I treated him, but he was very clear in every detail. I do not believe he invented this story. He even indicated that Corporal Carlyle looked at his compass before changing direction."

"But, sir . . ."

"Thank you, corpsman—I'll take it from here."

Dominic was so frightened, he felt as if he were about to lose bladder control. Riggins looked down and studied some papers.

Finally Captain Riggins looked up, his face pale. "Corporal Carlyle, I have no choice but to bring you up on charges of desertion under fire, with enhancements for abandoning a comrade in distress."

Dominic felt his legs buckle under him, but Riggins made no move to support him.

"But I can explain," he said weakly.

"You'll have the chance to explain yourself to a court-martial. Until then you will be transferred to our permanent base. They have a secure prison there where you'll be held until legal counsel can be appointed to provide representation and until enough officers can be cleared to spend the time to hear your case."

"But they shoot deserters, don't they?"

Riggins dropped his gaze. "If they're found guilty."

Dominic expected that his heart would start racing and he'd hyperventilate, but instead he just felt weak all over. He could feel the blood draining from his head, and he worried that he'd pass out. "I'm sorry that it's come to this," Dominic almost whispered.

Riggins looked up at him with an ashen face. "At last we've found something we can agree on, corporal." He took a couple of deep breaths to steady himself. "The corpsman tells me that Williams would have died no matter whether you had tried to help him or not. So his death's not the point entirely. But the battle went badly for our boys, in part because they didn't have the maps they needed to succeed. That's the price of failure—men who might have lived but who are now dead or wounded. That's the price of your failure." Riggins should have dismissed him, but he didn't seem to have the strength. "That's the price of my failure . . ."

* * *

London—November 1942

"Philip, may I speak to you for a moment?" Philip looked up at the sound of Ismay's voice. At first he was going to answer cheerfully, but when he saw the look on the lord's face he knew better.

"Of course, sir, what is it?"

"I'm afraid I have some bad news, Carlyle. Some very, very bad news."

* * *

Carlyle Manor—November 1942

"But this can't be true, Philip. There must be some mistake," Claire pleaded.

Philip scooted closer to his wife on the sofa and put his arms around her. Claire was trembling.

"Perhaps there is a mistake, but the only way it will be resolved is in a court-martial."

"But Philip, what will they do if they find him guilty?"

Philip was very quiet. He suspected Claire knew the answer. But maybe not, because she asked him again.

"It all depends on any mitigating circumstances, but desertion is punishable by death."

"Oh—" Claire exclaimed, and she started weeping. When she gained some control, she said, "We've got to go to him. We've got to go, Philip. How do we get there?"

"I've already made arrangements to fly there by military transport. Ismay himself made the arrangements. But you can't go—not in time of war. I can go by virtue of my appointment to the cabinet."

"But I've got to go, Philip. He needs me now more than ever."

Philip felt himself trembling, and he wiped away the solitary tear that had started down his cheek.

"I know he needs you, but I'm afraid I'm all he's got." Philip felt as if he were going to pass out. He had cried in the back of the automobile on the way home, but now he was too weak to show emotion. All he could feel was an overwhelming sense of dread, like a cold vise pressing on his chest, leaving him breathless and trembling. "I don't know what I'll do there, but at least I can be with him."

"But you're still not fully recovered from your injuries. You shouldn't have even gone to work today. If you hadn't gone to work—"

"If I hadn't gone to work this would still be happening, except that we'd have learned it from a telegram instead of from Ismay. It was kindness on his part to tell me personally."

"But your wound . . ."

"I'll be careful." The lump in Philip's throat made it very difficult to speak. "Besides, what else can we do? I can't leave him down there on his own."

"Oh, Philip. Be kind. Whatever has happened, please be kind. He must be terrified."

"I will, Claire. I will. It's all I have left to give him." Philip's stomach hurt so badly he felt as if he must throw up to find relief. But he couldn't just now.

* * *

North Africa—November 1942

Dominic's eyes grew wide when he looked up and saw his father. "What are you doing here?" he asked indignantly.

Philip thought perhaps he should use some cavalier remark like, "I was just in the neighborhood," but he quickly decided against it.

"I came to be with you. May I come in?"

"You can come in, but I can't follow you out," Dominic replied darkly.

Philip waited for the guard to open the door. The prison was an old African jail, and the sound of the ancient key turning in the rusted metal lock was loud enough to startle Philip, though Dominic didn't even look up. The iron door swung noisily on its hinges, and Philip slipped inside. Philip was disturbed by the sound of the door being closed and locked behind him. It was unnerving to be in a room that he couldn't leave except with the permission of another person. He had a brief moment of claustrophobia, but he forced himself to walk over and sit down next to Dominic. When he scooted close, Dominic didn't reciprocate, but, significantly, he didn't withdraw either.

For a moment, Philip was tempted to speak first—the silence in the place was overpowering since Dominic was the only prisoner in this section of the jail—but instead, he sat there quietly. Time passed. Philip had no idea how long. The nervousness he felt at first eased, and eventually it seemed quite natural that he was sitting there next to his son.

After perhaps three or four very long minutes, Dominic broke the silence. "Well, aren't you going to say anything? Did you come all the way to Africa to just sit here?" His voice sounded tired and drawn.

Why did I come? Philip thought.

"I came because I love you."

Dominic shook his head slightly from side to side. "Not a lot to love, is there?"

Philip returned to his silence. He just sat. Eventually he reached his arm around Dominic's shoulder and pulled him close. His son yielded.

"Father, I've done a terrible thing. I don't know why I did it." Then Dominic's shoulders started heaving as he sobbed quietly. Philip stroked his hair until the sobs subsided.

Eventually Dominic looked up, tears staining his face. "I tried to tell everyone that I couldn't do these things. I tried to tell you. I tried to tell Captain Riggins. But nobody believed me. It's hard enough having to admit to yourself that you're a coward—to live with the shame and guilt from day to day—but when they make you try to do things that you can't and you end up hurting other people . . ." He started crying again.

As he thought about it, Philip realized that Dominic had tried to tell him. He felt a deep pang of regret that he hadn't realized his son's weakness more fully. What could he have done about it? He had used what influence he could to keep him out of combat, but it obviously hadn't worked. He'd reviewed Dominic's record before meeting him in the jail and could see how much trauma his boy had gone through. It would have been difficult for anyone—but for someone as sensitive and weak as Dominic . . . He drew a deep breath to steady his voice.

"Has it always been like that, Dominic? Have you always been afraid? You didn't act frightened . . ."

Dominic caught his breath and pulled away. "There's a big difference between fear and cowardice, Father. Fear gives you adrenaline so that you react and face it. Cowardice fills you with dread that saps your strength. I didn't act frightened because I was often terrified—the English schools with all their recitations of lessons where you faced the daily reality of being humiliated; the rugby field, where everyone expected you to be as good as your brother; the family discussions where everybody had a better opinion than me and I looked foolish and uninformed . . ."

"And the father who always seemed disappointed when you got in trouble," Philip added quietly.

Dominic was silent again. After a moment he said, "Sometimes that was worst of all."

Philip's eyes filled with tears. "Dominic, I didn't want to hurt you . . . I just wanted you to be strong enough to face life's trials and didn't know how to help you do it. I'm sorry."

When Dominic didn't say anything, Philip turned to him and said, "I guess I was frightened too—frightened for a boy I loved but couldn't seem to help. None of the usual things seemed to work—expressions of confidence, reprimands to provide discipline, inspirational talks—nothing seemed to register."

Dominic laughed a humorless laugh. "I understand what you're saying. It had to be confusing—it was to me. I knew what you were trying to do, and there were so many times I wanted to respond the right way, but instead I'd go and do something mean or say something sarcastic. I'd hate myself for doing it the moment I did it, and I'd want to take it back, but then you'd get angry, which only made me stubborn."

Philip shook his head. For the first time things seemed to come into focus. All the disagreements seemed to flood back into his mind. Too late. "Why was I so stupid?"

"You, stupid? That's rich. You're the smartest man I know." Then, recognizing the old pattern, Dominic quickly added, "And I agree with what people say about you. You are smart and kind and good, and I admire you for it." The last words caught in Dominic's throat, but he managed to add, "And I could never live up to it."

Philip hugged him a bit tighter, as if to give him the strength to keep talking.

"The only defense I could seem to come up with was either to run and hide or to get angry. I know it probably sounds dumb, but I preferred anger because at least it allowed me to have some sense of control—I could manipulate Michael and make him mad at me, I could irritate you and get a response, or I could exasperate Mother or get her to comfort me. The only time I ever felt in control was when I did something to make people angry." He continued softly. "That's the only way I could look strong when I was anything but strong."

Philip felt a new wave of panic. He somehow felt implicated and was ashamed that he hadn't been able to read through the bravado. *But even if I could have, what could I have done to help him?* Philip resisted the urge to further implicate himself. It would do no good right now. In some ways this discussion was very much about him—about a father who sincerely loved his son but apparently with a type of love that had conditions.

The phrase *Charity suffereth long, is not puffed up, seeketh not her own* burned in Philip's mind.

"Dominic," he said, turning to look directly at his son, "you asked me earlier why I came. I didn't answer clearly because I didn't know for sure. But now I do. I'm here because the Savior loves you. He loves you without condition, and He loves you in spite of what you've done. He loves you for your goodness, and He loves you in spite of your weakness. He loves you so much that He wanted someone to be with you during this awful hour of your distress. And so He sent me." Philip's voice choked up a bit. "And even though my love has not always been as pure and unselfish as I would like, His is. I hope you will forgive me."

Dominic simply rested his head on Philip's shoulder again—this time without holding anything back—which was perhaps the most wonderful feeling Philip had ever experienced with his son.

"I'm in real trouble this time, aren't I, Father?"

"You are."

"The British have shot deserters here in Africa. I think they're going to shoot me."

"I don't know," Philip said miserably. "Perhaps there are extenuating circumstances."

Dominic laughed bitterly. "Circumstances such as cowardice?"

"No, that wouldn't work very well, would it?"

They sat for a few moments before either one could talk. The emotion was simply too great.

"I shouldn't have come back to Britain. The Americans don't usually execute their deserters. They send them to jail, where they do tough work assignments. Had I stayed true to my own country, this might not have happened. Maybe I would have served honorably."

Philip couldn't think of anything to say. What might have been . . .

Just as he felt he must say something to keep the conversation going, a guard appeared and indicated that Philip's time was up. Philip was sorry that it was ending. He briefly pulled Dominic even closer to his shoulder. Philip felt a deep ulcer of sorrow for his son while feeling the bittersweet joy of finally, tragically, understanding Dominic Carlyle.

"I've got to go, Dominic. But have faith that all is not lost. We were finally able to talk. Really talk. You aren't alone! I'll be back, and perhaps we can help your attorney develop a case that will give you a chance . . ."

Because he was sitting directly next to him, Philip could actually feel Dominic stiffen as the fear reinfused his body. Without even looking at him, Philip could sense that the old Dominic was back. Philip's heart ached, because for just a few moments, they had been one in spirit in a way he'd never experienced.

The guard told him he had to leave then and turned the key in the rusty lock. Standing, Philip said to Dominic, "I'm glad we could talk, son. It means the world to me. I love you." Whatever Dominic had done, Philip meant what he said. It was a liberating feeling.

To his surprise, Dominic stood up and hugged him tightly—so tightly that it made his wound throb with pain. As he released him, Dominic said, "And I love you too, Papa—I love you. And no matter what happens, please know that I no longer have any bad feelings for you. We're all right with one another."

Philip staggered a bit. Those words shook Philip—shook him to the marrow of his bones. Just the use of the word *Papa* instead of *Father* was disconcerting coming from Dominic. He looked searchingly into his son's face and was surprised, considering the circumstances, to see him smile at him. He returned the smile but felt sorrow and uneasiness.

* * *

Philip was startled by the knock on the door. It was dark, and he had no idea where he was. At first he thought he was in Salt Lake City in the small apartment he and Claire lived in when they were first married. But then reality set in. Someone pounded on the door again, and he heard a voice say, "Lord Carlyle, wake up."

He was immediately filled with a sense of overwhelming anxiety, and he called out, "I'm awake! I'll be right there." He reached to the night table and turned on the small lamp. Quickly he dressed himself and opened the door. "What is it?"

"You need to come with me to the commander's office. He wants to see you immediately."

"Now? In the middle of the night?"

"Yes, sir. Right now." Philip had never been so frightened in his life. Not even in the combat of the First World War. Whatever they wanted him for couldn't be good.

As they arrived, the camp commander stood, and Philip noted that his face was drawn and colorless. "Lord Carlyle—please sit down."

"What is it?" Philip asked quietly, remaining standing. Adrenaline was now flooding through his system. "Why have you called me at a time like this?"

Seeing that Philip wasn't going to sit, the commander came around the desk. "We don't know how he did it, sir, but your son somehow managed to hide a belt in his room . . ." the commander said as his words faded.

Philip staggered and reeled, bumping his back into the wall. "Are you—are you saying that Dominic . . ." He found he couldn't say the words. Even though the thought had been in his mind from the moment the guard awakened him, he couldn't say the words.

"The guard found him on his normal rounds. He'd looped the belt around a narrow pipe and tightened it around his neck, setting the buckle to the furthest notch. Then he'd stepped off the bed. By the time we found him, there was nothing we could do to revive him, though we tried."

Philip felt his legs buckle, and the commander, a tall man, rushed over to help him. With the commander's help, Philip managed to make it to the chair, where he slumped down. "So he's dead?"

"Yes, sir. I'm very sorry."

Philip steadied himself. "Will you please take me to him?"

"I'm not sure that's advisable, sir."

"Please . . . I'm his father."

"Of course. But in this heat—"

"I understand—I won't stay long. But I must do this."

* * *

Philip was surprised that Dominic looked as good as he did. He'd actually expected worse. His body was laid out on a table. Without asking permission, Philip scooted himself up and onto the table so he could rest Dominic's head in his lap. *Oh, dear God, please be kind to my boy. Please accept him into Thy presence and help him feel loved. Please forgive him his trespasses. Please heal those whom he has harmed. And please forgive me my shortcomings with him. Please, dear Father, please—make him whole.* And then Philip wept. He wept as he'd never wept before.

He had no idea how long he wept, but the guards respected his privacy and left him alone. When he finally recovered, he gently rested Dominic's head on the table, stroked his hair one last time, and leaned down and kissed his forehead. He repeated his prayer in his mind and then stepped out into the corridor, where the camp commander had been waiting for him. "We found this under the mattress. He'd left a tail of it sticking out so it would be found. We didn't think anything about his writing it because we thought he was responding to questions from his solicitor, which is why we didn't read it earlier."

The commander handed him the note. His hands trembling, Philip unfolded it carefully.

Father,

By now you know what I have done. Please don't be angry and don't be ashamed. I told you that there are certain things I simply can't face, and a firing squad is one of them. I'm afraid that I would cry out or otherwise humiliate myself, and I simply can't stand that. It's better for it to happen here in my own room with no one to see.

I was angry when you came, because I wanted to be alone. I expected to goad you into another argument, but when you said you loved me, somehow I knew it was true. I wish we could have talked like that before, but I could never do it. It wasn't your fault. I guess I needed something as dire as this to finally open my heart.

It wasn't all as bad as I made it sound. I had some very good times in life—particularly in New York. The people there were like me, and I didn't have to pretend to be someone I was not.

I'm very sorry for what this will do to Mother. She was always my friend. Please, Mom, don't blame yourself— you've always loved me. I knew I could trust you to be on my side.

I have a strange sense of peace about all this and must simply hope that sometime God can find a way to forgive me. I feel that He loves me—in spite of my weaknesses. You told me He does, and I believe you.

I love all of you and will miss you.

Dominic

Philip's hands slumped to his side. "Are you okay, sir?"

Strangely, there were no tears. Philip's heart was broken, yet in his last words, Dominic had been generous. In the most remarkable way, Philip felt grateful that his son had shown empathy at the end of his troubled young life.

"I'm okay, for now," Philip replied quietly. He dropped his gaze. Looking up again at the commander, he said, "Thank you."

Philip closed his eyes and leaned against the wall, because the world hurt just now. And yet the Spirit comforted him.

Chapter Thirty-Two

BUCKINGHAM PALACE

London—December 1943

"Marissa. You're angry with me again, aren't you?"

"I don't want to talk about it, Michael."

"But it's been two months since we've seen each other, and already you're upset with me. All I did was invite you to attend an awards ceremony with me. You certainly don't have to go if you don't want to."

She turned at him, her eyes flaring. "Not *an* awards ceremony Michael—the awarding of an honor by the king himself. You know that the circles you pass in make me uncomfortable. Why can't you accept that we're not alike and just leave it at that?"

Michael felt his stomach drop. He'd had such great hope for this luncheon. He'd even gone so far as to ask some of the men on his boat to recommend a modest pub for lunch so he wouldn't put her off. That had led to a great deal of teasing from them, but he considered it worth the trouble to put her at ease. Now it seemed to have been in vain.

"Please, Marissa. It won't really be that bad. And it might be interesting to go inside the Palace. You might like it."

Marissa turned and looked at him directly. "You just can't see it, can you, Michael? You and I are different—hopelessly different. You come from a world where I don't belong, and in spite of your protests that you're American and all that, you don't really belong in my world."

Michael didn't know exactly how to describe what he was feeling—desperate, perhaps. He liked the way he felt when he thought of dating a girl like Marissa. He liked the way the other fellows looked at him when she was on his arm. And the thought of losing that—of losing her—was overwhelming. But he also felt anger that they always ended up in a fight with him defending something that wasn't his fault. He couldn't help it that his father was prominent. Yet she held it against him like it was a curse. And he didn't like the fact that she made him jealous by always going off with other guys rather than spending time with him. That wasn't very kind either. He wanted to think of something clever to say at this point to break the tension, but instead he blurted out, "A lot of girls would love the chance to go to Buckingham Palace and meet the king and Princess Elizabeth."

Marissa shook her head and relaxed a little. It was as if she had made a decision and no longer felt the tension that had animated her just moments earlier. "I think I finally see why it's so hard for us to talk about this. In spite of all your years here in Britain, you really do see things from an American point of view. Over there every young girl dreams of growing up to be a princess. And that makes perfect sense in a country where anyone can grow up to do anything they like. But that's not my dream. Besides, you and I like different things—we have different personalities."

"What do you mean by that?" Michael said sullenly.

She spoke softly. "What I mean, Michael, is that you're the kind of person who will only become close to a woman in the proper way—through marriage. You're the type of man to marry—not to have a good time with."

"And why is that a problem?" Michael asked.

She smiled. "Michael, I'm not ready to get married. Can you accept that gracefully?" She looked at him earnestly. "Please?"

"But we have so much in common."

"We do? All we have in common is that you were sick, and I was there to help you. Aside from that, I enjoy a good night out on the town that includes pleasures you don't enjoy and dancing with many partners—many *friends*. And you don't really like any of that, do you?"

"Well . . . no . . . but . . ."

She smiled and took his hands into hers. "No buts, Michael. I know that what you do and don't do is your business—I respect you for it. But it's not for me. At least not now. So again I ask you, will you please just accept this?"

Michael couldn't hide his disappointment.

"Oh, no. You really did have hopes, didn't you?" she said with that marvelous voice that had first attracted him to her months earlier.

"A real invincible hero, aren't I?" Michael said with sarcasm.

"I think you're one of the best people I've ever known. And you come from such a marvelous family. If anyone could tempt me to marry up, it would be your family."

The lump in Michael's throat made it impossible for him to reply.

"Thank you, Michael. Now that it's over I can move on. So can you."

Finally yielding to the inevitable, Michael relaxed and let go. "Well, if I have done something good for you I'm glad, because you saved me at the darkest moment of my life. So perhaps we were good for each other—for a time." He smiled and squeezed her hand. That moment lasted for perhaps a few seconds, and then it was over and she withdrew her hand to her side of the table.

"I'm afraid I don't know exactly what to do at this point," Michael said. "Not only have I never had a girlfriend before, but I've never broken up with one either. What do we do now?"

She laughed. "We relax and enjoy the very expensive lunch you've ordered, and then you have your driver take me home while you walk back to your town house. Does that work?"

She smiled at his sadness. "It was awfully nice to share your world for a bit. Just think, I can tell all my friends that I dated nobility—a future viscount. Thank you."

At that moment the waiter brought out their plates, and both were able to focus on their meals. Later, when the time finally came to say good-bye, Michael gave Charles driving instructions and helped Marissa into the car. She leaned out the back window and said, "By the way, if you really need someone to go to that ceremony with you, you should see if Karen Demming would like to go. I'm sure she'd fit in perfectly there."

"Karen? What do you mean?"

"You realize that she comes from a prominent family, don't you?"

Michael shook his head to clear it. "She does?"

Marissa burst out laughing. "Yes, you silly boy. Her father is the third son of an established family, which means they're not particularly well off but certainly presentable in the best of social circles. She volunteers at the hospital."

Michael shook his head. "I'll never figure all of this out, Marissa. I promise I never will."

"Then just follow your heart."

"Well, good-bye then."

"Good-bye, Michael. And good luck. And please don't come back to the hospital all broken up again. I don't think *my* heart could take us meeting again." With that, Michael brushed her cheek one last time, after which Charles drove away from the curb and down the road.

* * *

London—January 1943

"Nineteen state rooms, fifty-two principal bedrooms, ninety offices, one hundred eighty-eight staff bedrooms. And more than six dozen bathrooms! Built in 1710 for the first Duke of Buckingham and made a royal residence in 1762 . . ."

"What on earth are you muttering about?" Michael asked Grace.

She took no notice of him but simply continued her litany, her face in her hands as she peered over a book at the kitchen table. "Today's ceremony will take place in the State Ballroom, the largest room in the Palace."

Michael shook his head in wonder. "What on earth is she doing, Mother?"

"She's getting ready for your ceremony. You know how she likes to be prepared."

"I don't think they're going to have you take a test before you can enter, Grace."

She looked up and glowered at her brother. "Well, if they did, I could pass it while you'd be thrown out for your appalling lack of interest."

He was about to make a comment about the whole reason they were going there in the first place, but he held his tongue. It was one of the most charming aspects of his sister's personality that she relished learning all about the places they were going before they got there. In a way, her research was very comforting because it reminded Michael of the prewar days when the family got to travel together to some wonderful places in England and Europe.

"Papa, do you think we'll get to see the throne room? It's covered in the most marvelous crimson wall coverings." Grace looked up from the page she'd just turned to, her eyes shining with excitement.

"If we don't, I'll arrange a private tour for you another time. I believe we could find an excuse to return to the Palace on a quieter day. Besides, this is Michael's big day. We're not going there as tourists."

"I would love a private tour," she said breathlessly. "I want to see everything! You've been to the Palace, haven't you, Papa?"

Philip put his paper down and smiled. "On quite a number of occasions—more when my father was alive. He was actually on quite good terms with King Edward VIII, particularly when he was the Prince of Wales."

"I get my Edwards mixed up," Claire said. "He was the one who served for less than a year before abdicating?"

Philip got a sly smile. "Yes—he had the audacity to marry an American woman, and you know how dangerous that is!"

Claire swatted him with the section of the paper she'd been reading. "I know she was divorced, but I think it's charming that he would give up the throne for love."

"Most people think it was disloyal," Michael said. "You have to put personal affairs aside for the good of the country and all."

"It's lucky, for your sake, Michael, that your father married an American," Claire retorted. "Otherwise you wouldn't be here to receive this award. Just remember that!"

They laughed, in part to cover the nervousness that was natural on such a day. Out of the hundreds of millions of British subjects around the world, only a small handful would ever be invited into the Palace in the very heart of London's fashionable West Side, and only several thousand had been invited there to receive the Distinguished Service Cross, one of Britain's highest honors for those who showed uncommon valor in the face of hostilities.

"It says here that the Palace is the king's primary residence. What does that mean?" Grace asked.

"It means the royal family has numerous palaces in England and Scotland and that they divide their time among all of them," Philip replied.

Claire snorted. "And that's because one palace, one castle, and one mansion aren't enough?"

Philip laughed. "Not by a long shot, my dear. You Americans are so parochial in your thinking. There is Balmoral in Scotland, where the family spends their August holiday; Holyroodhouse in Edinburgh, when they have official business in Scotland; and Sandringham in Norfolk, where they generally spend Christmas."

Claire shook her head in disgust. "It's just too much. No one needs all that, not even the head of state. The president gets by with just the White House, you know."

Philip continued listing off royal estates with their respective functions until Claire interrupted with, "Ridiculous—it gives me a headache just thinking about it."

"Better not think of it, then," Philip said wryly.

"Well, I suppose we ought to get ready. I assume we're walking to the Palace?" Claire asked, recognizing that the short trip by automobile wouldn't make a lot of sense since their driver would have a hard time parking.

"Well, since you ask, I have something of a surprise," Philip said, receiving curious glances from all. "But I'm not going to tell you until it's time to go—which by my watch is in thirty minutes. Meet me at the front door, or you're going to miss the whole event."

As the group got up and started to leave, Claire caught Michael's eye and nodded for him to come talk with her privately for a moment.

"So I take it that it will only be family members at the ceremony?"

Michael's face dropped. "Just family." He looked up and attempted a smile.

"I'm sorry. I know you cared a great deal for Marissa. I hoped that you might take her up on her suggestion to invite Karen instead."

"After what I've been through, I'm not sure the best way to approach a girl is to ask her to the Palace on short notice, especially as a second choice." He was quiet for a moment. "But I did ask her over for dinner later tonight. I hope that's okay."

"I'm glad to hear that," Grace said conspiratorially, obviously having caught the end of their conversation. "I like her a lot more than that other girl—what's-her-face."

"Oh, for heaven's sake!" Michael said as he swatted Grace.

For her part, Claire was relieved that he could smile again.

* * *

The surprise was a horse-driven coach that Philip had arranged with the Royal Mews to pick them up. The Mews were the magnificent stables and carriage house where the royal family's coaches and automobiles were cared for, adjacent to Buckingham Palace. On this occasion, one of the state coaches was put into service for the Carlyles, drawn by a team of four white horses. The short ride from the town house to the main entrance was just a ten- or fifteen-minute ride through the grounds of the Mall, but with a light dusting of snow, it was a magnificent trip.

Grace was gazing intently out the window. "Look at all those people waving at us."

"They probably think we're members of the royal family."

In spite of her enthusiasm for the grandeur of the whole thing, Grace settled back in her seat. "I guess I wouldn't want to be recognized everywhere I go. It seems like you could never fully be yourself."

"That's why the royals spend so much time in remote castles," Philip replied. "It gives them privacy." He winked at Claire.

Claire shook her head back at him.

As they arrived at the entrance to the Palace, the carriage passed through the magnificent 3300-pound black gates, including the fabulous golden royal crests that sparkled in the winter sun. Grace nearly burst with excitement as they passed by the red-coated guards to enter the inner court of one of the most exclusive residences in the world.

Walking through the highly gilded hallways, everyone at first spoke in whispers but eventually fell silent—in part because the walls were so highly reflective that any sound they made seemed amplified as it echoed back and forth across the hallway—but even more in awe for the sheer grandeur of the place. Philip, the history lover, could not help but reflect on all the great decisions and marvelous people who had passed through these same corridors, and he soon found himself lost in thought. Practical-minded Claire brought him out of his reverie.

"It's awfully dark, isn't it," she whispered.

"It's the windows—they've all been boarded up because of the Germans. The Palace has already been bombed some five or six times," Michael replied.

"And that's the worst indignity of all. What did England do to Germany to deserve this?" Claire was an eminently practical person who had little patience with international politics, particularly when it led to useless wars.

"We just got in the way of their ambitions," Philip replied. "It's as simple as that. And so millions have died, and millions more will die. And there's more coming if we have to invade the continent."

"Do you think it will come to that? Don't you think Germany will see the futility of it all and let the carnage end?"

"Not this time," Philip said sadly. "Both Roosevelt and Churchill have declared that they will accept nothing less than total and complete surrender. They will not make the same mistake they made at Versailles in 1918. This time it will be a fight to the finish."

At this point they were directed into the great Victoria Ballroom, where their breath was taken away by the magnificent chandeliers, parquet floor, and beautifully embroidered draperies and curtains.

"Wow," Michael said, revealing how nervous he was.

"Are you okay?"

Michael laughed. "Okay? I'd sooner be visiting a dentist. I should be out on my boat, not here!" Even though he tried to make it appear humorous, Philip could sense the stress. Since Philip had become Mormon, he had not enjoyed nearly as many invitations to the Palace, or any other events for that matter, as his father had. Consequently, his children did not have the same level of experience in dealing with this sort of thing.

"You'll be fine, Michael. There will be someone assigned to stand behind you at all times to help you respond properly to whatever situation presents itself. Just relax and remember to call the king sir, with a slight bow at the waist when he passes by."

"I'm glad you're here. I'd hate to face this by myself."

"I'm glad I'm here too, Michael. This is without question the proudest moment of my life." He looked around. "Of our family's life. Your mother and Grace are just as proud as I am," he said as he fell into a reflective silence.

"You're thinking about Dominic, aren't you?" Michael had hardly talked about Dominic with either his father or his mother since Philip's return from Africa, because they had little time together to do so and because he never knew quite what to say when they were alone. Whether as a direct result of Dominic's death or simply his age, Philip's hair had turned noticeably gray in the past few months, and they hadn't heard his usual easy laugh on anything but rare occasions.

Philip's lip quivered. "Yes, I guess I am." He tried to smile but found he really couldn't. "But that doesn't come at your expense. If anything, it makes me appreciate even more that I still have you and cherish the times we get to be together."

"I still can't believe Dominic was so distressed that he would take his own life." Michael realized that this was hardly the time or place to talk about his brother, but it was still a few minutes before the ceremony, and it seemed important to at least remember him, even now. "I guess I've never really understood what drove him to such a thing."

Philip nodded. "He deserted his post. He found himself in a very difficult situation in which nearly everyone he had traveled with had been killed, and he simply allowed his fear to overtake him. He abandoned the battlefield. There were terrible consequences because of his failure."

"So he really was guilty." After all he'd been through, Michael could easily understand that kind of fear, and he knew that Dominic would have trouble facing it.

"He was. And he felt terrible about it. I think the guilt and the fear of what was coming weighed him down . . ." Philip's voice trailed off.

"I'm sorry, Father. I shouldn't have brought it up."

Philip put his arm around Michael's shoulder. "No, it's okay. I'm glad you did. I've been waiting for the time when you were ready. The truth is that at first I didn't want to talk to anyone about it. But now I'd like very much to talk, to try to understand. I don't ever want to forget about Dominic. Ever. If we let embarrassment or hurt stop us from remembering him, then his life has no meaning whatsoever. In spite of his failings, I don't want to leave it at that." He paused to control his breath. "Because his life isn't over, and I believe we'll meet him again one day. I want to be able to tell him that we stood by him, even in the worst of his crises. So you can talk to me about him whenever you like."

Michael now felt his lip tremble. His heart ached for his father. "I'm sorry we weren't closer. And I'm very grateful that I have you and Mother for my parents. To know that you can love him in spite of his faults says a great deal about your ability to love." With that, he leaned in and gave his father a hug—which was exactly what Philip needed.

Pulling away, Philip smiled and said, "There, we've got through that. Now let's think about what's about to happen to our oldest son!"

"I'd rather not," Michael said. "Your oldest son is scared out of his wits!" Philip smiled and gave him another hug.

"I don't know what you two are talking about, but you're making something of a scene," Claire said as she came up. "I think it's time for us to take our seats or whatever we do."

Philip nodded and moved to her side. "It's not like that at all. There won't be a program. Each of the men who are to be honored will take his position in the receiving line. When the king enters, he'll pass down the center so that everyone can acknowledge him, and then he'll work his way back down the line, greeting each man one by one until he's met them all. One of his military counselors will present him with whatever medal the recipient is entitled to receive while whispering the man's name in the king's ear. The family gets to stand behind their soldier or sailor so they can see the king directly. It will be a most interesting experience."

"Just take my hand and guide me," Claire said. "After all, I'm just a country girl from Arizona who raised the little boy from Salt Lake City who's standing in the front row."

"And his is the greatest honor of all that will be bestowed today," Philip replied.

There was a rustling in the room, and the ushers quickly lined everyone up. As the king and queen entered, accompanied by Princess Elizabeth, the crowd grew quiet. The royal family passed down the line just as Philip had said, with everyone bowing slightly to acknowledge their presence. One of the king's courtiers announced the purpose of the proceedings, and then the king and his family started back down the line. A formal announcement was called out to the crowd generally announcing who the recipient was and which honor he would receive, and then the king stepped forward and placed the medal over the recipient's head.

Just as the king was about to reach Michael, Philip happened to glance down and saw that Michael's pant legs were trembling. *Unusual valor indeed!* He smiled to himself. Philip was pretty nervous himself, which is why he was almost startled out of his wits when he was bumped from behind. He turned to see who had intruded, only to hear the stage whisper of Winston Churchill himself say, "I had to put the whole war on hold to get here. I'm glad to see I made it in time."

Philip smiled and shook his hand. Michael had turned to see who dared to talk in the presence of the king, and his face blanched when he saw who it was. Churchill tipped his head in a small salute and smiled at the thoroughly flustered boy, who managed to smile back at him.

Michael barely turned in time to hear the words, "The Honorable Michael Carlyle, Lieutenant, Royal Navy. The Distinguished Service Cross." With that he stepped forward to face King George VI. The king was a tall and slender man, rather gaunt in appearance and solemn in demeanor. But his greeting was anything but solemn.

"Well, Lieutenant Carlyle. I read your citation personally. Your country salutes your bravery and devotion."

"Thank you, sir."

"Of course, I should specify that it is your patriarchal country—I've never had occasion to present an award to both an American and a British citizen. I'm glad you chose to serve England."

Michael didn't have time to think what to say, so he simply said what came from his heart. "I'm very glad as well, sir. I'm proud to serve king and country."

The king nodded and smiled. "Do you hear that, Winston? This boy's almost as eloquent as you. You'd better watch him when he takes his place in the Lords."

"I've always had to watch out for the Carlyles, Your Majesty. But generally I trust their politics." He smiled at Philip.

"Indeed. You must be very proud, Lord Carlyle."

Philip stepped forward. "I certainly am, sir. A man could not hope for a finer son."

"And would you introduce me to the rest of your family?"

Philip motioned for Claire and Grace to step forward. Grace simply beamed with delight when the king and queen each took her hand. She curtsied for them, which brought a smile to all who were nearby.

"And do you share your son's enthusiasm for England?" he said to Claire.

"Other than the rain, Your Majesty. I grew up in Arizona where we get approximately the same rainfall in a year as you do in a week." Claire's face immediately flushed to think that she had been cheeky in such a setting. The king appeared delighted, and Churchill roared with laughter.

"Yes, well perhaps I should get on with it." At that the king placed the Distinguished Service Cross on Michael's shoulders and then saluted him.

"Thank you, sir!" Michael felt like his knees were about to collapse under him.

Then the king leaned forward and said, "I love the Navy, you know. There's no time now, but perhaps your father would bring you 'round sometime so I can ask you more about both your exploits on enemy soil and even more importantly, this ramming of an enemy ship. I should be delighted to learn more."

"Yes, sir . . . of course. Thank you for the invitation, sir." Michael couldn't decide exactly when he should use "sir," so he put it in whenever possible.

"You'll see to it, Lord Carlyle?"

"Yes, sir. I'll see to it."

"Good." And with that, the king and his family moved on.

* * *

The Carlyles worked their way out of the Palace after the royal family's exit. Churchill walked with them partway. "I heard what the king asked you, Lieutenant Carlyle, and I should tell you it would be dastardly indeed if you should share your story with him and not with me."

Michael's head was so overcrowded now that he didn't know what to say. So he stammered, "Whenever you like."

"What I'd like," Churchill retorted, "is to hear the story on the deck of your motor torpedo boat! Now that's what I'd really like."

"It would be a bit dangerous for the prime minister to put himself directly in harm's way, don't you think?" Philip asked, in part to give Michael time to recover his wits and in part to dissuade Churchill from actually making good on the idea.

But Churchill wasn't deterred. "That's pure nonsense, Carlyle, and I'm surprised you'd try to pull it on me. Everyone else does, but I'd think better of a friend."

"Only trying to protect our national assets," Philip said defensively.

"I'm the defense minister as well as prime minister, you know, and as the chief minister tasked with prosecuting the war, it's vital that I get out to see the real thing once in a while."

"I suppose if you put it that way . . ." Philip knew there was no sense getting in his way anymore, although he couldn't guess what Churchill had in mind.

"You'd be welcome to come see us anytime you like, sir," Michael said quietly. "Of course, my captain and the other men would probably faint dead away, but once they recovered, they'd be quite honored to show you what a motor torpedo boat can do."

Churchill brightened up and slapped his thigh. "By George, that's just what I'm going to do. I'm going to come to—where is it you're stationed?"

"In Felixstowe, sir."

"Yes, I'm going to come to Felixstowe, and you're going to show me your boat. Philip, for your obstinacy in this thing, I'm going to require you to set it up. Do you understand?" Churchill gave Philip one of his famous scowls. In this case, it was done in mock irritation, but Philip had seen the real thing often enough. Churchill had a fiery temper, but he always made amends sometime later.

"I will accept my comeuppance with grace, prime minister. Perhaps you'd allow me to accompany you, since I've never received an invitation to tour my son's boat. I think he's embarrassed by me. But if you were there, no one would even notice me."

"Of course, sons are often embarrassed by their fathers. At least mine are. We take so much liberty in speaking of their younger days." He turned to Claire and Grace. "Of course, you're welcome to join our little party as well, ladies."

Grace brightened up immediately, but her mother quickly dashed her hopes. "I appreciate the invitation, sir, but it sounds to me like this is a boys' party. Men and their machines. I'm afraid that I'd simply put a damper on things. So you men go off and play and enjoy the sport of it."

"Well then, it's all settled. Let me know the time and place. Now I better get back in there and congratulate the others who were distinguished today, or they'll think I play favorites."

"You could have ignored the ceremony all together," Philip said quietly as Churchill got out of hearing range, "but you're too great a soul to do that. This is certainly a day to write down in your journal," Philip said to Michael.

"Probably the strangest day of my life. I'd agree that it might be worth making a note or two." Claire put her arm around him, and the family found their way to the doors of the Palace. The coach was waiting for them, but by mutual assent they sent it back to the stables. It was the perfect day for a walk.

Chapter Thirty-Three

A BOAT OF YOUR OWN

Felixstowe on the English Channel Coast— January 1943

"Well, then, Michael, do you think you have the crew nervous enough yet? Is it time for the grand entrance?" Lieutenant Prescott chided.

Michael raised his eyes from the soft drink he'd been nursing for the past half hour to face Lieutenant Commander Prescott directly. A hundred yards away, the brand new *MTB-982* awaited the arrival of its new commanding officer, none other than R.N. Lieutenant Michael Carlyle. In accordance with an ancient naval custom, he was expected to wait on the sidelines until the appointed hour so that the first officer could get everything ship-shape for the arrival of the commanding officer. At that very moment there was undoubtedly an excess of cursing, bumping, and colliding between the members of the crew and the dockyard workers in final preparation for the grand event.

"You know that the more usual course for command is to be in the Navy for ten or fifteen years, then get a small destroyer, ultimately working your way up to an aircraft carrier or battleship." Prescott turned and smiled at him. "But then, what have they got that we don't have, except for a lot of horsepower?"

Michael laughed. "And a turning radius the size of a football field. We can be home taking a hot shower in the time it takes them to drop anchor." This was the sort of usual banter that pitted the Coastal Forces against the regular Navy, who mostly looked down their noses at the little boats. But today the conversation had great significance for Michael since he was talking with Prescott as an equal. Prescott would still be his group commander, having received his own new boat after the destruction of the *960,* but Michael now had the full responsibility for the success of the mission and the safety of his crew. That was a charge that no man could take lightly, whether commanding a small boat or a battle cruiser.

"Well, I don't know how nervous the crew is, but I doubt that collectively they could equal what I'm feeling. My stomach feels like I've had the wind knocked out of me."

"You'll do fine, Michael. It's no different from when I turned the wheel over to you a hundred times before."

Michael finished off his soft drink and turned to Prescott. "It's a mystery to me how I can actually feel more alarmed at this little ceremony than I did lying there in the water after the *960* blew up, but I do."

Prescott shook his head slightly and then stood with Michael. It was a bit awkward not knowing what to say, but Prescott solved the problem by stepping forward and grasping Michael's shoulders. "There's never been anyone better qualified. So you step on that deck with confidence, and then trust your men to do their jobs." It was an embrace of more than rank or even friendship. It confirmed one of the deepest bonds that can exist between people—one forged in the extremes of adversity when life itself was at stake. Michael was moved beyond words by Prescott's gesture.

"I'll do what you've taught me, and I'll be fine. Thanks!"

Five minutes later, Michael walked with a leisurely gait toward the remarkably sleek craft that bore no traces of the war or nights at sea. It seemed so out of place here, with all the battle-stained boats in the nearby berths. The finish on the wood gleamed in the afternoon sun, and it seemed almost a crime to expose it to the inevitable scars and injuries that would soon befall it.

"Commanding officer on the boat!" There was a scrambling sound as all the men dropped what they were doing and rushed out to both the forward and aft decks to stand at attention. On a bigger ship, the entire crew would assemble in one place, but a torpedo boat was simply too small for that. The traditional ceremony would also have them all dressed in their best uniforms, but in this case they'd been busy working to get ready, and Michael noted that more than one of them had to wipe sweat from his brow, even though it was a bitter cold day on the English Channel.

"All men present and accounted for!" the first officer, Sublieutenant Charles Carver, said, looking so young. With more than three years of war behind them, the experienced men had all been promoted to a larger ship—or killed—so it was boys barely reaching the minimum age of service that were being sent to them now. Carver had been on the boats for more than a year in order to work himself up to a posting as second-in-command, and as the two of them had chatted earlier in the week, Michael had decided that Carver was more than qualified. It was a little hard to tell exactly how their relationship would develop since they had both been pretty nervous at the time, but in the long run that didn't really matter since they'd have to make the best of it.

There was so much to worry about with command—and not just concerns about the running of the ship. A commanding officer had to know the temperament and reliability of each person in his command to know how best to use them when an unexpected crisis arose. The next few days would be crucial to his success with this crew.

"Very good, Mr. Carver. Perhaps you'd make the introductions." With that, Michael was introduced to the members of his crew, chatting briefly with each of them to set them at ease and to get an initial feel for their personalities. While they all seemed reliable, they were also amazingly young and inexperienced. He'd have to spend hours drilling them so that their actions would be automatic when combat arrived. He could only imagine what their first gunnery practice would be like.

Once the review was finished, he ordered, "Stand at ease," and the crew relaxed for the traditional first speech.

"Well, then, for many of you this is your first experience on a combat vessel. You're probably nervous, just as we all were our first day. But you shouldn't worry since Sublieutenant Carver here knows what to do, and he knows just what words to use if you're about to make a mistake." Michael was enormously relieved when the crew laughed at his little joke. That was a good sign. "And for better or worse, I've seen a bit of action myself, so when the time comes to go into battle, we both know what to do, and you'll figure it out quick enough. You see, gentlemen, German bullets tearing through the air have a remarkable way of focusing your attention." They laughed again. This was going well, and Michael found he actually liked being the one giving the instructions.

"Some of you, if you could be entirely honest, are probably disappointed that you got assigned to the small boats rather than something bigger and more grand. It's okay if you feel that way because we don't always get to choose. But as one who first cut his teeth on the *Hood*, I can assure you that you'll learn more in a month on the *982* than you would in a year on one of the capital ships." He let his words hang in the air for a few moments so that their curiosity would be piqued. "You see, on a ship that size, there's a sense that there are always a couple thousand other men to act in a time of crisis and that whatever part you play is a small role. But that's simply not the case here. Take a look around, and you'll see that all we've got is each other. If any one of you proves unreliable, then the safety of the entire boat is imperiled. There's no one else to do your job, so you have to step up to the challenge each and every day."

He saw the men shift uncomfortably and realized that a message like this could be both inspiring and frightening, so he resolved to conclude on a positive note. "But don't be concerned. You'll do your job when the time comes. We'll drill and practice and drill and practice until there's no question how you should act or what you should do. Before you know it, you'll be the best there is, and you'd willingly place your life in the hands of any member of the crew, just as they'll place their trust you." After pausing for another moment, he said, "I know all this from firsthand experience. You will do your duty, and together we'll do our part to win this war." He nodded so that the men could signal their consent. Once it quieted down, he continued. "Now, gentlemen, prepare for the greatest adventure of your lives. There's certainly nothing I've ever felt to equal the thrill of those three engines as they come to full acceleration. Let's be done with the words and on with the action. Mr. Carver, make ready for sea!"

* * *

The English Channel— February 1942

"I rather like being out here in the daylight," Michael said amiably. "It's a lot more fun to sport about the English Channel when you can see where you're going."

"Yes, sir. But it's still rather cold for a pleasure cruise, don't you think?"

Michael had discovered that he liked his new first officer. At 6' 4" tall and probably 150 pounds, Joseph Carver was so gaunt and slender that it was easy to assume he was humorless. And at first he was. The men still hadn't seen the lighter side of him. But Michael got his first glimpse of his wry humor when Carver referred to himself as "the British equivalent of Abraham Lincoln, but without the sparkling personality." No one else on the boat had gotten the joke because they were British, after all, and didn't have a sense of the somber character of Lincoln, but Michael did and thought it a delightfully accurate comparison.

Michael restlessly watched the time. They'd been on station for nearly three hours, waiting for a flight of Allied bombers that was expected to return from a run inside German-occupied territory. It was usually pretty boring, but occasionally the small boats needed to act as lifeguards for any fatally wounded aircraft that made it as

far as the English Channel but not all the way across. The pilots
and crew would almost sooner die than land in German territory
and be taken as prisoners of war, so they inevitably nursed their
aircraft toward the water.

It was a risky strategy, of course, because at this time of the year
the water was bitter cold and a man could easily freeze to death
before a rescue could be arranged.

"Do you see anything, Mr. Renton?" Michael had also learned
that his young signalman had eyes that easily rivaled those of a
healthy young bird of prey.

"Sorry, sir—nothing visual or on the wireless." Michael
clapped his gloved hands together and shrugged. As a general rule,
the aircraft flew with radio silence so the enemy couldn't sight in
on them using triangulation, but in an emergency, they had a
special set of code words they could broadcast to any British ship
in the area. Today there hadn't been a sound.

It was a bit awkward to stay on the bridge, trying to keep up
any kind of meaningful conversation, so he finally resolved to go
below decks to work on a report. He had just managed to say to
Carver, "Call me the moment anything is spotted," when Renton
called out, "There's something on the horizon at ten o'clock."

Instantly, all eyes on the boat turned in that direction and
started scanning the skies. Michael and Carver scanned the skies
with the high-powered binoculars they each carried around their
necks. It took a moment to find them, but sure enough, a black
speck appeared where Renton had predicted and then another and
then another.

"Full speed ahead!" Michael shouted, and the young seaman on
the wheel sprung into action, the alarm sounding so that the men
below decks wouldn't be taken by surprise. As the engines churned
the water into a boiling froth, Michael was thrilled as the boat
leapt ahead, quickly planing so that the bow rose up and out of the
water. They were able to achieve incredible speed as the keel pulled
up out of the water, reducing drag.

They were running on an intercept course with the aircraft but were highly unlikely to get to a rendezvous spot before the aircraft had long since passed over it. But this course would get them in the vicinity if something should go wrong and would position them better for any subsequent flights that came across.

As they drew nearer, it looked like all was well. "Looks like they accomplished their deed without any trouble," Joseph was saying when Renton called out again. "It looks like a wounded one at four o'clock, sir." On their new position, they'd come around more than ninety degrees, so this placed the new aircraft he'd spotted to the east and behind them. Michael wheeled on the spot and could see this new aircraft without any trouble since it was streaming a trail of smoke behind it.

"He's hurt. Come about, helm, and let's try to get there at the same time they do." It was going to be a lot easier since this bomber was flying very slow and very close to the water. As they drew closer, they saw two smaller aircraft come darting up from behind the lumbering bomber. "German fighters! Our fellow's in trouble." Leaning into the communication tube, Michael shouted, "We've got some friends who are hurting, chief, and anything you can give us will be appreciated." His engineer acknowledged, and Michael heard the engines wind up even faster. Since they'd already been traveling at top speed, that meant they were now well inside the red line, where bearings would quickly overheat and the oil would lose its ability to cool properly.

"The moment we come into range, I want our guns to start putting up some resistance to those fighters. Anything to get them off his back!"

"Yes, sir," Carver acknowledged. As the first officer, it was Carver's responsibility to govern the crew under the direction of the captain. So he was the one who gave the men their assignments, kept track of the stores and fuel, and disciplined the men when necessary. He was also the one, when not otherwise occupied, to translate the captain's wishes into actions by the members of the crew.

"Coming into range now! Fire at will!" Carver's high-pitched yell had the disadvantage of sounding rather thin and squeaky. But it could carry over a mile or two, since it was shrill enough to cut through the roar of the engines and any other clamor on the boat.

Michael was pleased to hear the guns respond immediately. Without thinking about it, he'd actually ticked off the seconds from when Carver gave the order to when the first shot was fired. It was well within acceptable range.

Because it was difficult to see exactly where the shells were reaching, particularly in an activity as futile as trying to shoot an aircraft out of the sky with light weapons, there were tracer shells placed in the ammunition belts so that at a regular interval a brightly colored glowing shell could be seen arcing its way out into the sky. That way the gunner could quickly correct his aim if needed. The tracer didn't carry a charge, but it was still extremely valuable.

One of the German aircraft noticed their attack and immediately took evasive action. That brought a cheer from the gun crew, who turned and combined their fire with the second gun now aimed at the other German aircraft. Unfortunately, this fellow wasn't as easily deterred, and he kept following the stricken British bomber even when the tracers clearly indicated that some of the shells from the *982* had hit his fuselage.

"It's too late. The bomber is never going to make it!" Oftentimes a flight crew would ride the aircraft into the water, and then slip out as it was sinking rather than risk getting shot at in their parachutes when under attack by the enemy. But in this case it was clear that the aircraft fires were so intense that there was a risk of the thing blowing up before they could ditch the airplane. Accordingly, a string of parachutes started blossoming out the side door.

"Stay on the Germans!" Carver shouted to the gunners. "Don't give them a chance to harass our men!" Michael had been about ready to shout the same thing, but he was glad that he'd held his tongue long enough for Carver to give the orders.

"Right, then," he said to the helm, "you can see where they're coming down. Let's get over there and help them."

The ship swung a bit, which temporarily threw his gunners off their game, but they quickly recovered. The German aircraft were so fast that they could only make passing attacks on the men as they came down. It was infuriating that they'd shoot at a man while he was floating helplessly toward the water, but both sides had learned early on that the loss of an aircraft was relatively mean-ingless compared with the loss of a trained pilot and crew. Far better to shoot them than to let them be rescued only to meet them again later in combat.

"Let's get ready to start taking the crew members on board." Michael said this loudly enough that the men in the area started getting the nets ready. He motioned to Carver to come close.

"I need you to get to signals and tell him to send out an urgent request for backup. Those two Germans are going to do their best to sink us. I doubt that any boats can get here in time, but if there are any British aircraft nearby, we need them right now."

"How shall I send the message, sir?"

Michael bit his lower lip—hard. "Send it uncoded and clear channel. I want everyone who's in range to hear the message without having to think about it. The Germans already know we're here, so there's nothing to be gained by silence. Go now—send it fast!"

Carver bounded down the stairs with surprising agility. Michael personally took over the handling of the boat as they came up to the first survivor. The situation called for extremely quick reaction time, and he simply didn't have the time to help his young helmsman figure it out.

"Why isn't that man helping himself?" Michael called sharply. "Is he wounded?" He was mightily irritated that the man was doing nothing to aid in his own rescue, leaving the boat totally vulnerable and the members of his crew at risk.

The answer dawned on him the instant the two seamen turned to respond, and he instantly felt sorry for what he'd said.

"He's dead, sir! Shot right through the chest. And it was after he started down because it went right through his parachute pouch!" The men were furiously trying to untangle the body in the water.

Now Michael had to make a split-second decision. "Belay that! Let him go. We've got to get to the others. We'll come back if we can!" Of course this shocked the men, and they were nearly knocked off their feet when Michael shoved the accelerator to maximum and the boat leapt out in the direction of the second downed parachuter. If they had any reservations about what he was doing, however, they were quickly put to rest when the water was churned up by a string of shells from one of the Germans who roared overhead. Some of the shells tore into the aft deck of the boat, sending splinters flying, and the two men who had been working on the rescue dove down flat onto their bellies to present less of a profile.

The aircraft passed overhead quickly, followed by the furious fire of the *982*, but as a torpedo boat she really wasn't prepared to fight off an aerial attack.

By the time everyone processed what had happened, Michael pulled up to the second man who quickly scrambled into the nets. He'd had the presence of mind to cut his parachute loose, so he was up and on the deck in record time. Out of the corner of his eye, Michael saw another shadow and so did a quick 180-degree turn that managed to avoid the line of fire from the second German aircraft. He did this so quickly that his own gunners were disoriented by it, causing them to send a string of shots in a crazy pattern that wasted precious ammunition.

"I'll try to give you some warning next time," he shouted, but it wasn't really necessary. Everyone knew that they were fighting for their lives.

By the time they reached the third man out of the five parachutes that had exited the aircraft before it crashed into the water, both Germans were heading straight for them. Michael tried to calculate some clever kind of maneuver that would throw them off, but it was pretty hard to do. They were an obvious target moving on the water in broad daylight. It was extremely unusual for a December day, but that's what they had. As they reached range, Michael suddenly swerved the boat to head directly for the two Germans. That presented a much smaller profile, and it also meant that for either plane to bring their guns to bear, they would have to turn into the path of their partner.

"A very slick move," Carver said admiringly.

The two Germans figured out what he'd done just in time to avoid a collision and roared angrily past him as they went out to make a turn and come back. Naturally they would adapt to his strategy by approaching from different angles that would not get them as fouled up with each other.

"Slick but not very long-lived." They used the time to get the third man up and onto the boat. As soon as his body slid on the deck, Michael gunned the boat again, and they raced off to the fourth man. In his peripheral vision he saw a shadow again and found himself wanting to curse. "It's not fair—they killed the plane, now why don't they have the sense to run out of fuel or something so they'll leave us alone."

He started a zigzag pattern that would make it more difficult for the Germans to site in on them, but it was still pretty hopeless. He saw both of the Germans lining up from their new angles. One had been smart enough to figure out the pattern he was following to reach each of the downed airmen and was heading on a course to kill the next man in the water.

Michael abandoned the zigzag to try to get to him first by bringing the boat between the aircraft and the man in the water. Just as the first German was coming into range, Michael braced for the impact of shells, hoping that one wouldn't hit him, when the German suddenly veered off. He was traveling at such a high speed that the underside of his fuselage was temporarily exposed in the turn, and Michael was gratified to see his men shoot some of their own bullets into the aircraft. One of the bullets hit home, and there was a tremendous flash, followed by a shower of debris and the terrible concussion of the explosion. "You hit him in the fuel tanks!" Michael shouted to his men. They didn't really need him to tell them that as they were jumping up and down by their guns, arms raised in the air as they shouted with delight.

Then everyone on the boat was nearly knocked off their feet as a second aircraft passed perhaps twenty feet over their head at high speed. "Who the heck is that?" Michael called out as he recovered from the shock and stood up.

"It's one of ours, sir!" Carver called back excitedly. "They must have been in the area and heard us."

Michael turned to follow the trajectory of the British aircraft that was now turning after the second German fighter. He hoped there were more of them, but this one was all he could see. Fortunately, the German had been so intent on his mission that he didn't see the British pilot until almost too late, and the German took some shells to his tail section as well. As the German aircraft wobbled from the impact, Michael and his crew rescued the fellow still in the water. It clearly took some great piloting skills on the German's part to avoid losing control and crashing.

"What's he going to do now?" Michael asked out loud. Everyone waited in anticipation until they saw the German turn away and head off to the coast of Belgium at top speed, the British fighter on his tail.

Anxiously, Michael turned to see if anything else was about, but the skies were clear. He slowed the boat as he came up on the fourth parachute and was relieved to see the man in the water wave at them. He easily brought the boat into an arcing turn that presented the side to the man, who quickly grabbed the netting and was pulled on board.

As soon as he was safely on board, Michael took off for the fifth and final parachuter.

"It looks like we dodged it this time," Michael said to Carver.

"Yes, sir. A bit close at times, but we seem to have made it."

"Can you give me a damage report?"

"Yes, sir. We have one very angry chief, since one of the shells that penetrated the aft deck also managed to graze his right arm, but nothing at all serious. It seems that one of our engines took a shell, but the casing was so thick that it didn't penetrate. Other than some required patches to the deck, we're all clear. No one was injured."

"Amazing. Thank you, Mr. Carver."

"Oh, I did neglect to report that at least one pair of trousers was self-soiled sir, but I'll take care of that personally when we get back."

Michael couldn't help but laugh. "I think we can keep our own individual reactions to ourselves, don't you, Mr. Carver?"

"Yes, sir."

As sea captains throughout the ages had learned, Michael came to understand just how important it was to have steady officers to serve with.

As the fifth man came on board, Michael was pleased to see that it was the pilot. He returned the helm to its rightful owner and went down to meet him.

"How many of my men did you get?" the young man said anxiously.

"Four, counting you." Michael held out his hand. The poor fellow had been burned quite badly and had probably been in excruciating pain as he brought his aircraft down. Michael could see the pilot's disappointment. This particular aircraft, Michael knew, had a regular crew of ten.

"We had to leave one of your men in the water. He'd been shot and killed by the Germans on the way down, and I had to get to the rest of you. If you're not in any immediate need of assistance, I'd like to go back and get his body if we can."

"Thank you." The pilot's voice caught. "I'd appreciate that very much." Michael gave the requisite orders and then assisted the pilot down the stairs to where they could give him something hot to drink and attend to his burns.

Later, as they were heading back to port, the pilot came on deck and requested permission to talk with Michael. "I'm not sure I properly thanked you for exposing your boat to so much danger to rescue us."

"It's our job. But it doesn't always turn out this well. I'm glad we were able to save at least some of your crew."

The pilot hesitated. "I know this is probably a foolish question—the sort of thing that people ask when there's very little chance—but do you know a young man named Dominic Carlyle?"

That was the last thing Michael had expected to hear, and it took him so completely by surprise that he staggered as if from a physical blow.

"I have a younger brother, Dominic. How do you know him?"

"I went to school with him. He did me a great kindness once that I never properly thanked him for. He was the son of Lord Carlyle."

"That's my brother." Michael was surprised at the powerful emotions this released.

"May I ask how he's doing?"

Michael tipped his head to the side. Other than a few brief conversations with his parents, he hadn't spoken with anyone about Dominic. Those who knew his story were embarrassed to discuss it, and Michael had no one he felt comfortable bringing it up with. He'd sometimes wondered what he'd say if Dominic's name were ever mentioned. Now he was about to find out. "My brother died in North Africa."

The young man's face fell. "I'm sorry to hear that. He was a good fellow in his own way."

Michael smiled at the possible meanings of that statement. "You said he did something kind for you. Is it something you could tell me about?"

"It is. I was struggling in English literature—actually I was failing the class. Somehow your brother discovered my problem and volunteered to tutor me. I spent many hours with him patiently going through the material until it finally started to come clear to me. Eventually I pulled out a passing grade. I'd have washed out of school if not for him. I should have thanked him then, but we were in our ninth year, and appreciation isn't something that comes naturally at that age. But since then I've wished I could tell him." He looked thoughtful. "Now I guess I never can."

"What was he like?" Michael asked, feeling odd.

The fellow looked at him, puzzled, but Michael chose not to satisfy his curiosity and instead remained silent until he got an answer. "Well, the truth is that he was a complex sort of fellow. He had some very admirable qualities, like being helpful to me." He paused a moment to collect his thoughts. "He could be very funny with a biting kind of satire that was particularly hard on the teachers. There were times he'd have everyone in the residence cracking up at his imitation of the teachers and their peculiarities."

"I didn't know that about him. I never saw it." *Maybe I did—he used to mock Father when he was angry at him.*

"And he could be a loyal friend to the handful that he got close to."

Of course there was more. The word *complex* assured that. Michael didn't know whether to press the man, so he just remained silent. Finally, the pilot yielded to the discomfort of the situation and continued. "He also seemed to have a special talent for irritating the teachers. There were times when I knew that he'd completed a homework assignment that he didn't turn in. I could never understand that. It was as if he was inviting their scorn. Yet he always excelled on his tests, which aggravated at least some of the teachers, in view of his seeming indifference." He turned and looked directly at Michael. "The truth is that he seemed to spend much of his time in his own world. For all his ability, he remained mostly a loner. I doubt many got to know him even as well as I did. And somehow that's sad, isn't it?"

Michael nodded slowly. "It is sad. Really sad."

Michael bit his lower lip as he pondered what he had heard. *Why didn't I take time to get to know him? What was it about us that made it so hard to communicate?* A hot tear dripped down his cheek, another totally unexpected reaction. He reached up quickly and wiped it away. "You took me by surprise, is all," he said to the pilot. "I didn't expect to talk about my brother today."

"Are you okay?"

Michael's lip trembled. "I will be. Thank you for telling me all this." Then to his consternation he had to suppress a small sob, and he felt more tears start their way down his face.

The pilot wisely excused himself, and Michael stepped to the port side of the bridge, leaned his arms on the railings, and rested his face in his hands as if he were looking out to sea. Try as he might, he could not force the image of Dominic out of his mind or stop the mostly silent sobs that caused his back and shoulders to lift with each intake of breath.

* * *

Felixstowe—February 1943

For everything he had to keep track of, the prime minister was never someone to miss out on an adventure. Even though several months had passed, he still had it in his mind to see the war from the deck of a torpedo boat. And so long after Philip had forgotten about it, Churchill suddenly appeared in his office one night to demand that Philip keep his word and set up the rendezvous. Now, as the gray dawn brought the pallid colors of the harbor to life, Michael waited on the deck of the *982* for the next chapter in his life. He was so glad that his father was coming with Churchill, because he wouldn't be responsible for all the conversation. He'd always known his father was well connected, but he had no idea he was this well connected.

For security reasons, only a handful of officers and military police knew that Churchill was coming. It would be a total surprise to everyone else. Michael had been given permission to indicate they'd have a guest that day because he wanted the ship in meticulous trim, but this would still shock everyone right down to their boots. He smiled at the thought of Joseph Carver being shocked the very great distance down his legs to his boots. Carver always needled him a bit about his title, as if he didn't really believe someone with such an entitled position would be serving on a torpedo boat. Today he'd learn the truth, and Michael allowed himself just the slightest bit of satisfaction in knowing that he'd get his first officer's goat once and for all.

There was a stirring up on the ramp as a military car pulled up to the wharf. Two other cars followed it, and a small security detail got out of the first and third cars. Then the door swung open, and the prime minister stepped confidently out of the car. The rear admiral, who was in charge of the torpedo boats in this area, had been informed at the last minute of Churchill's possible visit, and so he materialized seemingly out of nowhere to greet him. With very little ceremony, the three of them, including Philip, made their way down to the *982*. At this point Michael had assembled all of his men on deck, and he was pleased to hear their collective intake of breath when they realized who was coming.

"You've got to be joking," he heard Carver mumble. When Carver turned to look at him, Michael simply raised one eyebrow and cocked his head a bit to the side.

"Fine, I'll never hear the end of this," Carver said and then went quiet. Michael stepped forward to greet them, and the admiral said quietly, "It's an honor to have you with us today, sir."

"You're coming with us, I presume?" Churchill asked.

The admiral smiled. "I wouldn't do that to the crew. The two of you are quite enough to knock them off their game. The last thing they need is an admiral on board. So with your permission, I'll let you get under way."

Michael attempted to protest, of course, but the admiral was firm. And Michael was grateful. He was absolutely right about the crew. They were all standing so stiffly at attention that he seriously worried that one of them would faint from locking his knees. To avoid any disasters like that, Michael quickly introduced each of the men. Churchill wasn't to be hurried, however, and he took a few moments with each man asking what his duties were, where he was from, and the like. It didn't take long, but in that small act, he created lasting memories for all those who would survive the war—memories they would share with their family and friends for generations.

At last they were done, and the crew was dismissed to take up their action stations preparatory to going out on a short jaunt on the open waters of the English Channel. Michael then led his father and the prime minister on a brief tour of the boat—brief mostly because there wasn't a lot of boat to tour. But there was enough to impress Churchill, particularly the engine room and the armament. He caressed the torpedo tubes with his hands as if, in his vivid imagination, he could see himself pulling the firing mechanism when the order to fire was given. When they reached the bridge, Michael said, "It ought to be exciting today, sir, what with the waves as high as they are."

"Just the way I like it," Churchill said with obvious relish. "This is where it's really at, Philip. Not down there in that dreary dungeon of ours. Out here where you get to face the enemy squarely and see who comes off the best of it."

"Yes, sir. I'm kind of glad to be here myself. But if the two of you don't mind, I'm going to excuse myself from the voyage itself." When Michael looked up in alarm, Philip explained, "It's my doctor. He says I've been a very bad patient and that something like this could aggravate my scar."

Michael's face fell, and Philip knew it was because he didn't want to be left alone with the prime minister. But this was one of those times when Philip couldn't help him. Michael shrugged his shoulders and said, "We're ready to depart whenever you like."

"Then let's be off!" Churchill said, barely containing his excitement.

"Now listen, lieutenant—I know how you drive our automobiles, so you be careful with the prime minister," Philip warned as he stepped off the boat.

"Oh, tosh—don't listen to a word he's saying," Churchill said. Then he smiled at Philip and moved up onto the bridge.

When they cleared the mouth of the harbor, Michael gave the order, "Full speed ahead," and the boat roared confidently to life. Even with all the racket of the engines under full acceleration, he could hear Churchill laughing as they did their best to hold on for dear life. He executed a number of tight turns and other close-order maneuvers, much to the continuing delight of his guest, and then, turning to a straight heading, he turned to the man who more than any other was responsible for England's survival, and said, "Care to take the wheel, sir?"

"I thought you'd never ask, lieutenant." And with that Churchill stepped forward and shouted into the engine room tube, "Take it into the red, chief. Let's see what you've got down there!"

Even Michael was rocked back on his feet as his engineer somehow managed to coax even more power out of the three engines that were now propelling them across the waves of the English Channel at nearly fifty miles per hour. Churchill roared with delight, twisting and turning the wheel until Michael felt alarmed for the safety of the boat. Stepping to the railing, he put his hand out to steady himself while calling out to his first officer, "Better hang on for dear life, Mr. Carver—the leader of the free world is in control and it looks like we're in for a wild ride!" The two of them laughed as Churchill led them on a grand adventure.

GLOSSARY

Anschluss

> German for *union*. This more specifically referred to the political union of Austria and Germany as a result of Hitler's annexation of Austria. In 1938, Austrian chancellor Kurt von Schuschnigg anticipated that Austrians would vote against a union with Germany, but he was forced into canceling the vote and Austrians never had their say. Schuschnigg then resigned, ordering the Austrian army not to oppose the Germans. When the Germans invaded on March 12, the Austrians' lack of resistance convinced Hitler to annex Austria the next day. France and Britain objected to Hitler's move, but they, along with other countries, tacitly accepted the fait accompli.

armistice

> A temporary cessation of fighting by mutual consent; a truce.

blaggard or blackguard

> A thoroughly deceitful, unethical person; a rogue.

Blitzkrieg or Blitz

> German for *lightning war*. During World War II, the Germans used the elements of surprise, alacrity, and arms superiority to stun their opponents, causing psychological shock and resultant disorganization among them. Blitzkrieg strategy immobilized the enemy by combining land and air attacks: it used tanks, dive-bombers, and motorized artillery to paralyze the enemy principally by disabling its communications and coordination capacities. The Germans initiated blitzkrieg in Spain in 1938 during the Spanish Civil War, and they used it in Poland in 1939, and again in 1940, successfully invading Belgium, the Netherlands, and France.

blockbuster bomb

> The name given to several of the largest conventional bombs used in World War II by the Royal Air Force. The press dubbed the bomb *blockbuster* because it had enough explosive power to wipe out an entire city block.

bosun pipe
> A small fluted music pipe that signals various shipboard activities. The bosun blows on the pipe to signal a change of watch, call men to action stations, welcome visitors or officers on board, etc.

despatch riders
> During World War II, despatch riders were able to quickly transport small items, such as packages, letters, legal documents, and messages, by motorcycle, especially when other means of communication were risky or ineffective.

Distinguished Service Cross
> The military decoration awarded to officers of the Royal Navy in recognition of extraordinary bravery during combat operations.

Dunkirk
> In what has been considered one of the most heroic actions of World War II, hundreds of civilian boats and naval vessels, under the cover of the Royal Air Force, helped more than 300,000 British, French, and Belgian troops to be evacuated at the French port of Dunkirk after they'd been cut off by Germans forces (May 26–June 4, 1940).

flag semaphore messaging
> The semaphore, or optical telegraph, is an apparatus for conveying information through visual signals, using towers with pivoting blades, paddles, or shutters, in a matrix. Information is encoded by the position of the mechanical elements; it is read when the blade or flag is in a fixed position. Today it refers to a system of signaling using two handheld flags.

Goering
> Hermann Goering led the *Luftwaffe,* or German air force, during World War II and was second in command to Adolf Hitler. But Hitler's confidence in Goering wavered after the failure of the Luftwaffe in the Battle of Britain. Goering then failed to deliver German troops to the Russian front, and Hitler became even more displeased with him. As the Allied armies closed in on Hitler and Berlin in April of 1945, Goering made a clumsy and premature offer to take over as Germany's leader. Hitler charged Goering with treason

and ordered his arrest. Seventeen months following his surrender to Allied forces on May 8, 1945, Goering was convicted of war crimes at Nuremberg and sentenced to death.

House of Commons

The House of Commons consists of citizens who are elected by voters in their specific borough and county. Elected representatives are known as Members of Parliament (MPs) and directly represent the interests of the people in their electoral area.

The members of the House of Commons belong to parties, and the party with the most members is called upon to form a government. Generally, their leader is well-known, but the actual selection and calling of a prime minister is a responsibility of the king. Thus citizens do not directly vote for their highest public official—he or she is chosen by the members of Parliament. A rough counterpart in the United States would be the Speaker of the House of Representatives.

Once the prime minister is selected, he or she becomes the chief legislative and administrative leader in the country. The prime minister forms a cabinet of secretaries that run the various ministries of government.

Generally, a government serves for six years before a general election is mandated. However, if a government is particularly weak, the House can call for a vote of "No Confidence," which, if successful, ends that government. A general election is immediately called, and whichever party gains a majority is called upon to form a new government.

Likewise, if a government is particularly successful, the prime minister may call for an early election to gain another six years. For example, if the current government is four years old and popular, it may call a general election to confirm their majority, which would start a new six-year period.

Jerrys

A slang term for German soldiers. The British were nicknamed "Tommies," the French "Frogs" (because they eat frog legs), the Americans "Yankees," etc.

Kriegsmarine

German for *War Navy,* Kriegsmarine was the name of the German Navy during World War II.

Lords, the Lords

The upper chamber in the British Parliament is known as the House of Lords, or simply the Lords. The Lords currently includes 730 unelected members, including 2 archbishops and 24 bishops of the Established Church of England (Lords Spiritual) and more than 700 members of the "Peerage" (Lords Temporal). Members of the Lords are known as "Lords of Parliament."

For many centuries the Lords was the dominant force in Parliament, but its authority has eroded over time as the House of Commons has gained power. Major reform at the beginning of the 20th century left the Lords with greatly restricted legislative powers in that it cannot take any action on "money bills" related to taxes or expenditures and can delay, at most, passage of nonmoney bills for twelve months (24 months in 1940, when this story takes place). In that regard the Lords' authority acts as a temporary veto.

The Lords also holds judicial power in that it can act as the highest court of appeals for most cases in the United Kingdom. The entire house does not act on judicial matters, but rather only those Lords with legal training. They are known as the "Law Lords."

In practice the Lords provides an advisory function in legislative affairs and holds a place of honor in British society. In many cases a prominent member of the House of Commons, such as a retiring prime minister, will be granted a peerage by the monarch in honor of his or her service. This grant enables the individual to continue to participate in the affairs of government for the rest of his or her life without having to submit to an election.

Lords sit for life. Hereditary peers can pass both their title and the right to sit in the Lords onto their heirs, although reforms are placing further restrictions on these rights over time.

Originally, the United States Senate was viewed as an American counterpart to the Lords with well-seasoned members who acted in a more deliberative fashion than the directly elected members of the House of Representatives. The U.S. Constitution calls for senators to be elected by each state legislature. That was changed by constitutional amendment for direct election by the voters in each state. In our time the British House of Lords has diminished in power while the U.S. Senate has increased in power and influence.

Lords Spiritual
>The 26 leaders of the Church of England (archbishops and selected bishops) who sit as members of the Lords. They serve for as long as they hold a position in the Established Church, rather than for life.

Low Countries
>The region of northwest Europe that includes Belgium, the Netherlands, and Luxemburg.

magazine
>A place where ammunition for weapons that can be carried by a single combatant is stored. Weapons are actually kept separate from the ammunition stores as a safety precaution.

Maginot line
>Constructed in the 1930s, this defensive barrier along the French–German frontier was named after its originator, Andre Maginot. At the time, it was considered a revolutionary fortification. Protected by heavy artillery, its barracks, supply rooms, and underground rail lines were housed in thick concrete walls. It ended, however, at the French–Belgian frontier, which German forces crossed in May 1940. They invaded Belgium on May 10, crossed the Somme River, struck at the northern end of the line, and continued around to its rear, rendering the barrier useless.

Messerschmitt
>Messerschmitt-Bölkow-Blohm was a German aircraft manufacturer, made famous during World War II by its production of fighter aircraft such as the Bf 109 and Me 262. During the first half of the war, Messerschmitt's Bf 109 and Bf 110 models comprised the bulk of Germany's fighter power. The Me 321 Giant transport glider and the six-engine Me 323 were also used by the Reich. During the second half of the war, Messerschmitt turned almost entirely to jet-powered designs, producing the world's first operational jet fighter, the Me 262 *Schwalbe,* or "Swallow."

Motor Gun Boat (MGB)
>A motor gun boat was similar to a motor torpedo boat except that it carried heavier armament instead of torpedo tubes. It could fire from a greater distance and with heavier shells than a corresponding MTB.

Motor Torpedo Boat (MTB)

    A motor torpedo boat was a small ship with a crew of twelve. MTBs ranged in length from 60 feet to more than 75 feet with a beam (width) of 13 feet to 19 feet. Their draught (depth in the water) was just from 2.5 feet to 5.25 feet, and they displaced between 22 and 46 tons of water (their weight). Typically they were powered by three gasoline engines with a speed of 41 knots (approximately 50 miles per hour). Armament varied from the various manufacturers but typically included two 21-inch torpedo tubes (launched from the deck), one single Oerlikon gun, and one twin .5-inch MG turret (used as an antiaircraft gun).

    These small boats were highly maneuverable and served as both convoy escorts and antisubmarine patrols, and they fought against the larger German E-boats (Enemy Boats) that were designed for the same function in the English Channel and in the Mediterranean.

nautical terminology

    aft. near the stern of a ship or the tail of an aircraft.

    bow. the front of a boat.

    amidships. the middle of the boat.

    battle cruiser. Used during the first half of the 20th century, these large warships evolved from armored cruisers, and in nautical classification they fell somewhere between cruisers and battleships. Battle cruisers, though much like battleships in design, were much faster because of their lightweight construction. These speedy warships dominated the smaller warships with their advanced weaponry and outran larger warships when their weaponry proved inadequate.

    bulkheads. partitions crossing the length of and separating portions of a ship, also known as the walls inside a ship.

    coxswain. a sailor in charge of a ship's crew and who usually steers the ship.

    destroyer. fast naval vessel used to protect other ships. The term was first applied to vessels built in the 1890s to protect battleships from torpedo boats. By World War I, destroyers were often sent ahead of the battle fleet to scout for the enemy, beat back its destroyers with cannon fire, and then launch torpedoes against its battleships and cruisers. When the submarine became the main torpedo-launching vessel, destroyers armed with depth charges protected convoys and battle fleets against submarine attack. In World War II, with the addition of radar and antiaircraft guns, the destroyer's escort role included air defense.

flagship. in a group or squadron of naval ships, the ship carrying the commanding officer. It is traditional to fly a distinguishing flag aboard the ship housing the naval commander.

flotilla. a fleet of ships or boats; a naval unit consisting of two or more squadrons of small warships.

hull. the frame of a ship or boat not including the masts, yards, sails, or rigging.

knot. a measure of nautical speed equaling approximately 1.125 statute miles per hour.

port. the left side of a ship.

rear admiral. a naval rank originating with the Royal Navy that is above captain and below vice admiral. An admiral leads a naval squadron of ships and commands his squadron from a center vessel. The admiral is assisted by the vice admiral, who commands the foremost ships, which bear the brunt of a naval assault.

starboard. the right side of a ship.

stern. the rear end of a boat.

yardarms. either end of a square sail. One of the harshest punishments aboard ship was to be suspended from the yardarm at a significant height. When the vessel pitched and rolled in rough seas, the convict could be swung anywhere from fifty to seventy-five feet wide, and hung for days without being given food or water.

yeoman. a naval petty officer who performs clerical duties.

Operation Barbarossa

Just before dawn on June 22, 1941, heavy German artillery began firing across the Russian border, initiating Hitler's Operation Barbarossa, one of the most brutal campaigns in World War II history. At the cost of seven million lives, the Red Army emerged victorious after nearly four years of fighting. The Barbarossa campaign included some of the greatest military events of World War II, not the least of which was the Russian offensive beginning in 1944 that would lead the Red Army to the historic meeting with the Americans at the Elbe and on to victory in Berlin.

Packard

> Initially an automobile manufacturer, Packard developed the engine that powered the famous P-51 Mustang fighter used during World War II. One of the fastest non-jet fighter planes ever made, it could fly higher than any of its contemporaries, providing a significant measure of security for its pilots. Packard engines were also used to power many of the British-built motor torpedo boats.

panzer

> An armored vehicle or tank. The German word *Panzer*, or armor, referred directly to the protective metal coating, or *Plattenpanzer* (German for "plate armor"), of which the German tanks were constructed. The term gained infamy among the Allies during Germany's successful armored advances of World War II.

Parliament

> The British Parliament grew out of the council that advised the king in medieval times aknd consisted of noblemen, ecclesiastical leaders, and representatives of the counties and boroughs. It was formally recognized in the year 1295. In the seven hundred years since, it has grown from an advisory body, in which noblemen had the greatest say, into the formal government of England, in which the elected members of the House of Commons have control.

> Of interest to Americans is the fact that the British have no formal written constitution. Rather the constitution is considered the body of common law that has developed over the course of many centuries as acted on by Parliament and interpreted by court decisions. Parliament stands supreme in its ability to make and change laws.

piker

> Someone who's thought of as small-minded or stingy.

prime minister

> The elected leader of the governing party in Parliament. Called by the monarch to serve, the prime minister is responsible for all functions of the national government and governs with the help of a cabinet.

Quonset hut

> During World War II, the United States needed a versatile, light-weight structure that could be shipped wherever it was needed and erected without much effort. Named after their first site of manufacture, Quonset Point, located at the Davisville Naval Construction Battalion Center in Rhode Island, the huts were made of corrugated metal and shaped in a semicircle. The interior of the huts not only provided shelter for the armed forces but also served as barracks, latrines, isolation wards, and medical and dental offices. Over 160,000 Quonset huts were used during the war, and many still exist throughout the United States. After the war, these prefabricated buildings were sold to the American public for $1,000 each.

Royal Corps of Signals or Signal Corps

> The branch of the British Army responsible for overseeing telecommunications equipment and information systems. The Telegraph Battalion was primarily responsible for signaling until 1908, when the Royal Engineers Signal Service was formed to provide communications services during World War I. On June 28, 1920, Winston Churchill instigated the creation of the Corps of Signals. Six weeks later, King George V conferred the title Royal Corps of Signals. Throughout World War II, members of the Corps served in every theater of war. By the end of the war the strength of the Corps was 8,518 officers and 142,472 men.

salvo

> The simultaneous discharge of firearms. Also, the simultaneous release of a rack of bombs from an aircraft.

Schnellboot

> The German name of their motor torpedo and motor gun boats. *Schnell* means "fast," and these small craft were very fast.

Second Battle of El Alamein

> This battle signified a major turning point in the Western Desert Campaign of World War II. The Germans meant to occupy Egypt in hopes of controlling the Suez Canal and subsequent access to Middle Eastern oil, but the Second Battle of El Alamein, which began on October 23, 1942, effectively brought about the end of German expansion in North Africa on November 3 of that same year.

star shell
>An artillery shell that explodes in midair with a shower of lights, used for illumination and signaling.

Swordfish bomber
>This hefty, metal-framed biplane torpedo bomber was covered in fabric and sported folding wings, which made it ideal for use on aircraft carriers. The Fairey Aviation Company manufactured these versatile planes used by the Royal Navy during World War II. Mainly a fleet-attack aircraft, it was also used as an antisubmarine and training aircraft later in the war.

tracer shell
>Ammunition whose flight can be observed by a trail of smoke.

Treaty of Versailles
>Signed in 1919 at the Palace of Versailles, this treaty brought about the end of World War I. The United States, Britain, and France orchestrated the agreement without the support of the war's losers, including Germany. The Germans were forced to accept the blame and to make compensation for Allied losses. Germany's ensuing bitterness over the terms of the treaty—a ten percent reduction in German territory, a significant cutback in its military power, and many of its overseas possessions taken—helped create the conditions that led to the growth of fascism in Italy and the rise of the Nazi Party in Germany.

turret
>A rotating, self-contained weapons platform housing guns.

U-Boat
>A German submarine. The *U* stood for the first initial in the German *Unterseeboot,* "Under-sea-boat."

viscount—peers
>A peer of the realm is an individual who holds one or more titles of nobility and whose estate was granted to him or an ancestor by the monarch. The five titles in descending order of rank are duke, marquess, earl, viscount, and baron. At the beginning of the 21st century there are approximately 250 individuals of English descent

who hold these titles (with approximately the same number of Irish and Scottish peers). The title of duke is often conferred on members of the royal family.

At the time this story takes place it was possible for a peer to pass his membership in the Lords to his eldest son. If he had no son, then the membership was passed to the oldest living male heir who could directly trace his ancestry back to a previous holder of the title.

Wehrmacht

The name of the German defense forces during the years 1935 to 1945. The Wehrmacht was made up of three branches: army, navy, and air force. The commander in chief of this defense force was the chancellor.

Whitehall

The government complex that includes Number 10 Downing Street, the official residence of the prime minister.

REFERENCES

Allen, Frank, and Paul Bevand. *The Pursuit of Bismarck and the Sinking of H.M.S.* Hood. *www.hmsHood.com*, 2005.

The Cabinet War Rooms. London: The Imperial War Museum, 1996.

Churchill, Winston S. *The Grand Alliance: The Second World War, Volume III.* Boston: Houghton-Mifflin, 1977.

Clayton, Tim, and Phil Craig. *Finest Hour: The Battle of Britain.* New York: Touchstone, 1999.

Cooper, Bryan. *The Battle of the Torpedo Boats.* New York: Stein and Day, 1970.

The H.M.S. *Hood* Association. *History of H.M.S.* Hood. *www.hmsHood.com*, 2004.

Konstam, Angus. *British Motor Torpedo Boat 1939–45.* Oxford: Osprey Publishing, 2003.

——. *British Battle Cruisers 1939–45.* Oxford: Osprey Publishing, 2003.

Nicholson, E. S. *Adventures of a Royal Signals Despatch Rider.* London: Upfront Publishing, 2003.

Van Young, Sayre. *London's War: A Traveler's Guide to World War II.* Berkeley, CA: Ulysses Press, 2004.

[i] This is a direct quote of Winston Churchill's own writing. Source: Churchill, Winston, *The Grand Alliance, Winston S. Churchill: The Second World War, Volume III.* New York: Mariner Books, Houghton-Mifflin Company, 1950, pp. 606–8.